John Kelley

Harbinger of Springtime

novum pro

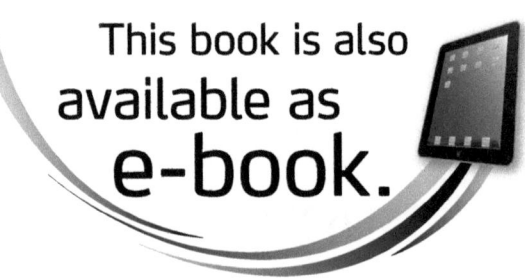

www.novum-publishing.co.uk

All rights of distribution,
including film, radio, television,
photomechanical reproduction,
sound carrier, electronic media and
reprint in extracts, are reserved.

Printed in the European Union,
using environmentally-friendly,
chlorine-free and acid-free paper.

© 2016 novum publishing

ISBN 978-3-99048-084-7
Editor: Louise Darvid
Cover photos: Soundsnaps, Paul Fleet,
Johnson175 | Dreamstime.com
Cover design, layout & typesetting:
novum publishing

www.novum-publishing.co.uk

Dedications:
Acknowledgements

The author would like to express sincere thanks to Jan Whitfield, for her continued enthusiasm towards me that acted as a driving force during the many months I was involved in writing: Harbinger of Springtime. Her rational gift was inspiration, remaining constantly in force whilst undertaking my research for the book. She reminded me obsessively of a quoted moment from a 'timeless' movie that we both knew, for me it became transformed into a cultural touchstone. 'If you put your mind to it, you can accomplish anything...'

Also in appreciation of Ian Sherman, who put up with me balanced on a tenuous 'learning curve' during my formative times with trepidation on the subject of word processing, allowing me to eventually reach the core of my computer. My everlasting thanks to him, especially his undying patience shown towards me.

Further, as a large part of my novel is orchestrated around the Herero people in the deserts of Namibia, therefore I have a sense of gratitude to express towards them by making the main theme of the storyline in all respects plausible.

On a personal note, a tribute to a name used in my book, the compelling ~ Anastasia. From the Greek originally, having a meaning of 'resurrection', personified as an iconic name for a daughter.

Finally to Novum-Publishing, thanking the company to the highest level for their acceptance of my manuscript, the progression by their commitment and dedication shown towards me as an author and excellence from all of the staff during the involvement of the publication process of the novel.

John Kelley

Chapter 1

Everything about him seemed in a state of aching, or was pain a more apt description? Neck, shoulder blades, to say nothing of the noise that since yesterday had definitely decided to take up residence inside his ears…

The tide was now in the process of slowly advancing. Early morning sunlight induced a clearly defined contrast of lighting, creating an overall appearance that is both recognised and appreciated by landscape artists frequenting this part of our coastline.

The inspiring view from his apartment window was not on this occasion apparent to Ian Harbinger. To escape his ailments he was sitting entombed by cushions in the relative comfort of the lounge sofa. He was consumed in a total sense of persistent worry, confirmed by the fact he was in the process of sipping yet another cup of black coffee.

He watched the array of subtle changes of light influencing the estuary view. His thoughts were not allowed to be there, they were fixed on one dominating subject matter aware there were to be no surprises. Facing him was a simple and vital task that needed his urgent attention; open the three envelopes addressed to himself, and then read their enclosed contents.

The letters requiring his vigilance were arranged neatly on the glass-topped table in front of where he was seated. Occupying the table was also a letter opener, he mused to himself at least that is ready for use. It did not however alter the fact that for nearly two hours it had laid there waiting in a redundant state.

Lack of discipline on his part had started to instigate noticeable stress levels, aided no doubt by his generous intake of black coffee. The austere official looking envelopes had their origins from HM Revenue & Customs, with the other two generated from banks, including his own business bank situated in Keswick.

Persisting for years, Ian had a self-inflicted and irritating trait concerning his incoming mail. Having recognised the possible content from the actual envelope, and if a concern existed to what a letter might regard, it would remain unopened. Eventually of course, following a protracted period of time, a day of reckoning would arrive and their contents finally revealed!

On this particular morning there appeared no exception to his irrational habit. He pondered on the realms of positive thinking, remembering those self-help books that are bought, read, and attempts made to act upon. The 'power of positive thinking' totally persuaded him this had to be his logical solution.

What is the worse that these letters might contain? After all he had passed through real dangers to life out on the drilling rigs in the North Sea. That was his job and his working background, there he would have total command of his circumstances. Given a well-known saying, that is supposed to be true, 'worse things happen at sea'.

Outside the apartment window birds that he recognised as swallows were enjoying a virtual fly past. Soon if he had remembered correctly they would need to undertake the task of departing to their overseas wintering grounds. By contrast on the chimney-stack of the old house visible below, a clandestine group of resident jackdaws were performing a quarrelling routine. Not until the order of importance for these birds had again been restored would there exist a fragile semblance of peace.

He was in the process of consoling himself. There are always difficult situations in our lives, which leave us no option other than to face them. He called out aloud, 'Come on it has to be done, they are only letters.' With noticeable determination he reached out and took hold of the letter opener, there followed a period of methodical ease as the envelopes that waited their execution with the letter opener were systematically dealt with, allowing at last an exposure of their contents.

His daunting task was showing signs of progressing. Removing the first of the three letters it emerged in an upside down position, he even attempted to read it in a reversed format. He shuddered, knowing whichever way it would be equally disastrous. Since his arrival on the previous evening, these letters had awaited his attention; now by his actions they had been opened. Ian however did not deserve their enclosed implications.

Appearing like a regimental arrangement the communications were fully decreased and laid out on the table. A pocket calculator had joined them, the last entered figures still remaining visible on the screen by the power supplemented from the window's sunshine. In consequence all three letters produced what would manifest and disclose a series of losses and probably that of personal despair, there were no surprises. He remained rooted, slumped in a protective wedge shape on the lounge sofa. This was too much to comprehend, what a stupid idiot he had allowed himself to become. But why? What a state of affairs; how could all this have happened?

Ian's stomach nerves were as tight as elastic string contained within a golf ball. A glass of water occupied the place where the coffee cups had been, headache tablets taken earlier were as yet to have any effect. His immediate future plans he had worked towards, focused on with a yearning for a change of life direction were appearing as if in tatters.

He accepted the fact, now what he had read was having the effect of taunting him, although he tried to remain cynical about his whole financial situation. By some strange macabre reasoning he likened his letters to that of bodies extracted from their respective body bags. He tried desperately to reason, snap out of it, be sensible, you need to get back in control. Face up to these hard facts, it is not like storms hitting a drilling platform out at sea, they do eventually blow through. In contrast he had no option other than to confront the issues, the letters had outlined his current predicament in both a transparent and precise way, his financial state was more unstable than he imagined!

The attendant jackdaws on the old house were once more fiercely squabbling over the territories that existed between the chimney pots. At least they have a simple, and what appears an uncomplicated life, unlike what had materialised out of all proportion for me to resolve.

Travel tiredness was having an inherent effect, resulting from yesterday's long journey, which had been fraught with endless difficulties. Due to prevailing weather conditions which affected flying, the company helicopter was almost cancelled prior to pick up from the rig. Following take off it was assigned in battling with head winds before eventually reaching its destination in Aberdeen. Ian considered he was still travelling, endorsed by pains emanating seemingly from every muscle, accompanied by this noise persisting in his ears. He was not complaining, but he rather favoured the noise from the drilling rigs anytime.

It did not end there, the ongoing flight to Bristol for an obscure reason was suffering delays. On finally achieving his next stop, the car hire company had made an error with dates that of course curtailed his booking.

An accumulation of events had transpired prior to leaving the rig. At the last possible moment he was organising schedules for less experienced work colleagues, amounting to an avuncular list of do's and don'ts which arguably really needed his attention; a result of his considerable experience in the oil industry. However, his leave entitlement was long overdue, and he was elated to have escaped, subject to receiving any communications via the company satellite phone in his possession. For him it was rather like encountering that situation known as paddling against the tide of life.

From Bristol the motorway resembled a sea of rain, causing significant flooding where it goes through the Somerset Levels. Do I have to tell myself it is the effect of global warming, knowing one of the main reasons that has supposedly caused this situation, then hang my head in shame, fossil fuel, and spending over 20 years of my working life supporting the oil industry. In blunt terms this amounts to one of the prime root issues regarding our planet's current causes of concern. Then what is my commitment? Drilling even deeper attempting to hit new oil reserves thought impossible a few years ago.

Recollections of yesterday's journey were not helping his predicament. No, enough was enough. A walk was called for, I need some fresh air. What was currently hanging in tatters would have to wait. The path leading to the estuary was waiting his urgent attention, he required thinking time and the sanctuary of some space. Somehow he must attempt to resist a habit of a lifetime; the figure of an 'ostrich' engrossed with burying its head in the sand.

He was mindful of one thing before leaving the apartment; the company phone was rather unceremoniously thrown on the kitchen table, the last thing he wanted were problems from the other rig engineers adding to his current burden, let them sort things. Defiantly his thoughts concluded on a salient note, this is my overdue leave it belongs to no one else.

Leaving the apartment he glanced reassuringly towards the parked hire car, noticing in daylight the vehicle's colour, having travelled the last part of yesterday's irksome journey in gathering darkness. No need for the car today, as there exists a gratifying walk towards the destination of the estuary. Zero carbon emissions, he laughed feeling somewhat smug, only my pure footprints, tell that to our esteemed government. His continuing defiant and assertive mood was beginning to percolate into his subconscious.

One of the main reasons that Ian together with his younger sister Julia had combined to buy their holiday accommodation on the Devon coast, reflected in the fact of the wonderful inspiring locations. Or put more simply at least from Ian's point of interest it was a good investment, a desirable property with views that were superb, no arguments. Julia was able to spend more of her time there, describing the apartment to most of her arse aching friends as that essential bolt hole to escape from where her work took her, that of London's fashionable area of Chiswick.

Joining the narrow lane he became embraced in a consoling feeling that the time of summer days were starting to wind down, you could notice the vestiges of early morning mists remaining noticeable on the overgrown grass, latticed with spiders' webs that only nature can replicate. He was conscious of those letters waiting his attention, but at this precise moment this walk was his undeniable therapy. It would not avert his problems, but it was that much needed relief, and nobody was going to stop that.

I have to think... I need to think and really hard; he was inaugurating a self-assessment process, believing this must help somehow? The background to all these events, how did he allow himself to arrive in this situation, to be misled and cheated by those that he knew and trusted? Face the facts he told himself, accept and recognise this cruel imposition. You have had your face pushed into the dirt, it's happened and unlikely to be resolved. He walked on wanting those headache tablets to take hold.

He started to recall the financial history appertaining to his hotels. This amounted to a joint business venture that was to mature and consolidate with its financial fulfilment; the investment had been his future. Ian had on occasions fallen in a trap that allowed him to be described as a selfish person, although not necessarily with any malice. In an analysis for his defence he considered himself a man of self-preserve, assured in life that his personal right belonged only to him. Now this attitude of self-preservation was undergoing its most stringent test; that of the embezzlement by his business partner. She had secretly contrived and succeeded in cheating him of his capital at the highest possible level.

The narrow lane gradually receded, into his view came the long sweep of the estuary, even the air seemed different, invigorating, totally up-lifting. His train of well-ordered thoughts were suddenly interrupted by a distant but altogether familiar note. A determined call that sounded regimental in its concept, the crow from a cockerel, it appeared to be originating from the yard of a small farm that he was about to pass.

A group of hens were hunched together enjoying the liberty of their free range orientation, scurrying as chickens do in a perpetual search for food. He looked on with genuine interest, but his attention was no longer there, as his mind had become a receptor flooded by a series of incoming memories, causing him to drift back to a time of his past and that of his childhood.

Another farm in another county had all but eclipsed his present location, for him a far off different world. For whatever reason he was unable to comprehend, there existed something of a transformation with recollections and events of a schoolboy. In his reincarnation he was proud and equally important, seeing himself all those years ago carrying an old dented galvanised bucket lined with matted straw. His pride was to demonstrate self-determination whilst performing the daily ritual of visiting the chicken coops, enjoying the privilege of carefully collecting the farm eggs for his aunt.

Chapter 2

Ian's noticeable appearance along the exposed estuary bank caused the flocks of wading birds to scream away in a universal flight of alarm. His panoramic view across to the sea revealed that the tide had already completed the morning task, those ebbing waters had left a glazed signature as evidence of its previous encroachment. Shadows created by incoming cloud were now responsible for the loss of morning sunshine. That no longer mattered, as what he saw was a reassuringly deserted landscape. This is what I need, personal solitude; my recipe for valuable thinking time.

An ancient bleached tree trunk resided above the high tide mark, providing a perfect, if not an entirely comfortable resting place. From this newly acquired seat he clearly viewed the meeting of the two rivers, their independent water courses having journeyed through the county, flowed as a united front of solidarity to finally discharge into the approaching sea.

He remained equally calm and self-disciplined, concentrating his thoughts on the English Lake District, and his involvement with the financial investment of his two hotels. The morning's location seemed far removed from where his thoughts lay, but he accepted his immediate environment was providing valuable escape. To himself there was an agreement that the process with his recollections should be straightforward. What was that quoted phrase? 'Begin at the beginning… and go on till you come to the end; then stop.' It's from such a classic book, but on this occasion the title escaped him, but for now that was unimportant.

Begin at the beginning, that was easy in recalling. Was I wrong with my plan to stay with the oil industry and bring in someone whom I knew as a business partner would have total control managing the hotels? Other people do the same thing, it made so much sense with my continuing disposable income simply directed to the hotel business investment. Now with hindsight that was my undoing, and it left me financially vulnerable. I was ruled by a passion for success in the hospitality business, and I proved myself, but failed in one department overlooking the vital fact that my eyes and ears were not there.

The first of the two hotels was the most demanding investment. Purchased at what would have been described as an attractive price, as anyone in the immediate area would endorse. It was waiting for that breath of fresh air the right calibre of new owners could bring. Success with this hotel was achieved, despite what could only be described as healthy and aggressive competition already entrenched in the surrounding tourist region.

One year into the running a decision was agreed upon for the hotel's refurbishment. The plan that was devised required a substantial capital investment. How delighted he had been by the fact it was generated without any form of financial loan. Ian thought back to those heady times of lucrative on target bonuses, the oil industry knew no boundaries. In comparison with the current climate of credit restrictions he was finding it hard to believe it took place, but it did. These inflated bonuses were allowed to be channelled into the vortex of his hotel investment.

We waited in a state of nervous anticipation to review the outcome. Thinking now it only seems like yesterday, our decision and investment worked, the bottom line figures spoke volumes. We could have kicked ourselves, why did we not capitalise with this refurbishment earlier? But no matter, it was done and worked to our advantage.

The English Lake District where the hotels are situated is inundated with every conceivable variety of outlets, both privately and group owned with the under belly of the hospitality industry eroded by countless guest houses, and of course our beloved B&B establishments. The strategy to stay ahead, and remain there was not always the easiest of tasks. True you could list up all the factors that spell out success, but it firmly comes down, if you ever need reminding, to that of your staff commitment combined with the quality of dedicated leadership.

From the onset Ian's associate as his hotel business partner was a woman whose particular skills originated from a background of knowledge accumulated in hotel management, and that was an education she accrued in particular from the best of the bunch. It became a pleasure to witness her superb and uncanny flair reflected in anticipation of customers' requirements. Demonstrating a quality performance to the point of being infectious with any of her staff who happened to be present.

He pondered, you really could assess any hotel's strength by the all important service apparent at its front of house, like a job interview, that's often decided in the first few seconds! All that aside you have to face up that eventually your hotel involvement progresses down to what your accountant wants to witness. The first investment was definitely on the surge of ongoing success. His business associate was excelling herself, Ian was usually domicile on some windswept drilling platform, but certainly not all at sea with his 'onshore' business concerns.

True, certainly with regret he accepted that he was the silent partner in the hotel involvement. However the partnership revolved around that dirty word called money; the commodity making our world go round. Then he never lost sight of the fact it was his sole 100% capital investment.

Where was all this now? There was an invasion of a noticeable low spot gaining access to his managed train of thoughts, understandable considering how he was feeling. How desperately he had wished to turn back the clock over the last few months. The tree trunk that at first provided some comfort was now having a reverse effect. Accept hard facts, like what you are sitting on, you cannot turn back time. Even if you are old enough to remember blue police telephone boxes, now used successfully by a certain 'time travelling doctor'. Who would have thought this stream of seemingly useless memories could possibly invade his thinking space?

This prevailing sense of despondency was interrupted in the real world by the noticeable arrival of a car progressing ruggedly along the estuary track. It came off the rough terrain and parked between an array of puddles, the result of yesterday's rain.

Ian's thoughts now snapped back quickly rejoining the present. He watched as the lady driver opened the vehicle's tailgate allowing the evacuation of two Labrador dogs. Eager to ascertain their freedom they gallivanted across the beach firmly believing that the world belonged only to them.

The dogs' arrival on the shoreline disturbed two elegant white birds that had been patiently wading at the edge. Showing disapproval by having to take flight, one of the birds flew in the direction of Ian. He could see that by its serene character it was no ordinary sea gull, the bird's leisurely flight went over a large rock pool creating a pure white reflection on the mirrored surface. His thoughts now returned to the Lakes, and were dwelling on a certain hotel sign, 'Swan in the Moonlight'. Always he believed it was pure inspiration, it had become his second hotel acquisition.

He remembered the name alone had sold it to him. This investment had not progressed as easily as the first, to be pedantic it had not come on to the market, it had been offered to them, which at that time he did not want to refuse. That rock pool reflection for those few moments directed his memory to the very hotel sign, the swan's profile was an artist's impression cleverly painted that created inherent blue effect of moonlight. You needed to see it against its rightful place, the backdrop with the hotel. Today by contrast this memory was vague, far removed from his present coastal location.

He aspired to be elsewhere invigorated by thoughts of weather in the English Lakes, accepting a love affair with walks in rain showers, unique qualities of our climate. The location of the 'Swan' was perfect for these activities, adding to a range of features that worked strongly for what your guests were seeking. The larger of the two investments had an ominous burden in proving itself against more aggressive competition. There was also a protracted gamble, as their latest purchase had previously suffered from the negligence of absentee owners.

The second purchase resulted from an element of astute guidance from their accountant, a local Keswick man who knew the unique pace in respect to this area's tourism. In the early days of this hotel the decision makers, which included their accountant sensed a feeling they were about to lay down foundations with this venture that would grow into a success.

Ian told himself, and that is where you started to go wrong. The word I believe is empowerment, exactly the motivation for what you allowed to be put into the hands of two people both of whom you totally trusted. Now he was sensing anger in his own hands, clenching them in the shape of tight fists.

Following the positive feedback he had received from their accountant indicating how this acquisition was progressing he could hardly wait to inform his business partner. He remembered the text he sent indicating that their accountant was worth every penny. To endorse this, he had added, somewhat tongue-in-cheek, please be aware our 'Swan in the Moonlight' was incubating their eventual business nest egg!

Then came the time when both the hotel investments had reached a buoyant state, realised in a much shorter time scale than was anticipated. He had opened the discussion with positive thoughts of selling the two hotels, which after all had been his plan. It was clear to him now, the input from the ever pragmatic accountant indicated there would not be a better time, then that was not surprising given the odious scheme that he with Ian's partner was secretly preparing.

All that was twelve months ago. As a diversion to his thoughts he became involved with a small piece of driftwood, attempting with a pocket knife to improve his carving skills. This he hoped would effectively stave away the feeling of bitterness starting to surface in his thoughts.

Over the sands he made out the lonely figure with the dogs making her way back, the loyal duo were close at heel, any enthusiasm to pursue sticks thrown by their owner was now sadly lacking. Reaching the parked estate car, they were systematically helped on board, in a state of total exhaustion they were soon strewn out on their respective blankets. Unlike Ian they had not a care in the world.

The car started and rejoined the track, as it trundled past he wondered what other people's lives consisted of. Undoubtedly for the driver there would be shopping, preparing meals, cleaning and whatever else, who would ever know? On passing him the driver gave a hesitant but assuring wave, a similar friendly gesture was endorsed by Ian. The vehicle was gone leaving a restored appearance of tranquillity to the estuary.

Now he appeared as a lost and lonely monolithic figure, allowing his contemplation of what had once been his investments in the English Lakes. Visualising the time twelve months ago with the two hotels on the property market. His business partners agreed both were to be sold as established but more importantly successful hotels, a time of anticipation waiting on their estate agents for sales to reach the point of satisfaction.

During this tense selling period by contrast he could not fail to recall the oil industries operations in the North Sea were coming under extreme commercial pressure, the lucrative days were drawing to a conclusion. Our heritage of being largely self-sufficient, even though we had traded vast amounts of our stocks on the world markets was closing faster than our government would like to admit. The industry was having to accept those feasibility studies which involved deep drilling into preciously unexplored reserves thought to be impractical in the early pioneering days of the industry.

Whilst the sale of the hotels in the Lake District was underway, Ian by contrast had been in the forefront of an extreme work load. As an engineer of practical hard core knowledge his involvement was desperately sought after; entering a peripatetic role with less experienced work colleagues who were eager to learn the latest amalgam of developments. Life was drawn back into the industry, by the expedient of exploring unknown drilling depths, a salvation resulting with new reserves of our precious commodity coming on line.

This desperate and new investment by our oil industry, costing untold millions of government capital was to a large extent open to all interested parties. By contrast what was happening at that time in a certain house in the town of Keswick was clearly not. Two people were laying plans for their financial future together, one of whom was Ian's business partner, whilst the other involved party was that of Ian's accountant. For this prevarication to work they needed to follow a route of absolute secrecy. During that time, the couple looked longingly out from the bay window of the accountant's semi-detached house. The tall privet hedge obscuring the avenue would not require them to perform its annual autumn pruning, as by that time their patience for the embezzlement of the hotels' capital would have materialised, and they would be long gone!

It was easy to recollect when the activity from their sales promotion got under way, he was too involved on the rigs to give this activity any of his stringent attention. There was no alternative other than leave it under the guidance of their estate agents. He remembered the surprise when he learnt that their original hotel, best described as having barely reached the estate agents books, was not only sold but had also achieved the asking price. Even dust had barely time to settle, as the new owners in the face of tourism competition were understandingly showing enthusiasm to get started.

Would their second hotel the 'Swan in the Moonlight' follow in a similar vein? That question after all this time was still ingrained in his memory, he could call to mind those emails sent out to his working rig following the various stages relating to the progress of sales. His concerns had been the hotel's more rural location, there were understandably doubts that this might possibly deter potential buyers.

Then came their reward with positive news, the estate agents admitted that following a time of inactivity, suddenly two interested parties appeared eager to outbid each other, an estate agent's dream. Following a period of nervous tension, one of the potential buyers dropped out of the race. It was over; the sale of the second hotel went through. Happily with a degree of satisfaction they learnt that the successful buyers were a local family group of hoteliers.

Those two precise words that he read on his text, 'it's sold', was enough for Ian. There had been no time for celebrations, work was hell on wheels, non-stop. What was it? Yes I remember, that coupling for the lifting gear, only available from an agent out of all places Texas, but the company had to live with it. For all that, and the work pressure I still remember the heady feeling of achievement, virtually intoxicated knowing that both hotels were finally sold.

By now his attention span and for that matter his personal comfort was calling for a change. He had remained dedicated to his recollection process, even though it existed as a jumbled mess. 'Get up.' Giving himself a verbal command. His active work lifestyle maintained a slim and equally well toned figure, not a man trapped in a sedentary state. With a height combined with weathered features, courtesy of his outdoor working regime, he gave the appearance of a man possibly many years his junior. For that, he knew he was in no position to complain.

For whatever purpose he continued his mutterings. 'Let's reach the headland.' Still maintaining the thoughts of the hotels, and how they following the sales passed from his possession. There were regrets, he was not able to return to either of the hotels to say personal goodbyes to his own staff. That important touch from him did not happen due as always to his work schedule. Realising how totally selfish he must have appeared, he could offer plausible excuses, but his absence at those changeover times had been most apparent and inexcusable on his part.

Somehow during that time if only I had got back from the rigs, maybe there would have been a clue to their schemes, instead of being told eventually and too late from an anonymous source. How cleverly they must have planned the whole course of deception. His own business partner, efficient, dedicated to the running of his hotels, then their astute accountant, he had always been an integral part of business minds making up the hotel management. How the romantic entanglement actually began, that was anyone's guess? He only knew that it was firmly based by their sickening catalyst of deceit. As for me my investment and capital growth is gone, stolen, and not a cat in hell to get any redress!

Ian attempted to imagine the whole sordid affair being orchestrated, probably from the house of his accountant in Keswick, in some 'Acacia Avenue' or 'Laburnum Drive'. All towns have places like that. Perceiving in his anger neat garden fences, manicured lawns, too late they were gone, long gone, and with his capital. The two of them intent with a life together, fuelled on a diet of deception. No doubt they had arranged to assume new identities in a far flung corner of the world.

Not able to disguise the fact, he continued fraught with worry, and what a pathetic understatement that was, not the guilty party, but now left to pick up the tabs. His future had financially matured but had as quickly evaporated. Those chequered windswept decks of the oil platforms which hopefully were for him to be a thing of the past. That was not going to happen. Why should he have fallen victim of their insidious schemes, he paused returning to the world of reality. The ghost of this inference was waiting in judgement on him, all contained and precisely explained in the content of those three letters.

Would he ever be allowed to put all this behind him? Now he had finally reached his destination, visible were the outlines of the distant rugged cliffs that offered a graphic backdrop to the coastal scene. On more tempestuous walks he would stop to take in this inspiring view, it never failed reach his innermost contentment, it deserved an accompaniment of music, what better he thought than Mendelssohn's tribute to Scotland that enigmatic overture, 'The Hebrides'.

Standing on the oozing wet shoreline he could not help noticing a coloured object marooned in a narrow elongated channel that was acting as its sanctuary. It was of all things a vividly green toy boat. On closer examination it was noticeable that an amateurish modification had been performed by the addition of a mast and sail. Perhaps the next outgoing tide would breathe life to the vessel? It was easy to perceive that the boat's recent make-shift handiwork was undoubtedly the activity of children.

Then something came chasing through his mind; boats should never be green. Ask any mariner that pertinent question, it's wholly unlucky. No it's more than that, there are greens of all shades each assigned a distinct name, no bearing on what this was to do with his stolen capital. Then for whatever strange reason he started to compile a list, like kids in the back seat on a car journey gaining points to overcome boredom. What are those greens? It's easy, try sea green then there's verdant not forgetting the flamboyant Lincoln green. Only then did he realise, and he had no idea why, another green, and that's the colour I want… 'Pea Green'.

Looking over the expanse of sea, recollections from his past were again encroaching for whatever reason, feeling at their mercy he allowed the intrusion. In particular there was a nursery rhyme from childhood, remembering a picture frame which contained the rhyme stitched with embroidery work. It used to hang by a cord over the mantelpiece of his very own bedroom in the farmhouse of his favourite aunt. He longingly thought back on those times of escape with lazy holidays from boarding school. Why did those times disappear so quickly?

Childhood, there was an element of sadness in his thoughts, those cherished seminal times, why such a long way back. He would often read that nursery rhyme aloud, there was an inspiring and strange appeal for him, why, he never fully understood. Perhaps by its words, he wanted to aspire to be that owl. The green boat, the toy boat, that is the trigger, and it's responsible for my past to reach into the present, Ian had not totally forgotten the rhyme, so much so its words were now starting to assimilate for him.

The owl and the pussy cat went to sea in a beautiful pea green boat... Maybe then I'm not at sea... *With some honey and plenty of money wrapped up in a £5 pound note...* But on the subject of money he could not lose sight of the implications those letters demanded, and there was no escaping. This is an adult world of reality where I live, not some children's nursery rhyme. Could there be a state of incongruity? Is my... How can I ever explain? The boat that supports my life... is now in danger of sinking?

Chapter 3

Ian turned the key in the yellow front door of his apartment. The colour appealed to him, not that it was noticeable but it was supposed to be lucky, the colour of his astrological star sign. On entering following his invigorating walk it was stuffy by comparison, he took the action of quickly opening the lounge window. He had returned as his new self, now approaching hopefully his changed outward image, that 'ostrich of life' was shaking off the sand and no longer prepared to bury one's head with the problems of life? Although cautious, as knowing that only time would possibly show results.

The answer-phone was displaying one message, his thoughts accepted that at least someone knows I am here. It was his sister Julia, aware of her brother's pending visit she had been trying to make contact, enquiring if he had arrived safely, whilst adding that the letters for his attention proved no way as problematical as imagined? Even as the message was concluding, Ian spoke out at the inert machine. 'Worse than I dared to imagine.' In doing so he turned his back abruptly on the answer-phone that was still in the process of concluding its deliberation!

With his thoughts poised in a positive mode he elected to do what we British aspire in times of adversity, make a cup of tea. He set about once again to read his letters responsible in starting his day. Self-blame was remaining heavily in his thoughts, what did I allow myself to get into? Seeing how relatively easy his business partner and her accomplice had organised their mutual embezzlement of both the hotels.

They were never content, they had added further greed to their viscous schemes, the whole travesty of events was catalogued by referring to his recent correspondence. The banks were showing concern to cash loans taken out by his business partner, large loans against the hotels, with no effort to start repayments, not surprising as they were both now gone. It did not end there, the business credit cards had been taken to their absolute limit. Hell, he thought, where does all this stop?

Struggling with his new image of not avoiding issues of life, Ian could barely bring himself to attempt to understand the implications surrounding his communications from HM Revenue & Customs. The missed VAT payments that in itself amounted to something of a crime, he dreaded the ramifications relating to the capital gains tax. What else could they have possibly done? Stole the charity boxes from the hotel's reception? Although trying, he was struggling and failing to contain his anger.

Pull yourself round, keep thinking possible solutions, he attempted to regain his self-control. The finger of guilt is pointing in no uncertain way in my direction, I have to endure that torture as if salt was rubbed into my wounds. Once more he viewed the letters, even down to their reference numbers, nothing would alter what lurked within their contents. He reasoned that the interested parties, not knowing who he was, so for that matter it could have been him who set up whole wretched affair. Any appetite for what he wanted to eat surprisingly enough had left him.

Self-inflicted isolation, that's my present state, not wanting any form of communication with anyone on these subjects, it's a complete and total embarrassment, that's a bloody polite way of putting it! He threw the letters back on the table, the whole series of sordid events was in danger of reading like a cheap article from a tabloid newspaper. He allowed his thoughts to seek the sanctuary of the drilling rigs, almost to the point of imagining the salt spray on his face. Believing that totally uninvolved work colleagues would talk away all his accumulated difficulties. Stop… Reminding himself, don't start burying your head in that sand.

Completely unrelated thoughts were invading his agenda, knowing on occasions that he had actually broken the law, for a start there are speeding endorsements on his driving licence, no good arguing with that. With fellow workers on the rigs feeling smug, isolated from the mainland we watched untold numbers of DVDs on the cinema, despite their rigid copyright implications. Fortunately his ramblings associated with guilt complexes came to an abrupt stop, isolation was shattered for him by the ringing of the lounge phone.

That has to be Julia; her usual professional way of trying to make contact. In his profound wisdom he had made his sister aware of the prevailing circumstances. Support he reasoned from at least one of his rather limited family was something of a possible and equally valuable lifeline.

'Hello.' He pre-empted the phone's last ringtone, expecting the offhand voice of his sister but had not anticipated the surprise.

'Hi, Dad.' The unexpected had struck, the welcome voice was more than he could have possibly hoped for, his eldest daughter Clare, the one that keeps in touch, even to the point of remembering the time difference from Toronto. 'I know you get that extended leave, Dad, how long have you being back?'

Ian was elated. This was his daughter; someone to talk to. 'Last night, not the best of journeys, but no matter, I am here at long last, get some time to myself. How's things with the media in Toronto?'

His enquiring question gave Clare the ideal opportunity to bring her dad up to date with all her latest endeavours for the Canadian Broadcasting.

The characteristics of Ian's family had produced something of a paradox. His ex-wife had returned to Canada with their two daughters, both of whom eventually joined their mother in the media of television broadcasting, where through her guidance they had both aspired to strong career paths. A pattern had emerged becoming apparent that the youngest daughter was very much towards her mother, whilst by contrast Clare maintained a loving devotion towards her father.

Although their marriage had failed by a simple expedient of diverse employment, and that was restrained in its context, but for all that it had generated an amicable balance that prevailed ever since. They both knew that accomplishments spoke as real time achievements and were equally proud of their daughters' careers. Ian had long since accepted what had transpired with his marriage, a common fact of modern day life, no point in fighting against it, but most reassuringly he never forgot that he had two daughters.

Right now it was wonderful to be listening to Clare, he had no desire to burden insurmountable problems in her direction, it was not her concern, she was leading her own life. He enquired, 'How's the rest of the gang?'

She was cautious, knowing that her mother was waiting to hear from Dad on some obscure family concern. Therefore she attempted in her opinion a perfect evasive reply. 'Now that you finally got all this leave, Dad, what about our wilderness trip together, just the two of us, as we always talked about?'

Ian listened knowing her request would not end on that point.

'Remember, Dad, what's it to be, the backwoods of British Columbia, or riding across the Mongolian desert? Got my sleeping bag ready.' His eldest daughter from an early age had always an enduring passion for the great outdoors.

He listened with heartfelt emotional feelings to his offspring's request, fully realising it was a perfect tonic for him. So much so it was having an effect of causing his current climate of difficulties to take a back seat. 'Clare it's in my diary, nothing better for us both. Keep your sleeping bag handy I will have some great ideas, that's a promise.'

She followed quickly with an assuring reply. 'Oh my God, keep you to that, Dad, you'll not escape. Anyway must go, have a scheduling meeting coming up in the hour. Call me soon, don't forget, love you.'

He reluctantly had to say goodbye, noticing a distinct Canadian accent that was getting stronger in his daughter's speech, but then he reasoned why not?

Reminding himself as if necessary, blood really is thicker than water. In doing so he glanced over to the collection of family photos, although now looking if anything out of date. Clare at her university graduation remained in pride of place, what a pity she is on the other side of the ocean.

Ian regained the lounge sofa, as the cushions were in the same arrangement he sank into their embracing comfort. Reassuring himself with what the phone call had meant to him, tough as he knew it was going to be, he was determined to come out of this. Reminding himself if that was necessary, you are a survivor, that is what really counts.

Could the answer for him lay in a change of direction? There is certain money for immediate needs. Perhaps it is a case of too long in the same employment? Realising the implication with this poignant and soul searching question, he pondered, have I grown tired of the oil industry, will it grow tired of me? His preconceived plan had now disappeared like a dream sequence. Justice had eluded him, that capital was no better than dry sand running through his fingers, dry desert sand. That seemed strange why refer to it as desert sand?

Much as he wanted to escape the issue of money it loomed again in his thoughts. Work colleagues on various North Sea rigs had lavished over what was on offer from the other side, namely the newly created fields in the Russian Caspian Sea. Expounding the virtues with their reserves of both natural gas and oil, added to this, they were crying out for experienced personnel that the Western world could offer, even prepared to pay a fortune with contracts. He cringed on one very thought the severity prevailing during a Russian winter, our climate change as yet had not reached that far.

Thinking of distances he suddenly remembered the two phones in his possession, they needed checking for any incoming communications. He quickly established nothing on the company's satellite, the situation was the same for his own mobile. Ian would freely admit he was not a lover of mobile phones, if anything he showed an aversion towards them. It is another of those selfish attitudes, but they always intruded with sets of problems, or worse, unpleasant news, even when switched off you are never entirely at liberty to escape.

The sofa, like the estuary tree trunk was exhibiting signs of discomfort, although boredom would be more correct. Get organised, that's the only way and start right now. What is the accumulation of what I actually owe? Get it down in cold print, start to think positively by making out a 'wish list' hard copy approach.

There was a PC kept at the apartment. Although only a reincarnation of a word processor and printer but that said it served its purpose. His tedious task was soon completed, on checking his copy he realised rather profoundly that a cheque for the closing amount would solve his… lifestyle. I suppose that's why they are called 'wish lists'. Wish for him was the operative word. Carefully folding the sheet, he secured it inside his jacket pocket, the visible evidence haunting him from the computer screen was with malice aforethought quickly deleted.

Since the morning down on the estuary he kept noticing a prevailing sense as what he would describe as moody which was supplying a transient thread reaching as it was into far distant locations? Imagining it was caused as a direct result of being away from the active involvement on the oil rigs, out there you could never escape that constant background noise, that for him was a million miles away. Looking out from the apartment's opened window there was an atmosphere encroaching, a noticeable presence of fog drifting in from the sea. For all that changing process taking place his thoughts were wanting to remain loyal to those episodes of past nostalgic memories. What had unfolded he was appreciating, soothing those mind-weighing financial implications that he could not escape.

Reasoning that somehow there has to be a connection, too many distant thoughts invaded his space, exactly what, he still had absolutely no idea. Spontaneously he urged himself to refer to his personal document file kept at the apartment. Hopefully there were bonds that could raise immediate cash for him, vital to survive, no option there. Storage of these items were kept in the ultimate of filing systems, consisting of a large carton, leaving a lot to be desired, it was all there, you only had to find it. He had not looked through the archive contents for ages knowing as well as all the family legal items there also remained more recent paperwork of what existed with his hotel ownership.

He attempted a vague mental diversion, is there really any value trawling through all this paper? It's the only way to find an envelope marked bonds. As his investigation began he could not escape smiling, letters and brochures were appearing like old friends you would meet at a family wedding or worse a funeral. The purchases, ongoing business plans, commitments to capital investments, and advertising proofs for the printers, it was as expected all filed. He thought, who would ever be interested again?

Personal items were lodged in the file for safe keeping, including one of lingering importance. It was his late father's wrist watch, opening its weary looking case it revealed a timepiece in the shape of a Rolex Oyster. As always without exception having wound and corrected the time and date, he was pleased that it started ticking away to resume its original purpose in life. He made a decision, it's left uncared for, we are going to change that, it is going to be worn, he whispered to himself. 'Times are changing'. That has to be the same for me, the newborn 'ostrich of life', there are no excuses only then would he have a chance to succeed.

Let's get on; urging himself to examine the collated history of his past. The letters, brochures, and the very first menu cards, he laid them out in front of him. This was having an insecure effect, a feeling of dealing with a past that now sadly did not merit recalling. Studying the advertising flyers for the hotels he accepted they had worked right from the word go. In reality it was no consolation for his current predicament, all this is doing is paying homage to past success with tourism.

In the veritable jumble there was a singular large envelope very securely sealed. Its scribbled title indicated, 'Magnus Field Dilemma'. Although going back years he did not need to remind himself, leave it alone it should not be opened. It might be old, but this is one genie that needs to stay firmly contained inside its bottle.

His brave thoughts were overcome by a virtual scent trail of self-induced curiosity, probably more associated with the 'killing of cats'. The tape on the envelope that was once clear had become opaque with age, one more look as a reminder, it's not going to change my life. Removing the envelope's seal it revealed the hidden contents, cuttings from both newspapers and magazines, and one full length article taken from 'The New Scientist' urging him to ponder on one thought from all these past events, if only we could have gone public on this one. He read one cutting that was adorned with photographs he knew they all followed a set agenda, recalling the consistent story line typical of what you would expect a government department to issue as an almost insipid cover story.

Unlikely discovery of Viking longships that contained remains of a diverse cargo found almost intact lodged out on the seabed in the North Sea… Ian read the notes that followed, the theories expounded were as diverse as a particular journalist wished to conjure up, the most applicable that he believed at the time he had highlighted…

Following much speculation the general opinion follows that the vessels were victims of severe storms that had swept them off course. Eventually causing them to flounder in the North Sea, sinking on to the regions of the sea bed that some eight centuries later were to become our present day lucrative oil fields. The longship's gruelling fate reached a final conclusion with their static graveyards together it was assumed with the Norse-men that formed the crews. Here they had laid undiscovered until the advent of our modern day oil exploration…

Then he recalled that diving operator crews assigned to the Magnus platform could not make out what they had stumbled across. Although Ian had always assumed it would have been a matter of time before seismic probing unearthed the vessels' whereabouts. But he never understood why previously deep trawlers fishing those areas had not connected first? Who knows, perhaps they were waiting in anticipation for us humble oil workers.

He could still visualise the first artefact lifted up to the surface, the remains of a ships timber rib, quickly identified to be of Viking origin, even before they were processed by carbon dating. That was the start of a whistle blowing exercise with flood gates opening with all number of archaeologists desperately wanting to visit the site.

Then suddenly it became very interesting, entombed within the vessels were found artefacts that did not relate to that, or any period of our history?

He refreshed his memory by reading another newspaper article …All worldly goods owned by the Vikings were always carried in their long boats… But what of those other relics lifted from the sea bed? Those assigned to assist in the recovery were amazed to reveal all number of objects in the ships planking that on rinsing showed no sign of salt water corrosion! There were several different sized black obsidian blocks of no apparent purpose, other than they at one time must have belonged to something?

Items of this salvaged collection if truth were known would be described in a present day catalogue of artefacts as deserving a description as 'state of the art'. It never truly added up, why was this technology found inside primitive sea going vessels? From their history, we all knew that the Viking fraternity certainly did not have anything like this at their disposal.

My ultimate money spinner, could I take the lid off this, even after all these years, the oil industry's cover story, or to be fair the government's cover up. Even rivalling the Roswell incident all over again, he started to experience a sense of goose flesh creeping down his neck and arms. Where is all the evidence now? For that matter those colleagues he was involved with at the time. Consider all the secrecy, it must have cost our government millions. One thing he had to admit the clever way it was all executed.

The best had to be the pantomime of staging an 'April Fool's' story, a deliberate ploy by our industry as a publicity stunt, they had to float that corker. After that, all those involved first hand, thought they needed to reinstate an allegiance and believe in Father Christmas.

One person was brave enough with this can of worms, Ian struggled to remember his name, yes Anderson, Jed, or something Anderson. Following his disclosure he was recalled to Sullom Voe, and then, it was heard, urgently wanted on one of the Texas fields or was it New Mexico? Put another way no one had any more contact from him again.

He abruptly stopped his rambling thoughts. All this has to be confined to history. Showing no reluctance he forced the cuttings and articles back inside the envelope. He was revealed as the goose flesh affliction left him now as quickly as it had materialised. If there are still any little grey men out there, perhaps they would focus their almond shaped eyes in a direction of recovering his stolen capital. In the meantime a safer course is to call time and believe in Father Christmas, too many questions and there never will be for him enough answers.

Showing little patience with the next phase he assembled all the various envelopes, and on that note staring in his face was by good fortune the particular one he wanted. It was wedged with those he had not bothered to investigate. The bonds, an immediate life saver to generate some instant money, although as he was to learn not what he had anticipated.

An attempt to organise some semblance of order was defying his efforts, empty the carton he considered, then put them all back and they would all fall into place. On this occasion all was not going as planned, one bulging file containing family documents escaped his hold and to his annoyance the contents spilled out on to the carpet, leaving him not in the best of humour. There was no option but to kneel and collect the debris. In doing so he noticed a curled white card lying vacant on the floor, by curiosity he investigated.

Turning the card over it revealed to be that of a historical black and white photograph, to which he could not fail to mutter, 'What's this one?' Barely finishing his comment, he stared at the picture's composition. The image was of a large rambling house, the property's exterior nearly clothed by encroaching ivy, whilst as a backdrop it nestled within mature trees. In the foreground was the well, clearly the source of water for the house, that would be achieved by what was plainly in view, a pail secured by rope to that of a winder. The photograph had a timeless quality prevailing, allowing its image for him to emit a calming and altogether inspiring warmth.

It was acting out an entirely visual spell. Ian now recognised where the photograph had been taken. Is this what's reaching out causing all my emotional turmoil? There was a feeling, if not bizarre, that he had just at that moment taken out a 'second mortgage' connected with his past.

The property in the photograph was acting as a bridge to his childhood. It was a farmhouse situated in a rural location near an unspoiled village in Cambridgeshire. From this very property those captured reminiscences of his school holiday legends had started and were never forgotten. Now, today this humble photograph was obsessing his centre of interest, having the means from within to throw a switch on a latent personal dynamo, that started to power up all his distant memories.

The farm belonged to the most favourite person associated with his childhood. Even now, many years after her death he continued to cherish that house and all the important stages connected with his early life. It was always known to him as the home of his beloved Aunt Anastasia.

Chapter 4

The five-bar gate appeared to give a brooding significance, creating a definite statement of 'no entry' further enhanced by a necklace of rusting chain wrapped to its support post. The days that might be attributed to its constant use seemed to have past?

Ian was struggling, teased by a question, realising his memory had failed. He was able to see that the nameplate on the gate was damaged, part of which was missing, leaving only the word 'Home'… what was the rest? Place or field, it did not really matter. All that did matter was beyond this gate is the farmhouse that was once owned by his Aunt Anastasia.

Parked on the driveway, he allowed the car's seat to be inclined in a more comfortable position. 'I'm here.' He teased himself that 24 hours earlier he had absolutely no idea, in fact he still had no idea why he drove nearly non-stop to a farmhouse in Cambridgeshire. It seemed since the events of yesterday, something needed answering, of what he had no idea? This was his challenge, which appeared to be the best description, it was akin to an assignment that he had walked into, somewhere there had to be an explanation?

He looked at the old photograph of the property that yesterday had decided to fall out of his family archives, reminding himself as if it were necessary, this is what started it. Now by contrast it can be seen in front of me, the real thing. Until now it was only a memory from the past. No, not a memory, he thought, something much more than that, it's where his childhood really began. There's scarcely a month goes by without recollections of past events from this very place, but what would this visit tell him?

The morning was stirring into life and the weather was noticeably improving. Now it felt it was worth all the effort. He had endured the awful overnight accommodation only wanting to reach his destination. Whatever had entered his world was strangely active, at best it was taking his thoughts away from his problems, which was a blessing. For that alone he owed his late aunt one enormous favour.

Realising he was becoming drowsy by the warm sunshine through the windscreen, even succumbing to be overtaken by sleep, that answered to him as a premium in the last few days, it was about time to leave the car. The driver's door certainly needed some adjustment and following the efforts of two good slams he finally succeeded in getting it closed.

So what's changed? The house exhibited a quiet atmosphere, devoid of life. Probably the owners were away, or had it now become a holiday home? All last night he had pondered exactly what he was going to say to the owners, and whether he would have the audacity to ask to look over their property. Was that now actually going to happen? But there was an ongoing mystery, why was the gate to the house so securely chained?

Walking over to the entrance, he saw that the grass on the front lawn was partially hiding a possible solution to his dilemma. Somewhat weather beaten with the supporting post broken was laying an estate agent's 'For Sale' notice. On his closer examination it was easy to confirm that the padlocked chain attached to the gate showed no evidence of any recent use.

Resting his arms on the top rail of the gate, and now rather annoyed with himself as he was again trying to recall the full name, Home… stead, place… no, they didn't seem right. Judging by appearances he could only assume that the property must still be on the market? Ian's presence had alerted the attention of one particular resident, whose territory was considered to have been invaded. An old holly tree was a convenient perch for the parochial garden robin, whose song was creating a distinctive pugnacious call, proclaiming… This is mine…

The brigadier's hands were no way as steady as some 30 years ago, however the qualities of his Zeiss binoculars remained unchanged.

With astute observation brigadier George Atwell DSO (retired) was methodically reconnoitring from his latticed kitchen window which served as his observation post. He focused on the stranger who for some time was content in supporting himself on the gate of his vacant neighbouring property.

Ian's slamming of the car door had alerted the brigadier, whose discerning views from his binoculars were now in the process of been collated in the form of a hand written report. The breakfast cereal carton on the kitchen table had been pushed aside to allow him some valuable writing space.

Height, build, general appearance, his dress, details appertaining to the car registration, were all logged, quickly, lest the subject move off. Now the mundane details were added to produce a comprehensive itemised report. This activity caused him to recollect, and draw a parallel, in how vital observation details were needed with his past military career.

George Atwell continued his observations with the stranger, who at this stage was intent in comparing the old photograph with the actual property. Try as he might the brigadier was unable to perceive what Ian was so intent on looking at. Patience, he reminded himself, one of the arts of good intelligence, something he had always on past occasions, instilled in his men. The binoculars were growing heavy, this together with frustration of not being able to add this missing detail, called for an alternative remedy, a cigarette.

The binoculars were placed on the table, conveniently alongside their case, its regimental insignia that once existed was long gone, the result of polishing by the owner. He produced a packet of cigarettes, and with a lifelong skill there followed a ritual tapping of the cigarette to secure the tobacco. When completed, his Dunhill lighter was snapped into action to finalise the requirement.

A calming influence followed, entering as it did George Atwell's realm of operations. Interesting he thought, even intriguing, if only I knew why he was so intent with that sheet of white paper? Anyway at last I can put through a new report. He stared down at the cigarette packet, although his close vision had long since expired, he knew that perpetually illustrated on the Players Navy Cut was the sailor who hailed from an 'HMS Hero'. Now currently appearing on these packets were also more ominous statements, try as they might they failed to remove his feeling of contentment. For him it was an interesting morning.

His observed target was returning to the car, obvious that he must be preparing to leave. The brigadier actively flicked through his address book, needing one important telephone number kept in the miscellaneous section. In his opinion it was high time that his report should be phoned through. He would encounter the usual irritating delays, as a series of sinuous diverts followed one another, security precautions he had always reasoned. It was an age since a report had been possible, for the simple fact that the property had experienced no activity from callers.

Eventually contact was established to a voicemail, 'Command Post calling'. It was his usual mischievous introduction. The brigadier presented his carefully worded report relating to the morning's observations, it lacked neither detail or accuracy, knowing how important it was that nothing should be lost in translation.

Justification, he was in a buoyant state of pondering at least today I have earned some of my annual retainer. How many years is it? He clearly remembered the arrival of the anonymous letter with its 'request' for him to consider monitoring activity at the empty neighbouring farm. Induced by the offer of adequate expenses, he, more by curiosity, had given the mysterious letter a favourable reply. For him having to pursue a route through a box number during these proceedings was enabling the other party to cleverly preserve total anonymity.

Although to a large extent housebound by an unpleasant leg wound the brigadier found the concept of his new task both easy and equally rewarding. Each year, it has to be three by now, there would arrive a Fortnum & Mason Christmas hamper. Followed by an addition of a 'special delivery' envelope containing a considerable amount of cash, compliments from an unknown sender.

Knowing this surveillance must be important, he suspected it was probably appertaining to some legal wrangle. Not my concern he always maintained, my remit is to report in an unbiased way and that's why I am paid my annual retainer, no more than that. George Atwell would agree that these little episodes made an interesting diversion to his life of retirement. Following the loss of his wife he had decided that a pursuit of a house with a large garden would be agreeable, although struggling with his ailment, there were rewards. Known as GA to his close friends it was clear even in his advancing years, that he still exhibited the stance and mannerisms of someone who previously enjoyed an active life in the armed forces.

With his ongoing scrutiny he noticed that his target having returned to the car was preparing to drive off. Good timing, with the message process now completed, and phoned through, no follow-on details appeared to be necessary. He remembered that at 1300 hours his taxi was due for his weekly sortie to patronise the local supermarket.

Now all I have to do is sort out that damn mouse, it's most likely in the cottage somewhere, the previously set traps had failed miserably. A wood mouse, an illegal immigrant from the nearby orchard had established itself in the potting shed enabling easy raids into the cottage, to feed on all number of interesting pickings. Until discovered it had wreaked havoc on a crop of sweet pea seeds laid out carefully on a shallow tray to fully ripen.

What had hit the nerve for the brigadier was the pedigree the precious seeds had come from. They were a unique historical speciality, a wavy sweet pea, the 'Gladys Unwin'. He adored his beloved affair in raising prize quality blooms, growing as they did on upright bamboo canes, to which his military mind could relate, as the flowering plants exhibited an almost regimental stance.

The starting of the car drew his attention back to the kitchen window, in time to see Ian drive away in the direction of the town. Our retired army hero tapped the ends of another of his cigarettes. Now with thoughts trained on a mouse as his target, new approach on tactics for the elimination of an unwelcome insurgent...

Ian rejoined the road listening to the tyres as they crunched on the gravel driveway. His time spent leaning on the gate had created an effect of a whirlpool drawing into its vortex too many past memories, all of which were unique and priceless. However he still failed to recall the precise name of his aunt's home, but in time that would come. At this moment he felt like a kid in a candy shop wanting to see and experience more. The estate agent in town was going to provide just that, although he needed to stoop to his ideas of low cunning.

Looking back at the farmhouse, the resident and protective robin was busy searching on the lawn before the morning dew finally evaporated. How sad to see the water well now devoid of the tiled cover and apparatus once employed for extracting water, that he still remembered was contained at such great depth. The well looked so differently inspiring in his aged photograph of the property.

Sunshine had started to envelop the house, whose top windows long since devoid of their drapes gave an empty and sadly uncared-for appearance. The property was old, having passed through many beleaguered stages of history. If there was a soul existing within its walls it was in effect weeping for the want of loving care and fortitude to return.

On those joyous school holidays spent at his aunt's home, Ian had not shown any great interest to frequent the town. After all his supply of sweets and desirable weekly comic was brought in by his aunt. All he ever wanted lay in the surrounding trees and fields together with the stream that flowed through the farmland; there was never enough time in his day.

So on this particular morning he would not be able to notice any differences that the market town could offer. One thing was for sure, his visits to dentists and estate agents did not always go well, but he was open for this to be disproved. Unwin & Hornby estate agents certainly commanded a prime site on the high street, you could not fail to notice their office. He glanced at the display of property arranged on view inside the office's bow-fronted windows. The open sign swung from side to side as he pushed hard on the latch of the entrance door.

What greeted him was a perfumed aroma hanging in the air of the open plan office. The reason became clear, when a woman, the only occupant turned round, holding an enormous aerosol can of wasp repellent. 'I am sorry, I did not realise you had come in, thought you were looking at properties in our window, so much trouble these days, all over the place, wasps I mean.'

Ian smiled and offered what he believed was a tactful reply. 'Probably caused by our excellent summer.'

'How may I help you, Mr…' over the noise of two wasps in the final process of expiring he replied, 'Ian Harbinger.'

How he was to continue was anyone's guess. 'I do hope you can, it's the property at the foot of Spring Hill going on if I remember correctly towards what I knew as Waite's Farm.'

A quizzical look came over the face of June Orpin the Office Manager, an inevitable pause preceding her reply… 'Homemead, now that's been with us for a while, there are some problems; nothing insurmountable. It's a listed building, you would have to be aware of that. Mr Jezzaid one of the partners would see you on this one. It's in a great rural setting, Mr Harbinger.'

At last, he thought, Homemead… why did I ever forget? 'Actually, Mrs Orpin,' having noted her name badge, 'it's connected with my past as far back as schooldays, with a lot of personal attachment to the property, family connected involvements. It's one of those life stories we all seem to inherit.'

Their mutually flowing conversation was interrupted by the inevitable incoming phone call. 'Please excuse me, may I take this call?'

Ian acknowledged the request, taking a vacant chair close by her desk. He could tell by the conversation, she was having to explain the finer details leading up to an exchange of contracts, and June Orpin showed a captivating telephone manner. Ian wondered how many dramas, so often connected in the buying and selling of properties she had to resolve. For some reason he imagined her active within amateur dramatics, ideally suited, commanding centre stage.

This had not been a good time for him to visit the estate agents. The phone call was finishing, and he decided on a course of action. 'Mrs Orpin I will be staying in town for a few days, here's my mobile number. Can you sort out a time when I can view Homemead?'

She was relieved to hear his request, as holding the fort today was not without its problems. 'Mr Harbinger, we will contact you by the end of the day, that's a promise. By the way where are you staying in town?'

He reflected. 'Not sure yet.'

June Orpin pointed in the direction of The Bridge car park. 'Globe & Rainbow, second right on North Street, and tell them that June sent you.'

She was right, the 'Globe & Rainbow' looked just what a tired traveller needed. This was a time for some desirable afternoon sleep, not hearing the North Sea dashing against the superstructure of the drilling rig, which with a degree of comfort meant he was still on leave. His thoughts became consolidated in one place in a resonance of all the times spent at Homemead, still annoyed that he had forgotten the name, but that did not matter, as now he was more than aware of the answer.

Chapter 5

'Ian, turn the handle slowly, it's not a race, you are trying to make butter.' Not really a job for a boy on his school holidays. It takes forever until the milk starts to turn, why isn't it showing signs of thickening? The one thing that did matter, was noticeable by an aroma emanating from the oven. Aunt Anastasia was baking his favourite plum loaf for tea. So he knew he had to show willing, at least until the appearance of the butter, accepting with regret that catching those minnows in the mill stream would have to wait. His slower and steadier turning of the churn's handle resumed, now under the stringent watch of his aunt.

What was that persistent buzzing sound? That does not sound like the churn, what's causing it? He grew concerned thinking it might possibly be his fault...

Ian's mobile phone was on the bedside table. Its ringtone brought him out of tranquil sleep, childhood dreams that belonged to the kitchen at Homemead coming to an abrupt end. Heart thumping and totally disorientated, struggling to know where he in fact was, the hotel... I've dosed. Reaching out for the cause of his interruption, he grabbed at the annoying oscillating device and to his relief he finally managed... 'Hello.'

The caller's voice had a distinctive accent, making him think that's Aberdeen HQ. 'Mr Harbinger, it's Unwin & Hornby the estate agents, my name is Fiona McRae assistant to our Mr Jezzaid, we have the details on Homemead. Mrs Orpin says that you are probably over at 'The Globe & Rainbow', if so it would be easy for me to deliver these, I pass the hotel on my way home.'

By now he was in control of his actions, aware it was not his Aberdeen office, but someone else with a noticeable Scottish accent. He responded with a more coherent reply, thanking them for their efforts, and looking forward to seeing the property details which he would appreciate being delivered to his hotel. Relieved and now breathing more easily he politely ended the call. His head was severely thumping, realising the effect of his afternoon's sleep would take some recovering. He recalled a French girlfriend of his who had said in the most intimate of situations… 'The sleep of the day is very 'eavy.' On this occasion her remark could certainly be endorsed.

He had finally managed to reach the reception, where he trawled through the property section of the 'Cambridgeshire Life Magazine' experiencing his feelings of regret, as the pages replicated a catalogue relating to his worldly losses. To obviate this he became engrossed in the magazine, with a riveting article on the subject relating to fence hurdle making. His purported interest was interrupted by a cultured voice that appeared and was audible from her reflection noticeable on the glass-topped table close by him. 'Now this must be Mr Harbinger, it's Fiona McRae, Unwin & Hornby estate agents.'

He looked up from the visual image on the table's surface, allowing the magazine to fall back on the reception's seating. Standing up he introduced himself. 'Hello, Ian Harbinger, pleased to meet you. Thanks for taking the trouble to deliver all about Homemead.' Endorsing his statement with a satisfying smile they both occupied seats around the reception's table, allowing Fiona to place her document case on its surface.

'June Orpin said that you would probably in addition benefit by having an overview with any concerns that Homemead has inherited over the years.'

For the first time since her arrival he was able to appreciate the second member of the estate agent's staff whom he had met. He made a rapid assessment. If this employee represented the Scottish patronage then without any doubt she alone would be an outright winner.

Fiona McRae was a person that we all at some time meet during our lives. She endorsed a noticeable constant attention span radiating from her eyes, not in any way soul piercing, just reassuringly warming. A person you would soon realise thrives on any number of topics relating to genuine in depth conversations.

He perceived she appeared more mature than her actual years. Of medium height, and what our current magazines on health and lifestyle would describe as a slim and equally agile figure.

By his continued observations it was noticeable that her coat was covered with rain droplets, promoting him to comment. 'Looks like you were caught a shower?' he added quickly, aware that she was ready to start explaining property details. Fiona nodded a reply, taking advantage of his comment to remove her partially wet coat the fabric of which was of pure woollen tweed, delivering a modern approach, perhaps best described as a cleverly calculated fashion statement. The water resistance of the material intrigued Ian, allowing him to drag up one of those life clichés. 'What do they say? "Water off a duck's back." What an expression that is.' His remark produced a thoughtful smile from Fiona, who at this point had finally opened her case.

The clicking of the catches restored Ian's attention. She rather nervously removed several sheets of paper together with photos, confidently passing them for consideration to the potential client. He studied the first page intently, in particular the updated photo of the property on the brochure's cover. During the vacuum of time that he was taking dwelling on the property's introduction Fiona's thoughts were buzzing with excitement. Would it be possible, just possible for me to start up the process that leads to an eventual sale? What a score for me with Unwin & Hornby. Then these sort of things do happen?

She prudently reminded herself, keep the conversation alive, show an outward going interest towards the client. 'Mrs Orpin tells me there's a family connection with the property. I personally do like the setting, I've often driven past and the house looks if it commands respect, it's a piece if I might use the term, of old world Cambridgeshire.'

By looking up he acknowledged her comments, there was too much, the estate agents certainly furnished all details, with an awareness to that of listed buildings. Eventually he replied, with an outward show of enthusiasm. 'Yes, at one time it belonged to an aunt of mine, goes back to my holidays from boarding school, all the countryside that I had at my disposal and me in my innocence, Homemead days will never to be forgotten.'

Fiona listened with her usual intuitive approach, fascinated by Ian's return to his childhood roots. In front of her was a man epitomising the wild outdoors, enduring something of a pioneering spirit? Yet he was at ease to describe his passion experienced years ago on a farm in Cambridgeshire. She tried making an assumption with his working background, realising it was an interesting challenge, calling for that of her female intuition.

'You see, Fiona,' he continued, but now having to talk louder over the sound of rain lashing on to the domed glass roof above the reception. 'The past, that seems to be the key feature, certainly since yesterday, I wouldn't say it's haunting me, but the last 48 hours need some explaining.'

Fiona sat forward, a better course of action than raising her voice over the incessant noise. 'This you believe could be associated with Homemead, how exciting to have a mystery connected with your childhood.' She stopped herself, remembering why she had called at the hotel, my job is representing the estate agents, not digging into people's past lives, no matter how intriguing they might sound.

Ian regained the conversation, welcoming the chance to speak to someone who at least he thought would be able to offer an independent view. 'Fiona, perhaps it's me, spending too much time out on the oil rigs in the North Sea, that's my fulfilment in life, or so I believe, maybe I've lost contact with matters on dry land?'

Fiona was delighted without having to use any devious feminine ways, she had been made aware what Ian Harbinger did in the big outside world.

Feelings of guilt caused by him acting out this pretence had entered Ian's thoughts; despite his show of enthusiasm, it was false. The estate agents were doing their part, but in no way would it ever be possible for him to even consider buying his childhood retreat. I have to persuade myself to stay devious, I must see inside Homemead again. Looking up from the property details his gaze went up to the ceiling and the noise created by torrential rain. It cried out for another rather obvious remark. 'This will certainly lay the dust.'

'Excuse me, sir.' Ian turned to see a member of the hotel staff. 'Are you joining us for dinner?' He was looking into a cheerful face, no doubt the hotel's head waiter who was standing poised with the menus. A flash of complete inspiration came over Ian, he looked back towards Fiona.

Aware that women don't like direct questions, he indicated. 'I'm going to dine, would you care to join me?' Quickly supplementing.'If you have no other commitments?' He did not wait for her reply, rather pensively he added, 'Then I can tell someone why yours truly is in the middle of Cambridgeshire on a very rainy night.'

When she was finally able to reply to Ian's invitation it was both articulate and precise. 'Thank you, I've heard the meals here are excellent.' She smiled whilst at the same time acknowledging the head waiter who politely handed her one of the hotel's menus.

Ian was content, if not entirely eager to continue his conversation… 'There you have it, one day out on the rigs with the oil industry, doubling up and selling my business assets, it's goodbye hotels, and currently trying to have some long overdue leave, if that's what passes for chasing all over the UK. But, and this is important, there is a plus side, I'm in pleasant company, who is prepared to listen.'

He had steered a calculated and careful course explaining these events, deliberately swallowing his pride by staying away from implications relating to his lost capital investments.

Fiona believed that her evening was infinitely better than at home watching television. She was genuinely interested and fascinated by Ian's past and even more so with his recent involvement. Amused by his description of someone oddly wanting to buy a property, in the middle of Cambridgeshire on a wet night. As she was aware there would be a lot of time over dinner, she decided to ask enquiring questions in a gradual series of instalments, reminding herself who she was still representing, her beloved employers.

'There is one thing, Mr Harbinger, with Homemead.'

At this point he interjected, 'Please, call me Ian.'

Following a hesitant pause to his request she resumed. 'Well… Ian there is more than a makeover needed, it's stood empty for ages long before I joined the firm, it's old, those blocked up windows over the front door, that's window tax days.'

He offered a rather stilted reply. 'Yes I do remember how dark it was in the stairwell, quite spooky, especially for someone like me, a kid full of too much childhood imagination.'

Their meals arrived, allowing them time for a ritual admiration of the food's rather artistic arrangements, which put them both in danger of resembling attitudes of television celebrity chefs. Fiona steered the conversation, with a question about her interest with the oil industry. Whist Ian was delighted knowing his appetite was finally restored, his money problems could not be erased, but at the moment their conversation over dinner was simply priceless!

'First of all, Fiona, forget the glamour that you might think exists. After years of sea spray and eating methane gas you might wish you had chosen a better vocation, but then to be fair the camaraderie is second to none.'

She decided quickly with a following and rather pertinent question. 'Are there any women in the oil industry, that work on the rigs?' Commenting, that whilst she would welcome the lucrative salaries, but would undoubtedly battle with the problems of seasickness, unable to describe herself as a good sailor.

He surprised her with his eventual answer. 'Yes there are women employed on several platforms to my knowledge, they can show the men they are not frightened getting stuck in.' Remaining cautious not to pursue discussions relating to current issues, knowing that fossil fuels were in the political firing line with global warming concerns. Ian really could not care as he was experiencing a feeling of relaxation, all the money stress, hell, did money really matter, what if the person in front of you could be a solution to happiness?

Ian smiled thoughtfully adding, 'Enough of the three letter word, oil. I've left the best bit to last.' He actively shuffled through the collection of papers, to locate the envelope containing his precious photo of Homemead. He passed it over to Fiona who by now had guessed what the envelope might be holding. Her patience was rewarded allowing her curiosity to remark on the photograph, 'Wow, it's certainly changed, that's from a time when loving care was shown to the house. Have you any idea when this was taken?'

He paused. 'No, only wish I had. What you are looking at is this mystery, anyway since yesterday when that photo fell out of the family archives.'

At that point in their conversation the waiter arrived to collect the plates, in doing so leaving the dessert menus. Ian became almost desperate to explain his personal connections with Homemead and what his aunt had meant to him. 'You know, Fiona, the last 48 hours for me, apart from everything else has also been something of a guilt complex.'

His comments started to make him nervously fumble with the menu folder. 'During the latter years of my aunt's life, all I was doing was sending her the obligatory Christmas card, far too involved, wrapped up in my own selfish world, what's more I don't even know if those cards were received.'

Fiona was both quick and prudent with her reply. 'If it's any consolation I would imagine we would all be doing the same thing. Your aunt no doubt realised your, how can I say, remoteness, oil rigs, nature of the job, you know what I mean.'

Perhaps she was really saying exactly what he wanted to hear, but nonetheless her remarks were appreciative. 'Thanks anyway for your support, I'm still feeling a guilty complex, my aunt is no longer with us, and I'm, well, unable to turn back time.'

He realised there was a danger of allowing his melancholy feelings to ruin their conversation. They had passed on the desserts, now the coffee tray had arrived. He took what he thought was an easy and feeble course of action, reaching across with the tray he offered her a dinner mint.

The conversations by the other diners had started to level out, as by now the restaurant was gradually emptying. Ian was determined to redirect the attention away from himself. Therefore needing to refresh the topic of their conversation, he decided on a concerted plunge. 'At the risk of being curious here I am in the company of someone originating from Scotland, I can only imagine you must like this area? Hopefully your job throws you enough interesting challenges?'

Despite trying to remain dedicated as a member of the estate agent's staff Fiona found herself victim of an enticing trap wanting to answer his enquiring question. 'Of all things it's down to a few chips.'

Her reply naturally left Ian puzzled.

'By that I mean the silicon chip industry here in Cambridge, to be precise it was two things, firstly relocation following the unexpected death of my father in Scotland, I needed a respite, wanting at least for a while to escape the confines of my much beloved Highlands.'

She became active allowing the cream to pour slowly into her coffee, creating a pause in her conversation that no one would have the audacity to interrupt. 'Then, here in Cambridge I met Robbie a fellow Scot who had just graduated, we got on like a house on fire.' She laughed, thinking that's a good expression coming from an estate agent. 'Anyway it all fell into place for him, a job here in silicon chip technology with an American parent company, he really could not believe his luck.'

Ian detected a feeling that all had not progressed according to plan, but he dare not disrupt the flow of her dialogue.

'Anyway, Ian, he'd only been there four months when he was induced by an offer of a serious promotion on the condition he moved to their main division in California.'

Ian knew he needed to add an obvious remark. 'Fiona that sounds good.'

She shook her head, clearly wanting to explain further. 'The promotion with a new life in the States hit him like a shaken up bottle of fizzy drink, exploding, like he did, either his character changed or I was not prepared to adjust, you guessed it, we parted… He's out there, loving the experience no doubt.'

Ian took advantage of the pause. 'Don't see you on the American West Coast, you'd soon be craving for the cool winds of the Scottish Highlands.'

Fiona replied with her characteristic smile, his appropriate remark had drawn her thoughts to Scotland with her total passion for the family business venture that she was still determined to both enhance and pursue.

An inherent and noticeable silence was having the effect of eroding the ambience of the restaurant, as now they were the sole occupants. In a most discreet manner, Fiona had glanced at her watch, what it showed required her to add the obvious comment. 'Ian, much as I am enjoying the evening I will have to make tracks soon, it's an early start tomorrow.'

He rapidly adjusted to reality. 'Yes, indeed, our conversation has been what a good dinner deserves, anyway, I promise to read through all the details of Homemead and contact the office for a convenient viewing.'

They left the restaurant, and on reaching the reception area they could see that the rain had finally stopped. Ian was struggling with his conscience, although taking the opportunity to thank her for her company, whilst at the same time desperately attempting to suppress a feeling of liability towards the estate agents by the consequences of him wanting to view a certain property, but as he knew as a complete time waster. Hiding his feelings of deception, he helped her on with her coat.

Fiona was determined to leave him a final thought which was generated from pure determination with the passion for her family's business. 'One day, these coats will be my venture, or to be pedantic the fabric they are made from, please let me tell you about that sometime.'

It was easy for him to discern the sincerity imparted by her closing remark.

Ian reluctantly said goodbye, leaving uppermost in his mind, why do the best things in life always end so quickly? It's like all those school holidays on my aunt's farm, I don't even remember it raining.

Standing in the hotel's entrance he became aware of a feeling almost as if a presence had come over him, reminding, as if he needed reminding of the expression that someone was walking over your grave, putting the cause down to logically that of draughts in the entrance hall.

By contrast he looked at the modern day picture of Homemead, satisfied with how it occupied the cover of the estate agent's brochure. Knowing what he saw was responsible for starting this whole mysterious charade of a man returning for whatever purpose to greet his childhood.

Chapter 6

Astrologers by their wisdom must have recognised this particular day as rather unique. Alignments, moon phases, in fact the whole cosmic circus was creating an amalgam for the ideally balanced horoscope. Therefore those affected within their own star signs by the various profound events, were perhaps to be rewarded with assurances of personal fulfilment.

In the quiet secluded cottage opposite Homemead the brigadier was at peace, dozing in the comfort of his armchair. Previously he had studied his report that earlier had been directed by him to the unknown recipient. Now the only sound in the room was a constant repetition emitted from an ageing gramophone… click – click – click; the stylus on the record had become redundant half an hour ago, when the record had finished playing.

His satisfying sleep was the direct result of a second glass of malt whisky, a residue of which remained in his glass that was tightly cupped in his hands, therefore it would be a perfect drinking temperature. The deep sided armchair had a reassuring feeling of almost consuming the brigadier, creating a situation like the snug fit he would have experienced in the turret of a Chieftain tank.

Some biscuit crumbs, surplus from his previously eaten shortbreads had fallen down to the wooden flooring, much to the satisfaction of the interloper in the guise of a wood mouse. Unconcerned by the repetitive sound it was busy enjoying a salvaged meal, life for this 'resident' was different since the cottage had become his new home. Food was at hand. Unlike out in the orchard there was not the risk of an owl's silent strike of death.

Now the crumbs available for the mouse were all consumed, there were no more. Perhaps the brigadier's ailing eyesight in the light of day would fail to notice the 'calling card' droppings left on the floor by our most grateful of lodgers…

Marcus operated the remote for his garage door, the black saloon car came to rest against the stop pad; with familiarity he slipped the select lever into park position. The driver had experienced something of a long and active day, but for all that, he was eager to reach his desk to view his incoming emails. Marcus had a distinct sense of pride with anything that he owned; on leaving the garage he demonstrated a ritual of wiping over the vehicle's rear blue and white circular badge. The business of the day was concluded, now the time belonged solely to him.

The voicemail by its pulsing light was patiently indicating two new messages, they would have to wait as he was far too involved logging on at his computer. Marcus noticed his mouth became parched with a sense of almost disbelief, the long awaited email had finally materialised, his dreams were about to be answered. His bid had been accepted, unless of course they withdrew, then why should they, not after all those delicate negotiations, firmly convincing himself that will not happen.

His obsessive side was rising to the surface, but he accepted this predicament. An enduring passion ruled his life. He inwardly smirked remembering the main reason highlighted with the divorce proceedings. The accusations of his obsessive nature, he reassured himself that was all history. It's my life now, that postage stamp is coming into my collection.

Marcus by nature was a cautious man, now however a sense of exhilaration had overcome him; desperately he was trying to remain in control. Examining the authenticity documents that had arrived from Melbourne over a week ago, remaining confident that all the essential requirements were correct, the bids hit the right spot. Given the hundreds of pounds he was about to invest in the deal, it did not surprise him.

It was time to celebrate, after all this does not happen every day, probably as well given all the excitement. He perceived to pour himself a large vodka. In doing so he would not admit, but his hand was showing signs of shaking. This must be what it would be like to discover, he did not even waver knowing exactly what he was referring to, a Victorian post office Mauritius Blue that had remained hidden for generations. But in his own diminutive way with his stamp that was how he was feeling. Alone but contented he raised his drink in celebration, soon he would be realising his latest acquisition, the five shilling New South Wales Air Mail 'Special'. Why the stamp had such a high face value he had no idea, then he reasoned, those were the pioneering days for the newly formed Australian Postal Service.

His second glass of vodka had the effect of promoting him on to a level of a leading authority in philatelist circles? In particular to matters relating with a compulsion concerning vintage Australian postage stamps. He sat relaxed on the white leather sofa, a contented man, from there he was able to hear the two messages which had awaited his attention. The first could be dismissed as it was a reminder to settle the plumber's bill. The second message caused Marcus to reach forward on the sofa, a slow aged and monotone voice was describing a man leaning on a gate looking at the property called Homemead.

He gulped at his drink, but the glass was empty. The description at last and what we have been waiting for all this time. Karl will be elated. All along, he said he would return. What if this is the person? Then our dreams might finally happen. His evening was getting too much for him, he declared it was definitely time for yet one more, much needed drink…

Fiona looked despondently at Ian's gift; the single dinner mint residing on her dressing table, unable to fully understand why she had collected it from the restaurant. No matter. She could focus on it, enabling her mind to retrace an enlightening evening. There are still men out in this world, mature men that know what life is supposed to be about, would she possibly find one again? Exasperation had probably taken over her quest. Was it worth the effort, believing it's more like solving the perplexing task associated with a Rubik's Cube?

Her coat was hung over a chair; the walk from the hotel had been achieved only by encountering another rain shower. Remembering Ian's remark, she watched the water droplets rolling off the natural wool. This fabric was the inspiration for her business venture, the prospect was generating excitement. Distribution, that's where my plan needs a new approach, I am determined to discuss that with Ian, he has that sort of active mind. Each obstacle will be beaten, even now in our austere times of credit limitations, my home community would be with me, and that will move mountains!

 Fiona's thoughts were a long way off, in the region of the Scottish Highlands. Their cottage industry had been founded by her late father, it was growing, but she wanted it to take off, not casual passing visitor trade, anyone could do that. There was a vibrant market on a global scale that existed that would encompass quality traditional material. Marketing awareness, as always when she put her mind to these particular ideas everything became embroiled, I must target our products at those sectors that still have money to spend. That was her planning strategy, wanting it to happen sooner rather than later. At this late hour her thoughts were no longer cloistered in a small market town in Cambridgeshire...

At the Globe and Rainbow, Ian Harbinger had ensured that his mobile phone was definitely off. The travel alarm clock was set reassuringly on the bedside table, tomorrow promised to be a day with an element of self-discovery. Now settled, and as promised he attempted to understand the documents relating to Homemead. Soon it was evident that he was reading the same sentence over again, his evening in the company of Fiona had claimed him; that perhaps sounded rather dated, not that it really mattered at this time of night.

The property details were on top of another copy of Cambridgeshire Life; out of interest he quickly scanned the articles. Although in a state of approaching sleep, his curiosity centred on one particular feature, the history with farmhouses unique to the county. What struck him immediately were the archive published photographs, there in front of his eyes was Homemead, the angle of view might look different, but there was no mistaking, that was certainly his aunt's property.

He attempted an instant comparison to his own photograph, with his verdict guessing that it was about the same time? Although the bedside light would benefit with improvement, there was no doubt, he was convinced, that's Homemead. The accompanying article could be read in the morning, he propped his beloved photograph against the bedside lamp, believing soon he would have answers to all these occurring events. The town clock was in the methodical state of striking the midnight hour. Ian was engrossed with images of listed buildings, farmhouses, mixed with a relaxation preceding sleep, he totally failed to register the twelfth stroke...

The African sun infiltrated through the office window blinds, an easy task as many of the slats were missing. A ceiling fan waged a tedious repetition in attempting to clear the air hanging in a state caused by cheap cigar smoke. Its pulsating drone continuing hour after hour, the centre hub had leaked lubricating grease over the passage of time creating a graveyard with an assortment of dead flies.

Karl's eyesight was unequalled. He was lying back on what passed as the office couch, staring at the fan to watch the lazy progress of his cigar smoke, attempting at the same time to count individual insects encapsulated in the globe of grease. This was the time of the morning with its silence he always relished, although accepting the noise from the swishing fan blades.

A tap came on the office door. 'Leave them,' was his retorted reply. The boy deposited the newly polished Veldtschoen boots on the veranda. That morning chore was completed for another day, more importantly on time for the 'boss'. He hoped that the rest of his work would progress as easily.

The phone started to ring, Karl reached over not bothering to see what the display indicated, assuming it's some early impatient customer, with a disaster to sort out in this humidity. 'Hello.' The hesitant intake of breath from the caller gave Karl the realisation who had phoned him.

'Leetle brother, 'bout time, Marcus, you made contact.' Offering to his younger sibling a jaundiced and equally curt reply.

'Karl, listen this time it's real news, positive news, he's arrived at Homemead, we were right.' Marcus failed to complete his excited sentence, as he was rudely interrupted by his brother.

'We were right, I was right, my leetle brother. How do you know for sure, or a false alarm, like last year, that salesman stopping at the gate for a piss?'

'Karl, please listen to me, it's the description, age is right, it has to be the nephew, the report is explicit and the time he spent there, the old brigadier is no fool all the detail in his message.'

A pause followed in their conversation, Karl allowed his cigar smoke to drain repulsively away from his lips. 'Leetle brother it sounds good, but only sounds good. Check it out with the description, be careful, I know you will, you're too damn careful, bro, for your own good. Remember our father's words, you get back, double quick, hell we could be on the road to millionaires.'

Outside the siren wailed calling his workers to the yard, he replaced the phone; there were no goodbyes in his conversations. He needed to start another busy day, a gruelling day. The only way he believed he could achieve much was by kicking arses, something that his men knew only too well.

Their boss stood on the office veranda, careful to avoid the flooring that creaked under his weight. Above him was the immaculately preserved company's sign, 'Botha Plant Hire' his greatest aspiration was the proprietor's name, Botha, his family's name, that he would jealously guard against all possible on-comers.

Like most other buildings on the 'HK Airport Industrial Estate' it needed a lot of much overdue attention. Situated at Namibia's air terminal of Hosea Kutako it had been the first built, when the country was set to expand with all manner of new found wealth.

Karl Botha had got out of South Africa some years previously, shrewd enough to blame it on the politics. The facts were more volatile, he was being pursued by his creditors, his involvement in the gun dealing business was getting just a bit too dangerous. Anyway that was in his past, a closed book, as he was always hoping. Now domicile in Namibia he had subscribed to the business of plant hire equipment, which he considered a more respected form of earning an honest living.

Over the years Namibia's climate had suited him, the African sun had contributed to a deep textured face that a wealth of skin care products would be wasted on. His appearance was noticeable by his natural red hair colouring, overflowing to a full facial beard, this on a man of creditable height and stature. In today's parlance he would be described as, 'don't mess with me', but nothing could attempt to conceal his hideously motivated temper.

Karl's laconic South African accent issued out the instructions to his workers for the days assignments. 'Today we start earning bloody money for once, get da dollars coming my damn way.' Not one of his employees listening to his orders would ever dream of offering him a reply.

His mind drifted back to the conversation with his younger brother, imagining him at his home, so neat and precise. The weakling in the family as his father had always called him, growing up thin and pathetic protected by their mother. Even now Karl would never forgive him for what he had done by changing his actual family's name.

But he had to rely on him, the 'mole' as it were, living in the UK. This time, if only my brother Marcus is right? The one they have waited for all this time has finally turned up. Just suppose, what Father had told us his two sons, and now it was about to happen. Karl never forgot as a young man visiting the penitentiary to see his father, and those last words he had uttered. 'Find them, they're out there in the desert.'

Looking towards his cherished Toyota pickup truck, he watched the 'boot boy' busy washing the vehicle. He was starting to imagine his future with money and what power that meant. Taking the cigar from his lips, it was thrown with disdain on to the broken shingle yard. Maybe this was starting to be a very interesting day? The boy noticed where the cigar had fallen, when there was a chance, and nobody was looking, that prize would be his.

Chapter 7

Ian's shallow slumber was dissolving away, as daylight was invading with its subtle presence through the breaks in the curtains so ending his vestiges of sleep. Any remaining dreams in his possession had no option other than fade as memories.

Appreciation of his good night's sleep was noticeable; perhaps his deficit score was beginning to diminish. More so as he was prepared to gamble with the perilous route involving the hotels make your own tea, knowing most likely what to expect. This get up and go attitude, hitting the road running was torture, but common practice for him working out on the rigs.

An early start for an interesting day was going to pay him dividends. But firstly he wanted to read the magazine's article on local farmhouses, content that he could understand it now without falling asleep. He noticed that the magazine was well out of date, thinking it ought to be consigned to a doctor's waiting room. That aside, his attempts to locate the article failed, he resorted to using the magazine's contents page, but still without success?

The front cover's the same, but then it's the only magazine in the bedroom, I could not have possibly imagined that article, not again, another absurd trick, there were three pages, and the photographs… Homemead for a start? He was becoming distraught, I need that appointment today, once inside the property, then maybe it will offer a plausible explanation. When that's done, I'm definitely out of here, go home and put a stop to this chasing around, I don't even know what I'm involved with.

Concerned how despondent he was feeling, he abandoned his cup of tea, believing things would improve with a good hotel breakfast. Looking towards the bedside table for a measure of reassurance, he could see the stack of property documents but not the photograph of Homemead… Hell that's missing also.

Last night it was propped up against the lamp, it must be in this unearthly heap of papers. When he wanted, Ian could be the most untidy of people, as confirmed this very morning. He searched through methodically, but the result remained the same, no sign of his photograph. 'Let's have more daylight.' Muttering all manner of concerns, he crossed the bedroom to struggle with the curtains, that after his sustained efforts they reluctantly fully opened.

His uncontrolled search was hectic and eventually resolved by the introduction of daylight, there on the floorboards was his photograph of Homemead. 'What in the name are you doing over here?' For whatever reason it was residing against the room's ornate mantelpiece. He was prepared to argue, it's all very odd again, but why, not another of those days?

Kneeling down to collect his valuable possession, he became aware of the answer to the mystery. Draught, a vast and unnecessary gap on the lower edge of bedroom door, that's the reason, how wonderful to find an answer to a dilemma, there's always an answer. A rogue draught caught my photo and that is all. The huge gap the result most likely at some time from an over-zealous carpenter.

Relieved with the photograph back in his possession, and for solving the reason of its temporary disappearance, he considered it must be breakfast time. On what is definitely going to be a very different day, knowing it was also the day of reckoning, dwelling on his plans with the estate agent to act out his deception, posing as the worst of time wasters. Was there any other way? No, get myself into Homemead, that's what I need, then hopefully bury all these 'ghosts' from my past.

The hotel continued to live up to its reputation, as the breakfast was like those he was used to on the rigs, unequalled. From the dining table he phoned the estate agents, much to his surprise Unwin & Hornby had pre-emptied his request. They had tentatively arranged a viewing for today at 11 a.m. Mr Jezzaid the partner dealing with rural locations would be there to meet him, the efficiency and courtesy that was shown only served to deepen Ian's feelings of guilt...

On reaching his destination he parked in the same position as on the previous day. Cool morning air, resulting from last night's rain showers, with an intervention of sunshine was responsible in lifting his spirits. Yes, it was causing him to recall the delightful evening in the company of Fiona, at least, it had created an intrusion zone against all these recurring events. But it was stronger than that, he was in a determined frame of mind, confident these happenings were to be resolved, and more importantly very soon.

Patiently sitting in his car, Ian became intrigued with activity noticeable from the car's driving mirrors. It was the same on both sides, spiders were spinning their receptive webs. Obvious they live in the void of space behind the mirrors, they set webs and survive by any resourceful means leaving him in wonder at the power of nature. The mirrors' reflections would have an appealing interest to any passing flies, but it left him one question, by wondering if the near and offside incumbents ever met?

The vigilant predators occupied their webs eagerly awaiting their prey, Ian watched, intrigued by the spiders' astute cunning. Whilst in the same context, and unbeknown to him, from his observation post brigadier George Atwell, binoculars in hand was paying full attention to his target in the parked vehicle.

Ian became conscious of a noise on the driveway as a car pulled up behind him, it was 11.10. He could see in the internal mirror, a rather sharp looking hatchback. There was an unexpected surprise for him, as Fiona was in the process of struggling with her briefcase at the same time of getting out of her car, of Mr Jezzaid there appeared no sign.

'Hello, Fiona, this is a welcome surprise', he remarked as he went towards the newly arrived car.

There followed an instant reply. 'Ian, it's one of those, you know, mornings. Our Mr Jezzaid is delayed, actually he can't make the appointment, all apologies possible, so I'm standing in for him. He would like to meet you, maybe he will invite you for lunch… I'm really sorry for arriving late.'

He could clearly see the magnitude of stress that her conversation was showing. 'Listen, Fiona stop, and mentally count up to ten and relax. Homemead is hardly likely to disappear off the planet.' She welcomed the relief that his reassuring words of support meant to her.

Fiona realised she was treating Unwin & Hornby's potential client more as a friend, but then why not, it caused no hesitation with her reply. 'Thanks, Ian, trouble is with this property our Mr Jezzaid always shows a special interest. That's true of any of the rural locations I suppose,' she quickly added as some disclaimer. 'Of course there are listed building implications to consider.' Careful to avoid referring to them as issues which could restrain his interest with the property.

He saw that Fiona had a collection of property keys in her possession. 'Right come on. In your time please show me round my childhood haunt.'

As they both moved towards the gate, their talkative approach disturbed the inquisitive garden robin, whose decision with this needless intrusion was to fly away in annoyance…

The brigadier could now clearly see the two visitors as they reached the entrance. He surmised that this did possibly look like a viewing of his neighbouring property, reflecting on the fact that it must surely happen one day. Anyway a further report to put through, activity on the 'front line' at last, and it looked like there's a response…

The gate's padlock was corroded, but with Ian's intervention the lock eventually became free, after further effort the gate swung back on the creaking hinges. Together they finally entered the grounds to the property. Fiona was becoming composed, to the point of resuming her conversation. 'That's it, you're back on the right side of the gate, after I won't ask you how many years. What's it feel like?'

He hesitated in his reply. Although conscious of the question, he was absorbed in a world of his yesterdays, the summer holidays away from boarding school. Now in the present day with all his personal baggage of immature memories, the added contrast for him in noticeably feeling strange to return now was with the aged maturity of an adult.

He slowly rejoined the present world of reality, unaware that he had not replied to her question. By now they had reached the front door of the house, which Fiona unlocked. On opening she paused to allow their potential client to enter first. Ian was restraining a melancholy feeling that had strangely gravitated towards his thoughts ever since he had passed through the property's gate.

Fiona taking advantage with the lull in the proceedings, opened her case to obtain the relevant documents. It seemed odd to her, the firm's client, known on a personal front, anyway, since yesterday evening, now I am trying to sell him this property. She need not have worried, as the 'interested party' was experiencing what could only be described as an earth shattering anti-climax. For whatever reason the interior of Homemead meant nothing. Running through his subconscious was one single train of thought, knowing it's been said before… 'Never go back.'

'Ian I have to say, it's a little more than a make-over needed, the problem it's stood empty so long.' Fiona was struggling trying to exhibit her skills as an estate agent, she received only a nod of confirmation. Since entering the hall Ian had become aware of the property's dank atmosphere, only confirming Fiona's comments. However, he still ruminated on that singular thought, reminding himself rather stupidly… 'Never go back.' How many times in the past he'd heard that expression, now even he had to retrogress in this situation. Homemead did not belong to him!

Unwin and Hornby's representative meanwhile remained impartial studying the property details, but for all that she could not help noticing the change that had clearly come over Ian, she thought probably an encroachment of childhood memories. A new angle of approach was her next attempt. 'Ian, let's look at each room giving them in turn entirely fresh ideas, say create a modern setting, bring it to life without losing their character.' With no reply forthcoming to her optimistically held ideas, she added, 'The previous owners, were some art design family business, don't know how long they were here.'

As they entered the main reception room their conversation was noticeably enhanced by the room's hollow void. Dwelling on Fiona's uplifting ideas, Ian was struggling to focus on the reality of exactly where he was. He mentally nudged himself, come on, you are inside the property, that's almost ruling your actions. He succumbed and offered his apology. 'Sorry, Fiona, this all appears strange, almost foreign, don't know why it should.' Worse still he was standing inside the house as a complete time waster, not able to fully appreciate what he had contrived. He desperately wanted to explain to her, but knowing that would only compound his now stressed predicament.

Exactly, what am I expecting to see? My aunt to appear and tell me that tea's ready, sliced ham, followed by chunks of buttered plum loaf? He looked into another of the reception rooms, some discarded packing cases remained, creating a forsaken appearance as if nothing belonged. Despite struggling he was unable to recall what this room was used for in his childhood. Now it appeared intimidated by having its windows partially boarded over, whilst gaps in the ailing mortar were allowing the ingress of ivy that had achieved a transient hold on the walls.

He issued himself another of those orders; let's pull out, with as little pain as possible. With his thoughts in a state of gyrating, and declaring there is no alternative, Homemead belongs to my distant past, I have no right anymore to intrude. If I continue with this escapade then all my treasured memories will be eroded, spoilt for all time.

Fiona's response of interrupting his recollections was getting quite a habit, although without her realising, she was at least responsible for continuing their struggling conversation. 'Ian, move on to the next stage, give the upstairs an airing, by my listing, you'll remember, it's certainly impressive, Homemead is not short of rooms.'

She held back to let him alone ascend the stairway, it was then he noticed on reaching the landing that certain floor boarding had been taken up, and left in that state for whatever reason. His assumption was this could be perhaps electrical installation. The limited area of floor space caused the remaining flooring to creak as he walked on them. Each of the rooms that he looked into, intent to show an interest for Fiona's sake were victims of bizarre decorating schemes. She watched and listened from the hall area, beginning to be concerned about both a new found friend, and equally important potential buyer, who for whatever reason it was clear to see had lost both motivation and interest towards the property.

Referring to her interior layout details, she made a decision to call out directions. 'Ian you have the final room at the end of the landing.' At last he thought the gruelling exercise is nearly completed, the remaining room was a long way from the rest of the bedrooms. The door was firmly shut, needing a heavy push on his part to gain entry, fortunately he was spared the effects of any more outlandish decorating, not surprising as for years this room was a repository for all manner of clutter.

Sunlight was entering the room, although limited it was illuminating the bedroom's ornate mantelpiece. He eventually let go of the door handle, he was looking for no particular reason at two tins located on the shelf of the dust covered mantelpiece, they were paint tins that through the passage of time had subdued to rust. Ian instantly relaxed, smiling to himself, a sense of humour was prevailing, the tins, don't remember them the last time I slept in here. Now things had changed he was witnessing a virtual spotlight created by intruding sunlight, whose ephemeral rays were now welcoming him, as a touching lament for a schoolboy that once had been a past occupant of this very room. His own childhood bedroom at Homemead!

There was a transformation happening, this person that had forced the door open was suddenly different, his shoulders were pulled back, a head up attitude became noticeable. His thoughts were whirling into action, more than that, his emotions, like the beams of sunlight in the room they were fulfilling inspirations. This is where it all started, right here in my own bedroom.

Maybe now all lost in the shadowy past, and he had no idea what it meant, but one thing was for sure he was feeling absolutely elated, like one of the diving crew on the rigs, that had become exhilarated with too much nitrogen in the bloodstream. His own room, here at Homemead, it was revealing reminiscences, resembling to him a cascading reservoir that had suddenly breached its dam.

The melodrama associated with his recent anti-climax, figuratively speaking was washed away, knowing it was gone he desperately wanted to see more of what had all those years ago became his own domain. The interior views were restricted, window blinds in a dilapidated condition prevented any significant light entering. Only the mantelpiece could be made out in the struggling sunlight, he stopped in his tracks, that's odd. Two old ornate mantelpieces in the same morning, the one in the hotel with the photograph, no not again, you off chasing coincidences, all this has to stop. Lights he thought, he reached over and pressed the switch, a pointless exercise as the property no longer had power connected.

He resigned to make the best of the circumstances, motivating his attention on to the wall above the mantelpiece, two hooks were firmly secured they had once served as hangers. On the right, the nursery rhyme would have hung, remembering to be able to read it I needed to stand on a chair. Who would have thought, with a lapse of all those years I am still able to recite from memory those same verses.

Edward Lear's quintessential nursery rhyme once more was having the desired effect, he could not resist the temptation... *The owl and the pussy cat went to sea in a beautiful pea green...*

Ian was interrupted aware of a sharp tapping sound on the door. 'It's only me,' Fiona whispered. 'Thought you've found a skeleton, you know in a cupboard.' She was growing slightly anxious, concerned about her next appointment involving documents needing signing and routing on to the courier.

He emerged, reluctantly joining Fiona in the present time. 'Sorry, must have got lost in my past.'

Fiona was delighted, for the first time this morning she actually saw Ian expressing some happiness, better still, he was laughing. Taking advantage of the relaxed situation she explained the importance with her next appointment, adding there was only one remaining room of sorts to see downstairs, the pantry and cellar. They both returned to the hall area, she consulted the property's endless sheets of paper, adding a vague explanation. 'The cellar, it's an earth cellar, not sure what that is, but our Mr Jezzaid, will certainly know.'

He indicated for her to remain in the hallway to save time, whilst he would do a quick look with the remainder of Homemead, the part existing from the days prior to refrigeration. He stopped suddenly, something flashed across his mind. 'Fiona what was that you said about the cellar?'

She clearly remembered the description. 'It's a tiled pantry and this so-called earth cellar.' Ian continued walking, aware of the time restraints, earth cellar, what does it mean? ...word association, ...*earth*, home, the lair of a fox, why the connection with foxes?

Yes the penny dropped. That's it, my beloved fox head, on its red plaque. Aunt had given it to me, some neighbour had passed it on for young 'Master Ian'. On gaining the artefact all those years ago he recalled his aunt explaining what a taxidermist did for a living, stressing to her nephew it was nothing connected with driving taxi cabs, the memories made him almost swell with emotion.

He visualised the fox hunter's prize staring down from above the mantelpiece. In his subconscious he was re-enacting his efforts to fix it there, resulting in the accident with a hammer. Now I have it all clear to me, the nursery rhyme was at one end, and the fox head resembling a heraldic beast was at the opposite end.

What a wonderful prompt Fiona had supplied… earth cellar, earth, the lair of a fox, he repeated it to himself, so no excuses to forget. That's where this mystery is located, in my old room at Homemead, laying inside the wall wanting to reach out for me.

There has to be a solution, I need a plan, and fast, I must get back again into Homemead, all by myself without anyone knowing. Then perhaps these questions could be finally answered, it could be possible, revolving around an old schoolboy prank that he used to play on his aunt. An unofficial entry could still give a way in, he had not forgotten the pantry's casement window. Walking across the stone tiled floor he was hoping to confirm what he was remembering about that particular window. Much to his relief nothing appeared changed.

It was the same as all those times back, although serious neglect was visible with the frame's woodwork. At first he was cautious, after a degree of hesitation, there followed a concerted push, causing the frame to be skewed slightly out of alignment. Much to his relief his trick still worked, this meant it was possible to open the pantry window from outside. The secret entry into the disused pantry was his way back in. Satisfied, he returned to the hallway and joined Fiona, perhaps a more observant Ian would not have failed to notice footprints of a recent nature left in the dust on the pantry's floor.

'All done, thanks, Fiona.' Without so much of a touch of guilt in his voice. There was one remaining task, needed to be put in place, carefully and cunningly, like the nature of his 'fox'. When he closed the door that led into the pantry, he deliberately covered his actions and failed to turn the key that resided in the lock.

He now needed a highly executed plan, and by using the right timing it should be easy, as he was alert, actively thinking on his feet for when he again would visit the confines of Homemead... alone.

Chapter 8

Ian rested against the gate to the entrance of Homemead. He achieved the final photo he wanted, conveniently as the memory card was now full. Those feelings of his guilt towards Fiona and the estate agents; would he ever be allowed to eliminate them, all those fabricated range of deception? With pointless audacity believing he was not the only person ever to waste an estate agent's time!

He attempted analysing the events that had transpired since entering the property. On reflection he was aware of the coincidences of the two mantelpieces, the one in the bedroom at the hotel, with the strange occurrence of the photo found residing against it, followed by the second one, here in what had once been his childhood bedroom. It has to be me, I'm starting to expect all these peculiar incidents to happen.

Was there a connection with the mantelpiece in the bedroom at Homemead? Why should Fiona quite unexpectedly motivate a link from the dim recesses of my memory? Earth cellar, that was the operative word, 'earth' having an effect of bringing Ian's fox head that used to be displayed almost regally above the bedroom's mantelpiece. Perhaps without that happening, then most likely I would have left by now, heading back home. These recurring coincidences, it's caused me to adopt an obsession like that of a gambler down on his luck that at all costs must carry on hoping to win. There has to be some logic behind these occurrences, now at last I have a means to find out.

Half an hour had passed since Fiona had left, very hastily as she was concerned with her next appointment. he had taken this situation to resume his deception, indicating he wanted to remain to take certain photos of the exterior of the house and also an interest with the old walled garden. Their amiable discussion concluded when Fiona knew that on his leaving he would secure the gate, and she would see him later when he called in to meet their Mr Jezzaid.

He continued to think of Fiona, knowing that an attachment had already started to happen, it had become clear, an interlude of this depth in his life was currently most welcoming. At the moment however the concern for him was with the property, feeling comfortably relaxed knowing that Homemead was now about to be all to himself.

Returning to the car he packed his camera away, hoping that the lasting nostalgia with the photographs would alone be worth his visit. There was that feeling of excitement starting to build, knowing he was back in control of his destiny. That's the way I need things to go. Rummaging in the back of the car he collected two items from its basic tool kit, aware of what he had planned they would become very useful.

Again the domain of the protective garden robin was compromised as an intrepid Ian walked with intent back towards the property. Nervously believing he resembled a burglar, no, reminding himself, a housebreaker during the hours of daylight, either way it fell within a criminal category. The imposing water well caught his attention, although now boarded over it once created a dangerous adventure for him and another like-minded boy, both of whom on a youthful escapade descended to the well's unknown depths.

Reaching the casement window to the rear and conveniently out of sight from the driveway, he quickly realised with his adult strength the prising of the badly adjusted window frame was now much easier, the securing lock gave way allowing movement with the frame therefore it was easily opened. As a boy, he discovered this trick more by luck and would not let on to anyone, least of all his aunt. That's how as a devious prank he was able to get back inside the house without her knowing, even though she might be defiantly looking out for him at all possible entrances.

All those years and the wooden frame was never altered or repaired who would have ever thought, and for that matter he presumed not even known about. Treading over the sill he was inside the familiar tiled pantry, his scheme had worked. Opening the door he had deliberately left unlocked it allowed access into the hall, believing he was a kid all over again back inside Homemead. What am I doing? If my work colleagues could see me now, it doesn't need thinking about…

George Atwell had been able to piece together the morning's activities from over at his neighbouring property. Surmising that his target must have organised a viewing appointment, the young lady he saw was undoubtedly from the estate agents. The viewing had concluded at least half an hour ago, further more he had witnessed her driving away. GA then noticed the interested party had remained, intent on walking around the grounds taking photographs. It all appeared normal, he had no reason to think otherwise, even contemplating maybe this will be my new neighbour?

It had now changed into a complex puzzle, GA's sense of curiosity was alerted, as his target had returned to the vehicle, only to leave again towards the property, but for what purpose? Surely he would not have the keys. On reaching the house he had gone to the rear of the building, therefore out of sight. GA was astute, reasoning there has to be something he wants to investigate, but what? It required further surveillance, unanswered questions needed to be established. The brigadier had in mind a deceptive approach, needing on his part to instigate a simple 'war games' scenario…

Ian alone and inside Homemead was in an enhanced state of expectancy, confident that all these events that were affecting him would soon be answered. Impatiently he clambered up the stairs as if running a ladder on a rig platform, he knew the exuberance with self-esteem was remaining, more than that, he wanted it to stay.

Once inside the bedroom his memory entered overdrive, remembering from years past, it had to be five, the number of bricks up from the shelf. It was always easy the same as digits on your hand. He visualised where the fox head had once resided, the hook in the wall was a lasting testament to what had once supported his prized tattered and moth-eaten icon. Directly below where it used to hang, was the precise spot he needed to start. Still noticeable under coverings of paint was the outline of the bricks, first it needed the modern decorating removed, the car tool would prove ideal, from then on it should begin to get interesting.

The emulsion paint was no match over the years from the progress of damp, it easily peeled in pliable layers revealing the brick facing. At this stage, it would be easy to imagine Ian as some intrepid archaeologist, about to unearth the rarest of artefacts, perhaps he would not have changed places. He methodically counted aloud the brick course. 'One, two, three, four, and five.' The mortar had relaxed through time, enabling one particular brick to be easily extracted, as a dentist perhaps would willingly pull a tooth from its life long position.

The surrounding bricks also needed removing, they readily separated and were carefully withdrawn. His satisfaction was realised, as now the cavity laying behind the wall once again was exposed to daylight. The void he stared into meant one thing, remembered by his schoolboy secret code, 'Harbs Strong Room' or HSR after Harb his school name. It was reassuring to look again into this virtual bank, those times for him at Homemead it had become a closeted hiding place, a storage for all worldly possessions, certainly not some nondescript gaping space behind a wall!

For all that it was a complete accident with his discovery of HSR. On that certain morning Ian had an important task to install the taxidermist's art, his new delight the fox head passed to him by a benefactor. He clearly recollected how wonderful it appeared, as nobody at school aspired to anything that desirable. His excited efforts with the hook and nail did not go well, the hammer's almighty first blow missed the nail and broke through the wall revealing its unknown interior!

He could not believe what he had done, even now he imagined himself staring at the void that had appeared, he was overcome with worry. Luckily on that particular morning his aunt had been out. His predicament was fortunately solved, or more likely salvaged by confiding to Isaac, the local man who did all the work around the farm. At that young formative age, Isaac who answered to Issy had become something of a role model for this particular inquisitive schoolboy.

His over enthusiastic accident exposing the cavity also revealed that inside there appeared a basic shelf that continued to form a brick tunnel that disappeared into darkness. This was no empty space, it was a school boy's expectation for a storehouse or treasure trove, which naturally he had a burning ambition to lay claim...

Ian bathed in memories of that morning, sheer infantile recollections, his admiration for Issy who as a veritable magician solved his problems with the wall's gaping aperture. Better still, saving him from any punishment that his aunt if she had discovered might have administered. Issy had cleverly reinstated the bricks using a cement mix he had managed to conjure up, more importantly, when the repair was finished he then fixed much to his satisfaction the fox head plaque above the mantelpiece. Which allowed its masterful gaze from its pair of inert glass eyes, to constantly follow your movements over the space of the entire room.

There was something else he still remembered, the remarks made by his saviour in this very room. What had he meant? Back then it had sounded odd to a schoolboy, like an utterance by one of his teachers, even now those precise words had returned to him. It was connected with his accident and the exposed cavity, those comments had always intrigued him. 'Be things in this world as best left as they be.' Once more, he could not help reviving that statement, but what had it been referred to?

How had he retained exactly the same words uttered by Issy on that morning, he found that astounding particularly after such a lapse of time. What Issy said had not meant too much, particularly to a growing boy; adults were constantly proclaiming pointless statements. However what he had stumbled upon above the mantelpiece suddenly became exciting, taking on the role as his new childhood centre of interest.

He selfishly wanted the wall cavity all to himself, remembering how in his pragmatic way he calculated that the cement mix would take time before it set hard. Based on this when Issy had left he hatched an ingenious plan, by removing the bricks before the mortar cured but cleverly letting it remain fixed to the edges of the bricks. Then they could be reinstalled to form a disguise, as once in position they would appear as the normal mantelpiece wall. With his ability to remove them as he needed to access his new secret hiding place.

He thought how cleverly as a boy he turned that accident to a definite advantage, the repository had many uses, it stored his spending allowance, but as the withdrawal visits became more regular this facility drifted into the realms of redundancy. That did not mean HSR fell into total disuse, to the contrary it became the schoolboy's safe haven for a wealth of essential items…

Ian had taken an empty packing case as a seat, on sitting down he wanted to believe that he had returned to his boyhood height when last in this room. But he still failed to understand why he had forgotten both the fox head and 'Harb's Strong Room'. It annoyed him, making him feel sad that earlier today those two childhood events were lost from his memory, although fortunately for him only temporarily.

This morning was different. As a fully fledged adult he was eager to start his modern day exploration of the magical wall cavity, any redemption on his part would have to wait. Now what did I ever leave in here? Reasoning that anything found after all these years, would he actually remember? Whatever the cavernous void held would be located on the shelf in the front section, as he never reached any further into the dark interior from fear of what might reside there.

As an adult, same as he was as an agile kid, his sleeves soon became smothered in brick dust from the cavity, but he became disappointed and had returned to his seat, although not entirely empty handed as two items had been retrieved. On examination there was a small copper coin, not really a horde of treasure, although remembering it had once held a special place, newly minted and foreign, originating from South Africa. It was paramount in his limited boyhood collection, more importantly as it had been given to him by his aunt.

His second item was broken, no longer of any use, a symbolic pocket knife, its single blade had snapped, with his efforts all those years ago to prise the bricks loose to gain entry into 'HSR'. It had been salvaged and hidden for one singular reason, the plastic sides on the knife portrayed a 'Pony Express' rider.

Looking at his clothing it was evident that brick dust together with assorted grime was all over them, was it really worth the effort? Contemplating on the hidden items that had been retrieved, a knife no longer usable, a coin, assuming it's still legal tender unable to buy much in its country of origin? It still does not make any sense, all these recent occurrences, surely it must mean more than this? That melancholy feeling was invading his thoughts, too much reminiscing, it had to stop. He found himself for no reason wantonly studying the paint tins left on the mantelpiece, whose labelled dates were long since expired.

'Come on.' Motivating himself. Get those bricks back where they belong. Tidy up, we don't want to end up having an ASBO for breaking and entering. After that we can say goodbye, and leave Homemead. Reluctantly he started to install the bricks where they belonged, believing his actions should finally seal the mantelpiece cavity.

On this occasion there were no concerns with the dark void that stretched into the sculptured tunnel, inwardly laughing to himself, back then his boy's fear of the unknown. To think of my vocation in later life, an engineer on the oil drilling platforms, where dark and tight places are now second nature.

He pondered as anyone would for that one final glimpse, festoons of hanging cobwebs were visible, appearing like an illustration from a spectral ghost story, but as for any mystery, nothing appeared. Why a builder all those years ago fabricated a tunnel into this useless void, I will never know.

He struggled with the task aligning each individual brick, made difficult as any precious light was now vacating the room. Why didn't I think of it before? My key ring torch. Bringing this into use enabled him to see where to position the masonry. The torch beam was not completely selective, his endeavours as a temporary bricklayer were to come to an abrupt stop, as the light had focused on something that lay further into the hollow void. What's that in there? Nothing I can remember leaving.

Ian tenderly by use of a discarded curtain rail liberated a dust ridden bundle from the brick tunnel, judging by its weight it must contain something inside its wrapping cover. Now he was speculating what the package of cobweb strewn newspaper might contain? How long had it been in there? Someone else must have known of my hiding place. Was this what he was expected to find? Whatever it was had instantly become a realm of complete speculation...

The brigadier had been patient, no denying that, but where is the target? What had started after the viewing of Homemead he was able to evaluate, the young lady representing no doubt the estate agents had driven off. He was adamant that his target who had remained would not be in possession of any keys, yet he had gone back, going around to the rear of the property. Labouring on this point the brigadier had reached a decision in breaking cover and investigating.

Exactly why he trained his binoculars on the property again, is anyone's guess, but he did, in doing so he awoke a skill from his army intelligence days. Light, there's no doubt about it, visible up in the top windows, a defined torch beam, he reasoned, it has to be, aware that the electricity supply to the building was off. However the long overdue answer for the brigadier had now materialised. So that's where you are...

The layers of newspaper making up the bundle had been carefully overlaid, easier now for Ian to see, as he was standing out on the landing using the enhanced light of his torch. He was beginning to believe that the purpose of the paper covering had a deliberate intent, as the particular publication was 'The Guardian' with its front page arranged on the outside. Although the bold title could still be read, he was failing to make out the exact date of its publication?

Nothing could save the layers of newsprint. Pulling each one apart they lay wasted and crumbled, throughout, no clues remained to the age of the decaying paper. Approaching its core, there were vestiges of a fungal substance, lacking any real strength it rapidly dispersed to dust. This was to catch him completely unawares, the heavy object he was so intent to reveal, without warning easily slipped from his fingers crashing with a resounding thump on to the floor of the landing.

'It's, it's nothing but a chunk of rock.' Following a quick examination he was unable to change his opinion. Why wrap this up? All that effort, what's the purpose, some poorly supported practical joke, not guilty with this one. Who could have planted it there? Aunt did not know of my hiding place, anyway he remembered, without any doubt her newspaper was most certainly 'The Times'.

This is one 'oil well' that's run dry on me, enough, is enough. This lump of rock might weigh heavier, but it's acting as my 'last straw' in danger of 'breaking the camel's back'. Let's put it all together, then it's time to leave Homemead, but for old time's sake keep the new found rock as a souvenir, or better still use it as a doorstop.

It was all done, he was sitting outside on the planking that covered the water well, welcoming the warm sunshine after the gloomy interior of the house. Satisfied his planned withdrawal had left everything as he would have liked, including HSR, with his amused thoughts, although historical in contense, secure as an Icelandic Bank? Apart from the salvaged artefacts, in addition he had retained as a melodramatic link 'The Guardian's' title, the relevant scrap of aged paper was filed inside his pocket diary joining his recently created 'wish list'.

Unlike his days as a schoolboy, where there existed too much in life to fully understand, the contrast existing now with his mature mind had grown to assimilate reason, and to ask relevant questions. One of which he was struggling to unravel; there has to be an answer why the package was placed inside the cavity and for that matter laying undiscovered. Only today illuminated by my torchlight was it revealed, at least to me, strange. No, enough, let the past rest, the cavity is now empty and by my efforts of brick laying it should remain sealed for all time...

The long history of Homemead would lay claim to an important type of 'assurance' that had remained concealed and undiscovered. All things in this world have a purpose, and that was the case when a young Ian Harbinger found by his misadventure the cavity located behind the mantelpiece in his room. There was more than the front shelf used as his storage safe, the brick tunnel was longer than you would ever imagine. As for its length that was a journey into an avenue of superstition, as out of sight at its far end laying in darkness was the whole intention for its construction. Undisturbed since its inception, and having become encrusted through the ages with layers of dust was located the 'witch's bottle'.

In the distant past this object had been 'laid at rest' in the house out of an apprehensive fear by the scourge of prowling witches. The common practice of installing a safe-keeping artefact within your property arose in the lonely superstitious countryside, we would one day come to know as East Anglia.

Your doors would be closed and bolted, the windows had their shutters in place, but that left the chimney of a house vulnerable for an entrance of demonology. Wise clerics, knew of a lasting remedy against an invasion from a witch. They made available a bottle to contain sharp objects, usually nails, the container was sealed over with wax, to be buried in an appropriate tunnel constructed against the chimney piece. There it would remain for all time to repel the malevolent forces of evil, that could if allowed enter and manifest your dwelling in the guise of a witch.

Two earthenware bottles in different locations were secreted away within Homemead, they had laid undisturbed for countless decades. Owners of the property, at least in earlier years would have known of their existence, they had a duty as stewards to jealously guard the whereabouts of what protected the occupants against demonic forces. In those such places they remained hidden as a testament to more rural and vulnerable times in the heritage of our countryside. Isaac would have been aware of their importance, his generation continued to uphold a virtuous respect with all those past superstitions.

On that particular morning with Master Ian's accident with the hammer, Isaac accepted the innocent mistake, and as his mentor, contained within his powers was able to put things to rights.

Ian was freely admitting how relaxed he was, the stress of these last few months had seemingly eased, finance problems he was stuck with, which allowed his mind to be intruded upon by one poignant thought, I'm a survivor, and for me there's no other way.

Leisurely he was occupied with an inventory of his recovered items, a pocket knife possessing a broken blade, a coin oxidised by the passage of time, not forgetting the newly acquired 'doorstop'. Then of course my recent adventure in the realms of housebreaking, something that I will never be in a position to discuss.

Remaining on the cover planks over the well, he was wondering when water was last drawn from this very source. One fact he was still aware, the depth of silt deposited at the bottom of the well, if it had changed, then it could only be even deeper. He cringed at the thought how all those years ago, he came upon this knowledge, Sibley had thrown up the challenge. 'Let's find out how deeps be the wishing well.' Recalling his friend's exact words, although not precisely in the grammar that Ian's boarding school would have endorsed.

Christopher Sibley. No, he always wanted to be called Chris, was a boy of similar age from a neighbouring farm. They struck up a compatible friendship during Ian's extended summer visits, Chris had the grass roots of the countryside, whilst his compatriot Harb would offer by way of an exchange his more townie background.

The boys exhibited that typical impish behaviour of what can we do next? The water well at Homemead had a magnetic appeal, its disappearing void was calling out to be explored. The combined op was planned as a covert mission on a day when Aunt would be out shopping, therefore making the coast clear for their descent. A borrowed rope was firmly secured to the winder, allowing Chris who had jockeyed in position to attempt his downward journey into the unknown.

His descent to the water's surface was further than imagined, against an echo chamber effect Chris called out his gradual progress until he literally touched the water, but it was needing a second opinion, that's when Ian had undertaken his eagerly awaited attempt. For all their combined efforts the 'would be explorers' were left with one burning question, what was the depth of the water?

Ian's ingenuity solved this, in the barn there were just what they needed, a series of short poles, by joining them together, it became a depth gauge. Neither of them knew their real purpose, they were a set of bamboo poles used for sweeping chimneys, but not on this particular morning.

Chris was impressed by the brain wave of his townie friend, although he would never admit to it. Ian remembered emerging from his sortie in the well shaft, with one advantage, he was in possession of the answer, his grimy face manifested over the rim proclaiming… 'Depth of water at least a metre.' But the sediment that was the surprise, it went on and on, he showed Chris where he had marked the gauge, they were both amazed what had been revealed. Chris, whistled its six feet, Ian continued in metric, they argued over the measuring, either way on that morning they had discovered the latent depth of oozy sediment contained within the well.

The boys' school holidays including this adventure in the well shaft all those years ago was making Ian shudder, did we really do all that, here, below where I am sitting? Only now realising the magnitude of danger they had been exposed to, a lack of inherent fear, innocence of boyhood, that's a poor excuse. Perhaps this is where it started for me, pursuing of a career in the oil industry, fascinated by drilling deep holes in the seabed, who knows?

On Ian's following summer holiday Sibley had gone, his father had sold and the family moved to a farm in Norfolk. However, he would always dwell on their very last discovery, a bird's nest in a tall hedgerow. Chris as always was responsible for the find, he had shown Ian the bird's habit of catching its prey of insects, and then impaling them on convenient thorns, so making up a 'larder'. 'This be a butcher bird, don't forget its name, Harb.' For what it's worth, from all that time back I haven't, although I've never seen one since, wonder what the proper name is? As a gesture to where Chris might be now after so many years, that question for me needs to be answered.

He reluctantly stood up, one perplexing question had become lodged firmly in his mind, if my financial situation was viable would I ever consider buying Homemead? I don't know, and the way things are I never will know, it's a broken question, broken, like the 'for sale' sign laying on the lawn. Strange, wonder why the estate agents have not reinstated it?

He cupped his hand firmly over the 'doorstop' rock, mustn't forget this, and started walking towards the gate. There's too much here, if I bought the property I would become engulfed with a reality of living with past memories. The warmth of the sun was making him feel complacent, adding a feeling of reassurance, he wasn't going to let a melancholy shadow block out his 'sunshine'.

At least he was totally unaware of two sets of eyes that were both independently watching him. The robin on the buddleia considering him as an inconvenient nuisance. Whilst the brigadier from his observation post accepted his target as a definite challenge, that quickly needed to be resolved.

Had Ian known, then neither of those onlookers would have dampened his spirits. He was uplifted, already feeling the benefit that it was over, the testament to his past politely put at rest. The nursery rhyme that he would always associate from his childhood here at Homemead returned, he was content, free from any inhibitions to recite it in his deepest thoughts …*With some honey and plenty of money…* If only.

Without any particular reason, he threw the 'doorstop' rock high above his head. Setting his sights to catch it on its return, the rock on reaching its zenith became as expected a victim of gravity. He had kept his eye firmly on the object therefore he could not fail to notice a distinct glare of light momentarily emitted from the rock. As it fell he was satisfied to achieve on his part a perfect cricket ball catch.

Intrigued by the rock's emission of light, a more stringent examination was called for, the rock's outer layer in effect was housing an obscured inner membrane. Holding the object to the sunlight it was easy to perceive what had caused the gleam of light.

Already he had decided to promote his 'doorstop' with a change of status, it was destined to enhance his coffee table as the centre mass revealed a display of beautiful and equally exquisite glass like crystals.

Chapter 9

'Thinking of buying?' Ian was struggling in the far reaches of the car's trunk attempting to secure his newly esteemed piece of rock crystal, the strange voice made him imagine by some divine providence the car radio had come on. Emerging slowly, to avoid bumping his head, he was looking at who had raised the very direct question, a young lad slovenly sitting on his bike. More striking as dressed in white coveralls and with sunlight behind him he produced an almost ethereal vision. His question was repeated. 'You buying? Saw you here yesterday.'

Ian straightened himself, realising the new arrival worked at Stubbs Dairy, an easy assumption indicated by the company logo on his clothing.

Perhaps, as the day wore on he had become jaded, the question sounded impertinent, but he remained polite and offered a brief reply. 'Early days, just thinking, there's a lot of work involved.' The enquiring lad showed an open and honest looking face, easy to surmise he had undoubtedly finished his work shift, and now made his way home. Ian warmed towards a more tolerant mood, preparing himself for the next question that seemed imminent, whilst at the same time he looked over towards Homemead, as if the very property was monitoring their conversation.

On cue the next enquiry arrived. 'You from round here?' His questioner had now decided to dismount, his intention no doubt to stay.

Ian decided to employ the tactic of answering his question, with another. 'No, it's my boyhood haunt though, many years ago, an aunt of mine lived here… Looks like you've just finished work?'

The over inquisitive new arrival demonstrated a habit of brushing down his coveralls for no particular reason. 'It's the dairy I work at, mostly on the creaming tanks, stayed on today to clean the steriliser, get paid overtime you know.' Again he actively resumed his nervous activity with his clothing.

'Mother would have known your aunt, we live at the Stagers place, grandfather rebuilt it, he was from Poland, served with the RAF during World War Two, then stayed over here, Sosabowski that's my family name, always prefer Coburn its easier.' Ian had naturally assumed that the lad's mother like his aunt were no longer with us. His fellow conversationalist demonstrated one redeeming characteristic, a totally open disposition that you could not fail to both notice and admire.

Ian was aware and appreciated the impact the Polish services had during the last war, but then everything around Homemead he was coming into contact with was centred in the past, I must lose this entanglement. With this in mind he introduced himself to Coburn assuming that was his first name? 'Yes, I do remember the Stagers, had those two big timber barns.' His new found local was delighted to get recognition of his family's home.

The next piece of information Ian was about to hear, although he would have no idea, was however to become a turning point, just one of those innocent remarks people have a habit of making in passing. 'You know there is still someone who's at Greycliffe that was friends with your aunt. Mother used to talk about her, it's a Miss Cleary, used to run the newspaper, that's it, our local paper.'

'Where's this Greycliffe?' was Ian's immediate reply.

Coburn really expected him to know. 'Why, it's you know, a residential home, it's been that way for years.'

Ian acknowledged his response, this valuable information he could investigate. He corrected himself promptly, recalling his recent train of thoughts; here we go again getting involved in the past, what for?

Coburn wanted to play his trump card to discuss with the stranger his aspiration and for that matter his family's activities with East Anglia's involvement in WW2 re-enactments. He was poised to give a comprehensive account of what this entailed over their dedicated weekend events, starting with his latest purchase, a replica sheepskin flying jacket, but modern communications were for Ian to thankfully intervene.

'Is that your phone?' Coburn whispered pointing at Ian's car, who acknowledged and reached inside for his mobile. As Ian punched the appropriate key, his mine of local information had effortlessly regained his bike, following a reassuring salute cycled away intent to gain no doubt his overdue meal.

'Hello… Ian Harbinger.' Nothing was keyed into the memory, that was his aversion towards intrusive mobiles, it could be anyone.

'Hi, brother, it's Julia,' was the short snappy reply. 'Ian where in the name are you?'

His younger sister had raised her head, at least I've have had some respite, there was not even the obligatory how are you? As by now Julia was already in her full swing. 'Called you in Devon, thought you were supposed to be on leave chilling out, or at best solving your finances?' He knew there would follow an injection of sarcasm, and he was not disappointed.

'Got the copy of "UFO monthly" I've scoured the back pages showing the latest alien abductees, you're not there, so, my dear brother has to be on the planet somewhere.' He was used to these pointless inventions of hers and long accepted the best defence was the inevitable attack.

'I'm in Cambridge at Aunt Anastasia's old property, Homemead, long story it's one of those events, dear sister, that has to wait until the next time I see you.'

'Knowing you, Ian, there would be a woman involved. Anyway why I wanted to contact you is I'm coming down to the apartment this weekend and I need to talk, we hardly ever meet these days, you supposed to be what was it, resting.'

He took an intake of breath, it was his turn in the battle of the Harbinger siblings. 'Julia, I never knew you cared, anyway I'm leaving tomorrow, so you can put up with me this weekend. What's your news, getting married?' Knowing he would get the last laugh by throwing that cat among the pigeons remark into their already terse conversation.

'Don't be so damn personal. Anyway I must fly or I'll be wheel clamped, see you at the weekend.'

Ian reckoned, his worst case scenario that he would have some company waiting at the apartment, and it was worth running the whole set of events past Julia, as Anastasia was her aunt as well as his.

George Atwell struggled with the sleeve of his old shooting jacket, but he would welcome its warmth walking across to the gate of his neighbouring property. He had concluded his observation with the lad on the bike, aware that the individual had been seen on many occasions going to work at Stubbs. GA could only surmise what the lad's conversation with his target had been about.

Ian was still musing over the vindictive input associated by his sister's phone call. Suddenly, he became conscious of a tall elderly figure who was approaching. It's all happening this morning; like London buses, miss one, then five come along. Brigadier George Atwell was about to change the 'Rules of Engagement' although he considered adjust would be a more apt description.

Not really his remit as army protocol, but his tactic might possibly work for him. His right hand occupied his jacket pocket, where there was lodged an empty yellow cartridge case, a lasting souvenir from a shoot on the Furlow estate. Recognition had been the order for the brigadier, scoring as he did with his 20 gauge shot gun a breathtakingly high pheasant in the gloomy light of the last drive of the day.

Today the pocket's extra contents had a far more pragmatic task, he needed further information and would play it the army way. He reached deeper into the jacket pocket, gripping firmly on the smooth sculptured sides of the 'ploy' he was about to unfold on his target.

Ian had decided to allow his second visitor to talk first. He noticed the man's upright stature although he would fail to realise the inward pain that the brigadier was enduring, especially as he had temporarily dispensed with the support of his walking stick.

'Hello. Walked across from my cottage. May I ask a small favour from you, young man?'

Ian noticed as his verbal request ended, that he reached into his pocket producing something that was almost thrust into his face.

Ian was staring at a jar of pickled onions, followed by a humble request. 'Strong wrists needed to open, don't enjoy that privilege these days, but still enjoy the onions.' There came over the brigadier a confident beaming smile, as he knew that his target was equally bemused. Allowing the jar to be taken from his hand, his needs were rapidly answered as Ian snapped open the container's closure lid.

Ian offered a pointless remark. 'Everybody's more concerned about sell by dates,' handing the opened jar back to the rather interesting visitor.

The brigadier acknowledged his thanks, whilst adding a very direct question. 'Are you performing an inspection of the property?'

Without any delay Ian replied, 'Not really, I've had a viewing of the property, taken a few pictures but now it's back into town.' It was easy for Ian to perceive that the enquirer must have a military background, which left him wondering how long he had lived opposite Homemead.

George Atwell knew his target was drawn into the ruse of his conversation trap, achieving exactly what he desired. The brigadier walked towards the gate, making statements relating to the property on an assumption that his target would follow. It worked, as Ian more out of politeness joined him. He needed his war game scenario to continue. Without wasting valuable time Ian had the next question fired at him. 'Have you a background here in Cambridgeshire?'

Perhaps a sense of false security had overcome Ian, created by warm sunshine and a genial companion. Both men were content to lean on the entrance gate appreciating the rural peace that was freely on offer. Ian's initial reluctance had caused his reply to be slow in forthcoming. 'No, not really, Cambridgeshire was a childhood home, holidays from my boarding school.' Again he could feel himself embarking on his personal saga, although now it had developed with a feeling of maturity. 'An aunt of mine owned the family property during my childhood. Looking back now as an adult, I'm reluctant to say how I wish it was still available. What's that expression we are so often using? Never grow up.'

That's it, thought the brigadier, the link I need. Carefully resuming his cleverly rehearsed narrative. 'Homemead must have a wealth of poignant memories for you, I did not know your aunt, only lived here a few years, very content, great people hereabouts; an asset when you grow older.'

Ian was guilty of allowing his concentration to wander, imagining the flock of geese that were always here in the front paddock, including the infamous gander that with any opportunity would aggressively chase you.

Hearing the word 'sorry' returned him from past escapades. It was the brigadier with the inevitable introduction. 'Let me introduce myself. George Atwell.' Ian shook hands, cautiously aware of his grip acquired working in the oil industry.

'Ian Harbinger, good to meet you, can't say at this stage that we will be neighbours, I've too much that needs considering.'

No, the brigadier thought, the one remaining question, posed too much of a risk, how and why did he go back inside Homemead? The 'game' had gone as far as he would allow, any more answers from his target would in his opinion undoubtedly be lies. 'Well, Mr Harbinger, a belated lunch calls, wish you well with your property ideas, if you move in at least I will have a neighbour who can open my pickle jars.'

Ian was left leaning on the gate as now his second visitor had gone. That person who could have become his neighbour was inside his cottage, eager and enthralled by adding further data to his next outgoing report. His soft option subterfuge game had produced for him the desired results.

Ian knew it was now time to leave, snapping shut the coroded padlock into the chain, there followed a sense of lingering curiosity as he looked at Homemead. The house continued to appear gaunt, reflecting an appearance that replicated a black and white photograph that was eagerly needing an injection of colour.

The remaining pale mauve buddleia at least gave a colour to the overgrown walled garden. He knew the house would never suffer total loneliness as it possessed a catalogue of history, far more than he would ever comprehend. He gripped the car's ignition key, there was a singular thought that motivated himself, hesitantly he uttered his… goodbye…

Cheese with tomato, he couldn't argue that, his appetite certainly needed attention; it had been an active morning. He sat expecting waitress service, also he was puzzled by the actual name of the restaurant, 'The Open Roaster'. The connection eventually became clear as on the wall was a large glass illustrated mirror displaying an open touring car, a 'roadster', he pondered more out of a feeling of sympathy.

'Take your order, sir. Snapping back to reality he dictated from the menu his order almost robotically, then as an afterthought adding, 'Would you bring me a tiny glass of coke?'

The bemused waitress was quick with her reply. 'Is that diet or normal?'

His answer indicated as if a religious ceremony was to be performed, 'Ordinary will do, thank you.'

He waited passing the time in taking stock of his situation. The car was parked at the hotel, after the snack it had to be the estate agents fulfilling his promise, and then at least contact that residential home. Let me find Greycliffe and what this Miss Cleary has to say about my aunt. I owe the assignment that much before it becomes stagnant.

His interlude had allowed him to resolve his promise made earlier. Now Chris Sibley it's your special day. Ian's pledge was to happen as witnessed by the book he had just managed to buy, '21st: British Birds Companion' certainly this will answer what I need. Running his finger along the index under B he had located bullfinch, but no actual 'butcher bird', his lucid investigation was to be interrupted by the waitress. 'Here we are, sir.' She arranged the plate of sandwiches together with the teapot to her precise requirement, finally placing the miniature glass of coke on one side. Ian reluctantly closed the bird book, at the same time as thanking the waitress.

Pouring his much needed tea, he could not fail to notice the grime accumulated under his fingernails; a little trace of Homemead stays with me, how reassuring. Fumbling in his pockets he located the coin salvaged from HSR and dropped it into the glass of coke. At this stage he realised how hungry he was, housebreaking must have that effect. He was relaxed and equally contented. Clearly thinking I need that residential home's phone number, give them a call first.

Ian motivated himself. A lot still needed doing, the day's running away fast, the snack was consumed in record time. He picked up the bill, not forgetting to fish out his coin that had under gone a transformation process, that's like it used to be gleaming copper. Aunt would be pleased. When I see the next charity tin it can be given a new home.

Unwin & Hornby on this occasion appeared very active. On entering Ian was politely acknowledged by June Orpin. He stood feeling exposed and guilty like someone in a witness box, indicating, look at me, I'm a complete time waster and what's more I break into vacant property! At this point in time a drilling platform lashed by a storm would be a more comfortable venue. 'Hello, Mr Harbinger.' The office manager had walked towards him. 'Do hope the viewing went to your expectations, we kept the appointment by our Miss McRae standing in at the last moment.' Ian had already noted her empty desk, therefore assuming that Fiona must still be out.

June Orpin was acting with stringent instructions from their Mr Jezzaid, ensuring that Mr Harbinger, reference Homemead, was directed to him personally. She wasted no time explaining that the partner would like to meet him, although he had already been made aware earlier of this by Fiona, Ian acknowledged the request that seemed more in the way of a command and was ushered into his office.

Following mutual introductions, it appeared that Mr Jezzaid was one of the three partners at Unwin & Hornby. Their conversation started on a negative note, with his apologies why Miss McRae had to stand in for him. Already Ian could not fail to be aware of a condescending approach originating from Fiona's boss, astute and unnecessary questions aimed at him, leaving him pondering was there some obscure hidden agenda? But there couldn't be, so why this approach; was there a reason? Unless of course the concerns with Homemead as a listed building could be the cause, so he side-stepped and went mute on that subject.

It was leaving Ian with no other alternative than to defend himself. Explaining the property was not to be utilised as a business or small holding, not even an escape to the country. He reassuringly thought, this should be easy, as tomorrow I will be gone. 'Actually, Mr Jezzaid it all belongs to my childhood school holidays, and as you might imagine the great adventures I enjoyed at Homemead.'

He sensed by the reply their conversation was starting to run a degree smoother. 'Did your aunt farm at the property?'

At last an easier question for him. 'No, not to any great extent, the property was in the family, had been for years. She lived at Homemead, but would often be away on business in Africa.' It left Ian one thought in his mind, more applicable to an oil rig disaster: 'prep for immediate evac'. This time waster needs to exit and fast.

Mr Jezzaid had directed his efforts in fumbling through what were copies of the sales brochure appertaining to the property. Ian dwelt on the spacious desk it was so precise, even the paper clips were arranged in regimental rows.

Supplementing was his irritating habit of rolling what appeared an expensive ball point pen between his fingers, Ian was intrigued to notice further, that his shirt was laundered to absolute perfection, qualifying it for a television detergent advert. The shirt's cuffs set off by silver, overlaid abalone cufflinks, perfection, noticeable but entirely in the right sort of way.

'The property has been empty a long time, Mr Harbinger, we actually own the deeds, although not in a position to discuss why, but that said it's firmly on the market.'

Ian was finding it difficult to actually hear him speak, if pushed you would describe the partner almost to a point of being timid. Therefore he wisely decided to decline from asking why the for sale sign was lying unceremoniously on the overgrown lawn at Homemead.

The remarks that were directed at Ian alerted his concern who up to that time was focused on Mr Jezzaid's neck tie, his attention to detail was in everything, visualising how long his precise attire would last on a North Sea drilling platform. Well each to their own. Ian at this point in their discussions was handed a business card for any further contact, at the same time there was for the 'time waster', a relief that the 'interrogation' process was finally concluding.

He managed to fudge the remainder of their conversation, satisfied in his mind that he had at least kept the appointment. 'Any further interest you have, Mr Harbinger, then please contact me directly, don't for one moment hesitate.'

It left Ian feeling, that somehow it's all very hollow, it didn't stack up. Once more he glanced at the contents that resided under his finger nails and smiled, he had left with the door closing quietly behind him, it allowed a pause for him to note the name plate. Mr M Jezzaid, followed by letters which were appertaining to his professional status.

Fiona had returned and was involved emptying items from her briefcase. Noticing Ian saying goodbye to her boss she shrewdly took the opportunity to cross the office and enquire if any further help was needed following his viewing. Keeping a low whisper Ian thanked her for the chance with the photos he had been able to take. 'After you left I met two interesting local characters, it was all happening at Homemead's gate.' He was still unable to shed his complex associated with the process of his deception, who here would ever believe, that earlier today I was pulling the property's brickwork apart!

Fiona poising herself rather precariously decided to jump in with both feet, after all he might be gone tomorrow. 'Ian I really would appreciate your thoughts and input on my family's business venture.'

Knowing the restraints of talking in the current environment, he resumed his soft spoken reply. 'Certainly, I'd like that, give me a call later, Fiona and we can organise.' He picked up from her desk a sheet appertaining to Homemead, to in effect disguise from the staff their private conversation. Welcoming the thought of seeing Fiona again making an assumption that her family's fabric business venture would if anything be unique…

It was answered on the third ring. 'Greycliffe Residential, how may we help you?' Again Ian explained his current situation leading to an enquiry to hopefully see Miss Cleary. It was understandable to note an extended pause of caution from the receptionist, quite simply he could be anyone. The strong point in his favour, was the connection between his Aunt Anastasia and their Miss Cleary. Waiting for the reply he tried calculating how old this lady would be. After a considerable time lapse the receptionist answered his request, indicating it would be convenient for him to call in the morning after the daily staff meeting.

Following this he was issued with directions and given explicit instructions as to the parking requirements, leaving him wondering what he had got himself into. Anyway perhaps some of those teasing questions he was labouring could be finally resolved…

Fiona was very determined, an attribute from her late father, she was adopting an intuitive selling approach. Whatever the portfolio contained, she was allowing its impact to remain until exactly the right moment. Let me imagine I am in a buyer's office, my delay tactic, explain and draw their attention then the impact with the product. Ian for this ruse was going to prove an ideal sounding board.

She had encouraged Ian for them to dine at a newly opened restaurant, which apart from an excellent menu enjoyed a river view adding to its atmosphere. Her portfolio of products contained an array of woven tweed cloth, if nothing else you could not fail to be impressed with the varieties of colours. She looked at him across the table, feeling tense but equally determined, the build up had now expired, she knew it was to rely on the impact of the product.

'You know, Ian, I'm going for the USP.'

He returned a smile only too aware that it was a test for him to know what those letters meant. Ian did not even hesitate, raising his eyebrows and exclaiming, 'Your products' "unique selling point", Fiona.'

He was not disappointed as the portfolio contents were staggering, augmented by her comment, that our heritage and proximity to nature is evident in all we produce. From his point of view, he was left imagining what a fashion guru would be inspired by when first seeing these natural yarns.

'Fiona, you're involved with all this?' allowing the swatch samples to lay over and display their quality. 'You, who sells houses in Cambridgeshire?'

She glanced back at him realising that her business interest had hit the crucial spot. 'Please let me fill you in with all the background.'

'Ian Harbinger, it' all down to Scotland, like what's on the plates? Our smoked salmon starters, local industries getting it together and having confidence. There's a viable market out there, not what goes past your front door in summer. Sorry I do really love tourists to bits.' Fiona as she admitted in an abridged manner explained how their family had rediscovered the virtues of the

Scottish wool. But more importantly what in their modern formats was poised to be offered to those on an eager global client base.

He was listening formulating a tactful and what he believed a positive reply. He had fully appreciated the tweed sample range, displaying a veritable kaleidoscope of inspiration that oozed one thing in particular, quality. 'Fiona if I was in fashion, all these products you've got here, they're so different, any of your would be contacts will undoubtedly be drawn in. But can your family business do the supplying when you get really busy?'

Fiona was intent, she was fussing with the cutlery on her plate. 'I've studied our competition for some time, both in their designs and obviously their prime markets.' She had by now diverted her attention to rearranging the table flower vase. 'Your point on supply is vital, my whole family is rigidly behind this venture, call it historical passion, you know what they say, where there's a way.'

There was no stopping Fiona, she was avidly continuing, aided by a fresh input of enthusiasm. 'You know, Ian, there was an article in one of the nationals, written by the editor of Vogue magazine no less, still remember its intro, "No, tweed doesn't have to be twee!" It was so inspirational, it's pinned up in one of our workshops.'

It had approached a number crunch time in their discussions, he knew he had to raise the question of finance. 'How's your cash flow and investments going to stack up in our current, how should I say, leaner climate?'

Fiona was expecting that rather pointed question. 'We've tried all possible channels with loans for new business, but confusingly we're not in that category or the next. Either way we need money for future development.' She paused, almost reluctant to follow on. 'Imagine if we secured an order, a big one from a fashion house in Rome, our equipment simply would be unable to cope.'

Fiona rearranged the napkin which had fallen on the floor, Ian was feeling awkward having broached the subject of finance, to restore confidence he quickly intervened. 'I don't usually offer advice, Fiona but it's easy to see your undying passion with this whole project, it's like that song "it's a family affair". Stay with it, the quality will win through.'

Her feeling which had wandered away returned with enthusiasm, perhaps on an higher note. She intended to curb their conversation towards Ian's direction knowing by now he certainly deserved her attention.

'Had any more thoughts on Homemead?' Her captivating look coupled by dark tousled hair rearranged for this occasion was in danger of overwhelming Ian, he was verging into a state of absolute honesty, with redemption his next possible option? How easy in the comfortable surrounds of the restaurant with such company to confess, the purgatory of an estate agent's time waster. How would she respond? It did not matter as the opportunity was not going to arise. I've had a share of heartaches over the last few months, nothing is going to change my mind, the deception will have to remain a secret that belongs only with me.

'Sorry, lost in my own thoughts.'

She offered an empathetic reply. 'Penny for them? That's what we're supposed to say.'

He smiled, despite his guilt and an outward veneer of deception, happiness appeared, not present on his itinerary for a long time.

'It's all in the past, Fiona, I really had no business going back to Homemead. There has to be an end. He looked carefully, examining his fingernails confirming that his scrubbing activity had removed all traces of grime from his excavations.

With that assurance he reached across and took hold of Fiona's hand, at the same moment their eyes met, aided from the comfort of wine he was prepared to make a thoughtful statement. 'The future, Fiona, that's where life happens, like you've told me tonight, a heritage that your family want to see emerge as part of their culture again, enough said, my lecture's over.'

Fiona inflicted a squeeze on his hand, equally as discreet as it was intimate, lasting precious seconds like colours that emanate from the rays of a passing rainbow, that he would never truly forget…

Marcus had grown decidedly tetchy. Overwhelmed by the brigadier's message he had kept replaying the voicemail, elated by its content. It was, so it appeared, beginning to fall into place. What a character their 'mole' was proving, no wonder he had once held the rank of a brigadier.

But it was leaving him with the unacceptable event, how had the nephew, accepting that's who it must be, managed to get back inside the property? Surely he would not possess any form of master keys? The last few days were in danger of overtaking him, he knew the reason, too much vodka, a complete contrast to his elder brother who was a confirmed non drinker. Thinking of Karl made him cringe, mentally he rehearsed over again the next phone call he was due to make, imagining the profanity he would undoubtedly endure, he hated him and all that he stood for.

The desk light was on, illuminating one small but highly valued item, that he was worshipping, a stamp, a piece of printed paper, it could for him as a collector induce something of the magnitude of orgasmic pleasure. Obsession he thought, perhaps the word was invented solely for me. Focusing the magnifying glass on his latest possession, he knew he was muttering perfection, others would argue how can a surcharged for temporary use postage stamp be described as perfection? They don't and never will understand, they follow my brother's mentality.

Did it all really concern him? He was lost in his world of Australian postage stamps. It pleased him in particular as values in times of credit limitations were making these investments financially sound.

But, it was not to be that easy. He had no alternative than to leave the comfort of his realm of philately to make his phone call. He hated the thought, if only Father was still alive. Marcus could already feel the slur over the phone that would ensue, however there was no other way.

In an effort to compose himself he thought rationally, who else but his brother could resolve what was out there in Namibia? I couldn't that's for sure, no, I'm the brains not the brawn in this partnership. Difficult though his involvement with Karl was, he knew that his brother would never let him down. His mind went back to a bullying incident all those years ago at their school, once Karl had found out what his younger brother had been subjected to then all hell broke out. Still remembering the sight of those domineering individuals; the cause of his heartache. Did they really deserve what his brother had administered on them? It had sickened him for weeks afterwards.

Come on, it's phone call time, sketched out on paper was highlighted the information from the latest report, he took a liberty of sneaking one tiny vodka. This is my life's turning point, power is an aphrodisiac, you will see a different Marcus emerging on to this world, and my brother will lose this strangle hold on me forever. The time difference would have to go tonight, he smiled looking at the drink, his pathetic crutch of life, whilst he punched in the relevant Namibian code…

Chapter 10

Ian was early for his appointment at Greycliffe. He obeyed the parking instructions, 'do not reverse into the bays' which aligned to cream painted walls. Naturally assuming the directive was in force to prevent vehicle exhaust fumes polluting and marking the pristine wall.

Everything about Greycliffe followed the same pattern of a refined excellence. He could not help but reflect on the magnitude of fees that would be payable in such an establishment, supposing they would literally take your breath away!

It continued with the sumptuous reception area, where he was asked by their staff to sign in. He took a seat in the lounge area, overlooking a tiered mosaic garden effect. It was for him projecting a sense of being on display, akin to a piece of ornate china. Finally relaxing in one of the armchairs appreciating the company of an aquarium where even these residents seemed to enjoy a state of opulence.

Ian's thoughts had drifted again, that had been the trait most of the morning, in fact he was not clearly in the confines of the residential home. Instead the feeling of the previous evening with Fiona was the highest profile on his mind. He had not expected anything of that intensity, totally unprepared for what had followed. Last night's shared taxi drive from the restaurant with, on reaching her house, the genuine invitation from her. 'Will you come in for a coffee?' He had not believed in all honesty that still happened. Obviously even now he was having difficulty to comprehend as how rather rapidly a professional relationship for him had become he believed, ignited!

What had so easily transpired for both was that they had so much to talk about, it all followed a common interest as the time had wandered unnoticed into the early hours, obvious by then a relationship was set to begin. At that stage there was no inclination to stop as both parties were adamant with mutual loving desire. Ian counted back the hours when this liaison for them had started, he needed everything right in the forefront of his thoughts, nothing of last night, not the merest detail would ever become a victim to be erased.

When he left her house and walked back to his hotel in the unearthly hour of the morning only then had he regained his world of reality. Now, however in the cold light of day with severe lack of sleep he was prepared to accept in his labyrinth of thought that even love and desire had found an avenue back into his life.

'Mr Harbinger.' Ian took several seconds before realising that he was being spoken to. The enquirer had blocked the light emitted by the aquarium, she stood anxious if not embarrassed awaiting his reply.

'Sorry, yes hello.' He looked up his thoughts for Fiona were extinguished, to be replaced by what in all fairness could only be described as a genuine 'daughter of the soil'.

He was looking at a fresh faced girl, an epitome of Cambridgeshire farming stock, a person you would expect to be ingrained in a landscape painting by the artist John Constable. Although struggling she was succeeding in explaining that her task was to take him to meet their Miss Cleary.

Understanding her difficulty Ian smiled and asked her to lead the way. He avoided comments on the weather, instead remarking on the flower vases on the hall tables, trying to radiate his impression of horticultural knowledge. There was really no point as they had arrived at their destination, room number 12, displaying a nameplate, Miss G Cleary.

His escort knocked softly on the door, there was a brief pause, followed by, 'Come in.' He pondered who he was going to meet, it was certainly to be someone of advanced years, it had to be. The young member of staff hesitantly managed a basic introduction. Once her ominous task was completed she made a rapid exit.

The long narrow room ended at a large desk, where Miss Cleary continued to sit, making no attempt to approach her visitor. Her only action was removing her glasses. He felt awkward, and fell in the trap of speaking first with a stilted admission. 'Miss Cleary, pleased to meet you.'

Her response was painfully slow, he could feel the effect of being looked up and down.

'Mr Harbinger your aunt was a true friend. Her death became a great personal loss and saddened me.' He clearly realised it was no good him saying call me Ian, as this had an appearance of a difficult conversation, exchanges of dialogue for him would have to be earned.

'Firstly, Miss Cleary, thank you for your time in seeing me.' Knowing it was touching on the condescending, but he could not think of an alternative, worse than that his thoughts were still dwelling on last night in the company of Fiona.

Miss Cleary had eventually diverted her gaze and was in the process of quitting the computer she was working on. 'So why has a long lost nephew starting to enquire about his departed aunt?' Her direct question was delivered with what could only be described as a touch of malice aforethought.

Ian could not fail to notice how frigid her conversation was directed at him, even though they had only just met. He thought there was one logical course of action, allow this lady to be privileged to the whole story. Then it's double quick time back to Devon, even my sister's company would be certainly more tolerable.

He noticed that this elderly lady like the residential home was neat and precise, it showed passion of an intuitive attention to detail. As she continued to remain seated he had no idea to her height or stature, however she exhibited an air of refined quality, that would have become esteemed during her more senior years.

Most intriguing were her eyes, a colour of the palest blue augmented by their visual piercing nature. Noticeable as he looked at her whilst attempting to explain the circumstances during the last few days. Which included his unofficial return into Homemead and the search performed inside the property, thinking what difference will it really make?

One thing he could have been assured, his listener was giving the account her utmost attention, she folded her glasses placing them on the desk. Ian continued explaining how the dairy lad had found him by chance at Homemead. 'So, Miss Cleary, a fortunate meeting with this lad from the Polish family provided valuable information which lead to me getting in touch with you, there's so many odd and reoccurring coincidences, for which I am unable to find satisfactory answers.'

'You were missing from your aunt's life, Mr Harbinger, for too many years.'

He cringed at her remark, that of course had more than a grain of truth about it.

His thoughts flashed rapidly through untold episodes which could only be described as guilt trips. Growing up, and no longer any more visits to Homemead, then marriage, children and the encroachment of his working life.

Miss Cleary added a further insipid remark. 'Not even in the latter years a Christmas card for your aunt.' She picked up her reading glasses, opening the frames ready for use. 'That would have hurt her, she found it difficult to make so many allowances for you.'

The virtual barrage of her remarks were becoming too much for him, why this obtuse approach, continuing as she was and lacking to understand his prevailing situation?

Ian had decided it was time to call it a day, his mind was immersed in dereliction of his family duties, like many things in life how can we resurrect the past? One final question for my adversary, that's all I need, he steeled himself. 'Miss Cleary,' aware of an extended pause in his voice, 'where did my Aunt Anastasia actually die?' If he had been subjected to a ticking clock somewhere in the room then it would have been most clearly heard.

As a silence had followed his question, the answer would be forthcoming but only allowed in her own time. Opening a drawer in the desk she removed a set of keys, the fraught silence finally concluded. 'Your aunt, Mr Harbinger, shared a common interest with me in fact that's how we first met.' She unlocked a filing cabinet occupying herself searching through the folders, by contrast her conversation continued. 'Mr Harbinger, are you familiar with the subject of Lepidoptera?' Whilst she avidly continued her search within the cabinet.

No not again, another mind perplexing puzzle, give me a oil rig anytime. He wanted to be facetious, that's not the ideal solution, but let's see what reaction this gets... 'I assume, Miss Cleary, it's not, how can I say anything to do with leopards?' He even came close to addressing her as dear.

A retort with her calculated reply followed. 'Butterflies, Mr Harbinger, butterflies. We were both enthusiastic lepidopterists.' With this endorsement she had regained her chair with the addition of an oversized manila folder.

By this stage he was able to see this elderly lady extolled a virtue of acute perception, further aided by a sharpness which he had already fallen victim during the short time in her office. By her authoritative manner he began to wonder if she actually ran the establishment?

Once more she had replaced her glasses, her continuing conversation resembled a series of proclamations. 'Your aunt had, if I may use the word, an obsession.' He could not fail to notice a degree of enthusiasm in her reply. 'The particular one was the Glanville fritillary, that is a butterfly to you, Mr Harbinger, a rare species only found on the Isle of Wight.'

It left him with an immediate thought, is that where she spent her remaining years?

He fumbled with the car keys in his jacket pocket. Is this my salvation and the answer I have been seeking? He risked gambling a further question. 'It seems then, Miss Cleary, that my aunt decided to retire there?'

The usual protracted silence followed his enquiry, it left him thinking perhaps this time it had fallen on deaf ears. But Miss Cleary was intent in resuming a search through the file. 'Here it is, the actual report she compiled all those years ago on that butterfly's fragile status.'

Ian stood up, this was getting stupid. What can butterflies have to do with someone's life? Even his questions were side stepped failing to get fully answered. A dejected state was adding insult to injury, as now he was noticing painful cuts on his hands; a direct result from yesterday's brick removal. He turned and noticed for the first time the section of the office to his left, one thing adorning the wall could not fail to catch his immediate attention!

Displayed in all its glory, a reproduction film poster, courtesy of the MGM movie 'The Wizard of Oz'. Without realising he was on a spontaneous course to enter into the realm that verged on Miss Cleary's alter ego...

Marcus was struggling knowing only too well that words were failing him, even his grip on the phone was covered with perspiration, this was one of those times he really loathed his brother. 'Please, Karl, show some patience, this is the best we've had, it has to be the nephew.'

There wasn't even a pause before Karl replied, 'If it's right, leetle brother, then he'll turn up out 'ere, and that in case you forgot will be my bit.'

Marcus was tired, the strain of all but battling with his sibling was telling, having stayed up most of the night waiting for him to return his call.

'Find out how he got back inside the damn house.' That for Marcus had been an easy solution, it worked on his previous occasions, hire of a white van, and with his disguise in coveralls, perfect for not drawing any attention on visiting the property.

'All right, Karl, this time I'll find out what's actually happened inside the property.'

Karl paused lighting another of his cigars. 'Talk to me, bro, stop sulking, just think what this damn nephew has in store when he reaches Africa. Man he'd be crying for damn mercy.'

Marcus knew that the protracted phone call was finally ending. He wanted to retreat into the enclosed safe haven of his world of stamps. Temptation however was to intervene, one more vodka, promising himself only a small glass…

Ian continued to stare at the poster, almost hearing the song, 'Somewhere over the Rainbow', a flight of fancy he thought. A ticket to a daydream, perhaps there are even butterflies in Kansas?

It was natural for her to notice his attention the film poster had motivated, she was about to comment when her visitor broke the silence. 'My favourite film of all time, and I really mean that.'

To her it was patently noticeable by the sincerity of his remark. 'Well, Mr Harbinger, we have at least one, if only one, common interest.' She picked up the internal phone, pressing two well used buttons, resuming her attention to Ian who was totally surprised by her request. 'Would you care to join me for tea?'

He really had no option, was the illustrious Miss Cleary turning into the 'good witch' of Cambridgeshire? In a state of surprise he found his reply. 'Thank you, most welcome.' On the tea's arrival silence was observed during the ritual of the pouring, he was presented in what he naturally expected, tea served in a pure white china cup.

Miss Cleary resumed her attention with the file. Without looking at him she allowed the conversation to continue. To Ian's relief the tonal quality had completely changed, those direct questions that personified such a sour note were now lacking. 'I run the care home business here at Greycliffe, not exactly demanding, my early background was as a head teacher following into the family newspaper business for some nineteen years.' Lifting her tea cup she added reluctantly. 'With my age I also need what a residential home offers.'

'But you, Mr Harbinger, need answers... Southern Africa, to be precise Namibia, I knew it when we owned it as South West Africa.'

He was thrown by this surprise announcement. 'Sorry in what respect do you mean?'

She placed the tea cup back into the security of its saucer. 'Why, your aunt's last... home.' He detected at vacant look in her eyes, as if she had only offered an abridged answer.

It was leaving him thinking have I finally earned myself recognition? Surely it must have been more than my remark dwelling on an old Hollywood film even though it's a masterpiece. He decided to adopt a strategy to hold back, let my interrogator take the lead in our conversation that way I am going to learn far more. Miss Cleary closed the folder again as if it guarded some hallowed secret.

'Mr Harbinger you must be aware of your aunt's expertise as a metallurgist with her geology assignments connected to the mining agglomerates in Southern Africa.'

He knew that an answer had been called for, deciding that it was time for her to witness a perfect example of politeness from an oil rig engineer.

'Well yes, someone of a leading authority in her day, I do know that De Beers retained my aunt's services over period of several years.'

Miss Cleary had reopened the file focusing on its content, her reply was noticeably retarded but eventually forthcoming. 'That's a company at my risk of understating that owes much to your late aunt's dedication and indeed her expertise.'

His interest was aroused, he was cautious, thinking, don't rush your fences. 'I do remember during my school days there were certain holidays when I was unable to stay at Homemead, Aunt having been away on business in Africa.'

She leaned back in her chair giving an appearance of a relaxed attitude. 'After her husband, your uncle, died in the mining accident in Swaziland, your aunt saw no alternative other than throw herself into her world of work. Do you know much about Southern Africa, Mr Harbinger?'

Ian reminded himself, answer questions, don't start going off at tangents. 'Not as much as I would have liked, my wife and I went to Durban and on to Johannesburg but that's years back.'

His reply was almost anticipated by her. 'There is so much more to see, don't miss those wonderful opportunities, Mr Harbinger, try and make up for it, sooner rather than later.'

She removed two sheets of paper from the folder, making a gesture for him to collect. 'Your aunt left me details of her final visit there, more an itinerary. In the latter stages of her work she had concentrated entirely within Namibia, to what purpose I do not know, therefore I am unable to elaborate further.'

'I believe, Miss Cleary, I am correct in saying it's one of the richest parts of Africa especially in regards mineral wealth.' He could feel a spasm of sadness entering his thoughts. All morning there had been a total immersion of conversation about his Aunt Anastasia. But his driven question was still eluding him, what had finally happened to her?

This cat and mouse conversation is getting me nowhere, let me risk one more direct question. Quickly he mentally rehearsed it, but too late the conversation from her had resumed. 'You would not probably be aware of your aunt's involvement with someone that she met out in Namibia, by her account they shared several mutual interests.'

Ian predicted a pause in her conversation cautiously taking the opportunity to intervene. 'This is certainly news to me, by that time I would have been involved in the oil industry.' Deciding to take this precious window of opportunity to gain himself further redemption points, he was prepared to gamble by confirming, 'That was when my selfish side of life was not one of my greatest attributes.'

He momentarily noticed a slight change, only slight, but did a visual smile of emotion exist momentarily on the face of this almost frigid lady?

She continued, 'I never met him, but your aunt had her personal life restored once more, she certainly deserved that. He was from one of the old Dutch families, Botha, mercantile traders, he was divorced from what I understand from that of a young wife. There was one serious stumbling block, he had the two sons, both at that critical age, not to pull any punches they were more than just trouble, in short your aunt was presented with a volatile situation. There's a much used journalistic phrase, Mr Harbinger, she became a victim of circumstance.'

A modern term ran through Ian's thoughts… baggage, he decided to take the initiative. 'I assume nothing further came of their relationship?'

Miss Cleary replaced her glasses, perhaps to answer his very direct question. 'Precisely, the father was besotted by his two sons. I believe it was more down to a clandestine affair of his old family's name.'

Ian nodded in recognition of her assumption. She added an endorsement. 'Whatever way, Mr Harbinger, it was the prime cause resulting eventually in the collapse of, as you put it, their relationship and of course the marriage.'

'More heartache for my aunt. Would I be right in thinking she remained in Africa?'

The silence was broken as she replaced her cup into the saucer. 'By that stage, Mr Harbinger, she had become involved with the indigenous people of Namibia. By her letters it appeared she wanted to extend an empathy to those that she had come in contact with during her work assignments, now in our modern parlance, putting something back.' Once again she removed her glasses, closed them and placed them neatly on the file, like a headstone marking a particular monument.

He knew that he had been treading carefully. Risking further comments he decided to add, 'My aunt was doing more than any of the big players would even think about. At least with offshore oil as interlopers we only have the sea under our feet.'

His remark was assimilated by his listener who singularly replied. 'Quite.'

She had no wish to have a spotlight focused on her to become interviewed, as a lady of considerable years she lacked nothing in her approach and tactful skills with people. After all her apprenticeship had been earned in academic circles which had later propelled her to the heights of running her family's regional newspaper. She knew far more about Ian Harbinger than he could have ever imagined.

More aware now of his character, endorsed by their continuing discussions, she was placing a proverbial 'bait' in front of young Ian, understandably curious to judge what his reaction would be.

'The answers to your enquiries, young man, lay out in the deserts of Namibia.' Pausing to resume her habit to reopen the file but this time with a distinct sense of purpose removing further documents that could be easily recognised as maps. 'Your aunt, worked and indeed was involved in these regions of Namibia, it is not a case of x marks the spot. They are remote and vast, not from my experience but by your aunt's involvement, and what she passed on to me.'

As the maps were offered he allowed his attention to be drawn to their content. 'Yes, I can see what you mean it's a huge geographical area.'

Collecting them from his protagonist he attempted to take in the magnitude of the region. Noticeable were the pencil shaded parts annotated with hand written notes. 'Mr Harbinger, do take care of them, guard them closely. You would agree they are rather precious?'

Ian nodded in agreement further endorsing, 'By what you have told me, Miss Cleary, my aunt had many attributes in her later life, sadly now I wish I had known more about, however it belongs to the past.'

Response to his remarks were quickly and precisely answered. 'There always remains much we have to discover about ourselves, Mr Harbinger, you will have to remember that it is never too late.'

Perhaps the length of time they had been speaking caused him to be rather indoctrinated with a complex of too many questions, reminding him like those shell fish the limpets firmly attached to his thoughts. Originating with, 'if only', all those regrets were to be a burden he clearly knew he would always carry. Why, why, Aunt, did I not keep in touch with you?

She could not fail to notice Ian's reluctance to continue their conversation, his attention had become entirely centred on the Namibian maps. She decided to intervene. 'To reiterate it is a vast country, your aunt would describe it as totally diverse. Unfortunately I can advise nothing on the final stages of your aunt's life. My notification of her demise was eventually by route from their authorities.'

He knew that their meeting was finalising, now so much at ease considering how they had started out, a mutual understanding had clearly materialised. He stood up with an intention of taking a final look at the film poster. This was going to be a difficult goodbye, noticeable as he had started to fumble with the maps in nervous anticipation. 'Miss Cleary, may I say a big thank you for sparing me your time. So much is now clearer to me, these maps you have kindly given to me will always mean a great deal, rest assure I will cherish them.' He paused and gestured towards the film poster. 'Take care of our magnificent poster.'

'The rest is up to you, Mr Harbinger, perhaps you have your very own yellow brick road to follow?' He smiled in recognition at her remark, content in the knowledge their common bond of interest continued. He could add no more; that feeling of personal sadness had returned, he closed the office door quietly, failing to hear Miss Cleary's softly spoken words. 'Goodbye, Ian.'

Her visitor had gone, Geraldine Cleary opened the file again in the knowledge that the photograph adhered inside the cover was for her eyes only. Not the quality of the picture that counts, but it was herself and Anastasia on that particular sortie on the Isle of Wight drawn together in searching for the elusive Glanville fritillary.

Inhibitions for someone of her age was not a concern, she 'talked' to the photograph. There 'Annie' you would have agreed I gave your nephew a serious dressing down, heaven knows I was in journalism long enough. He has turned into a fine man. You would be proud of him, like us all at that age there are so many things in his life he still needs to find and understand.

What an interesting morning. She had always thought that an appearance from young Ian would happen one day, delighted now to have been proved right. Geraldine continued to linger on the photograph, it was provoking from the recesses of her thoughts a suppressed desire that she could not prevent from once again surfacing.

No one would ever know or even realise, how deeply she had adored Annie, a precious 'love' that would at that time set her heart pacing. Somehow she had managed to privately contain such strong infatuation for her, even now she knew if only.

Her world at that time consisted of all number of permutations. She had clung heavily to her academic career, it was gone, safely lost in obscurity. Closing the folder for the final time she glanced over at the film poster. It generated one salient point, somewhere over that rainbow… where her precious memories remained, never to be uncovered.

Chapter 11

This was an occasion that it certainly was worth driving on our roads. The motorway was remotely devoid of traffic, for whatever reason Ian had no idea, it did not matter as he was enjoying the rather unique experience. All this and a weekend with the family, even if the company was singularly his sister Julia.

The hire car had the ultimate luxury of one CD, however its accompanying music suited his mood; contented now in his mind that many loose ends that surrounded Homemead and his aunt's latter days were to a large part resolved. Although realising consolidated answers were still a long way off, did those revelations really lie out in remote regions of Namibia?

The 'iceberg' Miss Cleary during her thawing process had enlightened him on many of the background events, but he was adamant she had continued to deny access to chapters that existed in aunt's final years in Africa. Perhaps this is where I am now destined to stop. Why am I so eager to pursue events that now are no direct concern of mine?

He could not help dwelling on what he had been told, imagining his aunt's disappointment caused by the breakdown of the marriage in her later years. He tried recollecting the husband's name but it was escaping him. He speculated that this person must have at least visited Homemead, but why should those episodes of life be ruined for both of them by the intervention of the two children? The car's fuel gauge was giving a visual warning, time for a necessary stop.

Today he was verging with an increasing passion to become organised. The two phones that had a residence in the trunk of the car were needing his attention as communications with a diverse range of messages had reached him. His oil rig engineers were even admitting that his expertise was sadly missing. His compatriots had struggled with relay pumps in the lower D section, but then by following his log notes had resolved the issue. It satisfied him, as that was the route by which they would become competent. At the moment apart from the noise from the rigs he was not concerned by his absence out there.

His personal mobile was littered with messages. Julia in her usual efficient way had reminded her brother more than once about the pending weekend, as if he needed a reminder. But his most recent text had originated from Fiona, having the effect of adding a new dimension to his day; things have started to happen. With his reply there was a sense of regret having to leave that piece of Cambridgeshire. He noted, but too late there existed several spelling mistakes in his return text, but she would hopefully understand the implications. Now for him what lay ahead was home and sister Julia…

'My brother, I almost forgot what you looked like.'

Ian was more than satisfied by his welcome, has she turned over a new leaf he wondered? Julia was right it had been a considerable period since they had last met. He speculated as when the 'oil and water' mix with their personalities would aggressively engage.

He was labouring under an apprehension believing that a new man could be in his sister's life. That would call for a lot of mileage from her once their conversation started to gain momentum. Anyway I've handled Miss Cleary and following that apprenticeship there's nothing that life can throw at me. If I'm right with my assumption then maybe after all these years I will finally understand my sister's reasoning.

Their meal had reached its closing stages, a jug of coffee had been placed on the dining table. Perhaps their mutual detached state was enhanced by Julia's remark. 'Ian it's such a rare occasion for us to share a meal let alone talk together.'

His attention had been drawn to watching the estuary, two fishing boats were returning, maybe they had secured their allotted quotas, either way it made a tranquil sight.

He was determined to avoid discussing the implications of Homemead events this early. He wanted an easy way to gain the upper ground. 'Now, Julia, how's your world of high finance, or more importantly when's the respite coming with credit limitations? You must know that one.'

Julia was thoughtfully engaged pouring them both a second round of coffee. 'Don't know the answer to that one, but I know a man who will be the first to know.'

Ian administered the milk into his cup. 'Come on, Julia who is he? I sense there's something happening?' His direct question resulted in a genuine and for him rare smile from his sister.

'How long have you got?' was her instant response. Following an unusual pause in her opening remark she continued to profoundly add, 'This is the type of man that was made exactly with me in mind.'

Ian thought, I've heard all that before.

Rapidly stirring his coffee he engaged a below the belt tactic. 'Has he got a name, Julia?'

She reached across for the milk jug and delivered her salvo. 'No, he's referred to as Mister X. Of course he has, it's Gerard, but he's Ged to everyone except his father, and you are talking money, Ian, real serious money.'

That delivered one thought straight for Ian, the flashing light of pound signs, my sister will never change.

'Ged's in with his father's business, take a deep breath Ian, it's coal.'

An instant wave of mischievous humour swept through his mind, a graphic depiction of Julia's loved one alongside his father on a coal delivery truck. Julia's intuition detected the wry humour apparent on her brother's face. 'Ian what's so damn funny, it's a multi-million business that's escaping our current credit fiasco, that's fact.'

'All right, Julia, it's that we don't seem to hear much about the coal industry these days.' Reaching out for the coffee jug its weight confirmed that it was now empty.

'Listen to this, Ian. How about an industry that's tripled its pre tax over the last two years, and we talking here in the UK, it's staggering.'

He replaced the empty coffee jug. 'Don't tell me the only thing that interests you in this guy is what's dug out of the ground?'

'Ian at this rate with you in oil and me in coal all we want is some distant relative in gas and then it's a full house of utilities, sorry if I forgot water.'

He decided that an element bordering on more sobering qualities needed adding to their conversation. 'Julia what's your feelings anyway on fossil fuel use, not to mention all the beloved emissions?' Unfortunately her elder brother had stood on the thin ice as he was about to realise.

'Don't get sanctimonious on that issue, Ian, how many years have you been active dragging oil up from the depths?'

He had failed to gauge her reaction, seeking a possible salvation by offering a quick reply. 'Hold on a moment, all those years you speak of, I've come to terms and live with, at least I can sleep soundly at night.'

Julia broke a habit of a lifetime offering an apology to her outburst. 'Let me organise some more coffee, to celebrate those oil profits I've read about your outfit made in the last six months, it's sickening in our austere times. How many billion? What the hell, crack that other bottle, Ian, then I need to know about you.'

He was calm and relaxed in a conversation where his sister had actually apologised to him, or was he in a state of a false security resulting from the intake of red wine?

'Anyway what's with my brother dashing all over the country? Thought you were down here to unwind?' Julia decided to go on and test the water with a deliberate tease. 'There has to be a women involved?'

'You're right on that one, it's our deceased Aunt Anastasia and my involvement with what was once her property in Cambridgeshire.'

Julia had only a scant knowledge of this member of the family, other than she was a geologist who in her life worked in Africa. 'What's all the interest probing into the past? She's been dead for years, thought you had enough problems with the capital you've lost?'

The recently opened wine had no time to become acceptable to the palette, Ian had poured two large glasses. 'Listen, Julia, hold any questions until the end, try and see this from my viewpoint, it's all about association, you know what I mean, a word or an event.' She was curious having never seen her brother in this light before, Julia prepared to follow his intriguing request, and simply listen.

'Here, down along this road, before you reach the estuary is a farm small holding, with amongst other things the yard has some free range hens. That's oddly where for me it all recently started... Let me call them links with my past.'

As her brother's account was assimilated, she became bemused by all the occurrences he was holding so much store by, why had he taken to wearing their father's Rolex? Guessing all this might be a direct result from stress recently endured and was now somehow venting through his past? Is that what isolation on a drilling rig can do for you? Humour him, she thought it's the best I can do, he's entitled to that degree of empathy.

Ian reached the stage of his re-entry to Homemead and then stopped in his tracks and without any reason blurted out a name. 'Steve Mitchell, got it at last, it's Mitch... Alpha platform fire.'

Julia failed to see any obvious connection. 'Sorry, Julia, it's a name I've had on the tip of my tongue that's just materialised, where was I?'

Julia on a laconic point of sighing intervened. 'This, what was it, fox head, Ian.'

Julia began to think, I need saving from all this, if only my mobile would ring. 'Never mind all that, Ian, spare me the detail. Where's this crystal you found? Surely I'm going to be allowed that hallowed privilege?'

A well known supermarket bag revealed its contents to his tolerant sister. 'Ian I could pick you up something like this from any number of stalls around 'The Lanes' in Brighton, twenty quid, top whack.'

Her brother, reminded her to listen. 'It's something more, why was it hidden in my childhood secret hide away, and by whom?'

She picked up the artefact holding it to the light fascinated watching the patterns in the crystals change to different hues. 'Nice touch, like you said give it pride of place on the coffee table, it will reflect on to the glass top, it's our tribute to dear Aunt Anastasia.' She instantly thought it will serve to keep everyone including my spaced out brother sane.

'So, Ian, high time to fill me in with your octogenarian lady, now that is something I must know about.'

He had wised up, realising the danger of falling into a virtual Venus fly trap with Julia's appraisal of his current status. 'Take it from me, this Miss Cleary is the sharpest of any elderly lady I have ever come across, probably became so bored as a resident that's why she's running their accountancy affairs.'

He predicted a typical Julia reply. 'Gosh, cupid must have been firing her arrows when you two met.'

The only thing that averted a rapid cross fire from Ian was a soft smile that came over her face, without any grace she quickly added, 'You know me, Ian dear, only my little joke.'

Desperately wanting to avoid their usual conflict, he endorsed what was for him the most important fact, confirming, 'The significant thing for me, Julia, she's likely to be the only remaining contact who can remember our aunt, in her latter years.'

Julia with a sense of reluctance and to hell with my alcohol units poured herself another glass of wine, then in recognition manoeuvred the bottle towards her brother. 'I've listened, Ian, heaven knows the last time we spoke like this together, that aside all I can make out is, you've chased around the country for a lump of rock and oh yes two maps, or whatever you call them.' Her intake of wine was having the welcomed effect, as she prepared a rhetorical testament to Ian's elaborations. 'Then I'm hearing about some elderly women who likes a movie about rainbows and witches, that's it, you're the one over this rainbow... get real, brother, you need rest, that's why in case you forgot you're supposed to be on leave.'

He surveyed the table knowing that any further conversation was pointless. The coffee was cold and the bottle empty, it had left a signature with wine stains resembling blood vessels splattered on the table cloth. Outside he noticed that rain had resumed, gradually enveloping his view towards the estuary, not that it mattered as darkness was beginning to fall...

Karl listened, he had to bite his tongue, their telephone conversation had progressed for some time. Marcus achieved a visit into Homemead, his brother on this occasion could not help but admire his meticulous attention to detail, suppose that's why he still collects postage stamps.

'This room, which one you say?'

Marcus for once was feeling in control of their discussion. 'One of the bedrooms down at the end of the corridor, it's full of junk, but those bricks had been taken out and pushed back since I was last in there.'

Karl exhibited his usual habit of interrupting. 'This damn phone line's acting up bad, like it all week, tell me again what you found?'

Marcus had no option other than to shout, 'After I removed the loose bricks there's a shelf, the dust had been disturbed, a cavity that goes right inside the wall, looks very old. I could make out a shape in my torchlight, used a curtain rail to hook...'

Karl retorted to a point of losing his patience. 'Never mind the damn details, what was it you found?'

Marcus resumed, shouting, 'Some sort of, looked like a stone bottle.' The telephone communication deteriorated further.

'You say a bone what?'

Marcus was struggling. 'No, Karl, a stone bottle, looked ancient, the top was sealed, anyway it didn't stay that way for long, smashed it, nothing inside except rusty looking nails.'

'Marcus, you can forget that, some kid's thing chucked in there years ago, he's found what he was looking for, must have known it was hidden in that tunnel. You still there?'

Marcus had decided to drain his ever present glass. 'Karl there's no sign how he got into the building, good job the old brigadier saw his torchlight.'

There was the inevitable pause while he waited for the next set of instructions from his elder brother.

'He's out of there, my leetle brother, forget the damn house, if it's gonna happen his next port of call is reet under my nose. I'm ready for that one, get back to your stamps. Father's looking down on us, it's all gonna be ok.'

The line had gone quiet, the harassing conversation had finally run its course. Marcus trawled through the events of the last few days, his fabrication with hiring the white van for his appearance as a tradesperson on visiting Homemead. His discovery and perception with the hiding place which had eluded him on the previous visit. But it was leaving him one nagging thought, how did that nephew get access into the property?

The cavity against the fireplace built at the inception of the house was once more sealed, if we accept that Marcus had only pushed the bricks back into position. The longevity associated with the history of what was entombed to protect its occupants had expired. The dust encrusted sentinel known as a witch's bottle had been maliciously smashed to reveal its hidden contents, the powers that had remained cloistered for generations were no more...

Ian speculated this has to be one of those Sunday mornings when the only task you should aspire to is reading one of the capacious newspapers. Slowly at first he started to recollect the events of last night's meal, the supposedly heart to heart, if it deserved that title between himself and Julia, from bitter experience he had endured worse.

His train of thoughts were distracted, I don't normally remember dreams, but on this occasion there are fragments of one lodged in my mind. It was in a bizarre sense reminding him of Tibetan prayer flags forever waving as tattered remnants in the wind. Where exactly was I, everything appeared hot and arid there was shade towards a canyon between tall cliffs. There was a dark entrance that lay ahead, in my dream sequence I was walking towards it, but too slowly, I could never reach it.

Noise was apparent in the apartment, unusual for Julia to be the first to rise. Don't tell me she's going to cook breakfast, if that's the case she must be in love. Her voice echoed along the corridor. 'Hi, Ian, got some toast on and real tea brewing.' What she meant by real tea he could only imagine?
'How's your head, sister? You know you…'
Julia was definitely not a morning person and today was no exception, she looked across hindered by the absence of her contact lenses, shouting, 'Don't even go there, Ian.' Pure silence reigned, broken only by the town church bells summoning all souls who were prepared to worship, missing from the congregation were certainly going to be the two members of the Harbinger family!
'Ian sorry about this but I've got to shoot off a bit earlier. Ged phoned me, he's in Hampshire doing some flying with one of his cronies, so he's asked if we can meet up later in Winchester.' He knew that at least his sister's request was genuine. When it came to a new man in her life she would follow them to the ends of the earth.
'Go for it, Julia, be good to see you settled again.' Although in the process of consuming what must be a glass of soluble aspirin, her raised eyes complete with historical traces of mascara indicated her approval.
Ian had collected the Sunday newspaper; Julia had given him a lift into the village. She had driven off content with her freely

offered words of advice, Ian could still hear her words. Did he need to be told to leave all the family past buried where it belongs, after all my sister hardly knew her Aunt Anastasia, she did not spend school holidays on the farm. Let it go, I'll walk back along the beach path, clear the head.

On his return the apartment seemed as he expected, quiet and welcoming. He noticed a sachet of some dubious hand cream left in the kitchen obviously forgotten in his sister's rush to leave early.

The weight of the newspaper acted like a thermal blanket creating a sense of warmth as he relaxed on the sofa. In particular as the weather had deteriorated with more rain almost hosing itself over the windows. Sleep, like a thief in the night had crept up on him, with a calculated result of losing himself in an afternoon doze. For all that an intrusion of what he will come to know as a recurring dream was imminent.

He was conscious of a feeling generated by the hot sun, aware of an obscure entrance set in the side of cliffs that towered high above, nothing he knew or recognised. Why am I here? The sunlight was highlighting the posture of a woman which formed only as a silhouette, whoever the form was it walked out from the darkened entrance and towards him. Ian could discern there appeared a long white scarf held by the figure. A following breeze causing it to shimmer like a plume of heat haze.

The apartment window received a strong blast of wind augmented by rain, the noise had the impact of snapping Ian out of his sleep, it was several seconds before realising he was not back on the drilling rigs.

The afternoon merited one description; melancholy, not the first time he had experienced such reactions. It would be easy for him to assume he had slipped into a state of depression but he knew this was not the case. A transition had taken place. All his devious running around had stopped, now what remained was his extended leave. Was it going to be worth all the effort?

At this precise moment he was at best content as an onlooker witnessing the coastal weather purging its fury on the apartment's windows. He finally relaxed taking a degree of interest with the newspaper supplements, easy to see a conscience effort had been directed to induce readers to exotic holiday locations.

Why not, anyway that's the operative word, a vacation, why not me? I'm entitled to some of that, say goodbye to British weather. He could not fail to notice that Africa had received a special promotion, he looked at his aunt's survey maps removing them from their protective sleeves, making an attempt to reach any possible conclusions to what the scribbled notes referred? These sheets only represented a small part of that country, he would need a full map of Namibia to gain any idea with these particular regions she had once surveyed.

He succeeded in rallying his thoughts and for that matter his inspirations helped by the ironic twist with the weather conditions which continued its fury. He had become an easy victim of seduction conjured by clever writing from journalism in advertising the African continent. Sun, that's my answer, perhaps our Miss Cleary was right all along, I'll have to follow my own yellow brick road.

No cheating, it's decision time, heads we go, only one spin, no best out of three tricks. His salvaged gleaming copper coin was seeing the genuine light of day. Shutting his eyes he flicked the coin.

'Heads.' Spot on, my lucky day, Namibia here we come. Oil industry engineers sometimes have to act on impulse, this was one of those occasions. Can the cost be justified? Heaven knows it's only money, and enough of that has gone already.

That certain dreary Sunday was beginning to come alive with his aspirations of a vacation. I can put it down to research let's see what the country of Namibia has to offer. That's it, there's the motivation – research, like an author involved with his latest travel log, well maybe.

He by now was already one jump ahead as at the moment he was waiting for a randomly selected travel agency phoning him back with the flights he needed.

I wonder… he hoped as the lounge phone rang.

'Mr Harbinger it's Vivienne at Umbrella Travel. Good news, we can do a flight, not direct, as I said when you first called, it's from London Heathrow to Johannesburg, then it's Air Namibia direct to Windhoek Eros airport. Most people car hire from there. It's this Tuesday. You'll be pleased with our price.'

Ian's attention had been diverted, the weather front was now gradually passing, endorsed by sunlight streaming through the window it had an influence on the rock crystal residing on the table top creating scintillating lights that played momentarily like a passing symphony of music, then as quickly that particular phase expired.

'Are you there, Mr Harbinger?'

He realised his lack of attention to the caller. 'Sorry, yes that's exactly what I wanted to hear. I'll give you my card details, thanks, Vivienne. All I thought was available on a Sunday afternoon would be an answering service.'

'Not so with Umbrella Travel, Mr Harbinger. There's our company logo to consider, we leave our competitors in the shade.'

Ian completed the transactions content in the feelings in what he was prepared to undertake. Wait till I see the look on Mitch's face, it will be worth it for that alone. His plan was clear, use up his remaining leave and then get back to drill even deeper into the sea bed, whatever else?

He remained hoping with a degree of anxiety for a further phone call which ought to be Fiona. He had left a message although he realised that was hours ago, but it was after all a Sunday afternoon.

The facets of the rock crystal by their angles of view were able to encompass the entire room, included were reflected images of Ian and like all lenses they are in a reversed. format. For years deprived in darkness for its existence the crystal had no option but to remain inert. Now all that was changing…

Chapter 12

Sanoon's nerves were starting to build up, his desperation was more intense than the first time. He craved to loosen his shirt's collar, but company protocol certainly would not endorse such actions.

He knew Captain Clements was right beside him, he wanted at this point one thing, please let it be a perfect landing. Approach speed stable, instrument check, final clearance from Eros Airport Control.

Air Namibia's Boeing 737-500 was on a satisfactory approach to the principle runway at Windhoek's Eros Airport. Sanoon flight pilot was demonstrating an efficiency combined with control that the airline would expect from a second pilot officer.

At last, that reassuring association of the tyres binding rubber on the runway's surface, abrupt vibration arresting the aircraft's momentum. Calmly he operated the following sequence, engaging the aircraft's braking systems. Sanoon knew he should not outwardly show his relief, I am a professional airline pilot, achieving my second take-off and landing. How his family were so proud of him, from his humble background in a country that was prepared to recognise equality. As a pilot he thought, with future landings, will I ever stop these nerves causing me a baptism of perspiration?

Ian was taking an account of his plan, the double thump of landing brought him up to date with reality. I'm here, this is my vacation, no what was it? Yes my research. He had been satisfied that all was in order before making his somewhat spontaneous decision for destination Namibia. Now he had arrived!

Did it really matter? No one waved him off, not that he expected such actions, Julia on hearing of his plan declared that she was washing her hands of the whole business. He could visualise what her actions would be, his next visit to the apartment and there would be a rock crystal to out do what he had discovered in Homemead, no doubt to get at him further it would have a ridiculously low price tag attached.

Dwelling on prices, during the flight's inactivity it had drawn him to examine the wish list created so as to establish the magnitude of his financial predicament. What am I really doing treating myself to a vacation? The list is a statement of my account and is not going to change, he knew that. The 'Guardian' title caption filed with the wish list caused him to deliberate. What was that all about? Why was that rock so carefully wrapped in the newspaper? Am I looking only at a coincidence, will I ever know? He folded the items together placing them back in his jacket's inside pocket.

If he looked for a way of compensation then his phone calls from Fiona before he left followed a refined course, understanding his interest with his now rather limited family, even if it meant delving into forlorn history. However the best news was for her to have the fortitude to wish him a good vacation, wanting to know all the answers as soon as he returned. Is that to happen, or is my only solution to really make it happen?

    Enough said, I have arrived, the company can still reach me via the satellite phone, that was the arrangement. Now the best course of action will be the look on Steve Mitchell's face, when totally unannounced yours truly turns up at his premises. Thinking of faces, it's a poker face when we do meet, although knowing Steve he would have conveniently forgotten about those past escapades.

He closed his in flight reading, at least I have given it a go, reflecting on his recent acquisition the book of 'British Birds' in an association with memories of his childhood buddy Chris Sibley, wherever he might be now.

The Sunday supplements that had engaged his interest with Namibia's capital of Windhoek lived up to their descriptions. If he had failed to read about its German influence then the street names would have clearly under pinned what he saw on reaching the capital. There was a noticeable coolness in the air further enhanced by surrounding green hills giving an appearance to lead him to speculate, is this what it looks like in a genuinely contented African City?

It could all wait, this is my vacation. Top of the list, number one priority in fact was find a hotel and one that suits the lonely and almost pensive traveller. He teased himself remembering the purpose of the whole event, his cover story, researching his latest novel. The cab dropped him off at the Hosea Kutaka Drive near to where it approached Windhoek Train Station. As his driver had indicated there appeared a multitude of hotels, somewhere amongst these one will undoubtedly reach his satisfaction.

He had not walked far to realise the temperature that the city offered created an almost hypnotic and soporific condition; welcoming the heat he was not going to argue in that direction. He stopped to take in an hotel frontage. What's wrong with this one, The Commercial Hotel? With one recent addition, it now ranked an upgrade as a newly added label had elevated it to a status of the 'New' Commercial Hotel. If it's comfortable and the meals are good then it's home. You can be won the world over by a smile; this establishment was a prime example. Ian's, 'Hello there,' gave the receptionist what she needed to know, allowing her to reply in English, from a variety of languages that she as a Namibian could fluently speak.

He congratulated himself on his perhaps his frugal choice, this is clearly not a typical tourist trap hotel. His allotted room offered what he was looking for, no way rivalling the plush hotels in Aberdeen he had frequented, but there's a difference; on this occasion it would be him paying the bill.

Any semblance of jet lag he had assigned was on hold, he was determined to appreciate his first meal that the hotel could offer. Sitting in a cool although dimly lit corner table in the dining room, a Namibian newspaper was bringing him up to date with their local affairs, realising that troubles are the same the world over. Creasing and trying to fold the paper he clearly noticed someone of obvious authority was approaching his table.

'Mr Harbinger, may I introduce myself. Jan Robinson I'm the owner of The Commercial. Now if it's your first time here, a very warm welcome to Namibia.'

Noticing that his table was cleared, the hotel owner sat down to join him; her polite intrusion was welcomed by Ian. Whilst the introductions were mutually completed he was able to make an assessment of the hotel owner. It was easy to discern that she had her eyes and ears on everything revolving around the hotel's performance, there was not a single thing she was prepared to miss, whether from her staff or for that matter her customers.

Jan Robinson was an attractive women that Ian could see was wearing her business face as an attire for her evening performance, everything was as it should be, leaving him to speculate if this career had always been her lifestyle. Did she originate from Namibia? The accent was certainly there, it did not appear there was a Mr Robinson in the wings.

He was drawn and fascinated to dwell deeper, beauty care was high on her agenda, confirmed by the dedication that must be lavished by her hairdresser. Coupling with her acute dress sense, down to the finer points of her jewellery, as each finger was suitably embellished with quality rings. It was leaving one question for him to puzzle on, not that it mattered but out of interest, how old would she be?

That could wait. He pre-empted the next set of questions, perhaps something that the single traveller has to accept. 'What brings you here to Namibia, Mr Harbinger, if that's not too much of a direct question?' His coffee cup was refilled by the waiter. When he left she enhanced her initial question. 'No, Mr Harbinger, let me guess. It's an easy answer, you're in the oil business?'

The irony of life, he thought, knowing what was happening off the Namibian coast. He needed all the allies he could recruit in an unknown country, deciding to just let himself go with the flow. 'Strange that you should say that, I have more than a nodding acquaintance with just that particular industry.'

'That's a relief I don't have to use my next guess, that you're a photographer?'

Ian returned a quizzical look. 'What's the connection?' His question coincided with the restaurant and bar lights turning on, reminding him from other African visits there is an instant transition from light to dark.

'All that you see around you,' was Jan's reply pointing to a range of pictures displayed on the restaurant walls.

Although they all attempted to follow a common theme of desert landscapes he had to admit they exhibited a breathtaking quality. Their conversation at this stage had gravitated to the comfort of first name terms. He really believed this holiday was going to be worthwhile, although thinking that beneficial would probably be a more apt description, even the all seeing Miss Cleary would have to confirm his thinking.

'That's the iconic favourite picture, Ian, they all want to do that one, a petrified forest out on the sand dunes, north-west near Khorixas. Those dead tree trunks in the desert are over 200 million years old, or so they say, that's even older than my hotel.'

Following a contrived laugh, Ian took the opportunity to chance bringing up a request in a guise of a question. 'Jan these desert areas of Namibia are vast and by what I've read the oldest deserts on the planet. I need some help to establish certain regions with two survey maps in my possession.'

Jan looked toward the bar and hailed one of her staff. 'Zappie will help you on that one, he does part-time guide work out there.'

Ian displayed the maps contained in their protective sleeves in front of their new arrival, who examined them from all orientations. After what seemed forever he eventually offered a reply. 'No detail on maps, boss, don't know this land, sorry not much help.'

Ian noticed a degree of reluctance with his reply, or was this part-time guide being cautious. Ian put it down his everlasting acute imagination.

Either way he thanked him for his efforts, Jan had now indicated that the evening bar was coming to life and it would need her attention. 'Don't worry about your maps, we'll sort that out tomorrow. You must be English, Ian, more patience than others I won't mention from overseas who stay here.' The closure of her pertinent disclaimer was accompanied by an intriguing wink.

The member of staff that she had requested assistance from was relieved to be active with the job of stacking the bottle cabinet. Zappie did not wish to associate himself with the regions of Kaokoland and the San tribes and others that lived there; he had heard too many stories from his own people of what laid in the deserts to the north-west.

Ian decided that his first day was about to conclude, he would engage a subtle disappearing trick, content that further research could be carried out in his room. Right at the top of the list of priorities was to locate Mitch's company and give him the surprise of a lifetime.

I wonder how he's changed since we last worked together? More importantly what lasting traumatic effects from the horrifying situation when he was trapped surrounded by explosive fires in the world's worst off shore oil disaster? Manifesting for all time to carry the ominous name of the Piper Alpha fire.

On reaching his room he placed his aunt's survey maps on a vacant chair, attempting for the umpteenth time to validate the area annotated with her irritating scribbled notes. Why were they merging with arrows drawn to specific points? Interesting, our beloved Miss Cleary I'm sure knew more than possibly she was prepared to divulge?

Why her reluctance? At the very least I am Aunt Anastasia's nephew, or is it now left for only myself to be allowed to locate the truth?

Chapter 13

'Excuse me can you possibly help? I need...'

Steve Mitchell looked up from his clipboard and stopped abruptly dead in his tracks. On this rare occasion his jaw really did drop... 'As I live and breathe, is that you, Harbinger?'

Ian was not taken to severe bouts of honest laughter but today there was to be a certain exception. 'I'm the genuine article, Mitch, not a cardboard cut out.'

He witnessed tears of emotion welling in the eyes of someone who had his highest respect; a man that had once cheated death on the working environment of an oil rig platform.

'Harbinger don't tell me you've gone soft, given up The North Sea rigs for the heat working over here off the Skeleton Coast? You won't pull that one on me.' Steve Mitchell had now come into full view, allowing Ian to see the extent of skin tissue destroyed by the gas explosions and fire from the Piper Alpha disaster. His disfigured face carried a haunting legacy that was visible after all these years.

'Mitch unless I'm out of date they haven't found anything off the coast yet.'

The two men shook hands both realising their last meeting had created a gap of too many years. 'Like the look of your business empire, even my cab driver knew of your address.'

Mitch pushed his baseball cap further back on his head. 'Not bad for an old bugger like me, Harbinger. Engineering supplies, they're wanted everywhere, but my real winner is supply and demand for the exploratory rigs off the coast.'

'The name's my own idea, yep, "3 Colour Supplies". Got the inspiration from the Namibian flag, the three colours you know, me a domicile foreigner, like to think it gives me an edge with the locals.'

The very last thing that Ian would dare mention was the fire back in 1988, knowing that he was standing in front of one of the sixty-two men that managed to get out alive. 'Mitch how's your poker playing skills these days?'

The answer to his question was genuinely delayed as Mitch's mobile phone balanced in his pocket decided to ring. '3 Colour Supplies... knew it would be you, they've arrived, get it all over before dark... that's a promise, buddy, bye...'

'Sorry, Ian, oil rig screaming out for more alloy lagging, you know silencing material. Poker, now there's a thing, last time I played was with you... must be?'

'Pleased you remember, Mitch old boy, as my reason for the unexpected visit is to collect my winnings, tired of carrying your IOUs around, all those nuts and washers I'm owed.' Try as he might he was unable to keep his usual straight face.

His compatriot fielded the question to perfection. 'Don't worry on that account, all your winnings have increased in value, price of base metals, gone out the roof.'

Ian could not resist one more tease. 'What a shame we did not play for real money.'

Mitch readjusted his cap, indicating to his ex-contestant that money back then would have shattered a long time friendship.

By this time Ian was so pleased to meet up with his fellow contestant from times gone by, a man you would have to describe as a genuine character from what the old days in the industry had produced. He oozed that charisma, you could without hesitation bottle it, and sell that very commodity.

'Anyway if my credit still holds, Mitch, I'm calling for some help, perhaps advice would be more precise. First how long can you give me?'

'Ian all the time in the world, after today that is. I've got to get this delivery out to the rigs.' Mitch resumed his activity picking up his clip board, he indicated to Ian wanting him to follow along an aisle between storage shelving. 'Now take a look at this lot, all the nuts and washers you could ever wish. Next game of poker, Harbinger, there's no mercy shown.'

His would be opponent raised his hands offering to pick up his next challenge.

The two men parted on an understanding that Ian would return early tomorrow when they would embark on a serious talk as to what he wanted to know.

He left the warehouses situated on Windhoek's Southern Industrial Area, full of admiration of what he had seen. He knew that Mitch was one of three work colleagues that formed a business consortium with a customer base in Windhoek primarily connected with Namibia's emerging oil and gas industry.

After what happened to him on Piper Alpha it would have been so easy to creep away and disappear, not so with Mitch, he was one of life's determined survivors. Ian didn't lose sight of the fact that Mitch's younger brother also in the industry was killed in a disastrous Chinook helicopter crash. It made him think, all for an unquenchable thirst for oil, what right have I to complain with the issues in my life...?

Windhoek Information & Publicity Office was an imposing building and as suggested at the hotel by Jan earlier that morning, was his next planned visit. Let's see how helpful this will be.

He welcomed the air conditioning on entering the reception area, as yet he had not acclimatised to the heat. Against a background of traditional African music, whose volume given his individual choice he would have preferred softer. His first ominous task was attempting to explain to the receptionist his tentative enquiry in relation with his two survey maps. Completely puzzled the desk staff called for assistance, resulting in a stocky authoritative figure of a man arriving on the scene. Ian noticed that the pocket of his immaculate white shirt was adorned with every conceivable type of pen, perhaps an indication of his status of rank?

The survey maps were taken from him, and the staff member purporting to be a wealth of information, or so Ian hoped, then disappeared behind closed doors, eventually to reappear with a stern request for his passport. What possibly do they need my passport for, it's only a couple of maps and for all that matter years old?

On his return to the front desk the senior staff member removed one of his pens from the selection to make copious notes on his pad. Looking up he enquired to the reason for Ian's stay in the country?

'It's my vacation and combined with some research for a future book I am hoping to work on.'

'Do you know the implications with these maps, Mr Harbinger?'

Ian cringed at his remark, what have I got myself into? 'If I may explain, they were handed down to me by a relative, she spent a lot of her working life here in Southern Africa, and that's many years ago.'

He was beginning to appreciate the air conditioning even more, this inquisition he was labouring was certainly not expected, leaving him seemingly one option to play with his next question. 'Is there something wrong?'

'It's the actual possession, Mr Harbinger, they are governmental geological survey maps therefore strictly confidential.'

Thanks, Aunt, he thought. That's a good start, I feel like a schoolboy again in the headmaster's office. 'That was her work, her profession being retained back then by all the big companies.' He was unable to add any further details as the receptionist gained the official's attention in order for him to take a call.

Ian watched obvious in his mind that whoever he was speaking with concerned himself. If I'd had any idea on this I would have abandoned the whole episode. The call he was witnessing was soon completed. 'Mr Harbinger, a senior colleague has confirmed by their references your maps are now long out of date, you may retain them.'

Ian desperately wanted to reply the like of which his sister Julia would use… Probably built a township out there by now, but wisely he remained silent.

The cause of all the concern together with his passport was handed back. Ian decided on a quick thank you and a rapid departure. 'Mr Harbinger, do have a good stay in our country and to answer your enquiry… Kaokoland over in the north-west.'

Ian left the enclave of the refreshing air conditioning. Quietly muttering to himself, officialdom it's the same the world over, mountains out of molehills, one difference I suppose they don't have moles in the deserts of Namibia?

Hal 'number one' was struggling getting used to wearing sandals, he much preferred going around bare foot even if it was supposed to be the rainy season, but his father had bought them for him as a present the last time he had come back from his work at the Rossing Mine. Not that he knew his father, it was Hal's responsibility to keep the family on course, reminding himself that's why I carry the title of 'number one'.

There had been some porters work at Windhoek train station, but it had dried up, so he decided to tramp off to Gammons station and hang out seeing what was happening? Might get a lift on a pickup truck, worth a try he reasoned, at that point he noticed a tourist getting out of a cab outside the Commercial Hotel. Hal One could not believe his luck. It's him, he stood and watched, soft touch tourist, which included the plastic carry-bag inscribed with 'Hart Travel' guide-books and maps.

Boss Botha, I need to get to him double quick, that's his man, he's worth $5 to me, let's hope none of the other boys have spotted him yet? What a reward, and Boss Botha always pays up, one day somehow I'll buy that cell phone, be like these oil prospectors in town. Get one so the ringtone plays our national anthem that's real cool. His sandals were quickly removed, he was running barefoot whilst at the same time praying for a lift towards the Airport Industrial Estate and Botha Plant Hire…

Ian really believed his research was progressing, now able to lay his aunt's survey maps over the capacious tourist map recently bought in town. This transformation was finally beginning to resolve his search. Like the information provided by the bureau employee there in the north-west was what he had indicated, an area shown as Kaokoland.

His continued interest was centred on the new guide books in his possession, beginning to come to terms with the vast size and contrasts that this country holds. What tasks those early explorers from history had to undertake, and with only limited resources at their disposal.

The obvious noise beginning to be generated from below reminded him that the evening at the hotel was under way and his meal was certainly needing consideration.

He declined a table in the conservatory preferring his usual corner dining area knowing it was and would remain cooler. Although he was to regret this decision as the adjoining table became occupied by three individuals all of whom were in the oil business, intent with conflicting discussions on the latest seismic survey off the Namibian coast. Which left him with only one salient point, do I really need this clamour of conversation, particularly on that subject?

An interruption by Jan was a welcome relief, more so as she joined him to enquire on his research progress, curious to know how a writer actually approaches their enquiries. Ian decided to make something out of his visit to the Information Centre, particularly as it was her suggestion.

'You telling me you had a third degree because you have two maps of the desert?' Turning in her seat she beckoned one of her bar staff. 'Ian, please join me with a drink, the rest of this I've just got to hear.'

He enjoyed a tongue in cheek presentation of his tangle with officialdom, but was quick to endorse that they had finally answered his enquiry. Which enabled him to indicate to her it is a region located in north-west Namibia that he was seeking.

'Ian, I'm not much on geography, now if it was Luderitz down in the South, that I would understand. It's not called a girl's best friend country for nothing.'

He looked up puzzled by her remark.

'Diamonds, Ian, you know square cut or pear shaped, diamonds are a girl's best friend.'

If he needed an endorsement of her remark he only had to look at the rings displayed on each of her fingers.

'I've never been down there, I'm a town mouse at heart, but if you drive through "diamond zone" it's verboten to get out of your car, a very sensitive area. You can pick up a diamond laying in the sand at the side of the road, personally I think elephants might fly.'

Ian dwelt on the implications with her reply deciding to add, 'Either way, Jan, there must be something, as they're prepared to go to all those lengths?'

'Not my worry, Ian, I've The Commercial to run, the politics here are a good deal less stressful than when I lived in South Africa, back then anyway, so this is home, and it will stay that way.' She had finished her drink and it was clear to see that impatience was motivating her to get involved in the hotel, it was certainly starting to attract the customers. 'Anyway, well done with the maps. You need guides if you decide on a visit up in those regions.' Following a quick wave and complete with her empty glass she made an exit by one of the restaurant side doors.

He was offered more coffee which he accepted, deciding to remain at his table interested to watch the variety of people that were swelling the ranks of those that were already staying at the hotel. Satisfied, in fact contented, this was a different type of holiday, however more importantly he was starting to enjoy what was on offer. The guide books were sowing ideas which he wanted to make reality, aware that his friend Mitch would be worth in gold his local knowledge. Or should that be diamonds? he mused.

The ponderous relic of a juke box in the bar had come to life spawning an incarnation of a song that ought to have been drowned at birth. He decided to vacate in an opportunity for the warm night air. Sliding his chair back he was unaware of a figure of a man standing behind him, turning he realised that his chosen exit was blocked at neck level, by an arm pushed hard against the door frame.

The area of his corner table was not well lit, although he could make out the rich red coloured hair on the bare arm that was forcibly determined to obstruct his way. There was enough illumination to discern he was wearing a masculine gold bracelet. Although many were missing it still remained partly adorned with segments of abalone shell.

The juke box had entered a silent phase and at that moment the individual spoke. 'Don't get many tourists in here, you gotta be in oil?'

Ian looked into the face of a giant of a man, although his features were all but lost by a full facial beard. Ian retaliated by deciding to snap an abrupt reply at someone with the audacity of invading his space and trying to spoil his evening. 'No, I'm a tourist, my friend, and wanting his solitude!'

The reply offered to Ian was slow in forthcoming, when it did he could not fail to be appalled by his opponent's deeply tobacco stained teeth. 'Sorry, mistaken, thought you were from the damn rigs, I'm nosey to find out what's 'appening out dare?' Finally and reluctantly the opposing hulk decided to lower his arm, whilst adding a degree of credibility with his continuing reply. 'I'm in plant hire contracting, out on da Hukato Estate, name's Botha… Karl Botha.'

Chapter 14

'Don't tell me you're here every morning nibbling on these snacks, Mitch?' as crumbs from the mealie biscuits unceremoniously dropped on Ian's tourist map spread over Steve Mitchell's desk. 'You're right on that one, all my boy's families look after me, makes me feel I'm good to work for.' Mitch cleaned his finger tips whilst offering Ian a sample.

'That's wild country up in those parts my friend, you've no metalled roads, all four wheel drive work, there's hardly any one that ventures up there, more interest elsewhere.' He waved a pencil at the map indicating the vast areas, further endorsing by carefully laying the precious survey sheets to register the contours in the same regions. 'There you go, Ian, they line up, and spot on, Damaraland then across to Kaokoland, up into those desert mountain ranges, if you've a couple of years at your disposal you might possibly see it all.'

Ian was occupied satisfying his taste buds with the biscuit, allowing Mitch to further endorse his informative conversation. 'If this aunt of yours had any contact with indigenous people in those regions, it probably happened over a long period of time, that does not mean you will. Not wanting to rain on your parade but they don't exactly wait around at, how can I say, bus stops.'

'Mitch let me try to explain further, there's…' He fell victim to be sharply interrupted.

'Whole story this time, Ian, you're holding back. I feel a sense of purpose in what you've in mind, but I'm struggling not knowing your true reasons.' He reached down to his desk drawer producing something like a magician in front of an audience of children would conjure a rabbit out of a hat. Although his more adult alternative consisted of two empty glasses nudging contentedly alongside a bottle of Jack Daniel's.

The incoming phone lines were put on to divert, Ian had played the full part at last, the total unabridged account was fully explained, nothing had been contrived, altered or further elaborated or put in context. Mitch had the full story warts and all, leaving him mentally exhausted, desperately Ian gulped at his iced bourbon. 'That's it, Mitch, the whole truth, nothing but, proving one thing, when you working on the rigs it's best to stay on them until you're fully retired.' As he concluded Ian knew he was offering a pensively weak smile.

His audience reflected and was quick to react. 'I thought you came out here just to see me?'

Ian picked up one of the survey sheets and waved it as a politician proclaiming some divine providence. 'It's the final bit, Mitch, it's a question, and out there I am determined to find an answer, my childhood hero who meant so much to me, I need to know because no one will tell me what actually happened to her.'

'Ian one thing before we go any further, I've an idea what her remit with these companies could have been, her geological surveys in these regions were most likely, and this will surprise you… it's uranium.'

His remark did exactly what Mitch had predicted, causing Ian to thump his glass hard on the desk. 'You mean the ore, actual uranium ore?'

'That's it in one, buddy. There's more than an assumption that other reserves of uranium must be known about in Namibia.' He adjusted the tourist map to show the regions to the west. 'This part over here, they've got it marked as Swakopmund, there's the Rossing Uranium Mine, now I went up there once, it's one of the world's biggest open cast mines, you're talking huge, producing what the world' developing countries want to get their dirty hands on most of all, uranium.'

'What you are saying, Mitch – if this runs out there are other known reserves that can be exploited, and my aunt could have been instrumental with their discovery?'

'It's all down to politics, Ian, this Rossing Mine is an eyesore on the landscape to say nothing of the demands of water needed in the extraction process. When it's at full capacity and no labour troubles it's pushing out a million tonnes of unrefined ore a week. Do you want me to repeat that? …A million.'

Ian assumed that serious environmental issues were at stake, with Mitch having lived here for many years he would be naturally sensitive to those implications. He attempted with caution to gauge his reply. 'I understand your feelings – it's this continued rape of our planets resources, at least with disused oil rigs we are now starting to decommission them sensibly.'

Mitch fingered as a lasting lament the now empty bottle of Jack Daniel's. 'We are getting certain things to rights, glass I mean, recycling empty bottles, you and me are doing our bit.' Laughing outwardly he placed the expired bottle on the floor. 'I've got an idea for you, Harbinger, think this one over. I do a lot of serious thinking in my life after surviving Piper Alpha.'

Ian looked up, only too aware that since meeting Mitch this was his first hint in reference to the oil rig tragedy. He was even inclined to bring the subject into their conversation, knowing he would be seeking out his friend's current feelings after a lapse of many years, but hesitated and decided against pursuing the delicate matter.

His attention had to be given to the idea that was on immediate offer, Mitch had already started his presentation. 'How about this one, Harbinger, a serious safari up into those regions that I now understand you're desperate to visit. I don't mean some organised trip, that's not what you want, this will be you, a guide that can be trusted, and transport; that's for me to organise.'

'Thanks, Mitch, this is starting to get interesting, very interesting.' He was surprised what was offered, but he remembered, not for nothing in the industry had Mitch earned a title of a 'Mr Fix-it'.

Although his outward enthusiasm was to be marginally deflated when taken out into the receiving bay and he viewed his allotted transport. 'Few knocks on it, Harbinger, but runs like a

Swiss watch, mean that.' He was staring in sympathy at a Nissan pickup truck which previous usage would disqualify from proclaiming a title of one careful owner!

Mitch was quick to explain his company had at their disposal a fleet of five pickups which were hired out, usually on a long term basis, however the old stager was kept strictly in reserve; despite its extending pedigree vehicle No1 remained reliable. Ian could see that the front winch fitted on the vehicle was at least a relatively new addition, allowing it to enter the realms of a mean machine.

'What you don't see, old boy, are the 'extras', it's what you need out on desert safaris.' Mitch placed his hand on Ian's shoulder and directed him to the vehicle's second reserve fuel tank, then to a lockable strong box welded inside the cab.

'How many, as you put it, Mitch, safaris have you done up there or anywhere?'

I had no idea that I had hit a rather tenuous nerve. 'Well, actually none. Don't worry, what I do know is how to kit one out, and that includes your first rate guide. Besides which this contribution is on me, put it down to clearing my gambling debt.'

'Mitch, this is more than I expected, but I'm going to cover the guide costs. One thing that's come to mind, is languages up in those parts. What's the situation on that one?' He had stopped fiddling with the key associated with the padlock on the vehicle's strong box.

'You get used to it with time, when I first moved out here I noticed the mixture, you know bits of this and that, these guides pick it all up from birth.; Afrikaans, German, and the San dialect's more than enough to get by.' He handed him the padlock key for the strong box. 'They're able to interpret back in English for you, trust me on that one, or you get practise with sign language.'

Ian appreciated the humorous remark. He did not need anyone to tell him life was improving, his troubles were definitely all back home. This is one holiday that's beginning to go my way, he thought. He was laughing as he shook hands with Mitch believing that only oil men could possibly act like this. After all, he reasoned the pickup truck would only need six months in a body shop and it would emerge like new.

The bond of camaraderie was to continue between them all morning as the logistics of his trip were brought together under one roof. Mitch had already obtained the plastic containers to carry drinking water, with other approved cans needed to hold the truck's reserve diesel fuel.

For the highlight of the morning Mitch had decided to keep it under wraps, at least until his visitor arrived. Through many of his contacts he had secured a guide that not only would Ian need, but he could relate in his tentative search for people he was so determined to make contact. He was not going to disappoint him, although his undertaking resembled a search for people akin to the proverbial needle in a haystack. A fact he knew that Ian would have to discover in his own time and to his and only his satisfaction.

Having not previously seen Grittan he liked what he saw as the young man, rather uncertain in his approach, entered the office. Des Montgomery over at the employment centre had certainly come up with the right goods. The introductions complete, this enabled Ian to explain his plan of campaign, underlined by Mitch's valuable if somewhat apprehensive attention to detail.

Both men allowed Grittan to speak freely with any ideas or for that matter concerns that as the guide he needed to discuss. As he was usually involved with helping as a backup guide this trip was going to be a refreshing change, allowing him to endorse a higher level of responsibility.

Ian added a strong emphasis with the implications for languages of the people he was attempting to make contact with, still noting a degree of reluctance that Mitch was showing in particular with speculation of reaching these local inhabitants. It was having an effect of making Ian more determined to prove that his apprehensions were unfounded. At this stage of the procedures, there's no way he was pulling out. Which led him to show good faith by paying Grittan a certain amount of dollars in advance. As his allotted guide left the office, Ian could not fail to notice that paying anything in advance was against Mitch's better judgement.

It was set, orchestrated as far as possible, leaving only the fundamental requirement of supplies. Mitch intervened in the proceedings. 'That's all at the moment, buddy, give it the day after tomorrow, in the meantime you can organise your foodstuffs. I'll give the co-operative store in town a ring, tell them you're looking in, let them sort you out.

'Which brings me to one thing; when you get back I'll want a full report. Better than that, you'll have dinner with us; chance to meet my new wife.'

Ian could not resist aiming one predictable and typically condescending reply. 'Mitch, what's happened to the old one?'

Having made his remark he was quick to realise it had fallen on stony ground, noticeable as there followed a pregnant pause. Mitch reached over pushing the buttons on the phone taking it off divert, he looked back towards him and much to his relief resumed their conversation in exactly the same tone.

'Scars of life, my friend. She tried over the years I suppose, but gave up the struggle, no longer able to hack it, living with someone looking like me. Sereena, now that's different. I met her in Jo-burg two years back, she understands what you have to endure. What happened on Piper Alpha will always be with me, Ian, it only leaves me when I die.'

He saw the build up of emotion that Mitch had to endure, he was prepared to risk the grim topic of their conversation further. 'As you say, Mitch, it's something you never can put behind you.' Wanting to endorse his empathy but feeling intimidated, risking unearthing too many memories, he sensed that Mitch wanted to explain his feelings on a more intense level, and he was right.

I'll only discuss that night on Piper, Ian, with someone connected with the industry. I'm one of the lucky survivors. When "The Silver Pit" rescue vessel pulled me out from the sea I was scorched alive. Like the others, our immediate treatment the only thing possible was having bags of frozen vegetables pressed on our burns.'

Ian knew he was lost for words, any appropriate words that is. What can I possibly add, what relief if any has the gap of twenty years since the horrifying tragedy helped the traumatised survivors? Ian knew his conversation had dried on him he desperately wanted to add his thoughts and feelings but his companion showed signs of deep distress. Silence was, he believed, the only action he could follow.

'You know, Harbinger I'm thinking of your departed aunt, I so admire your passion with what you are intent to pursue. But it's her name, it's different truly wonderful. To me it relates to Russian names, you know their royalty of years ago. Anastasia, by all it's priceless, my friend.' At this stage it was easy to see that the contained tears of emotion were draining from this tough old stager's eyes…

Karl Botha was frustrated, twice he had phoned his brother, on each occasion he had been out, using his messaging service was simply not the way he operated. At last his evaporating patience was finally rewarded. 'Leetle brother, where the hell you bin? I need you 'ere not wasting your time damn working.' Marcus knew his day had been going too well, all that had rapidly changed with his elder brother's call. 'It's bloody good news Marcus, he's arrived. I met the precious nephew in his 'otel, out 'ere he's like a fish stuck in da mud, ready for the damn net. It's gonna be easy, real easy, gonna enjoy the whole damn shoot-up.'

Marcus could hear his brother's raucous laugh as he resumed his detailed description of his meeting. 'Like taking candy from a damn kid, he'll make a move soon, and then, dear brother, it's to 'appen, that's when I need you 'ere, unless you wanta leave your slime trail for ever in your precious adopted country?'

Marcus was sickened at having directed towards him such an odious remark, he wanted to retaliate. Why is it that I always have to be treated in this way?

There were times when he seriously reflected was it worth all the planning and waiting? Their father had instilled the thought of wealth becoming available to his sons even though they might have to resort to unscrupulous means in remote regions of Africa, where it would always be possible to escape detection. His brother was relentless, an obsession of greed that he had inherited and was not prepared to let anyone stand in his way. I want my peace. Do I have to go through with all this? My satisfaction in life is that of the experiences of collecting postage stamps…

Ian's enthusiasm and organisation for the trip knew no boundaries. When he reached the co-operative store he took on the role, at least in his mind, of a supply officer that oil rigs have the good fortune to employ. Satisfied with the procurement of the food stuffs it left him one clear day to perhaps fully experience what Namibia's capital had to offer the visitor.

Having dined at The Commercial, he was ready to qualify what the guide books had described with Windhoek's night life. There was a variety available with sharp contrasts that ought to suit most tastes between the muted demands for tourists and the more opposite extreme where the local inhabitants were frequenting. Noticeable in particular he thought on entering the Flamingo Bar, would we ever know how many carry that same name tag around the world?

Had he been more aware on entering the Flamingo then he would have noticed his hired guide intent telling his fellow compatriots that he was set to embark on his first single handed safari with this guy from England, wanting to see Kaokoland, and make contact with those that are supposed to be living there? Ian's advance to Grittan had already been responsible for two rounds of drinks, which had in turn created more 'friends' than he knew, in frequenting the bar. One of whom was closely linked in his work of site clearing with having a patronage to requisition his hire plant equipment from one Karl Botha.

The Afrikaans and German parentage of Zwart Meyer was a unique mix, he owed a debt of personal gratitude towards Karl Botha that he would never forget. Anything possible he could contribute from town gossip he was only too pleased to pass over to his mentor.

For that reason alone Zwart called at the Botha Plant Hire first thing in the morning, fully aware that the owner would be at his office. It would be worth the visit for the friendly abuse he would be sure to encounter, he was not disappointed. 'What the hell do you want this damn time of day?'

His welcome did not surprise him. Stepping on to the veranda carefully avoiding the broken flooring he shook hands with Karl. 'Mr Botha, I know you have some decent coffee this time of day, and I don't come empty handed.'

Karl listened, the feelers he had put out to all the boys were coming home to 'roost'. So as expected the nephew was making his first positive move, leading him to raise a pertinent question for his unexpected visitor. 'Who's this guide he's gotta tagging on?'

Zwart placed his chipped and stained coffee mug down to explain what he knew about him, emphasising that the guide Grittan had made previous trips into Kaokoland.

An incoming phone call interrupted their discussions. Karl dealt with it showing his normal abrasive manner. His mind was in a state of turmoil, it's going easier than I thought possible. Already a perfect scheme that he could instigate had entered his realm of devious thoughts…

Later that day Ian's transport was dropped off at The Commercial, parked up in the yard out back, covered with a tarpaulin sheet, it was all but ready for the early morning start. Determined to return to the hotel when the trip was completed, certain items were to be safely stored for him. Jan was prepared to give any assistance to a writer seeking research for his next novel, believing, who knows, there might be a reference to her very hotel.

On arrival of the truck two large postal bags were handed to him personally. He was told they were for him only and had come from Mitch. His surprise packages judging by their weight rapidly got the better of him, calling out to reveal their contents. What do I need with a gun? was his immediate reaction, handling what was clearly a rather battered ex-service revolver with the addition of several rounds of ammunition.

On a more mundane level the other bag contained a vast stock of water treatment tablets and an engineer's compass. Although the vehicle was equipped with one fixed in place, an alternative compass could become perhaps a valuable necessity.

Paramount with his final inventory was the company's satellite phone with the necessary attachment for charging via the vehicle, comforting he would remain in touch if needed with Mitch, and if the company needed to communicate.

For all that it was the note that Mitch had tucked inside this package that summarised the whole organised affair. Apart from a usual well wishing remark, understanding his personal search, there was also included a poignant supplement originating from an ancient proverb, causing him to appreciate and dwell on what Mitch had copied for him… 'The mountain has only one summit, but many paths up.'

Two of the early morning boys at the hotel were actively helping Ian in a cold light of day with the pickup cover sheet when the 'guide' walked into the yard. 'You Baas Harbinger?' came an enquiring question. Ian turned and slowly realised it was not Grittan he was looking at.

'Cousin Grittan, him bad sick, I not let you down, Baas Harbinger, I do guiding for you.'

Ian tried to take in the change of circumstances. Looking at him they would have passed as peas in a pod, although he was struggling with his English you could certainly discern the family likeness, or so he thought.

At this late stage and everything in a state of limbo ready for the off he was not prepared for any delays or worse still a cancellation. Ian called out whilst continuing to load the back-up diesel fuel on to the pickup, 'Well, my friend, what's the name you answer to?'

His new guide worked out the implication of the question. 'Me Nassindu, always called Nass, good guide, Baas I knows that country you go to, being up there, no roads you need this truck.'

Ian resolved himself to accept the turn of events, considering at least they're related. 'Okay then, Nass, throw your pack in the cab and climb on.'

Perhaps he thought momentarily he was back on the oil rigs, as he could not fail to underline his orders. 'I want this show on the road and soon…'

Once clear of Windhoek the open Namibian roads really did belong to them, making Ian feel relaxed. His passenger was certainly reserved, generating only limited conversation, even this could only be induced as a direct result of asking questions. During the last two hours, Nass was seemingly content to aimlessly fold and refold the foil wrapper that had previously held a piece of chewing gum. Perhaps he knew and was attempting to fold the paper more than the recognised maximum of five times?

Ian was unaware of his passenger's nervous activity whose mind was going over the details associated with yesterday's deal that Baas Botha had made with him. If it worked out it could mean more dollars than he would probably ever dream of.

Last night he had achieved the easy bit when he was able to get Grittan drunk into a paralytic state, conveniently taking his place, now acting as his cousin. What guiding he had done was sketchy to say the least, but he would get by, he was raised to survive by that very fortitude. All I have to do is see where this guy Harbinger wants to go, Baas Botha said there be maps and most likely diaries or whatever. Get that right and the money is coming my way, Karl Botha had shook his hand on it.

Ian was pleased to be on his way. Mitch had done a truly excellent job with the logistics in organising what had been required, now the remainder was very much in his own hands. He reckoned by their progress that this time tomorrow they would have exhausted the metalled roads, with the true purpose of his endeavour under way at last.

Mitch of course was right, apart from its battered superstructure the honourable pickup truck was running superbly, long may that continue as he lovingly tapped his fingers along the steering wheel. His mind had returned to Greycliffe, with of course his meeting with the evasive, but knowledgeable dear old lady, Miss Cleary. Remembering without that film poster in her office and their mutual affiliation towards 'The Wizard of Oz', then perhaps I would not be this far. Recalling the precise words of her profound statement that was directed to him. 'Perhaps, Mr Harbinger, you will have to follow your own, yellow brick road.'

Chapter 15

Ian was in a deep reflective mood, contemplating that everyone should be allowed this exhilarating experience at least once in their lives. You can count them, singularly one at a time, untold millions of stars, you would although need to devote your lifetime with the undertaking.

This was his third night sleeping under the desert sky and nothing was eroding the spectacle. It reminded him of his aversion towards a word that had gravitated into far more common use, 'awesome', everything possible was having that tag attached. But here in the vast desert night sky was a sight that commanded that very purposeful description.

If enough time existed you could number every individual star, he had reached a point of understanding what is referred to currently as light pollution, but here in these wonderful remote regions you can really appreciate what the Milky Way has to offer a patient observer. Not even views from isolated oil rigs at sea can reconcile what on this sheer scale is so captivating.

His speed of living had gracefully slowed down almost experiencing that of verging on a reassuring stop, he was appreciating the inactivity. By direct contrast any positive results with his quest was remaining at nil, at the moment that did not entirely matter.

Mitch had endorsed real wild country, and as usual no question on that, fortunately as far as the mechanics were concerned all was going as planned, the 4WD vehicle appeared like Ian himself; in his element. Of his guide he continued to remain the silent type and noticeably withdrawn, he wondered if it was simply shyness? Either way he made up for this with his skills as a chef, the meals offered exactly what your would-be explorer at the end of a long day desperately needed.

All this, but he had to be realistic with his minus results. The trackless voids were hiding their secrets, Ian systematically was trying his best to cover definite zones that he had previously blocked out on copies made from his aunt's maps. Well organised but with day number four now emerging lacking any achievements. Calling on his speculative oil drilling background he was remaining forever optimistic.

He completed his almost religious morning checks on the vehicle and the supplies with the vital assessment of their drinking water. Remembering the advice from Mitch, by his reckoning there was less than three days of water left, they would today with necessary caution start a strict ration quota.

The ground over firm sand they had followed all morning had finally given out, the desert winds had chiselled away the scant surface. At this stage they had access to the end of a narrow confined valley, although there appeared from the maps no way through. He attempted to explain to Nass that American western movies would have affectionately described this as a 'box canyon'.

For the first time in days they had entered an area of scant vegetation, a change of environment that as his guide indicated would hold desert wildlife. Ian knew by what he had planned they had reached the most remote and further most point of their journey. But why, not just one sign of the desert inhabitants, people that his aunt had worked with and befriended?

Neither Ian or his guide would ever have the knowledge of how the light of the deserts are used, you would have to be born there to understand what could be 'read', unaware they were observed by an onlooker who was remaining mounted on the saddle on his stationary camel. Whilst methodically focusing on them using his ancient telescope that once in its history had seen service by the Kaiser's German army, not even a possible reflection from the front lens would ever be noticed by those under his scrutiny…

Nass could make out tracks in the softer edges of the sand that had not moved in recent wind disturbance. 'Bass Ian, elephant through here about two days, they fed and gone out.'

He took note of what his guide was showing him, even to the point of how many in a family group had entered into the canyon. Of human intervention there continued to remain nothing.

He referred to the maps, whenever they were laid out on the vehicle's bonnet for viewing this was when his guide for some reason came to life and any inhibitions he showed disappeared, a yearning of considerable interest in what detail the maps held? Ian made his next decision. 'All right, Nass, we make the best of the day, come out again into the main body of the valley and head towards what's shown here, this escarpment.' Having made his directive he noticed that Nassindu for whatever reason inwardly retreated into his shell again.

They lost valuable time as he got the vehicle stuck in a soft sand hole, however Ian was getting used to this recurring off road problem, in fact he prided himself how quickly he was able to bring the truck's winch into use and secure his way out, although realising so far how lucky, as there were available winch points. But with time draining away his plan to cover the whole region on his aunt's maps whilst supplies allowed, was in serious doubt.

By the time of the next stop he decided to make camp, they were in another inner canyon, it stretched into a broad plain that formed the desert floor which headed towards the distant escarpment that he was determined to explore tomorrow. Whilst Nass became busy organising their meals Ian headed out on foot, hoping by scouring the landscape with binoculars possible clues would, as ever hopeful, be forthcoming. He began to recall those profound comments from Mitch. 'They're not hanging around at bus stops.'

On returning to camp, signs of darkness were already showing, on this occasion with the bonus of available scrub wood Nass had established a healthy looking fire, staving off the cold of the approaching desert night. The cooking was in the final stages, Ian used the glow of the fire to again view the survey maps, as if they were not already imprinted on his mind.

Laughing, as in all his maps and notes and the Namibian guide book, if that was not enough there was also Chris Sibley's book on the subject of British birds. Now I really need that mine of information out here in the Namibian desert. If Chris could see me now what would he really think?

His train of reflective thoughts was interrupted by Nass calling that food was up. The bubbling menu in the cooking pot was about to deliver, when they experienced an arrival of unexpected guests.

Almost like a materialisation in the eerie desert half light, the obvious leader appeared, followed in single file by its clandestine attendants. Ian made out their shapes in the gathering gloom, although slow and in a dignified manner he was looking at a train of mules.

The lead animal stopped on cue within the glow of light from the fire, it was clear to see that they were not wild as in fact the first animal had a ornate carved saddle, the reins were not loose they were well managed and tied back. It did not end there, as following the lead animal was the team of like-minded beasts, with one difference they were truly beasts of burden, as each had a pair of panniers attached, as for any human attendants there appeared none.

Nass had joined him, able to offer profound wisdom indicating they were in fact asses which were used by the desert people, either way it did not answer the one fundamental point. Where are their owners?

Ian really had no option other than make a decision to tether the beasts rather than allow them to continue their wanderings into the dark desert void. Although judging by their lack of activity on having reached the campsite they looked set to stay.

'Food that's what we need, Nassindu, all your hard work at cooking.' The menu enthused a rich stew, although it was a repeat occurrence from his previous meals it was proving ideal. Ian reasoned that with the animals stationary it would at least give their owners a breathing space to catch them up, exactly what the panniers contained was another puzzling question.

Surely, he reasoned, this will bring people into the scheme of things, their owners and maybe answers might be forthcoming in his search.

Once the meal was finished he considered that an inspection of the pack animals' cargo was called for, at least on the premise they were now under his charge. By torchlight he examined the panniers' capacious skin bags, each needing releasing by undoing a cross-over lacing of cord. Difficult working in the limited torchlight they finally made out the exposed cargo in one bag. It contained sugar like amber crystals. Nass quickly intervened by smelling and then tasting the commodity. 'It's all salt, Bass, worth much money.'

He considered there was no need to open any more of the containers based on a safe assumption that the remaining panniers held the same cargo. Ian quizzed Nass on the implications in exactly what the value of salt meant to the desert people, fascinated when he learnt the wealth of bartering power that was secured on these animals. He remained resolute to keep their 'visitors' tethered on the grounds that their owners should locate their missing charges that much easier.

Ian gathered from the truck his usual sleeping kit and following the habit on previous nights pitched close to the vehicle's wheels. Under his torchlight he studied the survey maps trying once more to figure out his aunt's annotated pencil sketches and various arrow heads appearing on her maps, but with no logical purpose. He was interrupted by Nass bringing over a cup of his own concoction, it had become known as his 'special brew', a hot desert night cap. Ian would not be aware it differed from previous nights by the inclusion of extra ingredients, making something of a unique and insidious recipe.

The arrival of Nass caused him to inadvertently crease the survey map he was intent on studying. On resuming he noticed a change in the orientation of his aunt's scribbling, in particular the unexplained arrow heads. Interesting – as he focused the torchlight closer, it was totally different when the maps folded. It referred to an entirely separate part, revealing a valley area which as yet had not merited his attention. Could this be the clue I need?

He stared towards the fire, Nass must have made it up, as it was crackling with new found energy. He could make out his guide, intent with various duties it appeared that he was arranging the plastic containers that held their precious water supply. Ian wanted to call out but it did not seem to happen, although his memory was conscious, it was all in a muddle, sleep although he wanted to struggle against it was beginning to gain an intrusive hold over him.

The lonely desert night had ascended, Ian was not conscious to witness the following events, his guide had become active, water containers were taken from the truck and tied on to the panniers of the patiently waiting animals. Ian vaguely felt an intrusion but unable to physically respond he seemed to have succumbed to a remote and equally paralysed state. Nass was taking the survey maps, the watch on his wrist suffered exactly the same fate.

The leading animal was untied from the winch housing on the truck, slowly and creating virtually no noise the team of asses moved off under new ownership into the desert night. Nass could not believe the acquired wealth that was now under his control.

A light wind had risen since night fall, causing the fire to generate the warmth that was reaching Ian, who by now was lost in an unreal state of deep unsettling sleep. No further fuel would be added to the fire, his guide with the team of pack animals was gone. Nass welcomed the desert wind that was instrumental in covering the animals' tell tale tracks they were leaving in the sand.

Chapter 16

The light appeared different to Ian, as if dawn had happened hours ago. There was no activity at the campsite. He struggled to remember much of the night, it was nothing else than a blur. Did I look out, as on previous nights, the array of satellites tracing through the theatre of the desert sky? He felt cold, the fire despite its stack of available fuel had during the hours of darkness been allowed to go out. What was happening, no movement, nothing seemed right?

'What's the time?' automatically looking down at his left wrist, but the watch was gone. Had the bracelet come undone? He searched around the sleeping bag with no result. That was the first time he noticed his condition, his whole body was not fully responding to his actions, there was a thumping pain emanating from his head, like a hangover that was fuelled on steroids. He was concerned with his noticeable state, believing that he might have become a victim of poisoning from a bite or sting. He shouted out to attract the attention of Nassindu.

'Nass, you there?' Repeating his request several times, his response was completely negative… only his own echo reverberating through the darkened canyon. He struggled but it was apparent that he could not extract himself from the sleeping bag. He rolled partially to one side gaining a view of the surroundings. The pack animals were gone, is that the answer? Have the owners claimed their rights and then acted in an unfriendly way to his guide and for that matter himself?

He had no option other than lay still and try to reason what had occurred. Where's my guide, is he kidnapped, dead? Why did I sleep so sound and for how long? He then noticed something else in his catalogue of mysteries, his aunt's survey maps were missing, they were left inside the bird book, surely they would mean nothing to anyone, or so he believed.

One benefit at least, he was able to reach his water canteen, he stupidly gulped at the contents which offered some respite to an unusual thirst that had developed. His action immediately produced dire consequences, inducing a fit of severe vomiting. That's it, he thought. It's a poison from something, maybe in the water? He resumed this time, in a state of frenzy calling out for Nassindu; the response remained the same, only his personal echo. Now understandably he was starting to become alarmed.

The phone, my satellite phone, hell it's in the security box inside the pickup. How can I reach it? I need to contact Mitch; something's gone wrong, very wrong…

In the mind of Ian's guide Nassindu, nothing was wrong; nothing could be further from his thoughts. All night he had travelled at the head of his acquisition, the pack animals, blessing the desert wind that stirred the sand whispering as a secret the tracks of the asses. He figured in three days he would have reached his destination, the hinterlands which they had passed through on the way out.

Here the lucrative cargo of salt would be sold; there would be few questions from people that dwelt in those regions. Salt acted as a conduit establishing a life blood for the desert tribes people in these more precarious regions. Your position in their society could be measured with that precious commodity in your possession.

Payment in Namibian dollars, then home as a rich man, he laughed, and all for bags of salt. Boss Botha would still buy Harbinger's maps now in his possession, then there's the watch to sell. Rich, I'll be like the American oil prospectors in town, all will become available to me. Women in the clubs and bars in town, knowing his salacious habit would be satisfied over and over again, no hangers on, just me, big man Nassindu…

Ian had returned to an uneasy sleep, of its duration he had no idea, the consuming heat of the rising sun started to have its effect causing him to wake. The confines of his sleeping bag still remained his virtual prison, whilst the debilitating nausea had not in any way diminished, treating him more as a state of being paralysed.

He was not a man to panic, after the initial shock he was prepared to try and establish in his mind what had actually taken place. Firstly by his logical approach, where's my guide gone? The fact that the pack animals were no longer as he had left them seemed to offer some link to these events. He assumed whatever happened must have taken place during darkness judging by the amount of scrub wood remaining unused for the fire. The routine on previous nights was that Nass had continued when necessary to maintain the fuel demanded for their fire.

But what's caused my condition? His knowledge was scant of the desert environment, still concerned that he was a victim of a venomous bite or sting. He tried the water again, cautiously a few sips, nothing had improved, the vomiting continued to persist. The worst action he could take was consuming any fluids, the concoction that his guide had maliciously introduced into his desert night cap had violent reactions to liquids, further weakening any possible form of a recovery.

Nassindu had in his possession what his elder generations knew about, but that in modern times although able to administer he was by the consequences reluctant to use. But Ian's guide was driven by greed so he was drawn into his odious plan, to use the death sting poison that depending on its dosage would allow its victim a death by virtual instalments. A fine ground pulse vegetable was host for an inclusion of one of Namibia's prime and subtle killers, an essence from the thick tailed black scorpion.

The concoction introduced into Ian's drink would cause sleeping followed by acute nausea and invasion into the limbs. With no immediate treatment then death would be the conclusion by stealth of dehydration and probably heat stroke. Thus the desert would eventually lay claim to another seemingly innocent victim.

He knew there was one solution, the satellite phone in the vehicle, it had to be reached, send an SOS to Mitch. 'Come on I've got to do it.' His struggling was draining him, with no respite from the searing heat of the desert sun, resulting with him quickly overcome in a volume of unnatural perspiration, with his only immediate course of action to sink his face in the quilting of the sleeping bag's interior in an attempt to escape the sun's relentless power.

Ian remained in this sanctuary shielding the daytime fury waiting there for a degree of comfort that would only arise when the sun started to set. His condition had not deteriorated but for that matter there were no signs of abating. Time and again he directed himself with but one train of thought he must remain calm, believing this was the only solution to resolve his predicament.

The arrival of the desert night transformed his turmoil of the day to a state of at least partial sanity, knowing that the cold would be facing him as the night wore on. Punitive efforts on his part to establish the fire were not going to happen, or in blunt terms it would not be possible for him to get a fire even started. Although by a disciplined and determined need he was able at last to relieve himself, an achievement which yesterday had meant nothing, was now an accomplishment.

Darkness brought change to the wild desolate environment, a feline troupe of desert lions were attracted to the strong scent that the tethered pack animals had left by their urine stains on the sand. The alpha lioness of her hunting group was cautious as there was another smell in the air, unnatural, one that permeates from the presence of man, that of the alien sickly odour of diesel fuel.

The predators of the night had skirted the camp no less than five times, aware that food could be there and an urge of natural hunger was affecting them. As the sparse game of their hunting territory had now vacated to higher grounds.

Ian's dozing had helped his situation, appreciating the cool of the night, believing a new found strength would be enough for him to evacuate the sleeping bag and get to the satellite phone.

However renewed efforts on his part continued to show no positive results, other than generate a thirst which he dare not risk trying to satisfy.

The exertion whilst unsuccessful, had one outcome, it brought on a satisfying sleep, the scorpion-induced concoction in his system was going into another phase – that of inducing weird and unexplained dreams. During this period in the night he woke to vaguely witness movements at the edge of the campsite, creating an unnatural feeling that eyes were intently watching him.

The marauding lions were preoccupied with their search for food, they had cautiously circled the area on which the pack animals had been tethered, on the point of leaving to track down this potential source of food when they scented other prey that much closer; human kind which lacked any protection from a fire. The alpha lioness, only too aware her troupe like herself was hungry, would use the cover of darkness to her infinite carnivorous advantage…

Mitch hated stocktaking, but on this occasion he decided on a brainwave by working really late and getting it done in one lump, or so he wanted to believe. His discipline had progressed, promising himself on completion a reward with one singularly large glass of a certain bourbon. His desk was its usual mess, although firmly believing everything was at hand, that's when he noticed the photocopies of Ian's maps; gosh, how long has he been gone? It further propagated a rather mischievous idea, I'll break radio silence, get Harbinger on that satellite phone, least-ways leave a suitably rude message. Looking up the number he started punching in the required digits…

The alpha lioness approached her prey, needing only starlight as the coating on her eyes channelled all available light directly to her retinas. She paused cautiously separating the scents all too apparent under the night sky. The emotive diesel fuel she tolerated, what lay partially concealed in the cover of the vehicle was her eventual aim. The remote regions of the Namibian desert was her kingdom, she knew little of the value of humans, it was prey, food, life blood for her troupe. Remaining to seize her eugenic prize was a calculated leap from where this dealer in death was unflinching in her crouched profile.

Ian awoke coming out of yet another bizarre dream sequence. He stared towards the heavens; despite his circumstances he still marvelled at the expanse of the desert panorama. Would there ever be an explanation? His languid state still allowed him to trace the passage of those satellites as they put in their nightly journeys. He had no knowledge of his night visitor, she was barely breathing, acutely waiting, motivated by her natural urge in needing to kill.

As an engineer Ian should have known better than to allow equipment that relied on electrical storage to be left switched in the 'on' position. The lioness could feel the muscles in her hind quarters poised for the intended plunge, she was not prepared for the intervention of where her intended prey originated, that of the modern world of man.

In the cold vacuum of space the satellite received the signal from Mitch's phone. It could not think or intervene, it was purely a machine. A higher force on this occasion might describe it as a 'guardian angel', the signal had already transferred its energy, now it was earthbound. The receiving phone's ringtone set on maximum volume virtually screamed from inside the security box in the pickup...

The predator of the night could sense the breathing rate of what meant food for her troupe. Saliva showed as an outward presence draining from her fangs, all was shattered in a moment by an ear splitting noise, she spat in temper with a startled growl in an effort to warn her pride of an unknown danger. They were gone in an instant, desperate to escape the acute noise affecting their hearing. Now only embossed footprints remained as a legacy of the death dealer and her troupe. Ian went cold with fright, becoming conscious of the phone's ringing, but that was nothing in comparison to what he sensed through his primeval fear, the bodily movement of creatures that had rapidly evacuated into the desert night.

Darkness remained painfully slow before the long awaited signature of light, he kept remembering a certain bench seat along the coast at home. It carried an engraved plaque with such a poignant inscription: 'No matter how long the night the dawn will surely break.' Eventually the glimmer of a false dawn was heralding its purposeful approach. Whatever had ventured into the campsite had no inclination to return, but that had been at the expense of him remaining awake longing that a fire could have been possible. In the morning he made the first scribed symbol in the sand next to his sleeping bag, indicating, that's my first day of isolation done.

He crawled using all his strength planning on salvation by burrowing beneath the vehicle reaching life giving shade. On this, his second day of turmoil, he wondered why any form of an appetite had not returned, but he could at least sip fluid, cautious that his meagre water supply was now possibly standing between his life and death.

His efforts between the wheels of the truck were slow, his determination was realised by using, as a crude shovel, the bird book bought in memory of Chris. Slowly and by his arduous determination it was working, excavating a sand pit in the vehicle's limited shade that would offer daytime relief from the searing heat.

Would it be possible to lay quiet during the heat, wait until dusk, then an almighty effort on his part to reach that phone in the pickup? I must, it's my solution, seemingly my only solution…

Nassindu had become complacent, resting the pack animals longer than needed. The journey to his potential customers was getting drawn out, then did it really matter? This was a man set to become rich, wealthy more than in his wildest dreams. Everything would find its own time; he had no thought for the man he had so clearly left to die out in the desert. Greed was his newly discovered goal. He worshipped what had fallen in his hands and was set to make him a man to be accountable with.

It was at this point that he remembered the bottle of liquor tucked away in his back pack, that meant for him relaxing in premature celebration, content in the feeling of his immediate future wealth he was surely about to secure...

The camel would be the first to recognise the strong scent of the pack animals. The 'old one's' eyes could still follow tracks even when the sands had obscured them. The pressures and indentations they had left he could visualise, although not as well as in his previous years. He knew that the animals had not been fed, there were no signs of dung, he was struggling to discern where their presence had gone. He must rely on the herding instinct of his camel in naturally following the pack animals, animals that it knew only too well...

Ian had no idea of the time, all that mattered was that the fierce heat had finally abated. He was prepared as a matter of life or death to reach the truck's door and gain access to the security box which housed, among other things, his lifeline – the satellite phone.

Only now by standing did he realise how weak he had become. The convulsions had ceased but the unearthly state of nausea was still prevailing so much so that he believed it was affecting his sight. Slowly and with an almighty effort he reached the vehicle's door. Despite the approaching cool of the night he was soaked in a clammy state of perspiration. Nothing mattered, his goal was achieved, he grasped the vehicle's pitted chrome handle and pulled, but to no purpose, the door was locked!

This stark realisation made him want to scream. Looking through the vehicle's side window there was no sign of the key in the ignition, slam locked he thought. The truck's spare key was hidden inside only compounding the situation for him. In a state of desperation and using all his efforts he attempted time and again to smash the side window, but exertion had overcome him, there was no option other than to collapse his bodily weight back down on the sand.

That was the first time that he started to believe that this whole travesty had been orchestrated by his very own guide. He had to reach the protection of the sleeping bag. The bout of perspiration had ceased which was allowing the cold of the desert air to have its way. An almighty effort was rewarded by gaining the sand depression between the wheels and protection afforded by his sleeping bag.

Ian remembered nothing further that night other than the severe cold; the coldest desert night he had experienced, not helped by a progressively weakened condition. The water supply had all but gone, his thinking process was becoming seriously fragmented. The only tangible relief was the bird book bought in his school friend's honour. Early stages of delirium were having an effect; in the dark he thumbed through the pages, clearly envisaging much of what Chris had all those years ago told to his townie friend.

His lips became swollen and were reaching an advanced stage of cracking, although as yet any severe craving for water was not apparent. Now imagination was playing a series of tricks with him. Was he right, were the truck doors securely locked? All the events were polarising together, the silence convinced him that the oil rig machinery had stopped running, was there an electrical fault?

Did it matter anymore? The weakness was taking a further hold on his system, now there was a danger of reaching the point of no return; starting to lose track of the time scale. Just how many days have I struggled to survive?

It was morning again, another night had passed, noises had returned at the edge of the campsite. What were they? If only I had a wider knowledge of the desert's animals. Wild dogs he suspected, fortunately having no idea he was still been stalked by the returning desert lions. The prime lioness had renewed her interest, noting a stale scent of pungent perspiration from her intended prey.

Ian's progressive debilitating condition was more noticeable for him. Desert winds in the morning would frequently offer relief to the daytime temperatures, today they were missing. He struggled, burying himself deeper in the shade afforded by the pickup truck, but progress was limited – further excavation only possible by using the bird book as a crude shovel. At first his renewed efforts were showing some progress, but again he realised his strength was lacking.

He laid his head on the randomly opened book, creating a barrier against the evasive sand. His mind was ranging on what had caused all this. Why the hell did that picture of Homemead fall out of the file? It's going to be the death of me, he shouted in resentment, rewarded by way of a confirmation of the echo from the canyon walls.

Strangely it offered him some relief. He continued shouting, this time for Chris, imagining that he was there with him, as innocent schoolboys roaming the fields of Homemead. He spoke out to his imaginary visitor desperately wanting to tell him that he could still remember that bird with the nest in the hedgerow. You told me its name, Chris, after all this time I can still remember. 'It was a butcher bird see, I told you I knew.'

Tears streamed down his face inducing a salty taint to his already parched lips. They went further adhering to the pages on the opened book, he pulled it away from his cheek, listening as his beard stubble scraped the pages. What shade the vehicle offered was no more, light was on the illustration of the randomly opened book. He read the bird's name out loud. 'Red-backed shrike, *Lanius Collurio*.' When he first bought the book he had overlooked any of the text, he was drawn to this opened page and what it had poignantly revealed for him, the shrike's alternative country name, known as the 'butcher bird'.

From his low viewpoint he experienced the heat haze building up over the desert floor, that's when far out over the sands he first noticed the apparition. It was heading slowly and purposefully in his direction, the outline of the white shape was shimmering, constantly changing form, but for all those vagaries Ian was positive it was a woman, it had to be, something seemed familiar, exactly what?

He fell into yet another unnatural sleep. When he came out of the shallow slumber the figure was still apparent to him. The white clothing she was wearing he reasoned would be for protection from the unforgiving heat. She was holding up above her head a flowing white scarf, but why and who is she?

The face. I need to see her face. I must see who she is. Advanced delirium was beginning. The scorpion venom would soon claim its victim. The white scarf was now covering him with its life sparing shade. He saw colours that was reminding him of the rock crystal at Homemead with those facets of light that it had emitted. Of course the crystal, my secret artefact, it's not here, where, where have I left the crystal?

Water droplets from coarse towelling were falling in measured amounts. Their spangled light patterns he could see before they splattered down on his cracked lips. He had no other action than to lay prostrate on the sand, expecting another bout of continued sickness. His fingers were gripping firmly on the pages of the book. Desperately he wanted to shout out aloud, Chris listen to me I've found what I was looking for'.

Something was suddenly different, there was a noticeable sweet smell which he failed to recognise. Sarnesa knew what had to be done; she would not let him die.

Chapter 17

Ian knew that his father was watching him, noticeable by the cigarette smoke. His attention would not wander, each globe of water was the same, the trickle that merged into the burn was filtered through wet trailing moss, the water droplet would hang suspended and finally fall to merge with its predecessor on the rocks below. Trout came in from the loch, searching this pool where the burn joined the main body of water. They were definitely here, having just seen the proof with his own eyes, his father had caught the first fish, now Ian was confident, and at last it had become his eagerly awaited turn.

The light breeze was sufficient to stop the midges from biting, the orange coloured tip of the fishing float trembled, with the bait having been taken it was gone, disappearing into the sepia coloured water. He did exactly what his father had instructed, the line had become taut forcing the fishing rod to become arched into a curve. He stood up realising that his trousers were soaked from where he had been sitting, nothing mattered. Following his mentor's directions he had now at last secured his very first brown trout, more importantly for him he had become an angler.

Suddenly this boy away from his boarding school had become unusually tall and equally proud. What an achievement, he turned and looked at his father who was smiling. 'There you are, Ian, it's breakfast, let's get back to our campsite...'

Sarnesa had attached canvas on to poles forming a rudimentary screen, then allowing the coverings to be soaked with water. By her actions the concerns with the desert sun were not set to worry her patient. It remained necessary for his measured intake of water from the suspended towelling to drip slowly and deliberately on to his severely parched lips.

His language was unknown to her, if that was not the case then she would have listened to his pleas that he continued to make concerning a figment of his imagination. The spectral form of the woman providing shade from her white scarf. Sarnesa was aware that the poison remaining in his system was in an advanced stage. She was desperate, the white stranger in her care was not going to die!

Needing to prove herself with the elder women of her people, this was her challenge, she remained resolute to gain their respect. The running fever had to be taken from his body, how long this state had lasted she had no idea, her thoughts were concerned by his clearly weakened condition. Even his muttered ramblings so noticeable when they first found him were beginning to cease…

The cooking pan emitted a blue haze, Ian watched his father frying the spoils of their morning endeavours; the two trout fitted into the pan as a matched pair, like peas in a pod. He was so excited. 'What would Mother think if she was here? Two trout for our breakfast.'

His father looked up from his task. 'It's a brace, Ian, a brace of trout.'

Both father and son were strangers to each other, and neither were guilty in that respect. The Foreign Office wholly controlled his father's activity, therefore his home life was scarce, assignments for the government department required his presence in all parts of the world. Offering no other alternative than for his son and daughter with all the turbulent trials involved having to follow a route of boarding schools.

Except this one special summer, due to cancelled plans his father was home in the UK, to be involved in taking his son on his first camping trip to the Scottish Highlands. Father was attempting to recapture his youth, at the same time showing his offspring what life in the wilds can really mean. Creating an excellent job that young Ian would never forget, it was for him unique, full of first hand experiences.

The wood bark eventually reached the stage by constant boiling when it had become soft and tactile. Now she knew it would start yielding its properties, the glutinous substance was added to a mixture of dried bones, the resulting amalgam poised to save his life. For the coming two days Sarnesa would have to fight him, the devil concoction entrenched in his intestines and nervous system was not destined to leave him.

On her previous treatments with her own kind the poisoning invariably had only just occurred therefore with her rapid attention the patients were possible to save. But with the white stranger she had to contend with the poison in a far advanced stage.

Slowly she almost caressingly lifted his head. The medicine had cooled, it was ready to administer. As she allowed the liquid to drain into his mouth nothing could hide its hideous taste from him. For all that her patient had barely any knowledge of the event, as the advanced stage of his delirium would simply not allow that.

Ian's mind was no longer associated with the deserts of Namibia. He could not believe leaning over him was Mrs Wardorf, the school's robust matron. Also there was no trace of the perfume of lavender water she always wore. When he had been ill most of the medicines that he was subjected to were disguised, as to be incarcerated in spoonfuls of strawberry jam. He could not see any thermometers; where was the bedside table in sick bay? Why had Kilmington and Harvey not come in to see him? They both knew how ill he was…

Sarnesa would not leave his side, needing to watch for the first signs. If nothing happened before the second sunrise then her patient would have passed over to be lost forever. The vessel had finally cooled, she removed the bones which formed an important symbolic part of the ritual, now they required burying deeply in the sands.

The elders watched and patiently waited, the mature women knew that Sarnesa had this chance to redeem her patient to stay alive.

She had now returned to their camp, having buried the animal bones deeply into the sand where no living creature could find them, only she knew of their location.

She watched all night but nothing transpired, now the light of a new dawn was active, still her patient's state remained unchanged. There was too much of a risk but she craved for sleep, although not daring to leave his side, aware that when things started to happen it would need all of her resources. Despite punitive efforts she was only rewarded by spasms of fitful sleep, her patient's precarious condition would never leave her thoughts.

Following an uneventful day she was building up the fire prior to the desert night when she saw the first sign, excessive perspiration on his forehead, this would bring him thirst. Her attentive nursing continued by assuaging his needs for water. Ian had resumed his incoherent ramblings, it meant nothing, except for one person who nearby had listened and knew his language, Jhoin the leader of these, the Herero people…

Nassindu's complacent attitude fuelled by his intake of liquor showed contempt to anything he reasoned. Only one thing mattered above all else, the wealth that was going to come his way; salt, the animals' loads of precious salt. He looked over at the tethered animals that needed both feed and water. All appeared as it should, there was no reason for him to think otherwise.

The 'old one' from a distance had watched the pack animals until darkness finally masked their view. His camel had led him to the asses that carried his people's stolen wealth. He knew the laws of the desert, not those of our modern world contained within the 21st century. Their laws relating to stealing extended far back in time, now by this theft that had occurred to his people, he and he alone was about to administer the penalty.

Nassindu was remembering the scheme that Boss Botha had devised without his 'swapping' of guides for the foreign tourist, then he would not be in possession of the pack animals and their precious cargo. He even accepted owing this turn of fortune to Boss Botha. In his drunken stupor he admitted that this man above all others was his treasured mentor. Nassindu shook the liquor bottle vigorously, it was well and truly empty. He could not summon the energy to make up a fire reasoning that it was not a wise move. He dozed resting against the saddle he had removed from the lead animal.

The blade was thin, made from Toledo steel imperceptibly curved and incredibly sharp. The 'old one' had possessed it forever. Its task in his hands would be one of punishment; Nassindu in his drunken state would be spared the implication of what was about to take place.

The laws of his desert people were appeased quickly and without ceremony. The 'old one' was strong, particularly by deliberate actions of his wrists. It was over almost as quickly as he had started. He left the campsite and the incoherent Nass and returned to his faithful camel and reclaimed his people's pack animals. The blade of his knife showed signs of anointment with fresh blood.

Nassindu could not understand where the intense sensation sweeping through his body was coming from, only after the numbing alcohol had drained from his system would he then realise what had transpired in a region of his torso. He first noticed that the team of pack animals were gone therefore the fortune of salt was no more, then by his body's acute pain, a shock realisation that his manhood had been removed. The justice of the desert people had been administered, the thief's punishment was that of castration…

Of the man he had left to die in the canyon, his condition was on a veritable cusp, his precarious survival relying on the measured doses of Sarnesa's rudimentary medicine. Its effect was beginning, noticeable by his state of increasing rhythms of perspiration. As the day began to fall her battle was about to start, otherwise she knew all would have been in vain.

She added more covering on the tent above her patient, then took advantage of the sleeping bag ensuring that he was entrenched in its folds of material. Vital, as his temperature would rise dramatically when the clandestine tribal remedy that was countering the poison increased its ominous task.

For the first time in days Ian was noticing the effects of his pronounced temperature, slowly at first, now by contrast it was becoming more noticeable, drawing his memory back to an illness suffered years ago whilst at boarding school. Picturing the room known as the school sick bay, that particular night at the height of his suffering, there were lighted candles in the room. Their flames appeared as solemn plumes of radiance, they were sufficient to light the tall gabled ceiling. As always both his parents were away on diplomatic assignments; it was his Aunt Anastasia on hearing of his predicament who had rushed urgently to visit him. The following morning he was admitted into hospital diagnosed with acute appendicitis.

Now all these years later, almost another lifetime, by a quirk of fate he lay desperately fighting for his life under the dark of an African sky. His mind was firmly fixed, but not in his present location, it was remaining comfortable with a sense of security afforded from the days of his childhood.

There existed a connection with his past spent at Homemead, but it had become intrinsically linked with the present, leading to his recent discovery of the rock crystal found in his own secret hiding place. Then he became concerned with the bedroom nursery rhyme visualising it in his childhood days above the mantelpiece at Homemead, mesmerising him to recite it, he wanted to act with assertion pleading to be allowed one particular verse that he could read… *with plenty of money wrapped up in a £5 note…*

Sarnesa was fascinated by his ramblings although having no idea what they related to. Her concern was motivated solely with one purpose; waiting and watching her patient for the surge that the ingredients of her potion were to create in fighting against the hostile substance.

In those intimate hours prior to dawn, a time when all earthly spirits are pitched at their lowest, Ian's reaction to her medicine took hold. He had become vaguely conscious, growing concerned as to where he was; perspiration covering his entire raging body it was insufferable. He struggled to uncover his sleeping bag in a futile attempt to cool himself and breathe the cold night air. That was to her a clear signal, now she was aware that the torturous fight was about to begin.

What she had administered was in direct conflict with the scorpion-induced concoction given to him by Nassindu, left unchecked that would have now served a testament for his death. His fever was reaching its zenith; Sarnesa was worried more than ever, would the white stranger finally convulse and pass over. Her next phase was critical in saving his very life. She was to offer a notion of faith, mysterious and almost beyond comprehension for the Western world.

She had undone the sleeping bag to reveal Ian's body, as expected glazed by rivulets of intense perspiration. She offered a tribal respect that what had been administered was having its acceptance. Now her patient needed an equally intimate and bodily involvement from her.

The soaked towelling was wiped over his face and chest it served as a respite, refreshing but of no lasting satisfaction. Sarnesa stood staring at the spectacle of the sky, the time had arrived, she removed her clothing, quickly growing chilled by the night air it was resulting with her breasts gaining in a satisfying volume. She had adorned herself with red ochre paste, a tribal right of her womanhood, she continued standing under the night sky, her situation through pending confinement was poised to rapidly change.

Laying slowly on top of her patient she could feel the radiation of his intense perspiring heat, she drew the sleeping bag tightly over enclosing them both. This was now the time to validate herself to her elders and the man she had uppermost in her mind to save.

Ian's raging bouts of sweating were running as clammy moisture over his body. Relief came to him, as Sarnesa allowed herself to act as a sensual bodily mass taking away the intense heat from his advanced fevered condition. At this stage her patient was not fully conscious to appreciate what had been offered, that of a young and conducive woman of the Herero.

Hour following hour Sarnesa battled to hold her unwilling patient in the confines of the sleeping bag. What she allowed to exude was by this advanced stage mutually merging with that of her patient. As a direct contrast the red ochre adornment was no longer the dried, caked application, now having become soluble the demarcated area was streaming in rich artistic red, colouring chaotically merging both of their bodies. Despite his weakened state Ian was seemingly drawing new strength, even above his rages of delirium, whilst Sarnesa was maintaining her desperate struggle to hold him in control. The one she was driven to save had no idea of his circumstances, other than Sarnesa's weight enclosing his body and that his arms were rigidly held back and above his head.

Desperately his mind was seeking a sanctuary where coolness prevailed, his delusions had found the confines of the vast pantry at Homemead. He was able to stand barefoot on its rough hewn tiling, it offered relief, but then why was he naked? The pantry had sticky fly paper trailing in fronds each adorned by insects that were already dead or dying, resembling to him as soldiers of a long lost battle. By the bunches of dried onions were hanging two dead pheasants, they were hooked up in display on a high beam in shadowed confines. He unashamedly saw their firm dark breasts streaked with red stains of congealed blood...

The silver of desert moonlight invaded the basic tent that Sarnesa had implemented. He was calling to her; she wanted so much to understand what he was saying. Whatever it was the same desperate words were repeated over and over again.

Even Ian himself would not understand his own ranting. He noticed how acute his hearing had become. He wanted food; the blood on the hanging pheasants had not completely set, visitations from flies on the prize birds had previously laid eggs which now had become writhing maggots. If that was not enough other prey were at hand, those hundreds of insects trapped on the clinging mucus of the sticky fly paper.

But he was not alone! Another of his kind had entered his feeding arena. Ian in his state of rapidly advancing delirium, could not think of his own kind. His soul was in torment, hallucinations had entered and possessed his mind. Believing he was in the guise of a creature, that of a 'black scorpion'.

Voracious to feed he would fight the intruder that exhibited an indelible likeness of his own. He likened himself of masculine strength that caused his scales to elevate, leading to the predominant tail to surge in a rampart virile display, knowing only one sense of satisfaction. His erect ascendancy became readily accepted by the physique of the invader choosing to occupy his domain, his rightful mastery was established. Once would not satisfy his advances, time and again the searing heat contained in his body had to be quenched by whom had joined bodily forces with him.

Sarnesa could not enter his crazed realms of hallucinations, but drawn together by their entwined bond she understood that the conflict continued to rage within him. Her strength in his advanced turmoil was demanded to the utmost, knowing her liberating attendances towards him remained resolute. Now by contrast becoming enhanced through incantations she almost screamed wanting the bones buried by her beneath the sand to show their ascendancy!

His inner conflict showed no sign of abating, only by pinning down his shoulders taking all her fortitude was she able to subdue his sheer strength. Still the fever remained paramount, believing in the treatment and accepting his demands she had no other choice than to keep him close to her body throughout the long hours of darkness.

Then with the approach of daylight there was a visual change, his eyes looked completely different, for the first time they were focused. In his slumbering condition he was not aware of his predicament, Sarnesa knew at once a turning point had been secured. His relentless fever from those long hours of darkness was abating, but something else, the man's natural strength was gradually restoring, joining those of the living. She continued to remain vigilant, even though his temperature was declining, evident now by his bodily calmness.

Her battle was reaching a conclusion, the fever had finally run its course. Drained of all her strength Sarnesa remained with whom she had brought back from that of another world. Eventually in spasms of each other gaining breath they were both able to be enveloped by the light of a challenging new dawn.

At sunrise she became aware how the turmoil with her patient had racked her with aching tiredness, the rewards that she saw were self-evident. Dressing quickly her clothing absorbed the perspiration and ochre compound although by now in a total mess it was remaining over her body. She stared at the white stranger; slowly his senses were gradually becoming restored.

Sarnesa's achievement through the night long vigil would gain her a rightful place with the elders of her people.

When the sun rose she retrieved the buried animal bones, watched in an honoured silence by the elders, in particular the Herero women who fortified their whispering in admiration for the life she had regained. Sarnesa in a clandestine manner returned with the bones depositing them on to the fire, its furious heat devoured them in moments… Now he would live…

Ian was becoming conscious, although in measured stages to regain normality, more so as he was appreciating the warmth of a dawn sunrise. In his contented enclosure he noticed a craving was persisting; he was hungry, famished. Food, he wanted food. Aggravated now as he was picking up the aroma emitting from the distant cooking vessels within the Herero camp.

He began to notice things, his shoulder blades were sore, then he realised why. Scratches, deeply embedded in his back. Something else he could fail to be aware deep almost rank bodily odour from the quilted interior. This was not the Western world of sanitised masking deodorants, he had lived through tribulations with a women of the desert people, one that had returned him to life from an induced obsession of a 'scorpion'.

Remaining as a legacy in the folds of his sleeping bag were honourable excretions of sweat, even more acutely noticed that of coagulated semen, serving as it had in bringing him from the corridors of death.

Would he ever be aware of his cloistered ordeal performed by Sarnesa? His thoughts might try to gather in the events of the last two days but it was closed off to him. Ian Harbinger rested above the panorama of the desert sky, alone he was benefiting from the peace that it was offering. His tired and exhausted body was free from torment by hallucinations created in his mind by the creature from Namibia's 'dark side', that of the black scorpion.

That was when Jho-in had decided to intervene. He had watched from a distance, growing proud of Sarnesa's dedicated efforts, as she had known no boundaries. He walked over to join her resting his hands on her shoulders, a mark of honour from their leader. She alone had resolutely reached a life saving climax for the 'young' Ian.

Jho-in realised that something as yet unknown had occurred. The man they had found days previously in the confines of the desert canyon was young Harbinger, suspected from listening to his ramblings which alone Jho-in understood. There had been the house, none other than Homemead, but one other thing, far more reaching was concerning him, an entrusted item was moved… But why?

His attention was drawn towards their desert settlement, a camel and rider had appeared against the backdrop of the ascending sun it was the return of the 'old one'. Trailing behind were their pack animals, with the precious cargos intact. As leader of his people he turned towards the tents to welcome their wanderer on his return. Up to then his thoughts were far removed, dwelling amongst the green summer countryside of what he cherished and could remember of England.

Chapter 18

The days had created an indolence that formed a reluctant habit of running into one another. Ian slept more deeply than he believed in his whole life. At times during waking hours, at night he returned to his passion of gazing at the constellations stretching above him. When he found it necessary to sleep during the day he sensed an awareness that the canvas screen over his body that gave protection from the desert heat was always soaked with water.

Two young women had been assigned the task of caring for him, they were both proud of the stranger whose white skin at first had fascinated them. As time went on they both grew to understand his needs for food and rest, although sadly not his language.

His world was yet to regain its full perspective. He could only recollect parts of the confinement caused by his sickness. Time and again his thoughts constantly returned to when the woman had appeared walking through the heat haze of the desert sands. She had materialised from nowhere and above her head she was holding the long flowing white scarf, but who was she, and out here in the desert wastes, where had she come from?

He looked at his watch. He could make out the time, but had no inkling to an idea of the date. Then like a vacant and missing piece of a puzzle his memory jolted. The watch had gone but now it's back securely on my wrist, how had it returned?

His attention was rapidly drawn away from his incoherent ramblings as someone kneeling beside him was speaking to him and calling him Ian. He could make out his dark ebony features, then completely unexpected his language. It was English, it did not relate to others at the campsite that he was overhearing.

Ian in a renewed state of anxiety was struggling, believing he was in a process of meditation, far from it, the painful truth for him was finally becoming a reality. What am I doing here, me a qualified engineer from the oil industry caught up with a turn of events in my life?

Although he would have no idea how all had changed, he was recovering and at this stage really needed space to recuperate. The Herero leader clearly seeing his continuing condition wisely left him, understanding time alone for 'young' Ian still remained a critical priority.

When 'the old one' had returned on that morning to the encampment he alone had witnessed the events that happened to the white stranger that was so intent to roam the isolated desert canyons. He had seen the dust trail from their vehicle days before, it had fascinated him by the areas of remote country that the guide was leading the stranger.

But then a turn of events had caused 'the old one' in having to track their pack animals, through not being attended by a young Herero keeper they had become loose and were wandering aimlessly into the desert. When he eventually located them they were solely in possession of the white stranger's guide? Plainly the guide by his actions were that of theft, attempting to lead the animals carrying their cargo away from their homeland with intent to sell to outsiders. There could be no other explanation.

Jho-in had listened to what 'the old one' explained on his return, accepting from his wisdom the events of what was laid clear with the theft of his people's wealth. The Herero leader endorsed the action taken by him in respect with their laws of theft, the penalty carried out with the importance of what the animals possessed for the Herero and the judgement of 'the old one' was upheld. Further to this it was obvious that the guide had on his person items stolen from the white stranger, which eventually resulted with the return of Ian's watch and the maps.

Jho-in had scolded his third son, as he alone was the responsible keeper for the pack animals' errant departure, he would be made to realise the immense value the sacks contained. All in the cause or so Jho-in believed in bringing up his children, thinking back to all of his youthful failings with the inevitable punishments as he was made to realise he would eventually aspire to be the leader of his people...

That belonged to his distant past. Now he had other concerns on his mind in the direction of young Harbinger; what was this man doing in the regions of the Herero? Would he ever realise how close to death he was? Was it some divine providence that had saved him? It was a puzzle to him of an untold magnitude, certainly it was making no sense. So much so it was causing Jho-in's thoughts to be far away in a country that many years earlier had meant so much to him. That treasured land where water the bringer of life was never in short supply, so radically different to his own lands.

Within the camp dwelling 'the old one' always remained in his own company, he was active over the cooking vessel simmering his meal that included the manhood parts executed from the thief Nassindu.

A wrong to his people was resolved, usually a ritual gesture would be that of offering part of his meal to the stranger and in this case whose life had been saved by the Herero. How Ian would have responded to an offering that included testicles recently belonging to his guide, would be anyone's guess.

Jho-in had waited growing more anxious to move Ian and his people away from the dangers that were present in the desert canyon. When finally he considered that their invalid had recovered sufficiently a litter made up of tent poles was constructed enabling them to carry him securely. Once this task was completed the Herero were set on a journey to a place where all would be consolidated, namely the main encampment in their homeland.

Ian was now fully coherent, although his meals were different and the gradual reinstatement of his appetite was doing the rest, as a survivor he was growing stronger with each passing day. He assumed that of all his silent visitors, the tallest of these elders, the one with the neck array of carved bones was their leader. On the few occasions that he had briefly spoken to him it was in near perfect English, a style that would be familiar in any middle England town, but why English? Leaving Ian thinking, an alien tongue in the remote deserts of Namibia again for him it did not add up.

For nearly three days they travelled along escarpments of sculptured sand dunes that eventually gave way to low hills. Ian continued to be puzzled. Where am I being taken by these people? Only myself secured to this bundle of tent poles, am I now a hostage? Where's my guide, what's my next fate? On one occasion he noticed that his 4WD vehicle was following on at the rear, in the quiet solitude of the desert he could not hear any sound from the engine. Small wonder as it was now under the towing power of three asses that had in effect replaced the vehicle's 'horsepower'.

Towards the end of the fourth day their destination was finally reached. From his restricted position Ian was able to make out a camp dwelling where thatched huts of a more established structure were in evidence. He was feeling stronger and determined on one thing, confront his tribal 'host' on the next interchange of conversation; at least English would be the language of common ground. For now it would wait, nothing was clear, tiredness had ensured he entered into a slumber of sleep where as always his pattern of dreams were sure to intervene.

The recurring dream, was a soft focus effect, like a trailer that might be attached to a forthcoming film. The appearance of the mysterious woman with the long flowing scarf, but for all that never an answer to who she is.

He woke noticing a change to his immediate surroundings; he was in shade, the relentless sun escaping his attention. Once more he was dwelling on his historical conversation with the aloof Miss Cleary, and her prophesy that continued to haunt his train of thoughts… Mr Harbinger you will have to follow your own yellow brick road.

Why had I been so totally stupid? Look at the state I've arrived at, the whole saga has to be a dream, like those outlandish television serials when their storyline gets too thin, the writers solve the plot by immersing their characters in dream sequences. He looked at his watch, desperately he tried to discern the date. Unfortunately for him the minute hand was temporarily masking that valuable piece of information.

He failed to hear the approach of footsteps in the sand, his first reaction was that of noticing the shadow. By this time Jho-in his visitor had asked a radical and what could only be described as a mind blowing pertinent question… 'So, young Ian, what brings you to our deserts of Namibia?'

At last Ian knew he was in control of his thoughts. What am I hearing? One thing in particular was more than intriguing him, why this constant reference to me as 'young' Ian?

He waited in a state of caution letting his host assume the lead, the question that had been targeted was followed by protracted silence. He decided to play a waiting game with his host, and he was finally rewarded by his deliberate wait.

'You have been ill, Ian, very ill, close to death. Only now do I feel you are well enough and we can talk.' He held a cup towards him containing a potion which had he known was to the desert people an elixir for restoration of life.

His benefactor resumed. 'I am called Jho-In, these are my people of the Herero. Once when I was younger your aunt, your

Aunt Anastasia came and lived and worked amongst us in her role as a geologist.'

Ian's surprise reply produced a remark that he was barely able to utter... 'Follow my own yellow brick road.'

A profound look came over Jho-in's face, but it did not end there, his response was equally as quick... 'The Wizard of Oz, I assume.'

There followed a time when both parties were equally relaxed and able to introduce themselves. Ian struggled with pronunciation of his host's name further fuelling their conversation with one blessed ingredient, that of laughter. What a change of circumstances, reminding himself that earlier he firmly believed he was a victim of a kidnapping scheme. A quirk of fate he had finally found those of the desert he had been searching, or they found me.

Wait till I tell Mitch. Suddenly it hit him, Mitch, of course what's happening? What am I thinking? I've made no contact with him.

'Jho-in, none of this is making sense to me, I've no idea how long this sickness has affected me, I've lost track of days, and another thing keeps puzzling me, why do you speak such unusually good English?'

The very look on Ian's face was all Jho-in needed, now he knew their patient was finally making a recovery.

'One thing at a time, young Ian, you were at death's door Don't think for a moment that you had fallen sick. Your guide had poisoned you and left you for dead... As for your leading question I was educated many years ago in your country, Ian, to be precise at Cambridge.'

A beaming smile came over Jho-in's face as he could see by Ian's posture and that of his body language he was portraying a curious but nonetheless contented state. The patient in his people's care was on the route in restoring to the fabric of life.

Ian was overtaken in what could be described as a tidal wave of curiosity. In front of him was someone who had known his aunt in her later years, more than that, his language, the English language. Once again too many questions, but this time he was determined, as in front of him was someone who knew the answers he was seeking!

'Jho-in your people saved my life, but why did this guide of mine need to try and kill me?'

There was a long pause before Jho-in attempted his reply. 'You will know the reason, Ian... greed, man's incessant greed.' He pointed towards the outlaying tents of their encampment. 'Your answer is there on the pack animals, without their handler watching over them they wandered away and into your encampment. Your curiosity must have found the panniers contained salt, the wealth of my desert people. What your guide also saw was stolen by him taking away our animals with their cargos.'

Ian's mind was in overdrive channelling his recent memories which only now were allowing free access to his thoughts. The gravity of the matter and how he had escaped death, he could picture his efforts trying to reach the vehicle, fighting off his debilitating nausea. So it was his guide Nass who had been responsible for scheming the whole affair, finally he was aware, understanding the evil motivation by his guide's actions.

'Jho-in,' this time his pronunciation had improved, 'what was he going to do with your panniers of salt?' As an afterthought quickly adding, 'Especially out here in the remote desert.'

'Only one thing, Ian. It would have been sold, there's enough interested people as he gets towards the townships. They would buy the sacks' contents, your expression if I do remember correctly, no questions asked.

Ian finally understood the bitter truth, realising what had provoked his guide's action, but why had Mitch recommend him so highly? Then he bit his lip, it came back to him, of course there was the last minute swap with his cousin, or so I was told, I was running with the second choice.

Without the Herero I would be bleached bones littering the desert sands. He pondered in what he was to say. How was he going to even try an attempt towards his thanks to the saviours of his life?

Suddenly without warning a vital thought struck him. The vehicle, my vehicle, the 4WD. What's happened? It's got the satellite phone inside the security box… where is it?

Jho-in could feel the magnitude of concern that was manifesting from his guest. He needed to act promptly, concerned that he would grow weak from any induced stress. 'Ian enough for now, food is prepared and you must eat, get your strength back, then we can talk more, which means I will have to practise my English.'

As he stood he handed him a somewhat tattered book. The bird book found clutched in his possession when they first located him. 'There, Ian, we marked your page. You were talking aloud when we found you, a person called Chris, from your past perhaps, but I could not follow… a bird's nest, a 'butcher'. Anyway I am sure you will know.'

Two women approached, they were carrying food which at best resembled a nourishing porridge. Ian sat forward. Amongst a series of unrelated giggling by his young nurses he had no option than to be spoon fed, no doubt part of his recovery programme. It was followed by an almost ritual act of his face being carefully washed. Sarnesa watched critically from a distance reassuring herself that her assistants, although, young were both proficient with their acts of nursing her patient.

He was finally left alone to his own devices. What had happened to the bird book, the state it was in, why the crumpled pages? He opened the marked page, it appeared abraded by sand, streaked by what must be water stains. Ian would have no idea to their origins, that of his very own sweat. Studying the marked page he noted one significant fact, within the text was explained this particular bird's habit of impaling their prey on to thorns forming an effective reserve larder. But more importantly, one more piece of information, although he had discovered it near to a point of his death he had forgotten, now at peace with himself he reiterated the bird's country name, the 'butcher bird'.

Ian could almost feel a surreal nearness to his long forsaken school friend. Now I know, Chris, the bird you showed me with its nest in the hedge-row was a red-backed shrike. He slowly closed the book tapping with affection on its sand ingrained covers, if only I knew where you are, my friend?

The heat of the day had gone giving way to a valuable period of cool and brief twilight. He decided that he was in need of exercise. Let's see what exactly this encampment of the Herero people is made of.

The complexity of the camp dwellings suggested that this was a permanent and securely organised affair, although the Herero showed a tendency of nomadic people. Alone in his cloistered thoughts he walked to explore his surrounds, that was the realisation on how weak he was feeling, noticeably especially with his balance, it was leaving him concerned how vulnerable he had become.

His attention was diverted as something had caught his observant eye. He walked over to investigate, even in the falling light he could make out what he was looking at. It was all out of place, appearing not to really belong in context. poles, derrick poles, lots of them, rolls of rusted steel chain, instantly associated to him as drilling equipment. But what's it doing out here, and more importantly for what purpose?

Chapter 19

Mitch desperately needed his second cup of coffee, knowing from experience the machine would dispense it considerably hotter than the first. It was an early start, realising that the work load was destined to be colossal. However his morning's routine at the warehouse always continued in the same vein, quick check on the TV news, whilst he sipped coffee and nibbled a biscuit, then get at it, onwards and upwards reckoning that was his only tangible course of action.

He stared at the news channel in disbelief, as usual he was tuned to a South African station, a bulletin was breaking on an oil rig disaster. He had no idea where. Mention of a deep drilling rig, and its size gave him a sufficient clue to its possible whereabouts; it must be out in the Gulf of Mexico.

In the breaking news item they were trying to establish the death toll concerning the rig workers. Mitch did not need any reminding to what those horrific events would have meant. It was leaving him gasping for breath, nothing like that could ever be totally erased from the mind. He found himself tracing his fingers over the scar tissue still evident on his face. He contained the stress, or so he thought, but for him it was the horror of the gas explosions on Piper Alpha all over again… We had nowhere to run!

The TV station had moved on from what was happening on the other side of the world, as nothing was going to tarnish the forthcoming events with South Africa destined to be the host nation for the next World Cup. The country's emerging freedom was spilling over in celebration to what was about to take place on their own soil. The expansive world of football was now focused on them.

Mitch decided on an easy option, extracting the news of the rig disaster from what was posted on the web, even though he considered there was an element that was already pre-digested for you. But he could at least ponder on what was happening, from the web page news he became aware of the location, he was right about in the Gulf, and also the speculated cause of the explosion. As always the inevitable consequences, the magnitude of oil that was gushing from its source on the sea bed, the world's press was poised to have a field day despite what this major company would argue in its defence.

By now his warehouse staff were arriving, concerned to see their boss huddled over his computer screen and almost whispering… 'Why, but why.' They were his only words, although he could not contain himself by adding, 'What went so horrifically wrong?'

Outside at the loading bay a truck heralded its arrival by an artificial voice indicating it was in the process of reversing. It was the first of two early deliveries scheduled for today. Mitch drew his attention away from the screen, then the desk phone came to life, all at the wrong time he thought.

'Hello.' He expressed a self-imposed panic, his thoughts still firmly lodged with the horrific news of the oil rig disaster.

Then the caller's voice became apparent. 'Mitch… is that you old buddy?'

That voice, he would have recognised it anywhere, even over the noise of the truck still actively reversing. 'Harbinger… where… where the hell are you?'

Ian in an understatement breathed a sigh of relief, he had returned to normality, his phone call to Mitch was achieving that. Now and only now would he be able to establish exactly how long he had been out in the desert.

'Mitch, it's one hell of a story, don't even know where to start. You were right they don't hang around at bus stops, they found me, and I've a bone to pick with you.' Ian finished his comments with an overture of laughter, he failed to hear at the other end the enormous crash coming from the warehouse.

'Ian… call me back, we've had an accident here… damn truck just reversed into my loading bay… call me back… must go…'

Ian was sitting in relative comfort on the sticks, the camp's valuable stock of fuel. He blessed the satellite phone, and for once respecting telecommunication with the power of extending its range to the remote regions of the Namibian desert.

But then he dwelt on the gravity of his company's incoming phone messages. Naturally he had procrastinated with the concerns and they were still waiting his attention. The company needed his expertise, although he reasoned more likely they were now calling time with his extended leave.

Why are they chasing me? He had knowledge of the complexities and issues that were now showing concerns, but why? Isn't there someone else out there? That danger of burying his head was beginning to haunt him. Come on, it's only an oil rig complex after all. For instant therapy he decided to explore once more his surroundings and would have been under way but Jho-in was to intervene.

'So I see our patient is recovering and now dabbles again with his modern technology.' His hands made a gesture towards the satellite phone Ian was so intent on holding. Jho-in had noticed that a pivotal point had certainly been reached with his recovery, now was the time he knew he could safely intervene.

He sat alongside Ian though their combined weight on the fuel stack gave them both a precarious act of achieving a balance. For the first time Ian noticed the true strength of character that his tribal host displayed, a man of advanced age but still continuing to portray a young exuberance. His grey hair and cultured facial features culminating with his forehead that showed scared tribal embellishments, origins that no doubt extended far back in time.

'You want answers, young Ian and you deserve them.'

Ian's attention span was drawn momentarily to a group of children intent in starting to play what could loosely be described as a game of football. In the pause that followed he became an innocent victim of unwittingly butting into Jho-in's conversation.

'Jho-in, only a few weeks ago this oil rig engineer you see in front of you was embezzled out of more money than I dare think about, that was in my business life of owning hotels, then with my real employment I needed to take a chunk of long overdue leave. That was the easy bit, then and don't ask me why because I've really no idea, my past life has started to haunt me.' A piece of firewood he held between his fingers was divided in two for no particular reason by his action of snapping it.

'But I'm still confused, perplexed or any other description you care to use. Why did I really come out here searching your desert homelands where my aunt's working assignments originated? By what you tell me if it was not for your people finding me, putting it bluntly, by now I would be dead.'

Despite Jho-in waiting patiently to intervene he was all too aware of the reasons for this man's quest into their desert homelands. So much of his ramblings during his confined illness had centred on such explanations. He let him continue, noticing the relief and escape it was creating for him.

There was one thing Jho-in had in his favour, tactfully approaching from the direction of Ian's feelings associated with his aunt. 'Ian it is important you understand, like all the elders and more importantly myself, the time that your Aunt Anastasia lived and worked amongst us will never be forgotten.'

The two men's conversation continued against a barrage of arguments from the nearby football game, fouls by the young contenders were so easily noticed. 'Jho-in you must have a wealth of memories of her, how long did she actually live amongst the Herero?'

'Many years, let me try and explain, and correct me if my English starts to become muddled, it's a long time since I have spoken English. Now see if I remember there's an experience, no expression, that was the word, once you have to ride a bike you do not forget, that's not entirely correct but you know what I mean.'

Ian laughed unable to disguise the fact this was set to be an interesting conversation. At the moment their only difficulty was the noise from heated disputes by the football teams, further augmented by the arrival of girl players.

Despite the nearby fracas Jho-in was able to continue. 'At first and for a long period of time your aunt surveyed vast areas of our land within her remit, often beset by governmental pressure. She would at times return to South Africa and with her new husband. Although things became difficult in her relationship having how can I say, a burden of two step-sons.' Jho-in was aping Ian's habit with the firewood sticks although not to the stage of breaking them in pieces. Ian had no wish to spoil Jho-in's flow of conversation by awkward interruptions. But that inherent guilt complex was invading his thoughts.

'Jho-in it's important, I need you to be aware that I had hardly any contact with my aunt during her later years, my fault entirely, wrapped up in life, married and earning money working away on drilling rigs.'

Ian's remarks were politely ignored by his host who was set to try and explain the past history of his country. He consciously for no apparent reason followed Ian's complete example by breaking the piece of firewood that he was holding.

He smiled and faced Ian. 'You have to be aware that all of your early life was made available to me by your aunt, now that's where she referred to you as "young" Ian. If my memory of English is still holding out, there was constant, no I mean considerable, yes considerable passion always directed towards you.'

Ian became aware of his rigid features that were intent to stare at him, an invasion of his very soul. Although not that he would know it was purely an act of friendly interrogation.

The football game had all but diminished, the participants were in the process of having their daily chores issued by their respective mothers. Ian took clear advantage of the lull in the proceedings to raise his next question. 'Jho-in where's the connection for you with Cambridge?'

Again Ian's direct enquiry was fielded to absolute perfection. 'Courtesy of your aunt, too much she knew had been taken out of her beloved Africa, something desperately needed returning.' Jho-in smiled his entire face radiating in a total show of satisfaction.

'Ian you must remember this was many years ago. Your aunt worked closely with my father right up to his death. I only realised the schooling departure when it happened. Without my knowledge they had arranged the whole episode for my education in the mother country.'

Ian intervened more by adding support. 'So this combined gesture of theirs was to lay foundations for when you became leader of your people?'

Both men stared towards the cooking fires, the busy activity of a new day was starting to establish itself. 'Ian it was an experience like you could never imagine, from here not far removed from stone age times, then I am watching your… buses, yes those red buses in London.'

This time it was for Ian to enjoy a self-propagated spate of laughter. 'Jho-in I can only imagine it, I hope for your sake my aunt was giving you reassurance back in the old country.'

'Yes to begin with, she was able to assist, not the right choice of word but then it was up to me. I struggled knowing I was doing everything for my father, and more importantly for my people I was one day destined to rule. So, Ian, I have never forgotten your aunt who made everything possible for my English education.'

Ian's mind attempted to draw a reversal with himself, imagining that if it was himself sent here to Namibia with these people, the cultural shock of what we rather humbly considered an uncivilised world. Now first-hand he had experienced these Indigenous people how on finding him close to death had literally saved his life.

'Jho-in I can only imagine what you must have accomplished, and what your father must have seen in you, influenced as you would have become by our Western world. There has to be at least one poignant question, although it's a time away do you miss what you experienced?'

Ian's question was not really a surprise, eventually he knew he would be asked. Jho-in picked another loose stick from the firewood waving it reminiscent of an orchestra leader about to perform. 'It's too many years ago, Ian. As leader of my people I now have sons that are ready to take on this responsibility. But I owe you a reply. Many times I draw strength from what your Western world taught me. But food, Ian, is now ready. We will continue our conversation in more comfort.'

Ian welcomed the respite needing to consolidate in his mind with what he had been told, certain answers that were evading him were forthcoming. Then the thought of Mitch suddenly shot into his mind, their aborted phone conversation; it would have to wait for a moment, there was too much with Jho-in's revealing conversation…

'But then, Ian, you would know nothing of my people, we are not how can I say featured in your average tourist guide books!'

Ian looked towards the settlement where the goat herd was rounded together and with the children responsible for them set about their daily task guiding them to the scant scrub that served as pasture.

Ian suspected the next phase in their engaging conversation was going to both interesting and revealing, he was certainly not be proved wrong.

Jho-in watched as the young goat herders departed, pleased to see the activities of his people in another day of life. 'The Herero people, Ian, were at one time lost, by that I mean we nearly became extinct. You need to know our history long before the British Empire administered our land then known as South West Africa. Before that time back in the 1800s we were under the rule of the overlords from Germany.'

The information as he indicated was not described for your average tourist visiting Namibia. As Ian was unaware of any historical implications he decided on a safe course of action in allowing his host to resume.

"For your knowledge, Ian, the Herero people were amongst the first to be victimised in Southern Africa. The earliest genocide cases our planet has in fact witnessed, back in those times our German overlords, who became our suppressors wanted nothing in any form of evidence noticeable to anyone visiting this country.' Ian sensed a brooding forbearance encroaching with Jho-in's dialogue, he was shrewd to continue remaining silent allowing him to continue.

'You need to be aware of our history. Back in 1880, we were a desolate part of Southern African. As I indicated long before the British laid claim to us we were a colony under the flag of Germany, other than their farming in the fertile parts they had no real interest in the desert country, but, and it was a big but, that all changed once gemstones were discovered. A lucrative wealth that they were determined not to lose, which led to a decision for the German Kaiser to employ his elite military forces and to be stationed out here.'

Their conversation was gracefully interrupted by one of his people bringing over freshly cooked meats. 'This is ironic, Ian, what we see here with this food, at that time would have saved my starving people.' He could see the quizzical look that had come over Ian's face. 'Our colonial masters tolerated nothing, save we were victims of total suppression. Not the first however, the Namaqua people under the esteemed leadership of Witbooi yielded in the beginning and yield they did.'

Jho-in was momentary distracted, in a typical mode of a leader he became embroiled with issuing instructions to a group of his tribesmen. This completed he averted his attention back to Ian. 'It's all a long time ago in our history but it is not easily forgotten. When I lived in your country, I attempted to research exactly what the Western world knew of our plight, you might be amazed by my outcome, I found precious little.'

Ian knew he had to intervene, there was that begging question, what happened back then and why? It did not seem an ideal time for the snack of cooked meat that had been made available.

'Jho-in I can follow much of what you have explained, there appears one reason at least, that singular word again, that we both know all too well... 'obsessive greed'.

Jho-in paused, almost asking himself, why did I start this conversation? 'You are so right, Ian, what can I say? By this token once our overlords had sampled a taste with the Namaqua, our rulers then wasted no time and moved on to us the Herero. We were driven off our homelands but not before as a people we staged revolts against these acts of suppression.'

By this stage of their conversation the magnitude of past events became responsible for a sombre vein invading both of their thoughts. Ian listened as the terrifying part of the Herero history was further explained. 'During those far off days communications were limited, that said word eventually became available to us, then we knew that the next chosen people subjected by our masters, was to be the Herero.'

Ian sensed the tone in his voice, predicting the next part of his account was going to be extremely taxing.

'Death in far and unknown deserts was to be my people's lot. Annihilation, yes, Ian, that's the correct word.'

Ian noticed that Jho-in had made no attempt to eat the luxury of cooked meats brought to him; he could fully understand why.

Ian realised he needed to interject with their conversation. 'You say that your own people were subjected to such a fate, yet somehow they survived?'

The reply was surprisingly quick. 'We did, we had no choice or our culture would be no more.'

His reply left Ian still struggling to understand how they had endured. 'But surely no colonial country would want to eradicate its adopted people, change their ways, teach new religions. That happens, but why destroy, surely there's no purpose?' Ian on conclusion realised what in real terms his proclamation meant. The Western world does not have to go far back, knowing in his lifetime he could dwell on recent history with horrific examples of European ethnic cleansing.

Jho-in stood, allowing his back to take a more straightened position. An effect of angled sunlight produced a latticed pattern on his grey weathered hair. Here was a leader of people, a man that personified trust that galvanised integrity, making Ian realise small wonder that he is a 'king' among his kind.

He waited and wait he did before Jho-in resumed. 'First let me explain in a tangible way. See, Ian, my English is improving, for that I have you to thank, it would have pleased your Aunt Anastasia. Now to continue. Where Luderitz stands there is a causeway to an island that was named by our German masters as 'Shark Island'. Back in that time it was a real island that was to become the world's first extermination camp. The colonial forces enraged by tribal rebellions, took their Namaqua captives who had survived the war. They were massed into the crudely built camps on that inhospitable island to die.'

'You mean, Jho-in, without reason or even that of a trial?'

Jho-in resumed his seat on the wood stack, then appertaining to an eerie whisper he finally spoke. 'Once our masters had realised the available mineral wealth then nothing else mattered' They bought this country in the 1880s with an understanding it would be suitable only for cattle farmers. If I remember my history correctly it was about 1905 that 'Shark Island' took on its sinister role with the Namaqua. Our overlords' insidious plan worked, as a people they verged on annihilation.'

Although unusual for him, Ian was totally lost for words, leaving him pondering what African country is not without its macabre past? Jho-in brought him abruptly back to reality as he recapitulated. 'My people those years ago were responsible for uprisings against the might of our German masters. We the Herero people incensed by these events threw our venom against German settlers. Many fell to the fury of my ancestors, as you can imagine reprisals were to quickly follow.'

The food that Ian was attempting to eat was left on the piece of bark that served as a plate. What he was hearing he had not expected, his appetite was gone, now the role he would take was solely that of a listener.

'These revolts by us the Herero were more than just a threat to their newly acquired colony rich in diamonds. It created an insult to the power of Germany. That's when they made a decision to send in an individual, a ruthless Prussian imperialist. I struggle to pronounce his name, I will not attempt it. That said and acting on the Kaiser's instructions he forced a policy by sheer intent and savagery directed at us.'

Ian seized the moment, desperately interrupting by adding his feelings. 'Surely not this island, this "Shark Island" again?'

'No, Ian, a far more, how can I say, a devious plan, this is how it was explained to me by my forebears… There were "words" sent to my people at that time, they came from von Trotha. There I've managed the pronunciation. My people we were not to be classed as German subjects anymore. You must understand by this time a great many battles between us and our German suppressors had taken place, we were fighting for our very homeland, multitudes of the Herero had already been slain. But their plan became devious in wanting to drive my people out of our country. Now, Ian, where have you heard that term before?'

'But Jho-in I can't really see how all this could have happened otherwise…'

He felt the hands of Jho-in placed firmly on his shoulder blades, he interrupted his sentence by nothing more than a whisper... 'Wait, young Ian, let me explain further.

'There was a "letter" which preceded the next historical event, it outlined what nowadays we would call an "extermination order". As we were no longer deemed German subjects we were forcefully made to leave our lands, failure to comply was death. There were no exceptions, women and their children were all treated the same.'

Jho-in stared over the visible expanse of undulating dunes, he made a gesture, pointing in that direction, clearly visible to Ian. 'The Herero were driven to the Kalahari Desert. Their eventual fate was to die in the wastelands. Guards were stationed at water holes, many of which they had deliberately poisoned. There was no escape; those that attempted to return to our homeland were shot. Whatever they tried the thirst land of the Kalahari brought on the desert madness and as our suppressers surmised took its eventual toll.'

Ian could clearly see the degree of emotion that had overcome Jho-in, knowing that he owed his saviour the trust to maintain their conversation, he attempted to offer a humble understanding. 'You mean the Herero were driven out of their homeland without as much as a thought. But what I am unable to understand is the deserts of the Kalahari, surely your people back then would have all the skills to survive?'

As he finished and not for the first time he realised the answer, Jho-in had already explained, it was water, sealed off from the Herero. 'Water, Ian, water. They were denied a fundamental need, today it's our value of human rights, but not what happened during the days of attrition in 1907.'

Jho-in scooped up a handful of sand and allowed the dry substance to gravitate through his fingers, forming in both their minds where no words were needed. Presenting as it did a symbolic statement to what death from thirst in a desert meant.

Ian knew his course of action was to remain silent, a further explanation from Jho-in would become apparent. 'So, Ian, all those years ago the struggles for my people in the Kalahari were soon ended. There are accounts of this holocaust witnessed, where hundreds were left in the desert to die, even our children had no salvation. Those that had weakened were eaten alive by predators, so became the appalling crime levelled against us the Herero.

'Yes there were pockets of survivors amongst my people, but the death toll of my beloved forebears was eventually known as 60,000 souls.' Jho-in watched the remaining grains of sands spilling from his hand, when empty he closed it in a noticeably defiant mood.

'Even now all these years later one of my people has a duty, pointless I know but alone he spends his time respecting our dead by wandering the desert, his touching lament in keeping watch over their lost souls. You know him, Ian, he is "the old one".

'What I have described was a rehearsal for the future, the Nazi holocaust. Ironic as the head official for the colonial power was the father of Heinrich Goering who we know was eventually to become Hitler's most loyal supporter. Take note, Ian, that modern day Germany is now the most supportive aid donor, whilst the family of Lothar von Trotha has the audacity to humbly apologise to my people.'

He stopped talking and nudged Ian on his shoulder and pointed. 'There, over by the outer huts, Ian, aid to the Herero, metal poles and chain for us to put together and dig for water!'

Ian laboured attempting to offer a summing up as a reply to his host's account of the Herero suffering. He realised whatever he could offer would be nothing but pathetic. What had white dominance historically done to this country of Namibia, and for that matter the entire African continent? No explanations he could possible offer would suffice.

At the end he felt ashamed on an account of so-called white supremacy that had dominated Africa. Personally he became a victim of what could only be described as an enclosed melancholy. He battled with his conscience, a task he was surely not destined to win.

He yearned to crawl away and hide, even his overdue contact to Mitch was completely forgotten. Time and again one singular word hammered in his mind; greed, to spill over and rape a continent on such an immense scale...

The night sleep was eluding him. He re-traced the vivid events that Jho-in had described, in particular those horrors that the Kalahari Desert must have witnessed. Whilst trying to find peace in sleep his mind searched an inner labyrinth to draw strength but the reward he craved was not offered. When he finally succumbed his sleep was fitful, for an unknown reason his centre of attention was rooted on what Jho-in had shown him stacked within the encampment. He recalled his terminology, a stock pile of metal poles, welfare aid aimlessly dumped on these desert people in vain contempt that they could subscribe to drill for their own water supply.

He wondered how much his Aunt Anastasia had known or had been made aware of this chequered history. As always again why so many questions, but never the full value of having all the answers?

Another intrusion entered his disrupted realm of sleep; surreal horrific dream gothic in its concept, he could see the desert floor in startling reality, recognising the area where he had laid on the point of death. There was that chill wind that would come in on the cold light of dawn. The realism of his dream continued. On the sand lay a white bleached object, a human skull, something told him it was the fabric of his own skull.

But how could I possibly be looking at my own skull? It appeared moving in a slow rocking motion exposing the long vacant eye sockets. The skull was occupied by something causing this movement. What became visible was unreal and equally hideous; the occupant of the skull was slowly vacating the dwelling, now he could clearly see it was that of a scorpion. He sensed by its erect tail it gave an impression of radiating power. There was for him a sublime affiliation towards this creature; he desperately wanted to be in its presence. By what connection he had no idea?

Then all became hazy, like wood smoke from a fire on an autumn day. He sensed the familiar white scarf had fallen over his face, enveloping his vision. In a sudden start causing his heart to palpitate he woke in a state of soaking sweat. I'm alive. The Herero have saved my life. He was disappointed that no white scarf laid over him, however something else was apparent, he was experiencing a vital and fresh train of thought.

His senses radiated rapidly away from the visions of hideous dreams, now he really did know exactly what he was going to do. After all I'm not an oil rig drilling engineer for nothing.

Chapter 20

Mitch, listening to Ian's phone conversation, was inadvertently clenching his fist and not without reason. Slowly the consequences of his friend's ordeal in the desert were unveiled to him. Now he was asking himself the relevant question, just who was this 'guide' Nass, and how had he infiltrated to take on the role that had been previously assigned to Grittan?

'Ian I've no idea, perhaps it was a case of getting our lad Grittan sick, judging by what he did to you he had some practice in that art, and switching places as... what was that you said, a cousin?'

There followed for no particular reason an extended break in their conversation... 'Mitch listen it's in the past, I'm alive, or put it another way if it was not for the Herero then you would have never known of me again.'

Mitch sat back in his office chair still finding it hard to believe what had transpired, desperately he needed to know more. 'Ian where's this individual gone who purported to be your guide?'

Ian was alerted by his phone indicating low battery power, he still had the core of his conversation with Mitch to get across.

'I don't know what's happened to him, least ways my hosts won't tell me, what's more I don't much care. However one thing I do care about is what I intend doing next.' The phone started sending out it's warning bleep... indicating low battery.

'Listen, Mitch, I've got the biggest favour ever owed to these people, I'm putting something back, apparently following my dear aunt's philosophy. Water, getting them a supply of water. They have aid thrown at them but precious chance of getting anything into practice.'

'What you got in mind, Harbinger?' Mitch welcomed the turn of events with their conversation as he had a heavy feeling of guilt following what had taken place with the calamity surrounding the bogus guide.

'If, Mitch, and I know it's a large "if" I need drilling gear like of which I noticed in your warehouse, the static hardware is out here already, that's their so-called aid, but drilling and pumping that's what I need. Damn I'm losing the signal it's breaking up.' By this stage he was only intermittently able to discern any dialogue from Mitch.

'Get charged up, Harbinger. Let me have a think on things my end, get back to you.'

By some divine act of faith or pure luck Ian was able to get those last words before his satellite phone finally went completely dead on him.

He could feel the difference in motivations with his actions, although aware he was still feeling weak, it was his sheer enthusiasm for life that had returned. He took stock of the diesel fuel in the pickup truck, fortunately no immediate concerns there. Having connected up the precious phone to charge he was determined to seek out Jho-in for one very important discussion, although for him there was an unexpected surprise waiting.

'Nothing, Jho-in, not even a sketch map to the whereabouts.' Ian had made an assumption and after that negative remark his new found energy had collapsed like that of a pack of cards.

'Wait, Ian, our people know where to find water, think about it, this knowledge is handed down for generations. What's more that's why our settlement is here. I will show you where the water lays, if it could only be reached.'

'Sorry, it's me, Jho-in. I assumed that my aunt had been active with surveys and somehow had managed within her remit to bring to the front a few "seismo" probes, discovering strata bearing substrate. Do you imagine out on the oil fields our company's prospecting is done by sheer guesswork?'

Jho-in became aware of the dejected state that had so completely and quickly overcome his patient. 'Ian, listen, put aside your wonderful modern day science. Let me show you where the water lays.'

The area of sand and scrub looked to him no different than any other that surrounded the settlement. He looked in disbelief at Jho-in. 'Here... this very spot?'

The leader of the Herero had retrieved a substantial stick which he proceeded to push into the sand acting as a marker. 'Under there, young Ian, as my father would have said lays the life blood for any people of the deserts... water. What have you in mind for us?'

'Stay with me on this one. I'm organising equipment which will allow us to drill right here where you say water is located and that's a big change for me, when crude oil is always the target.' Ian pushed the marker stick with zealous enthusiasm allowing it to go further into the sand, he stood back almost proudly as if demonstrating a bizarre forthright act.

Jho-in had become quiet and an equally patient observer, now he knew it was time for his intervention. 'So, young Ian, you are converted to what my own father would have believed in, and by using your skills of modern technology will bring forth what has been known for so long.'

Following this almost biblical announcement it was Ian who could reassuringly tap his host firmly on his shoulders and risk his reassurance in needing to succeed. 'If it's there, Jho-in, then we will pull it up to daylight.' Having made his proclamation he underlined his speculation with a wry and noticeable smile bordering on the sympathetic.

Jho-in had left the proposed drilling site needing to attend with their indigenous stocks of cattle, which called for a decision only allowed by their leader.

Ian continued to try and assess the scrub land that he was standing upon. How would they have known? The work of divining sticks I suppose? His thoughts were brought to reality by the ringing of the satellite phone, the screen indicated who, the world of his work was calling.

McPherson was irate and that was definitely an understatement. 'Aren't you even bothered to reply to my messages, IH? Section five is in problems, it's pissing steam on all ports… why the hell, you lot solved it once?'

Ian could visualise exactly what was happening, same as before. They were overworking the line, how many times have I stressed that, but no, they will never listen.

'Mac it's the same as before. Your guys are pushing too much through, you need to run a by-pass, get the first unit back and use any of the inlets, take that build up away from that section. Wayne knows the procedure, heaven forbid ten years ago we didn't even have these luxuries.' Ian almost regretted what he had said knowing what these workers were up against. It all came down as always to meeting production targets, as now our rigs are more than likely to be run by accountants.

McPherson having vented his frustrations on Ian decided to fire a rather relevant question. 'Ian when are we to see you back where you belong on this rig? Shouldn't say this but Halley's on the damn warpath asking about you in particular, only yesterday, wondering how much leave you are taking.'

Ian was quick to reflect on what those implications meant, they think nothing of it when we are working fifteen hour shifts resolving problems week upon week, or is it that I'm getting too jaded for this damn game?

'Thanks for the tip, Mac, won't be long now. I've got one of life's little favours needs resolving, I'm out in the deserts about to start drilling for water.'

His attentive listener on the North Sea platform was not entirely sure what he had heard. 'You said drilling for water?'

At that crucial point the signal was lost, given the prevailing circumstances effecting Ian probably the best termination to their estranged discussions.

It was pure imagination that much he certainly knew, but there was that feeling he could hear the noise from a drilling rig in his system then thankfully his orientation re-tuned to the present and the sandy wastes of the desert. It's my job right here and whatever else this is going to be achieved or know the reason why. His satellite phone came to life once more. What now? Had his patience ensued then he might have noticed who was calling.

The voice of Mitch came over. 'Harbinger it's your lucky day, take a deep breath and listen to me for once.'
Ian Harbinger did exactly what he had been told, he was all ears and listened.

'You've one important thing to do your end, Harbinger, get a very big letter "H" laid out on a big lump of flat sand, so it will burn, hell that's the first letter of your name you'll manage that won't you? Now give me a grid ref from your survey maps I'll line up with my copies and we are on target. Your delivery will be with you tomorrow and early, set light to the "H" after first light.'
Ian knew once again why Mitch was called Mr Fixit, and it would appear he was not losing his flair.

Jho-in was bemused, his invalid had not only recovered, but suddenly was empowered with an urge to achieve so much for him and his people. 'What do you want my people to do?'
Ian using his foot scribed a letter 'H' in the sand. 'Jho-in it's a visual marker, and we set light to it. We have a delivery due in tomorrow, it's the gear we need that will drill your well.'

'Is this overseas aid, Ian?' He followed his question by raising his hands above his head.
'Not wanting to disappoint you, but what's on its way is how can I say... a really big favour, from a long standing friend. Jho-in in times of adversity it is surprising what can be achieved by human resourcefulness.'

Ian thought that he had verged on a state of lecturing, but given the circumstances he was excited as the next...

The morning's mealy porridge was only just cooked when the vibrating drone of rotor blades could be easily discerned. Overwhelmingly a state of hysteria swept through the campsite, it not only affected the children busy keeping the 'H' fire burning but had spilled over to the adults. Jho-in shouted out to his people to stay clear of the area where the embolic letter was blazing.

The Westland Merlin transport helicopter completed a circuit and then touched down nothing short of perfection. This time it was Ian's turn to warn of the danger from the down draft from the active rotor blades.

Now he himself was in for a surprise concerning the helicopter's pilot, who at this stage was climbing down on the craft's aluminium ladder. It was difficult to discern who exactly to expect, the complications about recognition was not easy as the pilot was wearing an oversized flying jacket complemented by of all things retro matching head-wear. Only after the deep black Oakley sunglasses were removed you realised the pilot was a woman. Further confirmed as by now her visible metallic flying coveralls looked as if they had literally been sprayed on her, qualifying for Ian the wow factor, forget the pilot designer label, this was a most attractive woman!

He had precious time to reflect on his reactions when he heard his name called. 'Mr Harbinger.' Almost on cue the rotors finally expired making a semblance of conversation possible.

Ian walked towards the pilot, he had met deliveries out on the rigs but not quite to this challenging presentation. 'Hi that's me, this is my cargo no doubt?' Realising what an obvious and stupid reply he had made.

'Here's your manifest, Mr Harbinger. I would appreciate a quick off load, your consignment's up in the front section.'

Realising the rising heat of another Namibian day she removed the head wear which released her blonde hair allowing it to unfurl as he predicted in a totally alluring state of suggestion. The image in Ian's eyes was nothing short of exhilarating. One thing was confirmed by the feelings in his loins, they signalled he was now completely recovered.

But more than that he was witnessing a figure you would expect to gravitate as a character from a surreal computer game, in his mind it appeared unreal. He glanced over to see the children that had approached the helicopter with extreme trepidation perhaps this was the first they had actually seen in reality?

The two helper lads on the helicopter were operating the platform hoist and already three palletised crates were down on the desert sand. Ian looked over the details on the manifest whilst at the same time instructing via Jho-in for certain of his appointed men to off load the remaining manageable items.

Ian could not resist trying to propagate a conversation with the pilot, opening with a tentative enquiry. 'What's there for me to sign?'
Her shades were adjusted back in place, but not yet her headwear, Ian surmised that not only could she fly this virtual beast of a transport helicopter, she probably held an esteemed black belt in judo.
He knew he needed to repeat his question. 'Any paperwork you need a sig on?'
The pilot was engaged in the process of removing the wrapper from a piece of chewing gum, careful not to let the foil paper fall as litter. 'Nothing logged in for you, Mr Harbinger, then I'm not actually here. Get your "tribe" well away from the "bird" ... I'm out of here.'

He attempted shouting over the rising noise, 'Have a good day.' If it was heard he had no idea.
Jho-in joined him making a rather mute statement. 'The machine of the air, young Ian.' This time it was a firm slap that Ian received on his shoulder, now becoming something of a habit.

'Let's see, Jho-in, what my friend Mitch has organised. I think we are both in for some serious surprises.'

If Santa Claus had delivered they would not have been more elated. Agricultural drilling gear, compressors, lifting cradles, fuel which would also cover use for the beloved pickup, nothing was wanting. 'Well at the risk of an assumption, Jho-in, if that waters down where you say this will do what's required to bring it up, make no mistake.'

Jho-in lifted one of the assignment labels on the crates, his knowledge of English snapped into focus, it was or should have been consigned to the drilling rigs off the Namibian coast. Before he could manage a reply Ian got in first. 'Err yes, maybe our pilot got a little lost?'

To avoid an over sensitive situation Jho-in looked up and smiled. 'The deserts of my land are easy to get things lost, perhaps we shall even see your lady pilot again, young Ian?' Ian knew only too well what this wise matriarch meant by his remarks…

Hal One raced all the way, at last the tattered sign of the trading estate came in view, between his intakes for breath he prayed that boss Botha would still be at the plant yard. Knowing his news was valuable and that meant one thing for him, precious dollars.

Karl Botha rolled his cigar to the side of his mouth, an action which he had plenty of practice. He listened but it was difficult to exactly discern what the messenger was trying to explain. 'Take your damn time, boy, dare's no rush, I'm not going anywhere.'

Hal One was mesmerised as he watched Boss Botha administer the teaspoons of sugar into his mug of black coffee. 'You telling me this stuff was picked up from the warehouse by helicopter?'

Karl knew the company only too well, by his early attempts to try and screw down Mitch on unrealistic discounts. 'One of da offshore outfits then?'

'How you damn know it woz for Harbinger?'

In making his direct remark he slid open a desk drawer retrieving a packet of cigarettes which he pushed towards Hal. Delighted by the offer he tentatively removed one, his next surprise was Boss Botha offering him a light.

The calming influence of nicotine made him respond and at a slower pace to the questions. 'Libby at the loading place, he read good, Harbinger's name on those notes Boss.' Karl placed his coffee mug slowly and quietly on to his desk, he was in a reflective mood. Even his reply was noticeably muted by its concept. 'Consignment... delivery notes... all damn interesting.'

'Tell me again what was sent out, and it was loaded on last you say, so that's first off, still interesting.'

Outside a van pulled up which was the reason Karl was still at his office, the delivery was hydraulic pipes for one of his out of commission digger trucks. The driver entered the office with the sections of pipe, whilst under his arm he was attempting to hold a clipboard of notes requiring signatures. As he approached the desk as a mark of respect the driver normally removed his peak cap, however on this occasion that did not occur.

'Your last delivery, Mr Botha, manager says settle your account, you now on stop.'

Karl did nothing other than scribble his confirmation signature, and almost threw the clipboard in the general direction of the delivery driver.

'Out of 'ere, he'll get his damn money. If my news stands up I'll buy his whole damn f-ing firm.'

One thing was placed in Karl's thoughts, it's happening, father was right, as an assurance he longingly recalled his words...
'It's out there in the desert.'

Now for me, Karl Botha, at long last the time has come to collect.

Chapter 21

Ian was sitting on an empty packing crate where in a moment of humour he had written in the inevitable block letters rather vainly, 'director'. Arguably this was his first rest since the light of dawn following his established routine of starting work before the rising heat of the desert sun.

Fabric material from unpacked items had been cobbled together to create what resembled an umbrella. It was attached to the back of the crate that passed as his haven of a seat.

He was still wondering where the puzzling phrase 'busman's holiday' could have originated, but it was certainly one that might be attributed to him right now. An oil rig engineer drilling for water in the wastes of the Namibian desert.

So far everything was going to his plan, the derrick trestle had been secured; not the easiest of tasks given the nature of the groundwork. For Ian however his greatest breakthrough was his work force. In the start-up their task had certainly created its string of difficulties, the language barrier was his biggest stumbling block, having in effect to translate his needs through Jho-in, however that said it was having its lighter moments.

Now he could look back over the meaningful events of the last three days. His sign signals to his enthused team were more than just working; in fact at times all his workers knowing the reasons for what they were attempting could not keep away from the field of operations both day and night.

Ian did not need telling how the bonding with the Herero people was working, his only niggling concern was what they were after, would it happen in reality, to be surrounded by the life saving substance of water. Inwardly he was worrying, they were engaged on a drilling exploration based on nothing more than simply a whim and fancy, a myth from previous generations of the Herero. He did not need reminding how different it was out on the rigs – the intensive seismograph surveys before any thought was given to costly drilling operations. But for now he was enthusiastically locked into his leap of faith!

One of Ian's men brought him a supply of water, measuring it out in a tin beaker, there almost appeared a sense of irony, would water be on offer from this prospected source? He was already cringing on thoughts of failure to deliver.

Since the helicopter drop he had become dumbfounded in what had been assigned to him, how it was managed was only a wild guess. He suspected an ample lubrication of old fashioned bribery, realising what methods are employed in the remote regions of Africa. Although on reflection that ominous word corruption had entered his train of thought, he managed to convince himself otherwise putting it down to the effect of the rising heat.

With his first phase completed he could at least reflect on what his crew had accomplished and that by sheer undiluted hard toil. The drilling cage was in place, having struggled with the instruction manual printed in Russian, accepting that beggars are unable to choose, clearly pointed out by Mitch in one of their phone discussions where Ian had metaphorically gone down on his knees to offer thanks for what had been supplied.

The time was now almost imminent, at dawn tomorrow it would come down to the acid test although he thought perhaps that expression was not entirely apt when drilling for water. All was set to provide what he hoped were to be the answers.

It was planned for the cool of the day, the start time had finally arrived; a buzz of activity through the whole community was patently noticeable. Ian had fuelled up the compressor, the auger drilling bit was clamped in situ, now all was set for discovery of what the Herero folklore proclaimed. Much as he wanted, Ian was still unable to create the full enthusiasm for the tenuous project…

Marcus tried but he was unable to concentrate, the email or more precisely its content was coming back with sustained regularity to haunt him. Brother Karl had committed to the written word, very much out of character for him, now as instructed he had to wait for his phone call. Marcus was sure of one thing, it was something of importance otherwise this circuitous route would not have been instigated.

The long protracted waiting irritated him, having to seek solace in trying to complete a batch of pre WW2 stamps that had recently arrived from Australia. Nothing of any value but always possible to barter with in negotiating future dealings. Whilst examining one particular stamp his lounge phone came to life.

Always late he thought as he lifted the receiver. 'Marcus, leetle brother, big news it's pay out time, this guy Harbinger… 'e's found it… Come on say something to me.'

Marcus as always was in his same agitated state causing tightening pains in his stomach muscles. Even his voice pattern had lost its impetus. Now he was relying, courtesy of the prop possible from yet another glass of vodka.

'Karl how do you know for certain?' He did not have to wait long for his reply, delivered as usual in the crescendo he was to expect from his elder sibling.

'I've got my contacts, Marcus, it's about whose got the damn muscle out 'ere, my dear leetle brother. Harbinger's still out in da desert, although heaven knows what's happened to the damn guide we worked in. Anyway what the hell, 'e's had drilling gear flown out, you don't need to be a genius to work out what dat's for. Marcus you know our father's last words to us, shout it loud to me, leetle brother!'

He was not in a mood to talk, let alone shout a stupid claim to his over enthused brother. 'Yes, Karl, we both understand what he said, you in particular believe it totally. An untold wealth lays out in the desert, Father thought he believed it from his second wife. You remember her, Karl, don't you? Our beloved stepmother Anastasia, whom you always wanted dead.'

At last Marcus no longer needed to contain himself; his rapid consumption of vodka was starting to talk on his behalf.

'Keep out of my hair, leetle brother, you'd be no damn use out 'ere. I'll find Harbinger and what 'e's got on to. One thing's for sure he ain't coming back into civilisation anymore. Don't worry, Marcus, blood's thicker dan water, you'll be out here when I want you, then you can buy every damn stamp on da planet.'

Marcus was left in a void with their conversation, listening to a respiratory cigar cough from his brother. He carefully replaced the receiver as if he was observed by an unseen source.

Now he had lost count. So what? He lazily poured yet one more, small glass of vodka. How he loathed conversations with his brother, why did he always become the whipping boy? But it was too late to resolve that issue, it stretched back as far as he could ever remember. When this happens, whatever this wealth is, then I'm determined to play my trump card, obtaining a new identity and disappearing from his clutches forever.

That made him feel contented, he was falling victim to a slow and comfortable sucumbed state although he would never admit it was the result of his intake of alcohol. He was puzzled, that was the way for weeks. What had this Harbinger individual found within Homemead? After all I went over the empty house with a proverbial tooth comb, it must have being something in that concealed passage by the chimney, but what were those secrets? It was obvious that Harbinger had been privy to knowing the whereabouts and that as Karl knows is why this nephew is after whatever lays hidden in the desert. What a mess. Is it really worth all this effort?

He picked up the tweezers anxious to resume the sanctuary of collating his new stamp arrivals.

Karl laid his shoulders back in his office chair with puny regularity the chair's arms creaked under his full weight. Hell, he thought, what's the point of getting my pathetic brother over here? He wouldn't have the balls to do anything.

He contemplated, going over in his mind a plan of campaign. He fidgeted, an unusual habit for him – he wanted to concentrate but it was getting difficult. Now he had resorted to using his freshly lit cigar in an attempt to burn through the string loosely attached to the recently delivered hydraulic hose still residing on his desk.

He easily achieved what he wanted, the two hoses released from the string slowly uncurled replicating the action of sinuous snakes waking in sunlight. Karl had averted his attention through the window of his office, staring at the black masculine stature of his beloved pickup truck, then in sharp perspective the answer conveniently dawned on him…

The auger was certainly biting into some form of substrate. Ian eased off the drilling pressure reminding himself that what he had in his possession was almost a DIY outfit in comparison in what he was normally working with out on the oil rigs.

He looked at his watch, confirming it was all but four hours of drilling and only soft peddling on our part, but it was remaining the same, nothing was showing. He was not expecting a deluge to erupt and up to now he was certainly not disappointed, not even just a damp patch in the sand. His loyal team waited in anticipation and were certainly more convinced than he was. At first Ian naturally thought it was sheer novelty value for them, all the equipment and the constant noise of the power emitted from the generator.

Mitch had contacted in the ensuing days prior to the drilling operation taking place. Given his involvement he was showing more a casual interest in what was going to happen. Whilst Ian was in one of those real life situations that commanded a high motivation as if running on a mixture of high octane fuel, desperately he needed to see results.

His enthusiasm to reach water for the Herero had created a retrograde situation with his lack of response to the company's requests that had arrived via his satellite phone. I'm still on leave, he tactfully kept reminding himself, and that's it.

But it was more, the news had really hit him with the oil rig disaster out in the Gulf of Mexico. Every time he spoke to Mitch he was informed on the latest development to quell the precarious situation. At this stage both men were mourning the loss of life at the onset of the explosion. Ian could understand the implications, but Mitch, his compatriot knew more on what that meant, overshadowing for him on a personal note far more than the actual environmental disaster poised to infiltrate the United States' coastline.

The full heat of the Namibian sun was now burning down on the drilling site, whilst it proved Ian's logic of starting work at first light the rewards with their effort had produced an absolute zero. He was seriously having doubts on what he and for that matter his work team had undertaken. Causing him to muse in a grave attitude, we are doing something based solely on events relating to obscure and for that matter what would pass as an ancient myth.

Jho-in joined the scene of operations, his people stopped and stood clear of the drilling derrick, Ian cut out the compressor so they could hear themselves talk. 'It should have happened by now, Jho-in, we hit substrate, that was an hour ago.'

The leader of the Herero looked down at the drilling auger that was above the ground level. He was feeling isolated in a vortex of modern technology, he looked up towards Ian noticeably by now soaked in perspiration. 'Young Ian, you are no longer a tourist in my country.' Then by his smile it told Ian all he needed to know.

'Ian if I remember the word correctly, then persistence has prevailed. Perhaps what was once there now is no more?'

By now he had taken the spare drill, he indicated to Jho-in it was worth the effort to replace the working auger. As he went to retrieve the tool kit needed to perform the task Jho-in moved away to the encampment, realising there was nothing more at this stage he could possibly contribute.

The noise of the compressor again infiltrated the quiet solitude to which the desert was accustomed. Perspiration was getting through the seal of Ian's safety goggles forming an ethereal mist inside the lens, so much so that he failed to fully appreciate the thump produced when the newly fitted auger penetrated through the deeper laying substrate.

But one important fact had caught up with him, the maximum depth of the drilling was reached, the final card was played, he switched off the running gear allowing the drilling head to rise. Only one thing he wanted to see when the spiral of the auger bit emerged, he lifted the sweat-sodden goggles, by now his work team had crowded around the trestle area. It was self-answering, only dry sand fell away almost apologetically from the auger's spiral core, of any moisture there was no evidence.

Only when he reached the enclosure of his hut he realised what the heat of the desert sun had done in particular to his shoulder blades, all for no purpose, that was the galling thing. Did his team, not wanting to reveal their feelings, believe the stranger in the desert whose life they had saved was not keeping his promise?

There could be no celebrations for Ian. Worse than that the imposition in understanding the drill would no longer be effective as its maximum depth had now been achieved.

He knew he was cheating on himself, unfortunately the temptation was too much, the bottle of whisky courtesy of Mitch was in imminent danger of being cracked.

Thinking of Mitch he was pondering exactly what he was going to say, he would have to own up to failure. Not so much my fault, could I really ask for a stay of execution as all had been based on a whim of tribal beliefs? Then his mind sunk even further thinking of the logistics to set up this whole episode to say nothing of the delivery, his second slug followed quickly.

Jho-in's decision was to leave him alone, knowing those of the Western world that had a need for everything contained in boxes of their well ordered lives.

Ian's mind was continuing to dwell on the news that Mitch had relayed on the Gulf of Mexico disaster. As an oil man his immediate thoughts would not leave his mind, understandably directed towards his fellow workers and how they would have succumbed. No one could truly understand the feelings of those trapped in a fireball explosion on a rig.

Now more dejected with himself, certainly not helped through further intakes of whisky, he had progressed to what he would have to describe as a real sour mood. What are we trying to do with our planet, again it came down to big business, could they justify the result of man's greed? He continued quizzing his inner most thoughts. Had the oil industry become too much for even him to handle?

Before sleep finally took a hold, his feelings had gone out to his loyal team of workers. How days earlier under Jho-in's care they directed their energies in what they all wanted to see, emergence of a water source they believed would aspire to come bubbling to the surface. His mind was dwelling on the area of scrub and desert sand where by now it should be happening; painful guilty sleep eventually overtook him.

Contentedly he watched the tyre tracks left effortlessly in the sand, he stared seemingly for ever into the vehicle's rear view driving mirror, behind and in front was nothing but open expanses of desert. But who was in the cab with him?

On the skyline there was an outline of the high cliffs which were now growing larger. As he drove closer they appeared strangely isolated, an outcrop in the already remote regions of desert. Why and where are we?

By now Ian knew only too well he was in a stupefied dream made entirely worse by his unnecessary intake of drink. Whoever was in the cab was directing him to what transpired to be a natural opening in the tall cliff face, but how are we to drive through that angled gap?

Was this happening or was he dying in that canyon where his guide had poisoned him? Never enough answers, suddenly his senses were alerted. There was a feeling of contentment; the figure was there, it had materialised walking across the desert floor, always so reassuringly with her long flowing white scarf

There was shouting; where is that noise coming from? He could hear his name called, but why so loud? He did not know if he was awake. Sweat had soaked him, but that was largely his own fault; the empty whisky bottle provided the evidence. Limited daylight filtered into the hut, which did not improve the thumping sensation emitting from his head.

But who is calling my name? His muddled thoughts were drifting between two voids; that of the North Sea rigs and a rudimentary hut shelter in the remote Namibian desert...

Again he heard his name shouted.

Inside the hut in gloomy early morning light he could make out a vague profile. 'J... J... Jho-in... is that you?'

'Young Ian, wake... you must wake... we had a "visitor" that came in the night.'

'You say a what?' In his alcoholic splurge they were the only words he was capable of even attempting to utter.

Chapter 22

His intake of the demon drink amongst other recriminations had installed for his privilege an almighty thirst. Almost supported on Jho-in's shoulder he was standing and in front of his eyes he was staring in disbelief at his immediate remedy. Even the sound was reaching him, that of gurgling water!

Jho-in placed his hand firmly on Ian's arm. He needed to shout in an effort to make himself heard over the noise of his excited people. 'Young Ian, I knew you had confidence in my father's convictions, clearly shown by your celebrations last night.'

Ian knew enough to get more than an inkling of what he implied but decided to answer with a strictly tongue in cheek remark. 'If you put your mind to it, you can accomplish anything.' But he added. 'No, I lost my faith when that auger drill couldn't go any deeper.'

It was Ian's turn to reciprocate with a slap on Jho-in's back. Both men no longer holding any restraints could laugh, and laugh they did whilst all the Herero cheered which had an effect of subduing the responsive sound of the life giving water.

The beating pulse of Ian's hangover was at its most intense, he tried focusing on the scene in the emerging light; his workers still wearing their newly acquired white hard hats were spellbound. He was starting to witness, a dignified and humble way the parents were allowing their children to paddle in the rising water that the desert had yielded, and it was all for them, the people of the Herero.

Ian walked towards what he trusted would eventually become a well. He looked in dismay at the drilling equipment that last night was abandoned in a redundant state, it was now slowly becoming submerged leaving him to calculate that perhaps its work was done. Looking back towards Jho-in he quickly took advantage with a poignant remark. 'Easy you see, Jho-in, give it a bit of time and up it comes, nothing else I can say, maybe if you believe that you'd believe anything.'

Then without so much as a thought he borrowed a hard hat from one of his team and kneeling down allowed it to fill with water, followed as if a ritual by simply pouring its contents over his head, to him it was an ultimate hangover relief.

Ian however was not going to get away with it that easily, Jho-in had issued instructions not that it was entirely needed. His people were now carrying him high above their heads. He succumbed, feeling a degree of self-consciousness, leaving him gripping the edge of the empty hard hat. There was only one course of action, keep smiling. This was a highly contented moment which he was determined to fully saviour...

Karl checked once again even if he repeated what was already done last night, the water containers covered by heavy sacking, then the fuel stock, enough diesel knowing he would refuel before hitting the interior. Everything was in order, there was food enough, but he knew from experience that was not an issue, it all came down to water, plenty of water, the lifesaver up in those regions.

He was ready, all important items which he considered were certainly going to earn their keep were secured in the vehicle, including the firearms. His beloved hunting rifle was stored separately for safe travel, then with prudence he checked the hand gun and the rounds of ammunition, more than he would expect to use.

The whole operation had the element of excitement considering the years of waiting for these events to transpire. Now at last he had an 'appointment' with this nephew Harbinger right out in the desert, in an area he referred as his own backyard.

His final check was cash in his money belt, bribery confetti that he would probably need to use. The last item he considered an ace in the hole; his latest acquisition, the GPS unit. Functionally tiny he was still struggling with its operational data, but he knew given time it would become clear.

At last he was free to drive out of the Airport Industrial Estate, its tattered appearance served as a reminder that his payment for the maintenance was long overdue, but like all bills they were definitely on hold. Other far more important things were on Karl's agenda which were set to become as he believed life changing implications.

Once he cleared the confines of industry he started to feel more elated. As was his habit he affectionately tapped his vehicle's mascot that hung perhaps unceremoniously from the interior driving mirror. It had a varied life span, always passed on from the types of transport over the years he had aspired to own. Its shape was that of a tribal doll, in the first place the artefact had been given to Karl by his father as a symbol of good luck. He had absolutely no idea to its actual origin and for that matter no particular interest.

But for all that he would not swap it for the world; it meant so much to him, perhaps the only weakness he would ever dare to admit. The charm that his doll mascot would influence was highly respected particularly as it had belonged to his beloved forebear. Neither knew that its actual structure was made from human bone layered with native fabric. It swung with a tantalising movement from its revered place attached to the mirror. Karl smiled inwardly, refreshing his thoughts on all those years of speculation and waiting, now finally poised to be solved, above all else those iconic few words… It's out there in the desert.

That thought promoted him to think of Marcus, although they had not met for years he continued to despise him, try as he might he could never forgive him for changing his family surname of Botha. Particularly as Karl was so proud of the strong foundation that answered to that name, mattering more to him as a person than he could ever imagine.

He was gripping the vehicle's steering wheel far too tightly. An action that resulted in a veritable white knuckle ride, excusing himself as an inward display of temper motivated through his thoughts surrounding his useless younger brother.

They all need leading by their precious hands, hopeless in every direction. After that damaging thought he switched off what he considered as infuriating music courtesy of his cab's radio. Once more he tried to understand what had happened to the guide Nass, that had been successfully infiltrated into Harbinger's realm of operations, then as his informant had recently advised, the prize idiot chanced his arm for a load of salt, lucky to escape with his life let alone losing his damn manhood. Now not even a sign of him anywhere, if he ever shows he will no doubt have the audacity to ask me of all people for compensation!

All his ideas of idiots surrounding him were now out of his thoughts as he had lost what there was of the urban crawl, the much awaited open road lay ahead. He would need one night's stay at a motel but from then on he would be in the early stages of the desert that he was aware those consignments were sent. Its' who you know, not what you know. At last something was pleasing him. The fact it was flown out was proof that Harbinger had survived his guide's botched efforts to kill him. He believed appropriately and whispered as he tapped the lucky charm. 'If you want a job done, there's only one way, do it your damn self.'

He soon acclimatised to a feeling of relaxation, his beloved turbo-charged vehicle in the evening light was purring a contented drone. A motel tonight, but tomorrow the open sky just like the old times in South Africa, I've never lost my skills. As he approached the township a group of street traders occupied the road in front of him; they heard the vehicle's approach but were not prepared for the vicious driving that Karl from the sheer hell of his temper was to throw at them…

For Ian Harbinger the feast in his honour was more than he would have ever imagined. Given their frugal existence it would have placed a burden on the Herero people. Knowing only too well that those of our affluent Western world would find these austere conditions of desert life hard if not impossible to comprehend.

Jho-in had bestowed on Ian, that of an honorary brotherhood to the Herero. The leader by direct contrast reflected on his time spent being educated in what he referred as the mother country. Vividly remembering the importance that he had witnessed so many times whilst in England, those 'labels' that were attached to selected members of the community.

But here in my country Ian had shown resourcefulness with his organising of all the equipment, shipped to our remote regions, eventually proving what his father had always foretold. Words transferred into facts, clearly seen as he stood in front of the miracle of water percolating from beneath the sand.

For Jho-in knew at last that his patient was ready, and it was now time that his newly honoured brother should be allowed to visit what he had more than earned a right to know.

Of whom Jho-in referred he was confined to the quiet of his inner sanctum, accepting what was bestowed on him, 'The Herero's Life Giver' as Ian appeared to be known as, that being the closest translated from the Herero into English.

All had transpired to bring an inner peace, the time of his day was now controlled by the forces of nature, sunrise which followed by merging naturally into sunset. There was a self-imposed comfort for the first time during his adult life, making him appreciate those virtues, time and its strict routines were becoming if he dared to accept a thing that belonged to his past.

In his satisfied state the drilling platforms in the North Sea were in danger to become nothing more than a memory. Although there remained one persistent and niggling concern, was the water strike only of a given volume? His knowledge of oil pressure strikes was haunting him, was the water only an enclosed reservoir which in a short duration would no longer exist?

Now he was to make contact to modern day reality and his communication with Mitch, ready for absolute elation in telling him of the water strike, more importantly as he would need to explain that the whole project had rested on one precarious thing, folklore. The reply he received was one of sheer exasperation. 'Harbinger you're telling me it was nothing more than a glorified fable that water was there in the first place, all that equipment we smuggled out to you, hell, how the devil were they so sure?'

Both men were eventually forced to admit there was more in the cultured races of remote indigenous people than we in our modern world would thankfully ever realise.

On the more global front it was sad for them both as exponents in the world of exploring for the earth's riches they were subjected to the continuing news on an unearthly scale with oil pollution invading the coastline of America, consequences of which were entering into realms of the highest magnitude. Both men were adamant on one point, our planet continued to be subjected to the hand of man's incessant plundering. But at least, Ian thought, what have I the right to make such stilted comments, it's my industry and for that matter maybe my continuing employment?

Had his reality now become the deserts of Namibia and his bond developing with the Herero lifestyle? One direct and very apt word summed up his present situation, a new found guise of contentment.

Jho-in's feast in Ian's honour, provided a veritable platform for him to take into account all the ancient knowledge handed down by previous generations. Resulting with the spectacle of water visible to his own eyes, there were no other options other than to believe in what he, like all the Herero could see.

The remaining work was the installation of a structure to act as a holding reservoir. During this stage amounting to heavy effort from his workforce Ian was to gain a feeling of gratitude influenced by camaraderie of working with such inspired people.

It caused him to recollect a much earlier phase at Homemead and the well that resides there, all those treasured times conjuring up what he and his childhood friend Sibley had undertaken in attempting to reach its unknown depths. Perhaps ever the romantic, one day I will return again and prise those timbers nailed over its top and stare into that nether pit. Who knows…?

They left in Mitch's ancient pickup truck in the cooler part of the day; previously all was prepared for the journey, aptly described as his further reward. Or in Jho-in's words, a journey into the interior for him where even today no tourists have ventured. Although he was not prepared to disclose any details, other than an experience that he would not forget.

Perhaps the leader of the Herero knew this was more than a journey for Ian, it would become a realisation for his life, and Jho-in was proud to be his mentor on such an undertaking. But for both of them it was to become life changing as the hand of fate was to intervene.

The vehicles track's followed a route which back in the annals of time was reserved as a premise for beasts of burden trading across the desert wastes. Ian had a natural concern with the vehicle's fuel stock but by what Mitch had flown out and by consulting Jho-in there should be sufficient. By what Ian was experiencing from the Herero he was believing anything was possible.

Following much deliberation from Jho-in and his wives, the leader of the Herero had through coercion decided that his second eldest son would accompany them. Ian through these negotiations had let himself go with the tide. In many ways it was self-answering as the eldest Herero was away attending to tribal cattle. So they had Santoo as their enthusiastic passenger exhibiting the strange awareness of what travel by a motor vehicle was going to mean.

There was an almost strange quietness in the beginning of their journey. Young Santoo naturally occupied the rear seats. It must have resembled a virtual palace for him; by this stage it was safe to assume that 'wild horses' could not have dragged him from his newly acquired stronghold.

Ian in the early part of the journey continued inwardly to remain puzzled, how could they have known of the existence of that underground strata. There was no other course of action than to seriously quiz Jho-in. He would wait his moment, perhaps around the campfire. Away from his people there should be more time to devote an answer.

Not only would he achieve perhaps a closure on this puzzle and further he would be able to answer what Mitch also wanted desperately to know. Which reminded him to contact his buddy at the end of the day having already explained the surprise journey he was undertaking, but no answer as to the reason why.

So all was settling, as guided by Jho-in they were heading off into presumably more remote regions of Namibia where no charts or anything for that matter appeared to exist.

His image that gravitated from the vehicle's rear view mirror showed his appearance the like of which he had not experienced before. A full facial beard which he no longer struggled to accept. More than that he only had to look at his skin that had not escaped the daily attention of the Namibian sun.

All that was not really a concern, too much was centred on the communications directed from his company, however they were all falling victims of his disinterest. At first he had thought it was the horrific news centred on the Gulf of Mexico environmental disaster.

Deep inside he had a sickening feeling of again treading the decks of an oil rig. Whatever was motivating him away from his way of working life he had no idea but it was certainly having a profound influence.

The ancient and reliable pickup continued its journey with an odd feeling to its driver that he was still not aware of their eventual destination? But Ian knew one singularly important point even though it had a selfish content, as a person he had become appeased by contentment.

There came a trigger response, causing him to reflect on his time spent in the company of the illustrious Miss Cleary, who he was convinced knew more about him than she was prepared to admit. For all that he was forced to realise at this moment he was following her express wishes.

The arduous desert sands harassed the truck's progress, but he dwelt on her acute words… 'Mr Harbinger you will have to follow your own yellow brick road.'

But to where? That for him was remaining the tantalising mystery.

Chapter 23

'Jho-in how do you possibly know the way?' Then he realised his question was somewhat pointless. I'm not even aware in the first place where we're supposed to be going. They had made their first stop, Ian was, if anything, perplexed. Nothing over the desert existed in the way of signs or features you could possibly relate with. Although he was totally confident that they were not in any way lost.

Jho-in endorsed Ian's subjective request by holding his hands to the skyline. 'There, Ian, part of our very lifeblood, you will learn more as our days unfold.

'Read the signs, look, see how the sand rests uneven against the smooth flow already caused by previous winds.'

He stared, and when his sunglasses were eventually removed he could finally discern what Jho-in meant, it appeared singularly different from the surrounding land. He was starting to appreciate what he was being shown. In no way was this the like of which he explored in the company of his ominous guide Nass.

Already Ian was more than realising the perception and foresight that the leader of the Herero was showing him, but then it was a completely natural discernment that had been instilled into him since birth. It would have been fascinating to imagine him as a young man at Cambridge and adjusting to that of Western ways. Behind him at that time would be his sagacity of the remote and arid lands of his homeland of south-west Africa.

Ian looked up as his mentor continued to explain. 'Tomorrow, Ian, we will see them as we cross their trail; elephants of the desert, then you can gaze on a truly magnificent sight.'

Again as if he needed any prompting, the prophesy was unfolding. All the morning of the second day he watched the signs having little doubt that elephants by their sheer weight could hardly disguise their bulk on the sand. Under the noon day sun the testament from his mentor unfolded, the manifestation of the elephant herd appeared, consolidated as one with their journey of purpose in locating food.

'There, Ian, is a sight; the true wild elephants of our desert race.' Ian was hard pressed not to be moved by the unfolding sensation of sheer weight and power. He attempted a mental count, difficult with the changing pace of the herd. Enclosed in the centre were the younger elements, that of future generations. Encircling were the females forming the main body of the muscular strength. In the lead position noticeable above all others towered the matriarch leader.

'Jho-in, back home we have a hack-eyed phrase all the vogue at present but I will use it. Does it get any better than this!'

By this stage the lead elephant was standing firmly between the responsibilities of the cloistered group and the interloper in the form of the pickup truck. 'There see, Ian, this is wild elephant, they are not, how can I say, pestered by tourists.'

Ian by this stage had switched off the vehicle's engine, it seemed a wise precaution. The stand-off by the herd's leader was further intensified by her guttural sounds as the dominant trunk was raised in a display of potential aggression. Just as quickly for whatever reason the herd started moving away oblivious of the uninvited invader determined in resuming their intended journey.

For Ian it was remaining a sight that would not easily be forgotten. 'Jho-in it's marvellous, you're right. That's nature in the true wild, as you say they're not subjected to camera lenses poked at them every day.'

Jho-in confirmed his reply in the person of a reassuring smile, whilst in complete contrast Santoo his second son was still remaining awestruck by what he was witnessing.

Soon the herd had moved from sight, their purposeful journey, although once interrupted, was set to continue. Jho-in indicated it was for them a seasonal movement to gain precious water from the sparse plant growth in the drying river courses. As Ian had grown to understand that wealth of water was the desert's very credential.

He had come to appreciate how the Herero would observe obscure and endless movements in the sands, reading past formations left by tracks which could equally be influenced by wind directions. The complexities of their homeland to an outsider would take a lifetime to assimilate.

Unbeknown to them one other was also engaged in tracking signs. A lonely camel upon which rode the 'old one' had trailed the pickup truck for two days. He still upheld the virtue to know what the desert held in store by all those that entered his realm. The Herero leader was considered as much his concern as any other, especially when he journeyed into the desert's remote interior.

Further behind these active parties and for reasons of covert exclusion another 4WD vehicle was making progress. That of Karl Botha. His feelings of justification were that the desert belonged to him. He had devoted a veritable habit of watching in a state of boredom as the slow vibration of his vehicle caused his lucky mascot to sway in a mesmerising action. He tapped the talisman of good luck believing although not admitting to its influential power…

The interlude with the desert elephants now seemed a long time back. Even the atmosphere inside the cab was far more relaxed to when they had first set off. Santoo under guidance from his father was at least attempting a course of everyday English. For Ian as a listener it was not without its humour.

The language lesson served as a sudden prompt, it came into his head quickly. Must make contact with Mitch, not that he would be able to endorse exactly where they were.

'It's never done this before.' Jho-in stared at Ian's satellite phone that he was holding but like the animal tracks to Ian it was a completely inert object. By now its owner had checked the obvious, it's fully charged, then the realisation came over him. I've been cut off by the company at their end, it's the only logical explanation. He was about to enlighten Jho-in with the circumstances when motivated by aggression he made a rapid response, lodging the phone back in the truck. Whilst facetiously thinking hell why do I need it? There's no pizza places out here to phone up and order...

The days were lost to him; perhaps he was starting to think like that of a Herero? Now the advancing landscape was subtly changing. He could begin to notice tall outcrops of rock formations for some reason best known to himself he began to believe they were approaching their intended destination. Aided with his new found confidence he was prepared to broach the question. 'Jho-in, is that our goal ahead?'

His reply had almost a hint of mischievous humour. 'Not your "football goals", Ian, by night fall you will enjoy making our camp in the sanctuary of Taroo, that is to be our destination.'

Whatever Jho-in was referring it appeased a feeling of relief for him, if this is our final destination then my worries with our fuel supply are resolved. It had been difficult to impress on Jho-in his concerns associated with the vehicle's precious diesel.

As they approached the towering outcrops they were met by a wonderful display of light patterns that polarised into the very structure of the cliffs. Forming an effect of no discernible defined structure to the cliff faces, strange, it showed an almost unreal trick of light. The more he stared at the representation of light patterns the more it became almost impossible to comprehend. He broke the silence in confines of the cab. 'Jho-in, that light ahead on those outcrops, don't believe I've seen anything like it, it doesn't look as if it's solid.'

His reply although slow in coming did eventually happen, Jho-in tapped his hand on to the vehicle's dash and then pointed. 'Ian what you see will be one of many sights to witness where we are travelling Perhaps even you will not be able to believe them all?'

He continued to give Ian only the vaguest of required directions. By now they were progressing in a steady pace towards the tall cliff outcrops, Ian was assuming they would be of sandstone, based on the ingrained wind erosion that was visible on the exposed surfaces.

One fact that was paramount which he had now become aware, that of the sheer distances that the desert portrayed. Speculating it was a direct result of nothing for comparison that you could therefore relate to size, confirmed as the outcrop was both larger and higher than he had first imagined.

Jho-in indicated another direction for them to take contrary to that of Ian's angled approach. At this stage he almost resisted his instructions. 'But why are we driving straight at a cliff wall?'

He laughed before his reply. 'Another of your English expressions I might venture using. "Oh ye of little faith", Drive on, young Ian, and you will see why.'

He had no doubt the leader of the Herero was his guiding force, however the surprise that transpired on getting nearer to the outcrop was dramatic. 'Ian you need to turn our transport towards that direction.' He did as instructed but he was not prepared for what his eyes revealed.

'It's a cave, Jho-in. A cave but you've no idea it's there, it emerges only when the light's at certain angles.'

He looked at Jho-in expecting confirmation that it actually existed, but was marginally disappointed. 'No it's more than that, it is the only entrance into what we know as Taroo.'

Unbelievable, Ian thought, no landmarks to work with, how would you ever find it again? 'Jho-in, it's uncanny, like a trick of the light, it answers all the points of a classical optical illusion.' It was leaving him so intent, drawn by the shapes of dancing shadows overplayed with light merging into the very fabric of the rock face. He was left reasoning unless you knew of its existence you would never find it.

'Ian you will have the honour of the first to drive a vehicle in recent times through to reach the sanctuary of the Herero.'

It seemed strange to him as the pickup truck passed the threshold with its acute angled light appearing to fold over on itself, akin to that of an expansive envelope that was closing purposefully behind them. Weird, strangely uncanny but for all that a refreshing occurancet.

'Jho-in, there's one question, have we enough width to get through?'

It was a wasted question. On the point of closing the truck's driving mirrors in he saw clearly that the entrance was increasing in width. He began to lose his fear of self-imposed claustrophobia. They progressed into what was a magnificent and vast hidden valley. 'There, Ian, you have your answer. This is the land of Taroo which for my people serves as our historical shrine.'

Soon the sweeping S bend of the entrance gave way to open sand, instantly there was as sense of quiescence together a natural dormancy laying ahead. At this stage Jho-in seemed more intent to guide Ian's progress as if the confines of the valley they had entered needed far more attention.

He could not lose his continued fascination by how the entrance had virtually swallowed the vehicle into its own singular domain, but how was it ever discovered? This was probably their last outpost when the German persecution had taken place. I need to ask Jho-in, at the moment it did not seen pertinent, it would have to wait.

Jho-in's earlier comment was correct. This was the first time in recent years that any tracked vehicle had driven into the valley of sand. The leader of the Herero people had traded the insignificant tracks of camels, their usual means of transport, to the impressions compounded by the tyres of a vehicle, proving to be a fatal mistake?

That night the camp was one of celebration, more available scrub wood could be easily salvaged turning into a substantial cooking fire. For food they were treated from the contents of two skin bags which Jho-in had placed personally on to the truck.

They revealed a range of preserved meats which as Ian was not surprised when cooked they reached perfection.

Ian in the quiet of the evening took the opportunity of checking over the Nissan, including emptying the next spare container of diesel into the fuel tank. He was more relaxed now as there was sufficient for their return journey. He marvelled at the fact that throughout the desert trek they had not become a victim of soft sand. Although they carried a pair of convoluted vehicle tracks, courtesy he imagined of some obscure army transport, thus far they had not seen service.

Having completed his checks he was more at ease. Regarding the actual servicing quality of the truck, that remained as a definitely keep your fingers crossed, he would be pushing his luck as to any rescue helicopter flying out here. He knew there was more in store, as Jho-in was intent in holding back, but he was prepared to wait in eager anticipation to what the following day held in store.

At the moment he had aspired to a realm of both teacher and entertainer as apart from the English language that Santoo was absorbing like that of a dried sponge, there was also an excitement from Ian's shiny copper coin. Since its extraction from Homemead and subsequent cleaning, the coin had resided in one of his trousers' cargo pockets. Now he was having to perform and showing Santoo the art of spinning a coin, resulting in the words heads or tails ringing in his ears. Now Ian had at least changed the calls to the Herero dialect, either way his pupil's enthusiasm had far from waned.

As time progressed they had moved on to the next level, his pupil had learnt more than the rudimentary rules and not wanting to lose games between his teacher there had been a move to the best of three. Invariably it depended on how the coin performed for Santoo who had aspired an insatiable appetite to win.

With the conclusion of the meal the fire was built up with heavier wood. Santoo was allowed to sleep in the rear of the truck, it was easy to see how excited he was with his departure from the settlement routine, in fact the whole atmosphere surrounding the camp was comfortably relaxed.

It had led Jho-in to discuss much of his time spent in England, reflecting for Ian his associations with his university studies. Underlining all the events were his memories how unbeknown to him his father and Ian's aunt Anastasia had conspired to make it possible for him, the eldest son who would in time be called to take on the mantle of Herero leadership.

An ambient setting together with their heartfelt conversations had weakened Ian to lower his personal defence barrier in a way that surprised even himself. 'You know, Jho-in, at times like these they're more precious than I can ever explain.'

His host remained silent, he could see enough by the light of the fire, Ian was intent, staring in a purposeful meditation towards the arena of stars.

'There's messages on the company's phone that need my attention, Jho-in, but the motivation has left me. Anyway that appliance of the modern world has now gone dead on me.' He stood and added more of the scrub wood to the fire. Although there was not an immediate need he'd rather do something than point a finger of guilt to himself. 'Its discovery, Jho-in, all starting for me a few weeks back, of all things looking at some chickens scratching around in a farm yard, it's all about my past, time staying as a boy like your Santoo, years ago on a farm in Cambridgeshire owned as you might imagine by my Aunt Anastasia.'

Jho-in continued remaining in quiet council, in front of him was a man that was changing, although tomorrow he will learn even more.

That night for no apparent reason Ian struggled to find sleep, believing that he was too occupied by evasive thoughts that were demanding his attention. This wave of intrusion was, so he believed, a guided alliance, but in direct contrast he quickly dismissed this train of thought believing those things do not exist.

Although one thing he could localise, it had been hitting him for days, here in the remote desert with what the Herero leader was showing him was the best thing that had transpired for him in years.

He only had to look at himself. Any sunburn had naturalised into his skin, as with his full beard visitations to mirrors to observe his facial change had now become less frequent. He recalled that on leave from the rigs several years ago he had stayed on one of the Caribbean lesser known islands. The sands of Namibia were serving to remind him although they were completely diverse. One fact had stayed with him; those words from the people he had met out on the island, their brilliant words were so apt. Staying three weeks was a tourist on holiday okay, but to stay any longer and you will go 'native'.

The cold desert air caused him to weave deeper into the sleeping bag, but he still wanted to watch the array of stars and satellites on their nightly excursions. This truly awesome spectacle, a sight that he would never grow tired of, he was thinking of his eldest daughter and how she would be in awe of this breath taking panorama.

The fire was past its glory, without fuel it slipped into a state of hot glowing embers. On the other side of the canyon the desert elephants had ceased their wanderings, they grouped together in an effort to protect their calves. The quiet of the cold desert night air was emphasised by the bellowing calls from these primeval giants.

Ian slumbered deeply in the comfort of the quilted covers. He was sure that he heard the testimonial calls of elephants, although by now he was entrenched in a satisfying sleep that the remote hidden valley could offer...

Out in the open desert barricaded by his tight pitched camp against the vehicle Karl Botha was content. He had spent the last hour of falling light in the process of zeroing the sights of his hunting rifle; it was as suspected near on perfect, reassuringly now confirmed by his action. Every stage was working to his satisfaction, pondering with amusement he remembered, 'slowly slowly catch a monkey'. The trail was easy to follow, not even the GPS had been employed, everything was going to unfold to provide, he reasoned, a final closure. If only father was with me, he would be so proud.

Chapter 24

Ian made a reliable assumption that the long awaited signs of dawn were finally filtering through the blankets draped over his sleeping bag. It was cold, deeply chilled. Perhaps this valley has its own climate? As he was considering his absurd theory he was interrupted by Jho-in's son offering him a precariously balanced bowl of steaming hot mealy porridge.

There was a struggle escaping the confinement of his sleeping bag and for some obscure reason he had Dickens' novel 'Oliver Twist' in his thoughts, but looking at the bowl's contents he would not even have the audacity to consider asking for more!

There existed a more relaxed atmosphere surrounding their campsite, the obvious reason was the fact they had reached Taroo, their intended destination. To what final purpose? That had Ian both prepared and waiting. There was no doubt in his mind that Jho-in had in store something of overall importance.

Despite the cold during the night that caused his lack of sleep, he was in a relaxed state of mind. Something was bubbling under although at this stage he could not even comprehend what it was? But his working environment of windswept decks of drilling rigs out in the North Sea, although he shuddered in his reasoning, it had now entered in a phase of being a lifetime away.

They were to continue their journey, although not of any great distance, all that was to transpire remained enclosed in the valley of Taroo. They mutually loaded the items back on to the truck, able to pack as to leave the tailgate area clear for a special privilege of allowing Santoo to ride there. Jho-in indicated they would cross the length of the enclosed valley towards the flat topped outcrops that appeared in the distance. Ian imagined that was the final leg of the journey.

As they resumed the sand itself had taken on a very different pattern from the open desert he had grown accustomed to driving through. Only certain areas were more consolidated than others, he wondered how often this obscurely hidden valley was ever in fact visited?

The shadows from the outcrops forming the valley's entrance in conjunction with an early start resulted in the sun's heat not reaching them by much later, so much so that Ian was experiencing an usual cold atmosphere even here in the Namibian desert.

The going for the truck was becoming difficult, but Jho-in had that quiet confident look that Ian accepted in a most reassuring way. There was an irritant, as the driver he constantly looked into his rear view mirror, his habit of a life time, as if anything would be following? He mused whilst watching the mirror's image of the vehicle's tracks leaving a reassuring signature as it trundled over the terrain that was by now deteriorating.

A self-imposed silence in the cab had resumed, Ian in his state of contentment decided to break it. 'What a team we are, Jho-in, look back at your son, he's in his element. I guess this is the lad's first visit to your valley?' Without any previous idea or warning, Jho-in grabbed the vehicle's steering wheel and pulled hard to his left. Ian, not expecting such evasive action, stupidly braked therefore stalling the engine.
  'Wrong way.'
  In the silence of the cab Ian stared in complete and utter surprise at his passenger... 'But surely that's our only direction?'
  'All is not what it appears, Ian, we go outside and let me show you.'
  The demonstration by Jho-in had been completed, causing Ian to stare in absolute disbelief. Jho-in had picked up one of the rocks that were strewn in a low dune, clearly indicating his intention he had thrown it out to land in the direction they were set to traverse. But now the rock, despite its reasonable size, was

no more, it had sunk to be totally engulfed into the sand with no sign of where it lay. 'Ian your truck by now would have gone, consumed forever by the sands of Taroo.'

Ian decided to lean against the vehicle's tailgate where all this time Santoo had watched intrigued by the disappearance of the rock thrown out by his father. Ian was not phased, this sight he realised was yet another of many incidents he would have to learn and try and understand within the valley's confines.

'Jho-in is this as far as we can go?' In making his profound statement he knew that he was staring in nervous anticipation at the wheels of the pickup.

His understandable concern was brought back to reality by that familiar embryonic laughter emitting from Jho-in. 'Have faith, young Ian… You need to know the way.'

It took Ian as much as the next hour before his natural confidence was starting to return, by then it was making at least a degree of sense. They followed undulating ridges along the valley floor, whilst Jho-in directed but never it appeared in a direct line, therefore the distant outcrops were taking longer than ever to reach.

As they drove, care was needed to avoid the perilous sand depressions that laid as inert traps for anything that was brave enough to venture into their domain. Ian scrutinised Jho-in as he was desperate to learn exactly what caused these zones of sand capable of consuming just about anything. Only after he raised the question of 'why' did he realise what an understatement he had caused.

Jho-in's description was precise. 'We have in the valley what you call puddings, if I remember correctly, that is how I need to describe what Taroo contains, like a thin caramel crust that for a moment supports you then collapses leaving you and your "camel" no escape.'

The Herero leader endorsed his statement by tapping the truck's dashboard. 'So, Jho-in, it's like I know as quicksand, water soluble sand, somehow it siphons upwards. But out here, putting it simply, it's acting the same, but of a fabric that is totally dry?'

Instantly he thought there has to be a paradox, it's almost a repeat, a biblical follow on, his ecclesiastical knowledge was not his best subject but he imagined the Kaiser's troops following the Herero into the sanctuary of Taroo. It's a Moses and the Red Sea remake. Let the Herero through and then swallow up their enemies, victims engulfed by sand, poetic justice, perfect. Somehow I need to ask Jho-in what happened back then and maybe quench my insatiable curiosity, who knows?

Ian had noticed by this stage how cautious and for that matter how painfully slowly he was driving. His severe grip on the steering wheel was soaked in sweat. Once more he delivered yet another leading question. 'But how do your people and those of past generations find their way through the valley and is it often visited?'

The answers to his enquiries were again preceded by laughter, however this time of a more restrained content. 'Knowledge, young Ian, that owes its survival from that of passing down to those that have entered Taroo before, see, Santoo riding high on the truck he must watch and then in time he will learn.'

'Jho-in I can see for myself how your predecessors the survivors from German persecution escaped, it's virtually impregnable, this is truly an ace in a rather large hole.'

It was Ian's turn to laugh, although as he was driving with restraint he hinged on a note of caution.

Their course continued rather intrepidly on an almost circular route although by slow progressive stages they were eventually reaching the distant outcrops. Ian was curious of the dry quicksands as he had decided to label them, anxious to learn how Jho-in's people had historically discovered the valley and to what purpose it served the Herero. Although he sensed at this moment his host was resistant to explain all of those details.

Why was there a purposeful direction towards this particular feature? It was certainly the largest monolithic structure the valley contained. He had established there was only one entrance and therefore he presumed that was also the exit? It had one familiar calling, once again reminding him of the term a 'box canyon'.

The terrain was changing, evident in that areas of rock were more prominent than sand. However what was becoming more interesting for him was that the facing sides of the tall outcrop, showed a variety of cave entrances. Jho-in directed the vehicle's progress to one particular entrance, certainly not the largest in size, in fact its darkened aperture had a rather insignificant look.

He could not help noticing that a solemn mood had ascended upon Jho-in; Ian's questions with the valley were going unanswered. Not that he was seriously avoiding the issues, but replies came back in the form of other obscure remarks.

Then there remained for him the overall mystery, what was in store, why had he been invited out to these remote regions? His only assumption was that the answers undoubtedly laid inside the caves they were about to investigate. Realising their immediate involvement he searched the gear on the truck knowing that Mitch had shipped out one item he imagined would be useful, a flashlight.

The passage leading into the cave that Jho-in was so intent for them to enter required a truly petulant approach causing Ian to kneel to gain entry wondering if this was set to be a pot-holing experience? However his intrigue was completely reversed as after a relatively short distance the cave opened to resemble a cavern, where a sense of coolness prevailed in the subtle half light. But Jho-in? He was now in a state of complete silence.

Ian's eyes slowly grew accustomed to the gloom. As he acclimatised he became aware of intruding shafts of projecting light, although what he perceived was comforting he could not escape a sense of apprehension caused by overall gloom of the interior. The internal rock faces were noticeably dry, creating a sense of preservation drawing you in a sense of seemingly drifting back in time.

It was then that he noticed what could be described as steps that had been hewn out of the rock face. He wanted to dismiss this as light playing on the rock strata, but not so, confirmed as now Jho-in was intent in climbing them to what looked like a form of an upper gallery.

For a reason that could hold no logic for him he thought of the pickup truck, he had not withdrawn the ignition key... Stupid, that habit of a lifetime what a ridiculous idea, who the hell would possibly be out here?

Without invitation he followed both Jho-in and Santoo as they negotiated the steps, believing this would possibly be a haven for bats. Whatever the contents that were to be disclosed to him they must be laying in the higher gallery.

The open desert was certainly silent, but inside here you were pained by the sheer ear pressing void of silence, what they would give for this out on the rigs. It was at this juncture that he sensed that Jho-in was waiting for him where the steps joined on to a broad ledge. Ian suddenly thought... Cathedral that's it, you feel you are in a darkened cathedral's interior, he was unable to elaborate his thoughts any further as in a whispered tone Jho-in broke his self-imposed silence.

'Ian you are in the burial place of our leaders, as wandering nomads this becomes where we finally rest.' Now it was apparent to him why the quiet and solemn tone had overcome Jho-in. It made him feel guilty with his over enthusiastic jabbering on his part with probing questions.

They had now reached a form of a gallery. The vestiges of available light were nothing but pitiful, Ian unaware of what was there made a gesture in total respect to Jho-in indicating in a request to use the flashlight he was carrying. As the torch beam illuminated the interior he could discern what he had been trying to look at, a vast open arcade which was supplemented with all number of separate catacombs perhaps best described as resembling portals of time. Overall the redeeming feature even by his torchlight was one of a distinct look of great age.

Noticeable was a state of preservation. He rightly assessed the dry air combined with a consistent temperature, creating a perfect ambient formula. As he lowered the torch he became aware of Jho-in's words as why? Individually laid out within separate chambers were what in Western eyes would be described as coffins.

Crude though by construction they had been shaped he suspected by the Herero, all had lovingly been toiled to achieve a clearly defined statement as to honour their past leaders.

He imagined by what he could now see that the caskets were relics that as he realised extended way back in time. Certain ones even in this sympathetic environment over decades had suffered depredations, exposing the interiors where the last vestiges of remains from past souls rested. At first sight to him almost of a macabre nature, but the sanctuary with its unique atmosphere could not fail to move the onlooker by an intuitive sense of peace.

Ian cultivated the whispering tone inherent with Jho-in, he made an enquiry as to the history and use of the caves, he was engrossed with his enquiring curiosity. It was for him a certainty that few people including possibly the Herero tribespeople had visited this desert sanctuary. The explanation was equally revealing, he was to learn that the caves had generations of use, as a wandering people they needed a form of permanence to consolidate as a place of entombment for their honoured leaders.

Time had come for Ian having recognised the privilege by his visitation bestowed on him worthy to be described as the most holy of places. 'Jho-in, this is one of those times when words begin to fail you. I know that probably no Westerners have ever frequented these caves, for me to say a thanks would not do justice.' One of those protracted silences from Jho-in was to follow. Despite the cool confines of the cave he began feeling the effect of perspiration inherently clammy against his shirt. Adding to this the batteries in the torch were fast approaching a state of diminishing power.

He returned to normality when Jho-in placed his hand firmly on his shoulder. 'Ian, remember that life has certain paths that we all must travel.' Santoo was looking up at Ian. The torchlight, although failing, was able to catch the highlights in his all seeking eyes, if the young Herero could have spoken English then he would probably have added further to his father's so very apt words.

Ian had acclimatised to the interior's gloom, making it possible to see more of the extent with the roof area, it loomed rather surprisingly into that of a cavernous void leaving him puzzled as why so large given the relatively small entrance they had crawled through to reach the interior.

Becoming less awestruck by the unfolding sights Ian was at ease to discuss what was constantly intriguing him. 'Jho-in how could such a place remain thankfully unknown which as I can see it clearly has?'

The torch by this stage had given up completely allowing near total darkness to resume. 'The valley of Taroo is its own keeper, Ian, as our German oppressors found to their cost all those years ago.' As he listened to what was said he was irritatingly tapping his beleaguered torch, trying by his efforts to restore it. Much to his surprise he succeeded.

'Ian please follow, you will see the place where my father is at rest.'

The upper region was that of a natural corridor where there existed further individual cells, whether these were developed by the hand of man it was difficult to discern. Together with Santoo he patiently continued to follow Jho-in. They entered one of the larger cavities where, supported on a dais of rocks was situated an ornately embellished casket, undoubtedly that of the previous ruler of the Herero, Jho-in's father.

Ian noticed draped on top of the casket was what he would describe as a hunting bow, the like of which he had seen with his time amongst the Herero. In addition were two arrows laid against the bow string for whatever reason.

Curiosity, as always, got the better of him. 'Why this bow with two arrows, Jho-in?'

In a flickering light the answer was forthcoming. 'It's, as you would say, a link from his world that he left. One arrow for that of danger that is ahead, the other for those that dare to follow him. I can add no more.'

Ian understood what it must mean for these nomadic people. With their leaders at a conclusion of their life they have a right to be consolidated together by interments within these clandestine chambers. There was an enormous show of respect to those that had led them through all of the vagaries that life in the desert regions could direct.

Now he realised this was the object with Jho-in's journey. For an outsider to see and understand the established rights of Herero leadership. It was leaving him struggling with the magnitude of profound thanks he would need to humbly offer.

However at this stage it was prudent to politely leave Jho-in and Santoo with their own thoughts connected with that of a great and respected ruler. Moving quietly away he saw more elongated corridors that delved even deeper into the very infrastructure of the caves. For no particular purpose he allowed his finger tips to trace over the wall's surface wishing that he knew the very nature of the rock.

He waited for the two to rejoin him in the corridor area. Desperately he was searching for the appropriate words for Jho-in as more than ever he realised the privilege bestowed on him, as allowing a Westerner to visit their revered sanctuary.

Words were not needed as on emerging Jho-in indicated for Ian to follow him, even further. Noticeable was that the passage way was becoming more restrictive, amongst the two men a silence was again prevailing.

Jho-in stopped and side stepped into another cavity. Within the walls it gave an impression to be further into the rock structure. Not helped as Ian's torch was reduced to a state of fits and starts, leaving him wondering how they managed when modern lighting was not available. At this moment he was not concerned.

He sensed that Jho-in was searching on a ledge situated above their heads eventually producing the remains of a large wax candle which he handed to him. 'Your technical light needs replacing, young Ian.' He laughed, it was inducing a comfortable feeling surrounded as they were by such an religious aura. He fumbled for the fire lighter matches and following a dextrous manoeuvre.

Ian for some obscure reason logically believed this burial chamber was to be the resting place of the one who historically had saved the last of the Herero from the foreign oppressor. Surely this past leader by saving his people from extinction would be given the highest accolade.

As before it was evident that the casket was raised on elaborate supporting stones. The hot candle wax needed his attention before burning his hand. It was resolved as a convenient splinter of wood acted as a holder; now safely secured he became aware of what was in front of him.

The flame caused patterns of light to dance on the chamber's interior creating an effect of offering views in a series of protracted instalments, focusing again he confirmed he was right the first time.

On the casket's wooden cover was a long white scarf arranged in a shape of a chevron. Slowly a realisation took its hold over him, he shivered as he was under the influence of invading 'goose flesh' whilst becoming intensified by the effect of even further bouts of perspiration.

A surreal mental force came to mind, as if he needed a prompt, of course, it's all those life saving dreams I've experienced in the desert, that figure of an unknown woman walking across the sands that always was holding her long flowing white scarf. Only now did he appreciate an emitting sense of oncoming déjà vu.

Why… he turned to speak to Jho-in but together with his son they both had silently and unnoticed left the chamber. Only the candle's flame of light was remaining with him; more than ever he noticed the acute prevailing silence. It was time to approach the singular casket, noticeably cautious, aware that the shimmering flame could be easily extinguished.

There was carving on the casket's cover, basic in its concept although carving none the less; the symbols would be Herero which understandably he could not discern. He moved the candle light progressively across the other raised letters, he made out they started to form into a singular word, beginning with an A… Now he could finally believe what he was slowly reading… Anastasia…

A rivulet of hot candle wax splashed down creating a star pattern on the carved letters. His eyes were forming tears expressing feelings of long lost emotions. For a few precious moments he recalled those poignant words spoken to him by Miss Cleary. … 'Mr Harbinger you will have to follow your own yellow brick road.'

Chapter 25

The loss of heat as the sun set brought on for Ian an unnatural feeling of a severe feverish cold, although the fire was already lit and deliberately forging ahead. Desperately he needed its warmth, one of the blankets normally used over his sleeping bag was employed as a shawl that he had despondently draped over his head and shoulders. All that was missing was a dog on a piece of string and the inevitable tin then he would have completed a pitiful example of a Westernised beggar situated outside a convenient shopping mall.

Both Jho-in and Santoo were actively trawling for wood litter at the base of the outcrop, by their combined efforts they had salvaged a valuable supply of fuel for the oncoming night. Whilst in complete isolation Ian huddled virtually on top of the heat generated from the fire, wanting only his yearning for solitude.

Sitting even closer did not improve his predicament, he found himself in a state of shivering as if he had become an unwilling victim of a severe chill. But he knew that was not the cause, it was more involved, he was even speculating with his spiritual side which he would agree did not rank high on his expectations of life.

Why didn't Jho-in tell me, give me a clue at least? After all she was my aunt. Then his thoughts became latched on to his personal recriminations, his years when only the obligatory Christmas card was mailed to her. Deep down he knew he would have to live with this, as there were no entitlements for any forgiveness.

The young Ian that all those years ago would run freely through the fields of a beloved Homemead, having his designated bedroom, complete with its secret hiding place by the chimney. He visualised the framed embroidery work on the wall, mentally retracing the words of Edward Lear's iconic nursery rhyme. That emotional lump that had recently formed within his throat was testament enough.

He needed answers. Why was his aunt interred in such a hallowed place, a revered location that was the province of the leaders of the Herero? What had happened to her in her latter years, was she with the Herero until her death? Why was Jho-in circumspect in a way to avoid explanations, or was it that the painful truth was laying with me?

He looked up to see the return of his two companions, their long flowing apparel for no reason made him reflect to think of his favourite and beloved festive song, the gathering of that winter fuel belonging to the annals of 'Good King Wenceslas'.

As Jho-in approached the camp he anticipated the feelings that Ian must be battling with, as he would have had no idea what awaited him within their burial cave. As the leader of his people he alone had the responsibility to offer what this man needed in the way of explanations.

On reaching the fire he added more fuel. Not that it was needed but he could clearly see the state that Ian was in and consistent heat would serve to soothe his current predicament. His action together with the fuel's dry state caused a blaze that you might argue was equivalent to a fire breathing dragon in a celebration of a Chinese New Year.

Darkness had almost enveloped before the cooking procedures were complete. He still could not bring his attention span to the reality of the camp, he struggled to finish his meal, even that was in silence and that for him totally out of character. There remained only one solution which he had to accomplish, a final quest to virtually interrogate Jho-in. Needing on his part to be aware of all the answers; the Herero undoubtedly must have laid witness to my aunt's final days.

Santoo had finally succumbed to sleep. In the fashion befitting a doting father, Jho-in secured to his satisfaction the blanket covers around his son. When he returned closer to the fire, it was in danger of resembling a volcano. He was about to speak when his prepared intentions were all but intercepted by Ian.

'Jho-in, I'm feeling hopelessly out of character, so much has happened none of which I was expecting. I'm not ashamed admitting it's left me literally as a shaking wreck.'

Jho-in turned and faced Ian. 'You are troubled, Ian, typical of those of the Western world that have no beliefs to follow but here with my people I have seen you grow strong. More so you were entitled to visit the resting place of your aunt. See, Ian, how my English is improving with practice.'

He stared hard at Ian, his dark sculptured features appearing gaunt in the fierce fire light, after his usual pause to ponder he smiled and resumed. 'You are becoming someone of our desert, more than just your sunburn. Think, my friend, what you have done for my people. Water where we knew it rested but had not the means to welcome it. My father that lies within would have been gratified by what you achieved; he would have seen the person of your aunt within you.'

The fire crackled, an echo as if offering an audible confirmation of Jho-in's remarks. Ian wanted to reply but his feelings were tinged with sadness. Resting on his repository of guilt, finding the right words was a burden. By pausing it resulted in his lost chance as Jho-in resumed.

'You are, if I remember the right word, indoctrinated in a world of haste and putting things of your life into "boxes". Yes, I remember the word is compartments.'

Looking at Jho-in who had again resumed his smile, Ian virtually stabbed at an interruptive reply. 'Compartmentalised!'

Jho-in laughed, endorsing his action by simply adding, 'There, Ian, you even have the right word for it.'

After that acute response he finally rested close to the warmth of the fire. He looked up at the spectacle of the outstretching vista of the stars, then as a gesture symbolically raised his hands. 'There, Ian, that is our "box", we of the desert races are in only one, always it remains above our heads.'

Ian was unable to contain himself any longer, despite his throat stifled by an emotional intent making even talking difficult for him, but for all those tribulations his question was poised. 'Please tell me, I must know all about my aunt when she worked here amongst your people.'

'Let me start, Ian, at the end, when your aunt worked surveying vast tracts of our lands, we the Herero had more than a curiosity as why. Heritage as I suppose you would of your Western culture describe it as.

'My father even doubted that a woman could survive in our deserts, he was to be proved wrong. Your aunt eventually became one of our people, by what she did for the Herero allowed this woman on her untimely death to be laid at rest as you have now seen with those of our bygone leaders.'

Ian finally realised that his nervous bouts of shaking were slowly ceasing, there was an obscure notion that had existed within him for several hours although he could not understand what. The rocks and crevices were calling him, as if he should ingress into their cover of darkness? Adding to this predicament he started to become noticeably dominant and equally aggressive with his urges, but it seemed wholly unnatural.

Only Sarnesa would be able to solve his dilemma as she alone knew the 'scorpion' within would always remain as his 'inheritance', ingrained inside her patient's soul. It would always be that way for him, however as quickly as he had sensed the thoughts and urges it would weaken and expire, until the next occasion!

Almost as if he was speaking like an out of body experience he could hear after this strange interlude of events that of himself talking to Jho-in. 'Therefore I presume she was amongst your people on her untimely death?'

'Yes, Ian, your aunt wished to spend her remaining time working with people she had grown to genuinely love and respect. Her death was the result of your Western world, that of stress, when a growth of what you know as cancer had developed. By the time it was eventually diagnosed it was too late, even for your Western cures.'

Ian did not have to pursue his question, now it was becoming clearer to him what had sadly transpired in the latter and brave years of his aunt's life.

'My father believed it had stemmed from your aunt's second marriage, I now find it difficult to remember all the details. She had to take on the responsibility of what amounted with two step-sons, at their ages difficult for your aunt to handle. With her new South African husband they did spend time alone at your Homemead, away from the offspring they achieved I imagine a degree of peace?'

Their conversation flow became easier and more open. Ian surmised that the marriage had ended motivated by the extreme difficulties of her trying to encompass two step-sons.

Ian was to learn that they finally parted and what followed came as a total shock to his aunt, her husband was arrested with evidence of the illegal importation of armaments into Africa on a large scale. Culminating for him with a custodian sentence served at the Drakenstein Penitentiary where he eventually died.

Having become the recipient of the details from Jho-in he understandably wanted to add his comments. 'Nearly all of what you tell me is largely unknown, by that I mean the second marriage for my aunt and all the inherent difficulties. This individual she married would have what now is politely referred as his "dark side", no doubt she would have had no idea what laid in store.'

He stopped clearly seeing that Jho-in had failed to understand his modernistic phrase.

'Jho-in, it's a phrase, a generic term I guess, to show that a particular person has an obscure side to their character with possible evil intentions, hence the word dark, it's become commonly used.

Either way it would have done nothing for making the situation easier in what my aunt must have gone through, enough said.'

Jho-in started his reply before Ian had finished. 'By her trial of embitterment she renounced her worldly ways to spend the remaining time amongst the Herero achieving what she wanted before her untimely death.'

Ian knew that his reply was to be choked with emotion, therefore he remained silent as if that was all he was able to offer in the circumstances. His question was answered, however the feeling of knowing for his conscious was mixed in an anti-climax of regrets.

'Take heart. You have now discovered where your Aunt Anastasia wished to spend her final years, she would not have known of my father's intention for her to become interned within our sacred chambers. That knowledge you will carry with you for all your future years, be proud, young Ian, of what has now become entrusted in you.'

'Jho-in, I'm wholly lost for words.' He knew there was one final epitaph he must add. 'These two sons you mention, the fact they did become her step-sons, is there any knowledge of their present day contacts? It's a thought that maybe I need to be aware.'

'There are no answers that can be given. One went to England to live, the other perhaps remains in Africa, it is all lost in past years.'

Ian rested any further need of conversation. He understood why she had been honoured by Jho-in's people, it was having a direct result of making him feel humble. That was not enough, he needed to pay an even higher respect to the Herero, his thoughts were interrupted back to reality by laughter from Jho-in.

'Ian this is a time for you to be made aware of an account my father was always telling me. I will be careful to get all the details right. On your aunt's final return visit to England before she came back here to what she called her new family, my father asked her a favour. The Herero had in their possession our symbol of life; to you it would be an artefact, it went back in our history, it had always travelled in our company, but the elders had grown concerned with its security.

'They saw the world becoming that of a smaller place, they decided that it should be hidden in England, secure for all time.'

Ian raised his hand reminiscent of a schoolboy at his desk. 'What are you referring to, Jho-in, by an object that your people held so dearly?'

Jho-in was cautious he wanted to continue but in recent days had become conscious that what Ian's aunt had secreted away all those years ago had recently been 'moved', although of course there was entirely no evidence. 'The point I make, please excuse the length of my story, it was of no value, only to my people. Stretching into the annals of time, it was known by a name from our first spoken language.

'My father tried for ever to get your aunt to pronounce its name but he never succeeded, finally in desperation your aunt decided to give it her English name, then my father struggled to pronounce that, the two fought over the name like sand geckos, all in good humour. As the story goes they rowed in our language and your aunt in her perfect English, but their dispute remained, solved only by a truce.'

'Jho-in, it's a great account, I can really imagine my aunt locked in a verbal battle, but for me you missed the point. What is it precisely, and what is it called?'

He relaxed, visualising his aunt in full confrontation with all the Herero elders, wonderful in its concept, one woman amongst so many men!

At that moment the fire started aggressively crackling, the result of the weight of wood falling into its heart. What with this and his continuing laughter he almost failed to hear Jho-in's reply to his pertinent question.

'Why, Ian, that's easy, even for me after so many years to remember... Your aunt called it... *The Guardian*.'

He almost asked Jho-in to repeat himself, but no point as he knew his ears had not deceived him. His senses were no longer in the deserts of Namibia; he was standing on the landing at Homemead, his clothing suffering depredations of plaster dust. He was holding an object that was completely covered with neatly arranged layers of an old and yellowed British daily newspaper. The Guardian…

Now he knew the definitive answer, he visualised his aunt actively buying a copy of that particular paper with one sole intent, that of encasing the object that was entrusted in her care. The unpronounceable artefact which she had decided would be safe buried within the fabric of Homemead. He realised at this late stage his esoteric cavity located in the wall was a secret that had not belonged to him alone. A continued wave of sadness relating as it did to past memories was in a process of returning and as usual laying claim to him.

He was remaining silent, frowning as if not understanding what Jho-in had elaborated on, his affront and feeble acting unfortunately had not entirely convinced the Herero leader.

Tomorrow they would be leaving the valley, sitting round their next campsite out in the open desert in his best composed manner he would own up, come clean, admit that this cherished object was resting, so he hoped, on the glass topped table in his Devon apartment.

Then he cringed. What if his sister had visited and… No it did not bare thinking about, right at this moment he was craving for something not in his possession, that of a drink!

There appeared no other alternative than excuse himself. There was no need to consult his watch as he knew it was late. By his feelings bordering on the distraught he assumed that Jho-in would fully understand.

Enclosed within the sleeping bag he was amused thinking of his aunt and how she would have all along known of the secret cavity. That's adults for you, making him wish that he could return to those treasured times of his childhood.

He was recalling the skylark all those years ago that he had so patiently watched all morning waiting for the bird's return to its nest hidden amongst the grass in the old quarry. Anything else was irrelevant as he became lost in a distant haze that drew him to be succumbed into the virtues of a deep and fortifying sleep.

How long he slept he had no idea, perhaps it was the cold or so much buzzing through his mind. He woke reaching for the spare blankets. On this occasion they had no effect, it was colder than he had previously experienced, or was it him? He stared to the palette of stars eventually locating one of the circling satellites, focusing on it he believed it was the equivalent of counting sheep, maybe it might work?

The confinement of the sleeping bag was growing more irksome, the past events were strictly ruling his thoughts. Now they had progressed into the next stage of controlling his actions. Realising that dawn was still a way off he struggled from the sleeping bag throwing faith that wearing his clothing was a better proposition to gain warmth. His actions however had a more divine purpose, collecting the torch and a set of fresh batteries he made his way back inside the darkness of the burial cave.

This time there would not be the surprise or even shock as to what happened previously. After scrambling the crude hewn stairway to the upper corridor he entered and kneeled by his aunt's burial casket in awe of the carving the Herero had created on the woodwork. It was so meaningful to acknowledge how these people of the desert would always be indebted to her as an outsider and then all that they had bestowed on her.

He found himself mumbling an account of the hiding place at Homemead and now of course his unwitting recovery of the Herero's artefact. Worse still where it was currently residing, a piece of rock crystal staring into the views of the Devon coastline. By his aunt's steadfastness, if she was still with us, she would have undoubtedly thought, whatever can possibly come next?

His reflections had returned merging on his feelings of guilt, his lack of contact with her over those years, just those obligatory cards, it was leaving him with no opportunities to possibly redress, even at this late stage.

But not so, it was up to him to put things to rights, it needs to start and start immediately

It was then he could hear the approach of what he assumed to be Jho-in, or as an alternative one of the many ghosts the catacombs he imagined would possibly harbour?

A firm hand rested on his shoulder. 'Ian another day has dawned for us all, come, join us, breakfast will be ready.' Yes, he thought, the world of the living awaits, swapping his tediously cramped position he returned to daylight and their camp and more importantly breakfast, or as he always respected the day's most important meal.

Turning he looked back at the burial cave, he dwelt on all those implications that had now since yesterday unfolded. Physically he reminded himself of those lonely and empty windows at Homemead when he drove away on that particular morning.

That lump of emotion radiating so firmly in his throat. Would there ever come a time when it would finally leave him?

Chapter 26

Ian knew it was all of an hour since for no reason he had last spoken to his passengers, the return journey on leaving the valley of Taroo was easier inasmuch that it only needed following what remained of the vehicle's tracks from their previous entry. For some time Jho-in had struggled to fix the ailing sun visor, eventually his patience was rewarded and only then was he free with the opportunity to actually speak with the driver.

'Ian I realise your experience of our burial chambers was more than you could have ever anticipated...'

The remainder of his sentence was abruptly shortened by Ian's abrasive interjection. 'Jho-in why did you not tell me about my aunt's internment earlier, or give a clue where I was going?' Having said that he desperately wanted to bite his lip, retract his outward remark. How many times had he made such blunders directly at Jho-in? His foot without any reason squeezed on the brake pedal with that strange feeling associated with a vehicle braking on loose sand.

'Don't say anything, Jho-in, I know the answer, I've learnt more about myself these last weeks than the rest of my life put together.'

He looked awkwardly at Jho-in whose face beamed with that unmistakable smile. 'You, my friend, as I am saying, have become a man of our people.'

Ian placed his head on the top radius of the vehicle's steering wheel, he was not ashamed to show tears.

'Come we must continue. My eldest son would have returned and will be eager to meet with you. The last time he saw you was when you were deep in the sleep that can come with death.'

'You're right, Jho-in, this means I will be meeting the one that in time will be ruler of the Herero?'

Jho-in did not reply immediately. When he did, Ian could clearly feel the strength of commitment that was directed towards his eldest son who in time was destined to lead the Herero.

He could not shake off his habit of looking at the view from the interior mirror, it was cultivating thoughts of saying goodbye in veneration to the rock outcrop that was from his perspective gradually receding in size. Rather quirkily he thought of it as some huge ice-cube that's only destiny in its ephemeral life was to melt into eternity. It almost became logical for him to think that what had transpired back there was contained within a world of obscure fantasy.

Santoo, who up to now had remained patiently inactive, decided that he wanted to occupy his seat on the vehicle's tailgate, following a lesson of teasing from both his father and Ian they eventually stopped and allowed the request. Reminding him that the fare increased for outside passengers, which given his background made that further tease difficult for him to even comprehend.

The vehicle stop gave a chance to add more diesel from the reserve canisters. Much to Ian's relief there would be more than enough to cover their return journey. All morning he was preparing for the camp fire confessional with Jho-in; subject on his agenda the 'acquired' artefact. It had to be done, disciplining himself, it's what I've got to do, my only possible direction, total undiluted honesty.

Jho-in had wandered away from the truck, as he was suffering cramp by his unusual sitting position in the cab. From this distance he looked back to see his ever inquisitive son watching and assisting Ian. It drew memories from all those years back when his father had brought him for his first time to Taroo.

Then for no reason his eyes focused and notice something that was rather strangely out of place.

On his return to the truck he had decided to say nothing, it puzzled him more than it concerned him. What exactly were recent footprints in the sand by nailed boots doing out here? Nothing else, no tyre tracks other than those they had previously made, so this had been done by someone that had walked out here, but from where?

Ian was busying himself checking the water level of the radiator, still in awe by the venerable pickup truck's reliability, but these were not times or the places to have doubts with your means of transport.

For reasons best known to himself the conversation from Jho-in had now gravitated to that of constant enquiries, wanting to be brought up to date with issues of the Western world. Given the huge time gap since his last involvement this became what could only be described as a prodigious but hopefully worthwhile task.

Satisfied with the truck's considerations they had resumed their homeward journey. Progressing by the circuitous and clandestine route there was appearing what Ian could make out as to where they had originally entered the hidden valley. He remembered the restrictive entrance gorge which this time would lead them back out into the open desert.

'Jho-in look, that's odd one of those bleached trees down and right across our track?' They were still some way from the obstacle but Ian from habit stopped the truck. 'Thought these trees were primeval, unassailable by time, yet since we came through one's gone right over?'

It was not a worry, a rope connected to the vehicle and round the relic and bingo out of the way it comes. One thing he needed to remember! Not to drive away from the track, or the pickup could become a victim engulfed by the dry quick sands...

Karl Botha was never without his lacerating wit. It's going to be like shooting damn rats in a barrel, couldn't be easier. Harbinger first then the natives will be scared stiff, take dem one at a time, da all end up as bleached bones, to make da matter worse, hell I'm going to enjoy it.

Then for me I'll be getting that fortune out of dose caves. Father you were right all along, your words... It's out there in the desert. Now I know where. Yours truly Karl Botha is set to be one 'ell of a rich guy!

His ambush was poised with nothing short of military precision, having the advantage of a high viewpoint coupled with complete concealment. Your professional hit man would give his eye teeth for this theatre of operation. As for his vehicle it was secured away from sight, residing in an entirely natural made to measure cavity within the entrance cliffs.

His ploy was engineered by the master plan to jam the narrow entrance by pushing over one of the ancient trees. Congratulating himself by orchestrating the ambush whilst endorsing that the film plots of western movies had not yet died. For them to leave the valley the only way was to pull the tree aside, an easy task but one that needed them to stop and get out, therefore becoming his exposed targets.

Karl checked his rifle, loaded, ready, the follow on rounds laid loosely in the open ammunition carton at hand. He was meticulous, satisfied with the rifle's telescopic sight, knowing from past experiences its unassailable accuracy. He had nurtured the Mauser 98 Kurz rifle for years, one of the few things he supposed it was possible to relate with his brother Marcus, that of sheer obsession.

Not many of this kind around anymore, single load bolt action hunting model they made rifles in those days. It was one of the few things when it was all going wrong for him he managed to excrete from South Africa. His thoughts in a rather jaded tone dwelt back to his rapid departure, it was sending shivers down his spine, that was an unusual state for even him to admit.

Reaching into his jacket he extracted the ever reliable packet of cigars. Soon he was composed by what the intake of nicotine allowed. There was time to contemplate, in fact time was exactly the pre-curser to his plan. This was easy, always get your target in a relaxed frame of mind, let them stay in their comfort zone, it's a simple job then. After they shoved that damn tree out the way they'll sweat, least-ways Harbinger will, a pause for them to gain breath and drink, then it's time. My appointment with Harbinger to jump a bullet right on its intended mark.

He wanted to move from his concealed position; he needed to pee, but consoling himself it would have to wait, he laughed inwardly. Maybe I'll save it up and piss all over my dead targets!

It was then that he noticed something, it was moving out from the cover of dried vegetation. Karl was to be joined by a resident of the desert outcrops, it crawled slowly on its agile and sinuous legs. To him it was a lizard, what particular one caused him no concern, after all it belongs here. It did however make him cringe and think of snakes.

Below in the gorge he heard the ancient Nissan manoeuvre into a prime position which would allow the vehicle's tow line to haul out the tree. Karl had one singular thought to deliberate, soon it's my time, Harbinger. His lizard companion apparently had concluded its journey, content to scramble on to a flat surfaced rock allowing it to merge like a statue. Had Karl any knowledge of the rudiments of natural history then the answer would be clear, the lizard was taking in the sun's heat which would allow the cold blooded creature to become fully active. On this occasion its daily schedule was overshadowed to a large degree by the prevailing stretched out frame of Karl Botha...

Jho-in tried to reason what had happened, the tree had not fallen on its own volition they're too old for that, then those boot tracks, although an effort had been made by scraping the sand over to cover up, but by his tracking observation it failed to hide what had been recently disturbed. Something was not right.

He could not contain himself any more. Ian would have to be told, let him come back from undoing the vehicle's tow rope. Soon the valley's entrance would be visible and once through then the open desert would be a better refuge.

Whatever it was it weighed on his mind, unless over time my tracking skills have evaporated it's only one set of prints to be concerned with... But who and why?

Ian returned to the truck, the gathered tow rope over his shoulder, only then did he realise how wet with sweat the task had made him. The tailgate was open making it easy for him to reach the much needed water container. Santoo joined him and was speaking slowly. Ian was starting to pick up brief words from the Herero language, however on this occasion there could be no prizes for knowing the chief's son also wanted water.

Ian was feeling contented, his 'ostrich' attitude was declining more so as he was at last pulling his head out of the metaphorical sand. Those answers he had searched so hard for were finally resolved. He continued to seriously reflect on the honour the Herero had bestowed on his aunt, if only she was present to be a 'fly on the sand' in hearing my rehearsed confessional due to take place at tonight's campsite.

A sharp tug on one of his cargo pockets brought him back to reality. Santoo looked up into his eyes; Ian knew what was required. 'Young man, you'll end up a gambler.'

He extracted the precious copper coin. 'What's it to be this time, heads or tails?'

His recent labours had more than tuned up his strength he only realised this when he spun the coin. Santoo was shouting, 'Heads.' It spiralled higher than necessary, glinting in the sun, a complement to that certain fizzy drink that had cleaned off the coin's oxidisation, all that for him seemed a life time away...

Even Karl from his hidden post was privileged to the copper glint clearly visible through the rifle's scope.

Ian failed to catch it on its return, but he needed to grab it quickly, it was imperative that whatever the outcome Santoo would be an automatic winner. He bobbed down before the young lad could witness any result, this unwilling action from Ian 'erased' the cross sight of the rifle that had been clearly manifesting on the back of his sweat laden shirt.

There were no winners, as the coin had fallen to be partly buried on its edge.

Jho-in could not contain his concern any longer, as in the air he was able to detect what he knew as cigar smoke. 'Ian we are not alone, there's something...'

But Ian could not hear as still kneeling on the sand he became subject to an ear splitting sound... A tyre, a truck tyre has exploded... What the hell's happened?

He regained his full height, the chronic sound reverberating in his ears, the acute noise was continuing although now going into the heart of the canyon. Jho-in was looking at him but he appeared different, no contact from his eyes only a transfixed gaze that was accompanied by his voice spluttering... 'W-h-a-t-s... happ...in...'

Ian shouted at Jho-in, whose distraught sentence was never finished as he collapsed head down on the truck's tailgate, the assassin's bullet had found an 'alternative' victim...

'Hell missed you, Harbinger... You son ov a bitch.'

Karl remained in his prone position. His practised fingers had already drawn the rifle's bolt back, the spent case was out and quickly reloaded, it was the skill of a hunter whatever his quarry. He buried his frame into the sand to improve the rifle's stability. He had no cause for concern, it's an arse about face situation, the native guide is history, now it's Harbinger and he's nowhere to damn run!

Karl's next prospect was in shock realising the extreme gravity of the situation. He attempted to turn Jho-in's body that had slumped forward on to the tailgate. He struggled feeling the restrictions caused by acute haemorrhaging from the exit wound. He had witnessed horrific accidents on the rigs, but out here there was no question, Jho-in was dead. A victim of cold blooded murder!

His sombre task was complicated as Santoo, alarmed by his father's lack of response was tugging at Ian's legs.

Ian finally realised and understood what Jho-in had been trying to tell him, but too late, the rifle shot and now his mentor was dead.

Searing adrenaline was purging his whole system without even thinking he was risking to stare in the vague direction from where the shot had possibly originated.

Only then did he stupidly realise the danger of his actions.

'You idiot,' he screamed, 'it's the coin that saved me from the bullet, if I hadn't had to bend down and pick it up. No it doesn't bare thinking about…'

Karl steeled himself, his prowess with a rifle would take a lot of beating. What had transpired was not a catastrophe only a mere blip. Momentarily he noticed the lizard on that rock close to the end of the rifle's barrel. Creatures of the desert meant nothing to him; if it was not for his onerous task he would have levelled the barrel and wasted a bullet blowing the insurgent into the next world.

The Husab sand lizard was finally 'cooked', the warmth of the sun's rays had brought its inherent chilled blood up to working temperature. Small, only the width of the hand of his companion laying beside him the lizard's daily warming requirement followed a rigid routine. But today the limited resource of its brain carried a message of fear, the invasion of an unnatural and intensified noise caused by the firing of the rifle.

Karl's interest was now focused with the true meaning of the word, through the rifle's scope he could see the dead body being slid on to the rear of the truck. 'Take you now, you son of a bitch, Harbinger, the runt of the party it be a damn knife at my leisure.' He exhaled, pushed the rifle butt hard against his shoulder then forming his index finger confidently on the trigger, the scope's cross sight was now where it belonged, aligned on Harbinger, his original target.

Primeval anxiety buried in genes of the sand lizard could not be suppressed, it physically jumped with a purpose to gain sanctuary afforded by the nearby ground burrows. Mercurial with its intentions, and propelled by fast palmated feet moving only on the filamentous powdery surface sand. There existed no inclination for this desert inhabitant to vary its direction, it was its domain, for the lizard the alien rifle barrel close to the sand's surface was not in any way an impediment

The dark shadowy world of hidden burrows was its sanctuary, its legs were a blur disturbing the powdery sand causing a bellowing cloud in its terrified wake. Karl was blinkered to all this, involved training the scope on his target. Confident of his immediate outcome, although annoyed by beads of sweat rolling over his temples.

The optics' precise clarity of vision was suddenly obscured by thousands upon thousands of propelled grains of powdery sand. Out of his anticipated reflex action the trigger was squeezed. The lizard reached the sought after protection of the shadowy interior, by contrast Karl Botha's bullet had failed to zero in, his intended target had again escaped the assassin's intention.

The bullet's course hit the tailgate's top rail and ricocheted into oblivion. Reeling by the acute report of the rifle, Ian resembled a protective member of the feline race by grabbing Santoo by his neck and lunging the frightened youngster into the truck's front foot well. Ian's sickening realisation had been driven home… Hell it's a damn ambush!

He desperately tried to stay calm, the rifle's noise again ringing in his ears meant he did not need a reminder. Stop looking where the shot came, hell it's like a cat caught in the headlights. Overriding was his sheer panic. Out of here… Get the truck started, it's harder to hit a moving target…

His would be assassin was now standing swearing at infinity. He recognised what had caused the sand cloud across his line of vision, then he started to laugh. What the hell, Harbinger, you might have a charmed life but you're not going to get away from my next bullet.

At that point Ian had reversed and was viciously driving the pick-up truck, hell bent with his only possible solution by heading in the direction they had come…

Karl needed to reload, one well placed bullet will stop the escaping wreck. Bending down not bothering to pay attention to where the opened ammunition carton lay, he was not aware what a certain lizard's cloud had performed; that of a confetti of grainy sand over all his spare ammunition.

'Hell there's sand over da bullets.' Worse, as the ammunition's protective coating with the addition of abrasive sand were not the ideal of bed fellows. To reload even if he could, would be the ruination of his rifle.

He tried to relax, reminding himself that only cats are afforded nine lives. Harbinger, your chances are gone, you want a chase, well we can accommodate, and when it's finished, Mr Harbinger, you'll scream for mercy. At the moment my comfort comes first, he laughed watching as his urine was having a pronounced action of creaming a froth on the sand right by his studded boots…

Ian's eyes glanced at the rear view driving mirror, he stopped, leaving the engine running. The horrific predicament was becoming fully apparent, Jho-in dead and now they want to kill us. Then his brain wave, the service revolver from Mitch he knew where it was packed, but how quickly could he retrieve it?

He directed Santoo to remain tightly crouched within the foot well, Ian had no way to explain what he had to do. Get the gun, he found the bag and having the presence of mind he quickly slashed the retaining straps, that's it, the gun and ammo. 'Got you.'

He pushed the tailgate up in a slow action as if to show respect to Jho-in, making sure his body was secured in the truck's confines. Placing the gun inside his shirt he climbed back into the cab, that's when he noticed what was appearing on the horizon and needlessly driving right at them.

Instinctively he knew this was not a rescue party, it was the biggest of the 4WD brutes, totally masculine. With exception of travel dust it wore a colour mask of black. For no reason other than war-like aggression the pickup truck's lights were on full beam including the formidable array of spot lights on its top bar.

The darkened privacy glass of the vehicle's windows made it impossible to see how many were in the truck. All he did know was that this gross creation of the automotive industry was aligned in his direction.

It's a chase... I've no option... what the hell's going on, who are they?

Ian pushed the gear stick engaging first. It's no contest... I've no possible chance against that horrendous thing... We're on their menu!

Chapter 27

Karl Botha momentarily stopped driving allowing him time to light his much needed cigar, he knew despite all of the relapses trying to zap Harbinger he of the Botha clan was back on form, and it was going to be easy. That pathetic heap of rubbish that Harbinger is using as a truck was about to see the end of its days. For me this is to be refreshing, I'm like a well fed cat playing with a frightened mouse.

Whilst stopped, he cleaned the sand deposits from the spare bullets and together with his rifle they were laid securely on the rear seat. He affectionately tapped at the tribal mascot that as always swung in attendance on the bracket of the mirror. Taking a deep intake of cigar smoke he resumed the chase appreciating the broad over-sized tyres essential for desert driving, but more than all that his mind was set on continuing his sadistic quest...

Ian reasoned that his only chance was to reach the sanctuary of the burial caves. They're using rifles which should mean they can only be fired properly if they stop the vehicle? Inside those caves I'm in with a chance, they don't know the layout, maybe with this revolver I could hold my own, but the anxiety of his thoughts was making him sick with fright... What's gone wrong, and who the hell are they?

His recent tyre tracks from the direction of the caves had remained visible, so vital for him as given the fact that he was in the area of precarious and unstable sand. He was aware of those dangers even as far as sensing Jho-in's words of warning, although struggling to try and remain calm, but for him it was verging on the impossible.

Nothing could help him, he was alone save a frightened youngster, and pursued by madness personified. The outcrop. Whatever else, I've got to reach those caves, now he was finding himself calling out in desperation... 'Come on, Aunt, you've got to help me... If only.'

His eyes became dazzled by the full battery of lights washing out the view on his driving mirror. His pursuer had continued and was now unmercifully tail-gating the Nissan. Ian slewed the mirror aside, as if by that action his troubles could be evaporated. Hell I'll never reach those caves, e thought, fully expecting at any moment to be rammed by the viciously encroaching vehicle...

Karl Botha had no such intention; his truck was far too well cherished, particularly as he had the presence to work out a solution. Painfully simple, high ground, gain the high ground, he saw up ahead the valley floor was showing a gradient. I'll detour and get ahead of this junk heap, once up and above then decent shooting by yours truly will end this damn saga. Result will be a certain 'late' Mr Harbinger.

I need that idiot out of my life now... Then the wealth that's in this valley is mine. Father, you were so right all along!

What had entered Karl's thoughts was his fixation in recalling the history of the American west. Proclaiming his wisdom he shouted above the noise of the vehicle. 'If General Custer had gained de high ground then he wouldn't have lost the damn battle at Little Bighorn. See, George Armstrong Custer, this ees how it's done ah...'

Without so much as a thought he drove off well the 'trodden track' that was visible by previous patterns from tyres. Changing down a gear he took an angled route across virgin sand in an effort to climb higher and get above the Nissan truck. Taking a discourteous action he spat his cigar butt through the open window. Sheer exhilaration was now coursing through his veins fuelling his mind.

It caused him to drift into a mode that made him feel ecstatic, Harbinger this is your modern day fight of the gladiators and our arena is right here in this damn canyon, feel proud, my friend, how you're allowed to be killed.

He had already calculated his next move, planned to take effect on reaching the elevated ridge… Stop truck at right line of sight, rifle out, climb on the cab's roof, load up, then perfection shooting… Blow away the fuel tank on Harbinger's damn pickup and put a finish to this story once and for all.

Traversing the rougher terrain caused his lucky attendant to bounce crazily in front of his eyes. Even to the point of annoying him. 'Damn stupid charm, Harbinger needs this luck, certainly in his next few minutes…'

Ian instantly sensed a change, then it came to him unexpectedly, his pursuer had suddenly changed course, and shortly that 'black beast' would be looking down on the Nissan. His furtive plan of reaching the Herero caves was rapidly failing, that option, and his only possible means for eluding them was gone, leaving him nowhere to run…

Whilst by contrast Karl Botha was so elated he had broken into song. 'Botha is top dog, he's gonna be rich… damned rich.' Suddenly there was a different motion with his truck, his foot was down on the accelerator the engine was revving, but nothing was happening. The truck was stationary. 'What da hell, tyre gone, hold up, not with dees brutes on board?'

'Damn I've hit a pocket of sand… Devil take you, Harbinger, you've a charmed life…Don't tell me it's a deeg out job?' He knew the excess weight his vehicle had on board, spare fuel, water, and a supply of petrol intent as he was to burn any evidence from this expedition. What struck him next brought him to the brink of sheer and undiluted panic.

'Hell we're damn sinking…' Karl Botha had no idea where he had ventured, an area of the valley's terrain waiting to claim any unwilling victim that trespassed on to its intangible surface.

At first it was gradual, hardly noticeable, but by the weight from the bulk of the truck the process was subtly increasing. 'It's like quicksand, damn quicksand, 'ees not possible?' He needed to vacate the cab and fast, it was then he realised the shock; he was trapped inside, despite using his ape like strength against the door, it wouldn't budge!

'Hell, Harbinger, you cost me dis truck.' Having blurted out his hate he grabbed the rifle. By now with the truck's acute leaning angle he was looking at the sky. There's only one solution, as the side windows were too small it's out through the damn wind shield. Despite his brutish efforts with the butt of his rifle it was his fifth attempt before eventually smashing the glass allowing his liberty.

Easing his way through the remaining broken glass he became entangled by his lucky charm, he ripped off the effigy before been able to finally deposit his bulk on the vehicle's bonnet that still remained above the sand. His heart rate was racing in cold realisation that he could have suffocated inside the vehicle's cab.

He froze in a rigid state although the sinking of the truck had appeared to stop, but still at the precarious angle. He consoled himself taking solace that he still retained his rifle, fumbling in his jacket pockets, he tried locate what he desperately needed, bullets. Then he abruptly remembered the ammunition was inside the truck where he dare not risk returning… No bullets, but wait only I know that…

Ian had stopped, he had watched the event, as without mercy the sands of Taroo were displaying an insatiable appetite for consuming the vehicle. Endorsing for Ian what the Herero people always knew laid within this remote valley that forever protected their heritage…

Long before they discovered and ventured to explore what they were to call Taroo, the canyon-formed valley throughout its primeval history had witnessed sandstorms severely funnelled into its restricted void, combined with their frequency had formed areas of huge craters that eventually over aeons of time became hosts for wind-blown sand. Resulting for the vast spreading depressions to accrue huge deposits of loose sand, which in itself had never became redundant in claiming any form of weight that ventured on to its vulnerable and equally fragile covering.

Not since the colonial rulers from Germany generations ago had pursued the Herero into the valley had any vehicles of recent times encountered the sinister secret of the valley of Taroo.

Ian through the binoculars had his view confirmed, there was his adversary and for the first time he was aware it was only one person that was forced to claim refuge on the truck's bonnet. Leaving him a pertinent question, was this precarious foothold by the vehicle doomed by its sheer weight to continue and to become completely engulfed?

Again he could feel the presence of his dead friend whose words of warning he had proclaimed on the danger of the sands of Taroo. It left him appalled and grieving with the fact of the cold blooded murder of Jho-in, and out on the sand was the stranded perpetrator. Whoever he is deserves only the very extreme of poetic justice…

Karl Botha could not believe the extent of what had happened, but he was already in a process of quick, very quick thinking. He could see that Harbinger had stopped and was resolutely focused on his life threatening predicament. He would drive back here, curiosity, sure guess on that, then it's going to take one hell of a bluff on my part, but there's no other way out.

By this stage he had the presence of mind to take his rifle and cautiously probe the surrounding sand; he could not believe the outcome. Hell it's the damn same whichever way. I've no way to get my arse off here, leaving him with the acute realisation he was marooned on the cab's bonnet that was by now becoming uncomfortably hot…

Ian was attempting to wrestle with his own consciousness. Over the years he had witnessed horrifying accidents out on the rigs, where men's lives were taken away in an instant. The contrast here was only he alone had knowledge of these 'dry' quick sands, assuming that if his enemy attempted to leave his precarious safety of what remained of his truck, then he wouldn't be able stand a cat in hell chance.

Surveying through his binoculars it was hard to discern any features of this individual as the shadow from his peaked cap obscured his face. It left him no choice, otherwise he would live with another chapter of guilt forever. Reversing the truck around aware of the surrounding terrain, he then cautiously drove to where his would be pursuer was residing…

Karl Botha saw the truck returning, he was rapidly rehearsing a tactful plan that just had to work. Furthermore at this stage and needing to add deception he had hidden his rifle, sick with the fact that it was useless without its precious ammunition…

Ian drew as close as he dared remembering there could be firearms. He double checked that his own hand gun was securely placed in his belt, not entirely unfamiliar with guns realising he possibly had an edge over his opponent with the current change of circumstances.

Now he was closer to what he had labelled as a hideous individual for whatever motivated his murderous actions. It was not that easy as he knew through that inner supposed voice of his compassion that he was not prepared to have a murderer's death soiling his hands.

At that precise moment he could see for the first time the features of the individual's face. Where in the Lord's name have I seen you before?

The 'coin' for his visual enquiry quickly dropped. That's it, back in Windhoek, my hotel, there's no mistaking that veritable ox of a man who elbowed my entrance in the restaurant. Ian levelled his binoculars again to confirm, no doubt, where else do you see such an abomination of a red beard? He scrutinised carefully; there was no sign of a rifle or hand guns.

He decided to get out of the pickup and gain protection of the vehicle's engine block between himself and his adversary. However what came next was a complete surprise for him, his name being called with complete familiarity.

'Ian... Mr Ian Harbinger, it's Karl Botha. We meet again. Sorry about your guide, damn accident... wouldn't have done that for the world, hold up, my friend, a leetle joke, went arse up, wanted da surprise for you ah.'

Ian took in what was said, at that point he even recalled, that's it, he's in the construction business. This guy, my adversary, what the hell is he after? Anyway at the moment he's stranded right on that tin bonnet, and certainly not going anywhere. What's more his life's in real danger, and the tables are in my favour for once.

He was not in any way motivated out of temper, but he wanted to express he was in control and therefore a new force to be reckoned. What was really directing his new train of thought he presumed was nothing more than his imagination as once again that inward feeling of an invasion of his body was apparent, but he mindfully pushed it aside as too much needed his forceful attention.

Firstly the service revolver was into prominent action, his aim was as cold as it was calculated. He fired a single round that found its mark on the edge of the cab's roof, close enough to leave an obvious message. Once the noise died he shouted a poignant statement at Botha who by the proximity of Ian's shooting was galling at the affront. 'There, Mr Botha, as you say life's full of those little surprises!'

The balance of the duelling power played out over the canyon's floor had more than found its equilibrium, as it was now 'clear advantage' Harbinger.

Ian opened the revolver to reload, removing the spent case he placed it on the Nissan's hood where it leisurely rolled away in a direction allowing it to fall on to the sand. Although no doubt only of a temporary nature a degree of calm was at least prevailing.

Santoo had joined Ian on the premise of safety to stay low and allow the bulk of the engine block to afford the highest degree of protection, although it still remained that there was no sign that Botha had any weapons…

Karl Botha was fumbling through the many pockets of his jacket attempting to locate his cigars, whilst resuming his stilted conversation with Ian who now had definitely gained the edge. 'Harbinger, listen don't act negative, bro. We damn well related. I've made a mistake ah, leetle joke misfired on me, hard luck on your damn guide. Hold up, my friend, he's not the only one left in Namibia, they're ten a…'

That was as far as Ian was prepared to listen. 'Botha that man you killed was a leader, the leader of the Herero. His people saved my life, now he's lying dead in the back of this truck, there's no answer, you've committed cold blooded murder.'

Ian was trying quickly to rationalise, with Botha marooned out on what was left of his truck, how would he be able to rustle up anyone to organise a rescue? I want that bastard back where he belongs in Windhoek on trial for murder!

But his thoughts were broken up by the response shouted back from the stranded Botha. 'Listen to me, bro, you've no idea what this is all about, man, we both damn millionaires. I can guess what you and dat sand spitting chief found out in dem caves, I've done you a big favour, him out da way there's no damn blabbering, we can share this, my friend ah, I've the gear to do any mining, you've got to listen, it's wealth and needs keeping low key, bro, and I mean low key…'

The seemingly everlasting shouting from Botha had finally ceased, leaving Ian to think what the deuce is he rambling on about this wealth in the caves, why did he pursue us out here? Whatever else he's committed murder, and that's the end of it…

Karl Botha's obtuse discourse had stopped for one singular reason, his luck had unexpectedly changed. In his search for cigars he had unearthed a salvation in the shape of one live bullet tucked in a jacket pocket, luckily left over when days earlier he had zeroed the sights on his rifle.

Now there was a challenge confronting him, without being noticed he needed to load his hidden rifle with the one remaining round. Slow and easy, its only the length of a damn cricket pitch to Harbinger, bide my time then I'm in with a chance, this bullet will do and then eez' blown away!

Ian was vulnerable by moving to face Botha in the front of his Nissan truck, but he was intent to examine the sand that bordered the track. Jho-in's words still rang in his ears, he remembered his demonstration of the rock thrown on to the sand.

It did not come as a surprise, as by way of confirmation Ian repeated what Jho-in had done, a convenient rock was thrown out as far as he was able to manage. Its weight held momentarily but as before once the surface crust weakened the rock was no more.

What's the alternative? He was not prepared to gamble his own life attempting a rescue of his stranded prisoner over such a perilous environment.

He tried putting it aside, but that inward bodily feeling had gained a hold on his actions leaving him believing it's a form of possession, a force from within? It always occurs in acting as a protective state of his surroundings, as a 'creature' in defence of its very world, isolated with a sense of rampant aggression. Then as quickly he knew the sensation would pass leaving him with its signature of chilled sweat…

Meanwhile Karl Botha knew that their conversation must at all costs be resumed, he needed to mask his actions as hidden in plain sight was his rifle which he needed to load. He turned away from Ian's view of him and drew the rifle's bolt back and loaded, easy. This achieved it required him to take the shot by jumping up and turning round, his one strong advantage the short distance to his target. But right now I need more patience.

'Listen, Ian, I'm gonna call you Ian, you've no idea bro where this could go. It's about wealth, don't you see? What the hell if a few locals get blown away ah, there's plenty more.' His satirical statement was ended on an almost hysterical note...

'Botha you're penned in right there, if you try and leave the truck the sand will claim you, swallow you up in a matter of minutes, believe me it will, and yours truly will not be your rescuer.'

'Ian, hold up, my friend, we've got off to a damn bad start, I'm the first to agree, what if that Aunt Anastasia was here?'

Ian was not expecting to hear that, before he could reply to Botha's out of context question, his opponent had continued, this time in a more subdued tone.

'Your aunt was also my step-mother... It's years back, but I've never forgot what she did for us all. I've a brother in England, Father of course is long dead, he was besotted with his wife Anastasia. They spent time together over in England, still remember, my friend, it was a farmstead, Homemead. There how else would I have remembered? So that's what I'm saying, bro, we're part of a family, give me a break ah. Get me off dis damn truck, time's valuable, bro, we're two rich men...'

To say he was taken aback by Botha's rhetoric was his understatement of the year. It had an effect on him to try and seek mental security of his boyhood times in the countryside of Cambridgeshire, temporarily taking himself away from all of this enforced danger.

In reality he was sick in the stomach with how the whole recent malfunction of his life had unfolded. It did however ring true with the two sons, and of course his aunt's second marriage. But for all that it made no difference, Botha had committed premeditated murder, and further with no sign of remorse he had been trying to kill Ian, as witness the pursuit in his truck. If that was not hideous enough, whatever was this obsession to kill for what he was forever hammering on about, untold wealth supposed to be laying inside the caves of the Herero?

He stared at the bulk of his enemy precariously balanced on the remainder of the truck, it made him shudder at the very thought of his aunt's involvement with this man's father. Justice is on your agenda, Botha, that's my purpose and nothing else, then cold reality came rushing back to him by Botha's next proclamation...

'Ian you not giving me any reply, you must believe me, bro, if your aunt was 'ere she show us da way. My younger brother is in England, damn useless, scared of his own shadow, we don't want him pissing with us out 'ere. Those tank tracks on your truck geet dem off, man, you can reach me, I know you can ah?'

For Karl Botha there could be no rehearsal for what was to be his next performance; his action needed to be instant. The grip he displayed with his rifle was struggling to suppress his inherent perspiration, he knew it solely hinged on a single bullet.

With Harbinger dead, the youngster would be screaming with fear, then I can crawl on my belly over this damn sand, ever if it takes me forever the rifle can be used as a paddle and I will reach safety. My truck's gone, but that rust bucket of Harbinger's will get me home, after what's about to happen to him, he won't be needing it...

Ian made a natural assumption that Botha's historical obsession with an unknown source of 'wealth' was a connection with his aunt's historical geological assignments for the mining federations. Perhaps those details of covert information had leaked by whatever means in the direction of her new husband? It was only conjecture on his part, but there had to be a reason? Was aunt's husband involved with a devious scheme with mineral discoveries in Namibia? But now like so many other things I'm up against they're are lost, all buried deep in history.

'Botha listen to me, my Aunt Anastasia is no longer with us, as for what you claim in valuable minerals I certainly have no knowledge. Show some bloody sense. If that was fact the mining speculators by now would have extracted anything of worth. You've got it wrong, you murdered for what you believed with this fixation of yours, and it will cost you.'

He waited for a reply, but in hindsight decided to add further, 'What you don't know is that Anastasia your step-mother lies interned in those caves you are so incensed about. They are the sacred burial chambers, the resting places of past leaders of the Herero.'

'Ian dat's all history ah, don't hide things from me, we gonna be partners, you found something hidden in Homemead, left there years ago by your aunt. Survey maps I guess for out 'ere with references to what she discovered. Hold up, my friend, why else deed you come out here, not for your damn health that's for sure…'

It was causing Ian to profoundly think, Homemead, was only a lump of rock crystal that belongs to a desert people, which this guy would not even be aware existed. So he's always believed there were other implications, and now he's coming to understand how wrong he was. Those tribal burial caves were his obsession; an Eldorado of riches, crazy idiot, and for all that Jho-in is dead…

Botha's shouting had resumed. 'Ian you gotta get out to me, bad cut in my leg, bro, caught it on damn glass getting through da windshield starting to bleed badly, it needs fixing real fast.'

Having shouted his needs he leaned over to his left, carefully knowing his life depended on his next phase of action, it was all down to jumping up slewing round and firing. Reassuringly he could clearly see that Harbinger's gun remained inside his belt.

But need to keep the talking going all nice and relaxed. 'Still bad, Ian, bleeding won't stop.' Satisfied by his convincing shamming he stressed his concern. 'Why you keep lying to me what dese caves have inside 'em? Heaven knows, man, there's enough out here for both of us…'

Ian was only half listening; he was making hand gestures to Santoo wanting the satellite phone from the pack, maybe it's come back on? He was marvelling at the youngster's composure given that he had only just witnessed his father's brutal murder.

Despite Karl Botha's ponderous size he was deft when needed and on this occasion he needed to be. He jumped frantically keeping his back to Ian obscuring the view of his rifle, his body crashed squarely on what remained of the cab's roof. Ian could not fail to see the sudden movement as he registered the rifle barrel swung in his direction, instantly he grabbed at his revolver but by this stage a valueless task.

The sudden heavy movement by Botha had tipped the balance relating to gravity, as on the truck's load platform were four large polythene containers full of water. On the first stage of the truck's sinking they had become wedged and unable to move. But his abrupt shift of weight released the containers and by their added impetus hitting the closed tailgate it allowed the continued descent of the truck.

Thus the 'scales of justice' against Botha declared that the volatile sands of Taroo were about to conclude its claim on its next victim.

Botha's horizon was no longer there. As the truck continued its methodical downward descent for no purpose other than a last desperate bid in his disorientated plight he pulled the rifle's trigger. The shot spiralled to nowhere leaving only its lingering resonance through the canyon. Still grasping his rifle he slid down from the metal refuge of the cab, there was no alternative. For a man of such outward tolerance he would have argued that his departure was nothing but emblematic.

In particular as to his relief what was under his feet remained stable. Beaten you, Harbinger, the sand's firm after all that, Botha's luck still holds. He lumbered hesitantly in Ian's direction, convinced there would be a way for him to gain the upper-hand. His lumbering stance allied by his weight was enough, the sands' outer mantle no longer had to bide its time.

For the murderer Karl Botha there was no escape, in moments his presence progressively disappeared into a vortex of sand. His repository for his anger was released by outright fear, like a hanged man's last cries on eventual suffocation. Even Ian could hear the screaming of his final words. Father... Father

It was more than Ian could take he quickly released one of the tank tracks from the vehicle's roof and grabbed the tow rope, it has to be done, it's a life. By his action the perforated track flopped down on to the sand, motivating his rescue attempt, then a sudden and vigorous pulling was noticeable on his trouser legs.

Santoo was the culprit by his action of aggressively pulling against Ian's would be efforts to resist. He was forced to stop with no other alternative than to stare at the action Santoo was making. He sensed that the young Herero was right, it was futile, idiotic to try, and now too late.

The sands of Taroo were answerable to no one, their victim had suffocated...

It had transpired all too quickly, he began to doubt what he had seen, even the act of Botha firing his rifle, was it really all imagination on my part?

Ian stood looking down on Santoo he appreciated what one so young had done, he was his heaven sent decision maker. He grabbed the youngster in a bear like hug hoping he would understand this strange Western custom.

An attempt at a rescue over the sands would have resulted undoubtedly in his death, it was over, leaving him nauseated but unable to show any remorse to the individual that was now consumed into the vortex of sand.

What did I ever let myself into? Again the reality that his saviour and loyal friend was laid out dead in the pickup truck by the hand of an assassin.

He wasted the drinking water soaking his hat to gain its cooling effect, he needed thinking time to resolve what had to be done. Staring hopefully at the satellite phone it appeared tattooed by no end of unanswered messages, but as for its usefulness it was as before disabled. Working out any possible salvation had landed squarely in his direction?

Staring across the expanse of the canyon he was finding the whole incident unbelievable, if he had not failed to catch the copper coin and then his following action to bend down to retrieve it he would be dead, obvious in his mind that he was the first choice by Botha. Now that assassin was suffocated and entombed with his pickup truck, there was a familiarity like that of a low-budget horror movie.

But from where Ian was sitting in his exhausted state it appeared all was not entirely concluded, as an item was remaining on the surface above where the vehicle and the driver was devoured. Whatever it was had no apparent size, almost insignificant, he had no idea until bringing into use the binoculars.

The eventual answer was bordering on the bizarre, its ritualistic origins must have saved it from burial? On the sand's surface it would remain until the next strong wind through the valley would claim its final dispersal. Even through the binoculars it was difficult to fully discern, although he reasoned it would serve as an iconic marker to Karl Botha. Of the object itself it must have hung from the interior mirror, nothing more than a faded effigy of a doll that Ian presumed served as Botha's 'lucky' talisman.

He returned to the truck, fully aware that the body of Jho-in must be securely covered with whatever material was available. His only appropriate course of action was to return to the caves. Once there he would be able to improvise a burial thereby securing the leader's body, later the Herero elders would travel to Taroo to perform the final rituals for their leader.

At this heightened stage he started to shake, at first he thought he was shivering with cold but given the heat of the day that was not the cause. It was venting a suppressed fear of how the Herero people would react to the news of Jho-in's murder? There was that 'word' again – murder. If I had not undertaken this whole involvement then all this would not have happened, hell this is my guilt that I have to live with forever.

The sands across the valley's expanse were shimmering with a phenomenon produced by heat haze. He reluctantly gained the shade afforded by the truck, by this stage even his teeth were subject to chattering. Perspiration had enveloped his whole body, he sipped water in an effort to allay his dilemma from dehydrating.

He stared through bleary eyes across the vast expanse knowing what comfort he wanted to see, but this time there were no white scarves as her appearance was not to be. He was overcome by a grasp of invasive tiredness and severe aching, with these conditions he became an easy participant for sleep.

Santoo watched over him, perhaps he would understand in time what course of their history on this day had occurred in the valley of Taroo.

He continued to remain vigilant, therefore his sharp eyes and senses were quick to notice a change of events.

Ian although in a fitful sleep knew something was happening. His arm was subject to vigorous shaking by Santoo, dragged out of his sleep he tried focusing between the shade and the sunlight. A long way off but outwardly visible was a vague shape on the track that led into the valley, whatever it was produced a slow lumbering motion as if only one speed was possible.

'Santoo what's happening?' As if he was able to understand his English. The binoculars were inside the truck out of his reach, but by now they were not necessary as he understood who was now gaining an appearance into the valley.

The spectacle he could see was formed as a silhouette against the light, it did not matter in the least as what epitomised was to become his immediate salvation. On the approach was a camel with its rider, as the beast of the desert drew nearer he was able to discern what he was praying to see. The camel was reined in and staring towards him from the ornate saddle was the 'Old One'…

Chapter 28

Ian was relieved to see that all the cushions occupying the sofa were as he had left them, meaning no visitations from his sister Julia had occurred throughout his enforced absence. In fact as often the way, the complete apartment was subjected to a time warp, you could experience faint spider's webs broken by your face as you went into the various rooms. At this precise time nothing mattered for him other than he was cloistered at home.

He stared in utter relief as the piece of rock crystal extracted months ago from Homemead was exactly the same as he had placed it on the glass table top. Although to be pedantic, maybe its surface had accrued a slight film of dust.

He could hardly contain a smile, reaching a point of laughing, imagining his aunt in her dictatorial way, how she would have told Jho-in's father of the artefact's new title that of her translation into English, and hence forth to be called the 'Guardian'. All that involvement by her was years ago, how arguably so precious, and for him certainly not to be swept under the 'carpet' of life.

Of contemporary times he had hatched a rather clever scheme during his flight back home. The crystal was going to transform itself, but only that of a small segment for a definite purpose needed for our 21st century...

He was feeling cold to the point of struggling to maintain a semblance of warmth. Although the imminent springtime with its early arrival was upon us, he concluded that he had returned to a bizarre comparison to that of watching the world through television that had gravitated back to those dreary images in black and white. That said it was at best a respite compared to what he needed to think about.

Having confirmed the room's radiator setting, he decided to add a fleece jerkin over his existing sweater, producing a virtual cocoon, allowing a degree of comfort from the ensuing cold. At this stage he remembered his ominous medicine, another dose of which would certainly help, although he was wondering if it was in anyway addictive?

The Herero ancient elixir once more had brought him back to some degree of reality following all the hideous incidents that had transpired for him in the valley of Taroo. Whatever it was had the desired effect, although heaven knows what the concoction consisted of, but it had managed to clear UK customs on the remit it was only herbal.

Today was going to be different; it will be a night of satisfying sleep. The route to his recovery was finally set to commence, or he would have to know the reason why.

But there was one serious aspect that as before needed his consideration, pondering on that very point he reluctantly glanced at the envelopes of his incoming mail, trying to visualise their contents. Life in the UK would quite simply never be the same following his extended time in Namibia, but the letters were his concern. Within the veritable pile were those appertaining to taxation, certainly no surprise there, they will have to wait. Then amongst the motley bundle was one envelope with a hand-written address that he could not fail to recognise.

Opening this particular letter he instantly reacted to its contents, an invitation which he correctly pre-empted was for his sister's forthcoming wedding, its immediate effect left him entirely with a feeling of isolation. The event was months away, but what riled him was the impact of the enclosed note, dictating that if you are back, do join us, and while I am thinking about it, brother Ian, please bring someone with you!

Well done, sister, cold and certainly straight to the point, not much empathy thrown in for luck. The silver embossed invitation was unceremoniously placed back in its envelope, in doing so he almost admired his deeply sun tanned hands enhanced against the white purity of the oversized envelope. It created a sense of sheer contempt, all his life he was witness to Julia and her motivation with selfishness, she ought to try living a couple of weeks in the wilds of Namibia. At this moment he had a cringing feeling firmly fixed in his mind, Julia dear, this is one potential guest right now you can scratch off your damn list!

They would never be any different to each other so what was any point of even trying. His thoughts had changed direction drifting back to Namibian deserts, there still remained too much for him to take in, why in heaven's name had it all occurred?

Once again he tried to reconcile those final events in the canyon of Taroo, he had witnessed far more than he was prepared to accept, was all of what he attempted to conciliate a direct result of his intervention with fate?

At this juncture his thoughts were invaded by the figure of the 'old one' as he had virtually morphed from the desert heat haze, taking on a role of a timeless figure resembling a lost crusader of old who was impartially observing the occurrences on that tragic day. What if young Santoo had not been in attendance, then how could he alone have possibly explained to the 'old one' the magnitude of events?

He continued to dwell on that return journey to the settlement. There were times when he struggled to actually recollect what life had thrown at him, culminating with the cold fact that Jho-in was dead and laid within the burial caves. Small wonder in view of what he had experienced his immediate concern was that of Santoo, as one so young had to witness his own father's vicious murder.

Although by contrast it paled into insignificance with the act of primeval justice handed out by that of sheer fate in the direction of the sadistic Karl Botha. Although he knew he was still trying to live with those graphic events of the vortex of sand and the horrific gurgling screams from his adversary, believing that it would always cause him visionary nightmares.

He, at his worst, had entered a realm of blaming himself, it would not leave him. If I had not gone to Namibia on what he now considered a fool's errand then all of what had happened would not be even a subject for discussion. I guess I should have returned to those rigs out on the North Sea and earned myself money. It was one of those occasions when all number of life's ramifications are thrown at us to settle, even more grief and we are left with no way to even comprehend an outcome.

However he was finally accepting the memories of the Herero funeral for their leader. Vaguely aware of the event and those rituals that had accompanied the clandestine event, as if he had attended a long lost primeval theatre which had left him pondering if the same platitudes of a departing life were observed when his Aunt Anastasia was finally interned within the burial caves.

Although when the elders had returned to perform the rituals of burial associated for Jho-in, he was there but patently not involved. On thinking back he realised that he had been under the influence of a potion administered by the Herero people in an effort to restore his well being.

Even now he continued in a vain response to have some form of recall, but strangely the Herero's new leader instantly was upholding his responsibilities following the tragic death of his father. Ian was repeating family history as he had fallen into the same state of his aunt unable to pronounce the denser side of the Herero language, leaving him to struggle to even pronounce the new leader's name.

For all that the honour in being allowed to accompany the elders of the Herero back into Taroo again for the enhanced burial rights of Jho-in their past leader. Although on that occasion he had forsaken motorised travel to join the elders on the camel train as in the tradition of these the people of the desert...

Ian had abruptly gained his focus and realised that he was still intent with fumbling unnecessarily with the envelope that symbolically contained his sister's invitation. In contempt he annoyingly flicked it aside directing his attention to the rock crystal, lifting it off the table and turning it several times as if it contained a sense of an obscure purpose.

The exposed facets virtually danced welcoming the intrusion of sunlight, by what he was seeking to use there was more than enough lucid crystals. On one edge they clung like icicles totally unblemished, whilst on the opposing side there was an impression as if the structure had been substantially fused by a form of heat.

They needed cutting out and he believed the term was lapping to fabricate into small separate pieces that could then be fixed through cords to create necklaces. With an eventual result to adorn the Herero elders. Only as a tongue in cheek thought he considered it a 'gem' of an idea, allowing small fragments of the 'Guardian' a new birth for our new century, an easy task he surmised for any reputable jeweller.

However more importantly this would give him the opportunity to return to Namibia and visit his respected people of the Herero.

He placed the crystal back on the table with its purpose as a coffee table ornament if only temporary. He smiled inwardly imaging his aunt all those years ago at Homemead prior to concealing the artefact how she must have intently wrapped the rock securely in that certain daily newspaper, proclaiming what she desired all along, the English role of a 'Guardian'.

There was a positive wave of unexpected feeling sweeping over him, his sanctuary of the apartment was in a process of play acting for him. Staring out from the lounge window he visualised the constant rise and fall of the tides, appreciating just how many times from this very window they would have occurred since his involvement in Namibia. He could not fail to notice it was giving him a personal and equally sensitive layer of contentment.

Would it last for long, as ahead lay a decision relating solely to one vital aspect of his working life, exactly what was going to happen next? He needed to make a decision as his employers wanted an answer to their enquiries and for that matter quickly which only he would be able to provide.

Despite his best intentions he was plainly realising with this inherent dilemma that his old habit was gaining a hold, continuing to bury his head in the sand of life.

Could he ever claw anything over to his side for defence? What had transpired over those intervening weeks in the Namibian desert, would he ever recall let alone recite those events no matter how diverse on his return to Windhoek. But he was able, although they consisted of protracted discussions running into the early hours with the ever stalwart Mitch. A man that by his dogged salvation was responsible in restoring a normality for him.

Ian was aware that he could seriously dwell on the fact that Mitch was the one that had salvaged his mental balance, given the conditions in the deserts he had endured. On reflection it was strange and out of place remembering it had all started on his search into the desert on that certain morning as he climbed behind the wheel of the pickup truck loaned to him by the ever resourceful Mitch.

Later on his return to Windhoek the same man together with his wife had endured his torment augmented with horrific dreams as he all but relived what had occurred in the desert canyon. Was there ever to be an escape from reliving the murder of Jho-in, and again that question, why did I venture there in the first place?

Did it help that justice by sheer irony of fate had been duly administered to Botha? But it made no difference to all the twists contained in his continuance of nightmares that always found him in a state of struggling to the point of suffocation in the engulfing sands of Taroo. Would his apartment, this veritable bolthole on the Devon coast be the salvation he desperately sought?

He drew comfort from the episodes of help and support that Mitch had offered, and this coming from a man that years previously faced death squarely in the face on the gas ignited platform of Piper Alpha. More than life's survivor, the man aspired to become head of a resourceful business group, ready on the ground for when Namibia eventually made the off-shore oil strikes.

Ian knew his thoughts were still out there, such was their enormous help they had extended, although as time went on he gradually began to feel claustrophobic, as they insisted with attending to his every need. Cleverly he had transferred on a pretence, getting himself into the town centre and within the confines of the New Commercial Hotel. Only to find a situation of out of the frying pan into the fire, as the Jan the owner attempted to offload his catalogue of stress by offering him her much beleaguered carnal support.

It became funnelled down with long nights in her company doing justice to bottles of red wine, whilst bizarrely between them yet another version of an obscure card game was in a state of play.

Their friendship gravitated by a natural impetus which culminated into a tottering relationship. Whether this was the constant overindulgence of alcohol he would never really know or even attempt to understand. Although in fairness he still could not forget the endless night excursions laying together on mounds of pillows allowing a state of mutual satisfaction, their only intruder that of Jan's ever present cigarette smoke, which predictably followed a path to disintegration from the oscillating blades of the ceiling fan.

Outside through the long nights, the street sounds of Windhoek continued with a relentless throb of life of a cosmopolitan African town, it was however quieter than oil rigs, but its purpose was more enveloping. That's when he finally came to his senses, believing he himself resembled a wayward plume of smoke from her cigarette, equally as vulnerable to the same fate that of oblivion, but not by the over active ceiling fan.

Ian Harbinger was in danger of undergoing a confinement, an appendage that belonged to Jan's business at her Commercial Hotel. They parted eventually on amicable terms; she was the one that controls her hotel, that was her idol in life readily absorbing her multitude of talents...

His doze had naturally expired, caused by the unprecedented intrusion of cool breezes, that the coastline of the south west uniquely offers. But like many things in life's pattern one set of problems could be exchanged for another, usually consisting of a higher magnitude. That was certainly the predicament as the global news was rearing its head again, the particular media coverage indicating an insidious horror of an oil disaster from the Gulf of Mexico. As pollution from an undersea burst of an untold volume was intent in heading straight towards the American coastline.

Why was all this happening? We are all becoming losers in our precious global structure, and the fault comes from one singular direction – that of human greed. Ian stood up to allow, so he hoped, to vent his feelings which he struggled to contain.

'Hell, not any more please, don't ask me to support this industry, I've finally had enough.'

There has to be an answer which only he had the power to execute. It was a bitter sweet word he was dwelling on: out, that has to be my answer. 'Out', get away, leave it to others. I'm resigning and it needs to be as painless as possible.

The sea gulls were squabbling along the guttering, one had scavenged a piece of bread, although short lived when his attendant gulls saw the bounty. Following raucous behaviour the pecking order was eventually restored, silence on the tiled roof was established, if only as a fragile peace.

Cool air through the open window refreshed his imagination, he needed the input given his payload of too many things on his mind, with the dire consequences in his overactive state preventing any worthwhile rest or sleep, nothing unusual there. Who knows maybe that insurmountable hurdle in his life would eventually end?

His natural curiosity prevailed as again he lifted the rock crystal from the table, looking more intently at its structure the shapes attempted to follow a pattern although it was in no way regimented. He was further intrigued by the portion that showed where the crystal had fused, which again made him think it was a direct result of severe heat.

Then he changed his thinking, pondering how long it had been encapsulated within the folds of that certain newspaper hidden away inside the walls of Homemead. My clever aunt had known about that 'hidey hole' all along. What a shame I'm lacking relations of that calibre any more, then I could discuss my life issues with them right now. An invading melancholy feeling was gaining a hold, high time to make a rapid change of thought. Come on, get myself organised.

At the very least he could attempt a course of action to resolve around moving, no longer his lethargic state he had drifted into. Opening the lounge window to its full extent allowed the sea breezes to infiltrate the apartment, but the gulls normally accustomed to privacy on the guttering by his sudden action flew off squawking their annoyance.

So what's to discuss? If I finally get off my backside and leave the company and he needed no reminding that was the master plan prior to his capital embezzlement. That resurfaced and he had no recourse other than grow bitter at thoughts of his business partner and the precious accountant holed up in some obscure tax haven no doubt?

What a severe contrast with what he had grown accustomed in those wild and remote tracts of Namibia, he found himself wondering as to what at the moment the Herero people would be involved in doing?

That train of thought returned to his idea with the crystal and the jewellery pieces he was determined to have fashioned from a small part of the rock. Rather stupidly he surmised that your average high street jeweller would be organised to perform what he needed.

However what was weighing on his mind concerned the issue that more and more was niggling away at him, his involuntary involvement with Karl Botha's death. True the Namibian authorities were prepared to accept a closure on the event, his time spent with the regional police in Windhoek had accepted his account, but he was anxious how in the future things could easily come back to haunt him.

Much as he respected the findings in Namibia he was determined that their embassy in London would be exposed to his personal account of Botha's accidental death, on one premise as somewhere in the UK there exists a brother to be contacted.

Then on a far more enlightening front closer to home he wanted to contact Fiona and not forgetting a promise to himself in visiting the incongruous Miss Cleary, almost relishing how he would be able to explain all the events that had unfolded since they had last spoken. That proposed meeting he would appreciate, reminding himself that the whole motivation was her inspiration that she directed straight at him all those months ago. Never forgetting her words to follow that certain brick road…

His plan was formulated, loose ends maybe, but it was at least up and running. Sadly there was no room left for his precious sister. It left him feeling sad, family blood is supposed to be thicker than water, how many times had he contemplated on that remark when trying to resolve yet another issue with Julia, it would never be laid at rest.

The remaining part of his day was disappointing as he tried unsuccessfully to reach Fiona on her mobile phone, not so much that but it was clearly not working or had it been changed? The only thing it acted as a reminder to himself he needed a replacement cell phone, heaven knows what happened to his last one?

If that annoyance was not enough there was an incoming call to the apartment phone on pure speculation from the company's Aberdeen offices. In curt terms he was summoned to attend a meeting. Instinctually he sensed that he would be heading into a black hole suitably primed with that of a hidden agenda, a content of this magnitude he had not unsurprisingly grown to expect.

Ian could almost calculate what that meeting would consist of, he likened it to that of 'a dusty road to his crucifixion'.

Things did not improve in his favour, as when he managed to go to town with what he thought would be an easy task for your high street jeweller they did not even bother to look. 'Nobody available to do those jobs, these days we only buy and sell.' Their only constructive note was a suggestion that the outlets of jewellers in Exeter may help?

Ian warded off any lack of enthusiasm by treating himself in visiting a restaurant and the luxury of an overpriced fillet steak, but where's the special person he wanted to share his meal with?

The diminutive restaurant looked over the modernistic shopping mall, where one of its stores caught his interest as its front window boasted a display of hats… Word association hit him, 'hat', yes that's the answer, the crystal can be cut. His optimism struck a definite high. I know exactly where, and I can be there tomorrow.

Chapter 29

Killing two birds with one stone was in his mind, and metaphorically speaking it was having an effect of improving Ian's morale for the day. Firstly his early start and the journey to London with his proposed visit to the Namibian's London based Embassy, which though he had enquired, it did not appear he needed to make an appointment. With the second 'stone' it should resolve his requirements in fabricating the cut pieces of rock crystal.

Emerging from London's Oxford Circus underground station he welcomed an intake of what he believed to be re-used fresh air, accompanied by a visual dose of weakly nourished sunshine. It was beginning to really hit him how claustrophobic the environs of a city are, then he rightly surmised the time he spent on the rigs out at sea, added to this were his recent protracted weeks in the remote regions of Namibia. Both of those diverse backgrounds had a well being that he was more than content to accept.

A tight formation of commuters assembled as a gregarious flock staring for the pedestrian crossing lights to act favourably on their behalf, ultimately allowing a safe passage across Mortimer Street. Ian made up the rear of the throng sensing a self-conscious portrayal for whatever reason.

Crowds of people were not really his thing, now it came across even more of an irksome task. Eventually, based on a premise that everything comes to he who waits, the green figure signalling pedestrian clearance morphed into life. He had a feeling of 'toothpaste' subjected to be squeezed from its tube and was jockeyed across the road with the rest.

He paused checking his bearings, from Langham Place it was easy to reach Chados Street and recognise the building that was his destination, Namibia's London Embassy. Further leaving him the task in locating the respective department able to deal with his enquiry.

In almost clinical surroundings his thoughts had abruptly returned to the desert valley with the stranded vehicle slowly sinking set on a purpose to avenge Karl Botha to a hideous fate. He nudged himself hard, there could be no sign of any retribution; that individual was a murderer in anyone's book.

'How may we help you, sir?' Ian snapped back to a world of well ordered administration, he was clutching his document case that at times grew heavy with the crystal that was due to be his next London involvement. In a robot like fashion he removed a file of loose papers that had originated weeks ago in the confines of the Windhoek police department.

He started noticing the power of the reception's central heating, far too hot for him, then he did understand that since his return from Africa he had acquired a habit of wearing too many layers. His mental rehearsal left no other course other than hold back until he was in conversation with those of authority. This was a subject that you were not accustomed to discuss every day, but he wanted it resolved in all possible directions, determined as ever that it would not return to haunt him in years to come.

He tactfully declined the offer of coffee as he was all but summoned into their External Affairs Department. He needed to be comfortable and by the same token get right to the point, which he most certainly did.

Acting on a shrewd premise he provided a printed bullet point type report prepared by him previously. What he was tactfully demanding in return was written confirmation that he had acted in the only way possible given the events in the desert canyon. The embassy's appropriate staff must further understand the horrific circumstances that had on that particular day prevailed.

His consensus of opinion had led him to a conclusion that in vast countries such as Africa inherent dangers with potential of death were waiting around every possible corner, perhaps in as far as putting a value of human life in that of a lower order? As he did not originate from there was it for him to argue otherwise?

Ian had the value of a fair and lucid hearing, with a pensive outcome as what was the value of further life being risked in an isolated region of Namibian desert to recover the remains of a body and that of a wrecked vehicle?

One final direction he dwelt on with his conversation amounted to be invaluable. 'Please could it be put in writing for him?' His request was noted, leaving him to wonder if this concern of his would materialise in reality?

Now it was over. It had seemed like hours, but by his watch it was only one hour precisely. He sat nearby at one of the tiny licensed restaurants that even this early was a hive of activity. The outside tables were a refuge for smokers, the available seating bathed in sunshine lifted his spirits. What he ordered quickly arrived, a Danish pastry combined with a generous cup of coffee. It was worth the wait, if not the over inflated price.

He was reasoning had he simply been a victim that was transferred to the embassy's various departments until he had gone almost full circle? Then how often does their London Embassy deal with such matters; should I have left it all over in Windhoek? Enough. I've done what I set out to do, my time, my effort and I'm the innocent party.

The remaining, what he called puzzle, was finding the location of Botha's brother domiciled as he had been told in the UK. Although if his memory was correct his family name was changed making he imagined a extremely difficult search.

Let me concentrate on a more rewarding task, having the contents of his document case worked on with my ideas, with an end result that will be a reward for the Herero.

'H' equals hats or put another way his quirky power of word association, none other than London's enigmatic Hatton Garden, home of the gem stone trade upheld worldwide, perhaps also with its respective twin, the city of Amsterdam, where it would be so easy to cut pieces of crystal to what he needed, with the added bonus that it was close to his first visit of the day. He all but congratulated himself with journey planning. Yes more than precisely it was two birds with only one 'stone' or that's what he was hoping?

Ian attempted to get some idea to when he had last visited Hatton Garden? What he recalled was an ominous occasion of a stag party organised by one of his fellow engineers, years ago. All lost now in hazy interludes and the so-called organised bash ending up in the wilds of Soho's red light district. But that was poles apart from Hatton Garden's main players that owe their presence revolving in the world sphere of buying and selling diamonds.

Where was he to go exactly with a chunk of nothing more than he surmised quartz and only wanting pieces cut off and lapped to shape, but he was determined, so keep looking, it can only be in a place like this?

One thing was utmost in his mind, that he was not a buyer of diamonds, given his precarious almost broke financial situation, that thought was ingrained with pain. His ramblings had now taken him into the lesser walkways and alleys that had probably existed since the foundation of the market that he imagined was during medieval times.

Now at last it was getting more interesting. In the haven of smaller individual shops that related to the trade, one took his interest, a supplier of machinery and tools associated with the jewellery industry. Through a jumbled shop front he could see a vast array of equipment that supported a pragmatic establishment. Behind the counter was the type of person he knew he would be comfortable to talk with, although he guessed they were both in their own right that of 'engineers'.

A sudden impulse of thoughts raced ahead of what he had in mind, I need urgently to make contact with Fiona, must not leave it any longer, by this stage he could only assume her mobile was permanently off. This morning history again was continuing to repeat itself, but where is she? He looked at all the office workers that were surrounding him, all of whom had their mobile cell phones stuck permanently to their ears. He wondered if these appliances were surgically removed at the end of each day?

He pushed open the door to Hatton Garden's, almost he was ashamed to concede, an impoverished shop. 'Nothing too big or too small.' It caused Ian to laugh at such outdated blur of advertising, on a plus side it would be certainly more relaxed with the content of conversation in direct comparison to his last call – that of the embassy.

Two engineers were about to meet up, he marvelled what exactly was on sale, everything he was looking at was in extreme miniature not exactly any use for his crew out on the drilling rigs.

Raphael Dupuis heard the outer door open and then close, a customer this early, his cousin and business partner Solomon the usual front man was out on a call, which left Raphael not at all comfortable out on the sales counter, unless of course it was one of his long standing associates from the Garden. These days he was troubled by focusing, he made the situation worse as he tended to keep his close work glasses on nearly all of the time.

The Dupuis business established by his father in the 1930s would cater for just about anything the jewellery and gemstone trade would ever likely need, probably now the only London source for these unique range of implements.

Solomon his cousin was out on a valuation, both partners had extensive knowledge in the diamond trade, Raphael himself had worked in Amsterdam for many years, and he had failed to be exposed to the intimate nature of this singular and clandestine business. But for all that, the Dupuis partners were the last sad survivors in their line, by normal events they would have both retired years ago.

Ian stared at the huddled figure as he looked up from the counter, had Raphael a choice in the matter he would have preferred his safe haven of the rear workshop. 'Good morning, sir, this is an early call?' The very content of the welcome made Ian feel he needed to apologise for his very interruption.

'There's a reason.' Ian placed his document case on what passed as the shop's counter. 'Now I don't want to waste your valuable time on a trivial request, I was in London and knew around here someone could say yes to cutting and polishing pieces from this chunk of crystal.' In a state of almost cringing with embarrassment he produced and placed the artefact on to the counter allowing shop's owner to view what had become Ian's inspiration.

Raphael was not able to take this in, granted it was early, but did he have a customer with a lump of basic rock which any London builder might possibly use as hardcore? A state of uneasy silence ensued.

Ian broke the stalemate. 'As I said what I would like is at best a few basic pendants cut and polished so as I can put a neck cord through them. Would you know my best port of call?'

How Raphael contained himself was beyond belief, probably it was that this off the street customer was wearing a neck tie saved the situation, it took him back to how things in Hatton Garden used to be.

Ian added on a futile remark. 'Naturally whatever it costs I'm happy to pay.' His hopefully generous comment coincided with the shop's ageing clock which hesitantly performed a ritual of striking the quarter hour. Ian remained in strained circumstances waiting patiently for a reply.

By now Raphael had at least condescended to take hold of the raw material he was supposed to be assessing. 'Let me take it into the back workshop, I can see it in more light.' More than that with his abysmal eyesight nowadays he needed everything on his side.

The door that separated his beloved workshop from the shop area was allowed for whatever reason to be shut behind him. His anxious potential customer was left to stare at the vast range of items that in due course were destined eventually for the gem stone trade.

Raphael had a mind to do his old trick, wait maybe two minutes and go back in the shop with a sage-like judgement revolving around, sorry, sir, not possible. Why he looked at the rock in his mood of contempt no one would have guessed, but he did.

It all came at once. He placed his correct glasses on then to finally confirm matters by using his jeweller's magnifier glass. With that he achieved a more precise and enhanced view. His mouth suddenly went dry, more so as the whole of his scalp was pulsing in a state of a rushing paralysis.

'On the love of my father it's not true.' He stopped whispering to himself… it's all, no it's not possible… Diamonds… It's pure solid diamond!

There were no ifs or buts about what he was drooling over; he had too much experience in handling gem stones. The Dutch had taught him all you could possibly learn and diamonds don't change over time. But this man out in his shop, his customer, had he any idea?

He suddenly became oddly frightened, he knew he was vulnerable. Who was the person out at the counter? Raphael wanted to rush out and decline the odd request, although heaven knows why but it was not that easy a magnitude of curiosity had swept over him, he desperately needed help. There was one way. Quickly he needed to phone Solomon, fortunately he was only at one of their clients almost round the corner.

He reassured himself that the door was closed, then without hesitation he dialled the number. Much to his relief it was answered instantly. Recognising the receptionist, he blurted his response, 'Raphael Dupuis, I need to speak to Solomon, he's with you, quickly please, hell woman it's urgent!'

Solomon was not used to this, least of all from his business partner. 'What's a matter, Raphael, they said it's urgent?' Fearing the worst he listened intently to the staccato whispering uttered by his cousin. Slowly he was able to discern what was said, although by contrast nothing was making any sense.

He had to take a stand on what was going on. 'Listen, Raphael, go back in the shop get him talking, play up to him. I'll grab a cab be with you in minutes. What you say must be right I know that, but your man there he has to be a sham?'

At the shop counter the protracted wait was meaning only one thing to Ian. His little task was undoubtedly going to happen and done here at this very shop. He calculated that he would have to pay cash, that was the least he could do, probably have to call back later.

Suddenly without warning the shops outer door was pushed inward creating a brisk draught from the street it preceded what he witnessed in absolute precision, as the 'postie' materialised and keeping one hand securely to his delivery trolley whilst making the customer's mail delivery by throwing the bundle with precision on to the counter top, blink and you would have missed it. There was even time for a smile by the exponent of these events. Ian was left to look at the bundle of letters comfortably corseted by the inevitable red elastic band.

No sooner had he taken this undoubtedly daily routine on board then Ian heard a voice, making him acutely aware that the recent intake of draught had the effect of causing the adjoining door to the workshop to come ajar. It was obvious the owner was engaged with a telephone call. Nothing unusual, until he started to hear the call's content, drawn out in a completely subdued state of almost whispering… But why the whispering?

The next few moments was set to virtually frighten him as he had fallen off a drilling platform. Although only allowed the home base side of the conversation it did not take him long to evaluate its content.

'Solomon, it's from Africa. No doubt – you've only to look at this man's sunburn, it's not done under a blessed sun lamp. How's he got this in the country, it's huge? No, I'm not mistaken it's one cluster of diamonds… diamonds like you've never seen, get here quick, or I'll have a heart attack, cos something's seriously wrong.'

Ian did not have time to believe what he had heard. He needed to act fast and that did mean without exception fast.

He went behind the counter pushing the half opened door. He was left with no other course than to confront the old man in a demanding manner.

'I need to leave urgently that means now.' The artefact was on the work bench subjected to the scrutiny from the focused light, Ian grabbed hold of it without any fear of hesitation.

'Thanks for your time.' There was no further thought, he was out of the shop as if an errant valve on an oil rig was about to blow.

He heard the shop door slam behind him he had to negotiate two street flower sellers narrowly missing both of them. He cleared the alley way and went into the morning sunshine hell bent in getting to Farringdon tube station, running down the steps gave him an impression like bath water disappearing through the plug hole. But it doesn't make any sense, why am I running...?

Solomon dropped a ten pound note at the cab driver, time was of the essence, his ailing business partner needed him quicker than he could have possibly imagined.

'I don't know Solomon, he barged in my workshop grabbed the cluster and ran.' Raphael hated confrontations in particular with his cousin, who was by far the stronger of the two on any discussions. He by contrast the more quiet one in his advanced age needed far more respect which Solomon always fell short of.

Their conversation was rudely interrupted by the phone ringing. 'Leave it, Raphael, I need to know what happened.'

Solomon had calmed to some degree he needed to listen intently to what had taken place. By the end of his cousin's jumbled account there appeared nothing of any tangible consequence. 'Raphael if he knew the value why was he carrying it around of all places here in Hatton Garden? He must know this is the fountain of knowledge, with all things diamond.'

On the top of the counter there was a polishing cloth. Solomon developed an irritating habit of arranging it squarely with the frame containing the actual glass. His thinking was completely divorced from what he was involved with, there needed to be an answer, what exactly he had no idea.

He continued to quiz his cousin on where he could possibly have come from. They discussed his accent, coupled with the visual fact to prolonged exposure to sunshine, it left them naturally to assume it had to be taken from Africa. How was it possible to smuggle this chunk of diamond into the country?

'All right, Raphael, let me ask around Hatton. Someone will know, or maybe your contacts in Amsterdam. We do this now and fast, if not we go "insurance", no stone unturned.' His little inappropriate pun of humour went unnoticed by his cousin.

But he did look up from the counter.

'You heard me, cousin. If that all fails we go "insurance". Hatton Garden pays for that.' An insipid smile came over his face.

Both partners were aware as to what was being referred. It was a principle that was set up ages ago, from its inception a successful solution had been found amongst the guilds of merchants and jewellers in Hatton Garden and Amsterdam.

None of the merchants would tolerate any significant loss whatever the magnitude of reason. As no outside insurance company would dare to consider let alone be prepared to offer this particular industry any form of insurance cover, premiums would be too astronomic to even contemplate.

To any outsider it could be considered as sadistic, it was not likely to change with an industry built solely on roots of trust going back in history. They took care of their own, retained in Amsterdam and also within London's Hatton Garden where individuals that within their remit were able to assiduously hunt down whoever, and nothing would be too much trouble. There was no escape from those that were tracked down, only a final closure was inevitable. Even the protection premiums paid for this unique service remained and always would be a closed secret...

What was discussed within Hatton Garden centred on his behalf and that of the raw diamond was no immediate concern for Ian, who by now was currently within the trains in London's underground system. His concern had centred on why, and what was it all about?

Only at this point he sensed that bodily change of his taking place, it's even starting to happen here at home. He had lived with this malady to a large part back in Namibia, but was not expecting it to rear its head again on home soil. That very self-imposed description, nothing I can recall but there is a connection if only it would come to light, 'rear its head'. It's deeper, right inside my very body. The closed packed corridors of the tube network a haven of cover that a 'creature' would take advantage of, no it's all my supposition again acting completely wild.

Nothing was making any sense. He certainly believed what he had heard, he could not accept however what had transpired, no one ever stumbles on such wealth. Who could it have belonged to? That's when he noticed how soaked with sweat his shirt had become. It was only now he attempted to take stock of where he was travelling, nothing came as a complete surprise – it was entirely the wrong direction. It did not matter, all that was necessary for him at this tenuous stage was to clear a distance between him and Hatton Garden. He almost reached a point of shouting at himself. Why, what have I done wrong, why should I be running?

Did my aunt have any idea to the value? A whole solid mess of raw diamonds, heaven knows what the value would be? Perhaps there was some knowledge or maybe a connection with her second husband or even his offspring, he loathed the thought that they were also his aunt's step-sons.

Was that why Karl Botha was chasing me across the Namibian desert, or did in fact that ape of an individual know anything about all this to begin with? Then his thoughts once more tried to focus on the younger other son now domiciled in England, it's all beginning to get too complicated.

His attention had drifted, the previous packed tube train had to a large extent disgorged most of the band of gregarious office commuters. He shuddered at the thought of the value of what he was carrying.

Opposite on empty seats were scattered today's discarded newspapers, one of which was the Guardian. He retrieved it, acting as a feeling of security, visualising his aunt at Homemead using this very calibre of paper before entombing what she referred as that of her 'Guardian'.

Back at that time this daily newspaper would have been of a much larger physical size, but no matter, for this morning it was serving with a profound sense of purpose almost covering his document case. Was this simple act that reached across time to what his Aunt Anastasia had inspired all those years ago?

Strangely by draping the newspaper over his case it was having the desired effect, of becoming comfortably lost in a world of hay meadows unique to those long summer school holidays at his beloved Homemead, if only.

He needed to change trains, go in the right direction, get back to main line at Charing Cross and on to where he had parked up his car. His plan was to be rigidly adhered to, get up to Cambridgeshire and fast. Like an outdated criminal on the run more than all that he wanted to find out why he was unable to contact Fiona.

Eventually on leaving Charing Cross Station he noticed how empty the trains were running, he reasoned with the high value in his charge it was safer around other travellers, lost in the concept of a crowd. He continued to pinch himself realising the magnitude of what his case contained.

He not unreasonably speculated about Botha's brother. Was this sibling also connected in any way with what had become exposed from the 'woodwork' of Homemead and what he now carried with its modern day updated price tag? It really didn't bear thinking about.

It had all become a serious state of guessing games. Firstly did the Herero people have any understanding to the ancient relics prodigious value? He was convinced the answer to that plaintive thought would be a very definite no, realising all the time he lived amongst them nothing connected with wealth from whatever source was ever a subject of their discussions.

Now it was becoming almost overwhelming for him, had his aunt been of the same opinion? Hopefully as myself up until an hour or so, nothing more than a hallowed piece of glass crystal that was the reserve of one of the earth's oldest living people.

It could not stop him from cringing at the very thought of its wealth, and it had laid open on view for months at the lounge window of his apartment!

By the time Ian had reached the suburban parking lot that secured his hired car the selective few in Hatton Garden's diamond fraternity had closed ranks in an unshakeable display of solidarity and were buzzing with what had occurred at the Dupuis shop. Based on the size of this raw stone you could re-write the Guinness Book of Records. Their consensus of opinions had by now established a common ground, there was no other option than to find whoever this stranger to them was.

Fortunately not considered difficult as the shop's modest security camera had recorded an admirable search image of the 'customer'.

Chapter 30

The journey 'escaping' from London with his intention of reaching Cambridgeshire combined with his thinking was fraught to a point of deep concern. That concern centred on the object which he had dragged out from behind the walls of Homemead.

Moreover he began to know what he needed to do, a semblance of an idea had formed, inspired whilst on the tube train, not so much the transport system but where it was situated, namely underground. That was the operative word, now he was determined to implement his idea into a newly formed plan to achieve what was desperately needed.

At this early stage he was suffering only one negative thought; was his beloved Homemead now sold? If so that would seriously curtail what he had in mind, but only time would allow him to know that answer.

All day he had laboured with his mobile phone in trying to reach Fiona, something was perhaps wrong. There was only one solution which meant visiting the estate agents where he assumed she was still working.

When he stopped for fuel he was prepared to gamble on the one overriding concern of the day. What if he had misunderstood what he had heard from the one sided conversation in the Hatton Garden shop?

All his stress and panic could have been for nothing? It was brought more to light by fumbling across in his jacket pocket the Hatton Garden's shop business card, obviously collected from the counter, it had what he needed; their phone number.

Ian relished his next direct move, give them a call, use a pay box, touch of old movies, nothing can be traced, or so he believed, hit them with one poignant question: Is it the genuine article?

The phone cubicle he used was even presentable, his call was eventually answered and by the outcome he needed to increase his speech volume to overcome impaired hearing with whom he was speaking.

Solomon as usual had taken the call, he all but froze when he realised what was transpiring. 'Who are you? Please tell me on my dead father's name where you got that stone, you must, heaven above it's priceless beyond recognition...' Even Solomon heard the phone's receiver click back, but it did not stop him from shouting... 'Hello, please hello.'

That was the affirmation Ian wanted to hear, now he became more buoyant with life, certain ideas perhaps are not so crazy. But he deliberately slowed himself down, his self-discipline had surfaced, be very careful, only one thing at a time.

The first stop once he reached Cambridge was important, into a convenient DIY store, there were items he needed and the only solution was to buy them. On his intended shopping list was a crowbar, which appeared masqueraded under another description and two heavy weight club hammers.

Next and at last his important location to reach Homemead with ever hopeful and fingers crossed, pleading that the house still remained on the property market.

Then the hand of destiny grabbed hold of him and others for that matter as the particular road was suffering all number of irksome delays by major road works, with of course the necessary outlandish diversions.

Ian's delay created a situation which he would have no idea of whatsoever. Homemead's neighbour, that of the Brigadier, had the dubious pleasure to be collected for a few days to be spent in an area of Norfolk, without respite to even his beloved Players cigarettes. His instructions were to enjoy sea breezes, his wife when alive would have simply got out of all this encumbrance. Therefore away from his cottage he was not on 'duty watch' over Homemead when Ian eventually reached his intended destination.

Who now having laboured all the delays finally approached the property and from an entirely different direction, a road he was convinced that he had not travelled before, then he did remind himself that his times spent there were exclusively during his boyhood. Which today were creating precisely those longingly reminiscent feelings as he tentatively approached Homemead.

He was in a state of escapism, as his thoughts were employment orientated to what the company would come up with, a personal change was with him, metamorphosing wholly from the depths of his system. He could not escape the implications of having to answer what was steadily becoming transparent to him, even if he stooped to that stilted phrase, 'Absent without leave'.

The brakes on the car were applied as if automatically, his mind was all but tortured to be in two places at once, however he was scanning and hoping. Bingo, his puny aspirations were realised, and to his relief nothing had changed, suspecting that the weathered for sale sign was laying where he had last seen it.

With an urgency of desperation, the result of a call of nature, he climbed the entrance gate; the broken nameplate, the rusting padlock and chain all as before. Gaining the sanctuary of the garden wall for his task he could see the estate agent's dilapidated sign lying where he had hoped. Now a certain Ian Harbinger was able to be fully relieved in more ways than one.

He was acting with a sense of well deserved caution, what his plan entailed would require no witnesses, like the driver of the tractor in a field opposite, however judging by the involvement it looked very much that the task on the land was reaching a conclusion.

No matter, as there was time for one more look inside the hallowed confines of Homemead!

Falling victim to an inward compression of laughter, remembering his aunt all those years ago and here I am again, my same party trick on her, as before slewing the casement window frame allowing a covert access into the kitchen pantry. Apart for him feeling a genuine desire to roam his childhood stamping ground once more, he wanted to know since last time if anyone had ventured inside the property.

Not unnaturally he quickly gravitated to the stairway and accessed his most cherished domain, the old bedroom. One final look at the mantelpiece and perhaps the not so secret hideaway that his aunt had either discovered or knew of all along where she had surreptitiously hidden the Herero's artefact all those years ago. Ian was sensing in his veins akin to a feeling of uncontrolled blood pressure, realising exactly what that crystal was in reality, diamonds, beyond anyone's dreams, he went as far as correcting his thoughts… Wildest dreams.

He found himself contemplating someone's been here. What he was witnessing was nothing short of a complete mess, it wasn't making any sense, lengths of skirting board thrown in no semblance of order, making him think all this was a result of possibly a visitor letting their feelings rant in a show of viscous temper? But there was more which he became acutely focused on, although residing in broken pieces it was evident it had once formed a large earthenware bottle, noticeably old but the damage was recent. Scattered around the debris were crude rusty nails, as to any theme of an explanation none seemed to exist.

His attention continued to the bricks above the mantelpiece which he had carefully returned to the wall cavity. They were not the same, now they appeared only crudely pushed back, could the shattered bottle and its contents also have been hidden inside the extreme depths of the cavity.

There was a return of his senses, nothing I can do, it's all history; I have one singular purpose and no more time can be lost. He allowed himself a privilege with his last lingering thought visualising the tapestry with those heart pulling words of proclamation for him as a school boy. Even now over that gap of years he could still describe the ramifications of Edward Lear's 'owl' and that of a certain solitary 'cat'.

From the landing window he noticed the agricultural activity was finished, it meant the coast was finally clear. On returning to his car he collected the items together with the object of the whole exercise.

Now his scheme would be laid bare. Homemead's water well where the 'Guardian' was to find its next and what he wanted, final closure of a resting place. A 'burial' in respect to the people of the Herero, the imminent action he was about to undertake was his recourse and he believed a logical conclusion.

As all day he had dwelt on the magnitude of events by his discovery of the objects wealth, but then he knew he was the steward of what he had in his keeping. The new found responsibly rested with him and him alone, furthermore his decision was about to be implemented.

How the task would go was unknown, he needed to act clever, very clever. The batten timber that closed the well's aperture was extremely secure, leaving him to wonder how many years had it remained in this particular state?

Anyway his ingenuity of an oil platform engineer would do. With these positive thoughts he applied the flooring lever to the nailed down battens. By hefty blows from the club hammer he loosened the rows of securing nails, whoever had previously performed the fixing had done an extremely sound job. To complete a removal a continued heavy force was still needed, eventually he was rewarded by a satisfying sound of the nails creaking as one by one they were withdrawn.

Now after all those years he was allowed to stare into the black abyss of the well shaft, an ironic twist of circumstances given his current employment. Enough reminiscing, he was determined not to waste valuable time. From under the cover of his jacket he collected the object about to be deposited into the depths of the well shaft. There was only the refining items to do, an empty onion sack was destined to contain the object, in compassion he let it remain clothed in the newspaper, a lasting sentiment.

The extra hammer went into the sack as the weight of ballast. He dare not dwell any longer with his motivation, adroitly reaching to the very centre of the well, and showing only the merest pause as an ambient moment... It was gone!

He listened almost praying. The longer the wait the better, nothing disappointing, there followed a hollow glutinous splash as if it was devoured at the end of the well shaft by an alien syrup. Leaving him to reason even if they sludge pump this hole in years to come it will still be coagulated in that vortex of ooze.

The planking needed putting back as it was before, meaning driving the nails into their original positions, not easy as time had rusted them into a natural concealment. Made worse as speed was his concern, he did not want to be seen by anyone.

That was when annoyingly he suddenly noticed some basic carving that existed on the inner wooden rim of the well.

Instantly he knew he had not seen this inscription previously, it was new, by that it was not there in the days when Sibley and himself had explored the depths. It intrigued him, who, what and when had this happened?

He could not think of an immediate answer, he reached for his ball point, and copied the detail of a few numbers on to his shirt cuff. Moments later he was busily involved closing over the opening, with the best of his knowledge hopefully unobserved.

Only fate was staring at him had he only known, and what he had scribbled on to his shirt, perhaps his aunt had instigated a thought, that one good turn really deserves another?

It was done. He stood back, all the nails were as he had found them, a piece of broken wood from the garden was used to stop the hammer blows erasing the rust corrosion on the nail heads. It looked totally preserved to any would be onlooker as it had appeared this way for ages.

Again he duplicated his reassurance to himself; even if they pump the water out of the well they will never lift what was now reassuringly deposited in its ultimate depths. There was a sense of satisfaction for him and if they knew he believed the Herero people would be of the same opinion.

Sadly it was time to leave. Climbing the gate he looked back at the house; like all those months ago the top windows radiated a feeling of lost souls desperately seeking a semblance of love and understanding, but he knew in his heart he was unable to do any more.

There was a wrench on having to leave his embryonic haven in the deep surrounds of Cambridgeshire. It became more than he could possibly endure, far too much history. He fell into a trap by mesmerising himself as a young exuberant school boy on his holidays all those years ago, how different now in these contemporary years with his knowledge that his beloved Aunt Anastasia was laid at rest in a far off country, back then for him he supposed that he did not even know of its existence. How remotely strange it was all appearing, especially as he was at the very home of what he had recently yearned for whilst in the desert canyon at death's door, Homemead, in his cherished English countryside.

At this late moment he was able to recall what one of the early 1970s North Sea drilling prospectors told him, and it had stuck word perfect with him ever since. More importantly it would act as a fitting tribute for his departure from Homemead, which he was certainly loath to perform... 'Let your ears gladden, and drape your very soul with joy.' So a reluctant Ian finally reached his parked car, his last response, that of a glance to what he knew was the property's new and concealed hiding place.

Only at this late stage did he give any real thought to the value of what he was responsible in just doing, to think at one time it was earmarked as a doorstop for my apartment. Not so, but a truly colossal wealth in terms of man's recognition was once again gone from sight. It would have more than written off his personal debts a billion times over, but what then? Look at the resources that mankind has exhumed from the world's oceans in my lifetime and to what avail.

His calm repose was broken rudely by the invasion of noise as two fighter jets that had their course over the fields that surrounded the property; it was then that he became aware of tears that had welled and were draining from his eyes.

There was no other course left for him, he all but pleaded to himself. 'Leave. You must leave now.' Once you were for a short time the keeper by inheritance of the 'Guardian', you have done what was needed, it was your decision, Aunt surely would have endorsed your action. The past, it must now all belong to the past, and believe that the long line of Homemead's 'ghosts' will secure it for all time!

Ian's activity as always was noticed. The observer was the resident robin that viciously guarded his inheritance. Past generations of this bird had known times when the soil of the garden was tended by long gone generations that understood horticulture, one of whom would have been his aunt. Those gardeners by their activities had brought forth nourishing meals for past avian inhabitants.

Soon once the interloper Ian had gone then this latest in the line of robins would rightfully regain its territory as no cession from others of his kind would ever be tolerated…

Paper towelling in the car provided Ian with a ready means of cleaning the worst off his hands. He drew an odd parallel with his recent escapade making him feel like a 'murderer' full of remorse having just disposed of the victim's body.

The feeling rapidly left his senses, the task was done, so a priceless object of man's desire was gone, least ways from sight. It said something for the skill of those at Hatton Garden able to recognise diamond in the raw. It would always puzzle him, not so much all the intrigue behind the actual artefact but where had it originated?

His thoughts for a need of sheer comfort had gravitated to the deserts of Namibia, wondering once again on the origins of what he would always know as the 'Guardian' crystal. He hardly needed to remind himself of the loyalty he owed the Herero and the last true custodian of the crystal his own Aunt Anastasia.

What stories existed for those that had possessed huge diamonds over time and the eventual disaster that overtook so many. He recalled the huge diamond which he believed was known as the 'Hope', and its chequered history of personal grief to its lineage of owners. That would never be a concern for him as his task was resolved, albeit laying in the sludge of Homemead's well shaft…

Another chapter had entered the realm of history for the two diamond crystals that once had fallen to our world, but that was centuries ago. Their journey had taken them across the trackless wastes of the heavens only to find a conclusion when they became unwittingly imprisoned within the gravitational pull of a planet which would be called Earth.

There were at their inception of interstellar travel two almost identical shapes of carbon crystal, originally it was one, but a separation had occurred aeons ago forming mirror images of each other. When the gravity of our planet claimed them one had plummeted into the ocean whilst by contrast its twin had gained a sanctuary over what would become the Skeleton Coast. Its destiny was to end its journey by illuminating as a night star across a land that already was instrumental as the birth place of mankind, that of the continent of Africa.

The itinerant nomads of the Herero all those generations ago had witnessed its glowing arrival as a zenith of fire, by the sunrise they had located where it had made earth-fall. They would have no knowledge of its origins or for that matter what in future generations its value would become, it was not a concern to them, this appeared as a god like gift from the stars. They were to be its sole claimants and so remained through time.

There would have to exist in our modern sphere, generations of scientists that would expose the world to knowledge of carbons and the specific form of what man would eventually label as diamonds. Further enlightening studies in later years would reveal that certain planets inhabiting the cosmos consisted almost entirely of carbon, the raw ingredient that interprets what we know as gem stones.

We would in time begin to realise the supernova explosions that took place long before any life form of man's beginnings had even approached its infancy. Those symbolic white dwarf stars possessing as they did carbon cores, an eventual catalyst to form as diamonds of the gods.

Parts of these porous charcoal-like structures would break away to drift through the trackless wastes of interstellar space. Those that mankind found during their early history were to be hallowed for their unique and equally intrinsic creation of nature.

What however had appeared over the skies of Africa all those generations ago to the wandering Herero was without equal.

They embraced an object that had glowed and once cooled had exhibited natural uncut crystals, unique by a skeletal carbon growth formation. They knew of nothing like this before in their history, therefore it was ordained to be of mystic status and became entrenched in a historical worship.

So through the course of time the artefact was carried wherever the Herero peregrinated in their travels. Until a time when the father of Jho-in became worried by inroads made from outsiders to his people's lands. Alone he had made a judgement that surprised even his elders, he was to entrust its future keeping to one that had come to work and even toil amongst his kind.

Therefore on one of her return visits to England Anastasia had included in her shipment of core samples one extra piece that by now she referred as the 'Guardian'. Thus it became secretly lodged for its future keeping within the walls at Homemead, unbeknown to any outside influence. The Herero's most treasured possession, like other things in Homemead's history was concealed away from man's eyes and intrigue, the house had perhaps rather reluctantly become its new keeper.

But Anastasia had not entirely considered the implications of that of her young nephew and what his actions would do in the future…

If she could see her nephew now then she would be bemused by the dirt and grime left embedded on his hands; the direct result of his furtive task to open up the well shaft to lay the artefact into the glutinous mud layered depths…

Her nephew by this stage was driving purposefully towards the town, he wanted more than anything to see Fiona. There were a host of reasons but above all else a feeling augmented by state of loneliness that had been present for too many days. Not unnaturally at the moment he was seeking the need of her company.

Even the car's radio had no appeal with all the bulletins and traffic updates he elected on a course of fulfilment, by switching it off. At that precise moment by some ironic twist his mobile phone bleeped signalling that a text message had arrived. Ian ever the optimist as he approached the car park had simply one thought, surely it has to be good news?

Chapter 31

Ian stared in disbelief, he would have to admit that the text message on his phone was read by him at least six times before finally registering. This was one occasion perhaps the most crucial in all honesty he needed to proclaim to the world that he loved his sister Julia!

Of course it was scripted in her usual curt approach, but what the hell, it was the content that mattered. Shared out family money, he had to be honest with himself it was something that he had completely forgotten about, the long legal wrangle was stretching back before the dawn of time, he tried to guess the number of years since it was first muted? Now it really had transpired, equally shared between himself and his 'beloved' Julia.

It was a life saver, or more precisely a salvation, so good things do reach you on mobile phones. To say that my basic savings were draining away was yet another of those pointless remarks we all become guilty of expounding.

This found him elated and with his hand almost shaking tapping a badly spelt reply to his sister confirming what unbelievably he had just read. For no particular point he noted the time of her message, odd, as he remembered it was the same moment he had dropped the incumbent crystal into the depths of the well.

On reaching the estate agents of Unwin & Hornby he had to juggle round the window cleaner who was labouring intently on the individual panes that made up the bow fronted window. Rather pensively as he entered, Ian scanned the open plan office, but of Fiona sadly for him there was no visible sign.

June Orpin looked up from her onerous task of checking a spec sheet that needed entirely re-writing. Where are the standards these days? She did pride herself in her ability to place the face with the property that they could possibly be intent with pursuing, not always the name though. On this occasion there was an exception. 'Mr Harbinger, it's good to see you again. You're our listed property namely Homemead.'

Momentarily Ian fell under a spell of being impressed, either he was famous or they exhibited a desire for clients to close deals? 'That's right, Homemead, good of you to remember me.' He was attempting a double task, a polite reply whilst further hoping that somewhere within the office Fiona might appear.

'If it's still an option for you, there's no offers outstanding, it's a long time since we saw you, busy no doubt?'

The window cleaner had entered the office placing his invoice on June Orpin's desk. When she finalised this task connected with the windows Ian had no alternative than a straight question. 'Is Fiona McCrae available? I have some questions that she could possibly, how can I say… unravel?'

He did not even have to wait for his reply as the outer door opened and balancing two filing boxes with uncanny trepidation in came Fiona. For all that she was able to instantly recognise Ian, wanting to throw caution to the wind but the presence of their office manager made her act astutely with restraint.

'Mr Harbinger, I have your "letter" we can discuss that now if you wish?' Her female intuition cleverly acted with absolute perfection, thus extracting Ian from the all encompassing attention of Ms Orpin. Fiona ushered her potential client to her immediate boss's office. Once the door was closed she relaxed and by this stage Ian had done his part by playing dumb and cleverly going with the flow.

'Well, Ian, you are a sight for sore eyes. I'd all but given up on you, wow look at you, sun tan, how long were you out there?'

'Fiona it's the longest story you'll ever imagine. Firstly I've tried to contact you, your phone's never in use?'

Fiona reached into her pocket and produced the object of their discussion. 'Don't talk to me about mobiles. I've had a spell of disasters that you'd never believe, that's why… Anyway hang on, I'm only just back in action now, even got a new number.

'Enough of all that, Ian, you look fantastic, I'm impressed, you look more relaxed, composed might be a better remark.'

His reply to her was that of a smile, at last in her presence he assured himself what he wanted to do in pursuing all the events surrounding his aunt's chequered life. He was ready and verging on a desperate pitch to share his adventures with someone he knew deep down he was genuinely in love with!

Fiona broke his train of intimate thoughts. 'For your peace of mind and reassurance our Mr Jezzaid is away, some personal matter he's lost his only kin apparently, anyway he won't be barging in on us.'

Ian sensed at this stage before jumping in with all his adventures he was duty bound to enquire on her passion with the family business in Scotland. 'Fiona I've wondered how your clothing concern is progressing given our austere times, please tell me the news is good?'

There was too long a pause preceding her reply, it worried Ian. 'Doubled edged answer for you, or should I really say what do you want first the good or the not so good news?'

He didn't hesitate for a second. 'I'm on a roll today so make it only the good news.'

Based on an assumption that his day had progressed this far motivated with all the right positive vibes, he really did not want it to continue on any form of a shattered note.

'Ian last year was cool, more tourist trade, lot of fuss attending to their needs, our family never complains. But we've hit the big time for supplying tweed cloth to an Italian company, went against all we expected, and before you ask, we're struggling to supply. Not enough, I hate using the word capacity to produce, if only we could invest in more equipment, we are struggling with what Father started the business using.'

He could see the initial enthusiasm drain rapidly from her face. He needed to interject into their conversation real valuable and worthwhile support and quickly.

'Surely there must be grants available, Fiona, you know they are always talking of cash injections to help our industry, after all Scotland's got the oil wealth.' He wisely stopped, as not for a moment wishing to labour the magnitude of his reply.

She poised knowing only too well what answer was needed. 'It's the cart before the horse scenario at present, but we are pushing our luck on borrowing ever harder, how many times I've wished my father was still with us.'

He had seemingly no other option than reply in a hand above his head gesture, the time and place of an high street estate agent's office was not conducive to further discussion.

By now the outer domain had sprung to life by the arrival of an extremely well dressed young couple that June Orpin was attending with in her usual professional flair.

Ian became distracted. It was more noticeable than when he had first sat down, the whole office of their legendary Mr Jezzaid was faultless, everything as he remembered since his first visit was neat and aligned almost to a point of being absurd, there was no doubt that the boss occupied this area.

Fiona pulled his attention span back into reality. 'The work at the moment is killing me. I'm off again in five minutes, we've three people including my boss out of action, if I carry on like this I'll be a professional estate agent before long.' Her comment was ended on a smile that due to what she had said was virtually rationed.

'Let me get out of your hair, all my overseas mishaps can hold, how about possibly this evening at the usual restaurant, see if the meals are just as good?'

By now in her haste she had stood up attempting to pack in her case more than it was designed for. 'Ian go for Saturday, gosh it will be the end of another week, and then it's full attention from yours truly on Mr Harbinger's adventures.'

This time she ended her suggestion on one of those enigmatic smiles that came from the heart. Ian on a note of spontaneity quickly ratified her request.

As he stood his usual observant self focused on a fabric covered tribal shield fixed to the back wall of Jezzaid's office. Strange, it was of Namibian culture, he had seen the same type with this particular adornment out there.

Fiona picked up the note paper where she had moments earlier written her new phone number and whispering discreetly handed it over to him. 'There, Ian, see you in our restaurant, this Saturday evening.'

He quietly left satisfied at best by their mutual outcome...

The town shopping centre was privileged to be bathed in warm spring sunshine. For Ian it appealed more as he welcomed its inherent glow. The reason; since his return he was deprived of the African heat.

He knew that for the first time in days he had actually slowed down, almost stopping. The outside table of the cafe where he was sitting was rather exposed to passing traffic but on a plus side he was bathed by something that passed as seemingly warm weather.

A small tray with far more paper napkins than was needed was placed in front of him, that said it was service with a smile which he reciprocated. His thoughts were fixed, he was dwelling on Fiona both as a person that he was more than just fond of, he wanted to help but then clearly knowing it was not feasible, if it had not been for his embezzlement then how different it would be.

A sudden vibrant noise interrupted the organised peace of the shopping community, sirens from an ambulance that needed to rapidly invade into the paved walkways, it was out of sight from him. He hoped like others maybe an unexpected early birth? A local couple tried to see what was happening; in doing so they pushed against the empty chairs adjacent to Ian's table.

Their action unwittingly dislodged what was hiding away, so much so they rolled leisurely over the paved blocks their progress ceased eventually by the bane of our civilised culture, an inevitable lump of compressed chewing gum. Ian watched the progress and choosing his moment he reached down to retrieve them... Pristine coins of the realm that even included a pound coin.

The ambulance was leaving in a more sedate manner than its arrival. Ian like the other shoppers would have been relieved to know that its passenger as they all had hoped was a young mother to be, that would be welcoming her new offspring into the world in a short space of time.

Mainly by an irrational gesture Ian removed his sun glasses, which had an immediate benefit allowing him to clearly see a sign of 'crossed fingers' above the gift and newsagents shop. He walked across with a sense of real meaning to his newly motivated errand.

Now he was back at the table where even the sun umbrella was in place. All of that was not an issue at the moment, he needed to ponder and eventually decide on six numbers, numbers to go on his newly acquired National Lottery ticket. The salvaged coins were destined for one specific purpose, or so he believed, as to his inspiration of success he could only hazard a guess.

But what numbers? It was years since he had undertaken any form of gambling; currently it was certainly way down his list. Some odd remark stuck in his feeble endeavour... You always win on 'borrowed' money, but he still needed a decision on what Lotto numbers.

Aided and fortified by the increase in temperature he was even prepared to run in the face of adversary by removing his jacket. It was at that stage noting the grime on his exposed shirt sleeves he hoped that Fiona had not noticed the depredation of his clothing.

Then and only then did it occur, those numbers on my shirt cuff, crudely copied from the inside rim of the well, they were what he needed, just six numbers. He studied them for the first time in more detail but nothing appeared to turn on a light bulb with any logic behind them. One thing he was adamant on, during those school boy holidays at his beloved house he knew they were certainly not in evidence back then.

Whoever carved them really was not a concern at this point in time, as a rather oddball conclusion had entered the arena, they could answer the criteria needed to adhere with the lottery requirements. Blocking off each number in turn on his ticket and without hesitation he went back into the store and completed his transaction using the treasure trove of salvaged coins.

On leaving he allowed himself an almost sneaky look at the vast range of magazines, his mind was switched by default to a juvenile mode, mentally asking himself where are all the boys' comics? If only my favourite the one that Aunt would have returned to Homemead for me on those market days. He laboured his 'if only' ambition but sadly there was no sign of his cherished weekly publication. Since his long off times the minds of our modern boys had moved into more flamboyant directions…

Ian rallied his mental 'to do' list. Next was something he was going to really appreciate, without any previous contact he decided to drive out to the residential home and seek out the illustrious Miss Cleary. Total surprise visit, his aunt would have more than endorsed what he had in mind for one of her lifelong friends. He recalled that his initial adversary had turned out to be what he would now tentatively describe as his guru for the Namibian undertaking. Even if he was prepared to accept it was largely the result of their common interest with a certain Hollywood movie. He knew enough to understand at best she was going to be intrigued by all that had transpired…

Greycliffe's residential home's reception on his arrival was unoccupied, nearly all of the reception floor was stacked with a range of bulging cardboard cartons.

His waiting time was not in vain as situated on the wall behind reception was one of those quintessential English paintings chosen by the establishment to add that perfect tone required by a residential home of this opulent quality.

On this occasion Ian, very much the onlooker, saw the water colour image as a noticeably penetrating effect. It had taken him back to a time where with his wife they had stayed at the very hotel in the picture; their room had looked over the quaint bridge enhanced by the artist's work.

It was unmistakable. It brought back so much, there was no name indicated, but for him there was no doubt. It was a village along a river valley in the county of Kent, he would for one special reason never forget. The river was the Darent meandering through the village known as Eynsford. The painting induced a dated period of time belonging to the past when pressures from the ramifications of motor cars were yet to arrive.

Ian and his wife had discovered a degree of peace there on a long overdue weekend retreat. Even now years later one single event was uppermost in his mind, this is where their daughter Clare was conceived. Ian had slipped into becoming bemused with himself, all this self-generated sentimentality was fast becoming reminiscent of an article you would expect to read in the latest soul searching pages of a woman's magazine.

His daughter was his motivation at the moment, waiting on a reply from her, no doubt it would explode to life with his text messaging service. Especially by what she had tantalisingly been offered.

'My apologies, sir, I was not aware anyone was in reception.' Ian hardly heard the remark as he was following a virtual path returning to modern day reality. By now Linda the receptionist had taken her rightful place behind the reception desk.

'Now, sir, how may we help you?'

Ian's attention had been drawn to one of the seemingly bulging cartons, an item that it contained had caught his interest. 'You look very busy, Linda, spring cleaning I guess?' The intro done Ian asked his purposeful question. 'It's Ian Harbinger, I've really called to see your Miss Cleary. My aunt was a great friend of hers, I was here myself months ago.'

His awkward disjointed group of statements were after a long pause finally answered.

'Mr Harbinger, sorry to be a bearer of bad news but Miss Cleary died over five weeks ago, it was the result of a bad fall she had. We all at Greycliffe miss her terribly!'

Ian momentarily visualised the lady at her office desk the first time they met, that singular dominant figure which eventually merged into the person that his aunt would have been proud that her nephew had warmed towards.

It left him no option other than briefly explain what the connection had been with his aunt and the deceased. It was with sadness to note that all the cartons were contents from the late Miss Cleary's office, leaving him nothing but pangs of genuinely deep rooted emotion.

How he had looked forward in having a lengthy talk in her office over tea served in those refined teacups, to follow on with a spice of adventure if that's how we would describe all of his accounts from Namibia. He knew by astute presentation he would have easily made all that captivating for his singular audience, but as many things in life it was not to be.

'That's what all the cartons are, Mr Harbinger, her life I suppose all going to the next phase for re-cycle, the van's expected soon. Sad it's sweeping her away from us.'

There was little doubt by what he could see that the dear old lady was already sorely missed and that was not going to be resolved very easily.

Ian on his point of leaving was set to ask one request. 'In that box I can see a movie, you know a film poster, I'd really like it, if as you say it's all going out, it was a strong topic of our mutual interest when I visited her all those weeks ago.'

As he finished the reception phone started to ring, Linda answered it immediately, whilst Ian received his favourable reply through a wave of her hand, enabling him to collect what he had asked for. He acknowledged by a genuine lip readable 'thank you'.

Walking back to the car park the warm sunshine had increased causing the brightness from the loose white marble gravel to reflect strongly into his eyes. As he passed the raised flower beds he could not fail to see the disappearing tapestry of colour in what still remained on the ageing wall flowers.

He could sense a connection from past times which he knew only too well, then perhaps all memories like those colours from the fading flowers in time will finally die.

Tinged by the recent news he showed nothing but despairing thoughts that the only remaining person that once knew my aunt has gone. No one would witness the tears of his emotion that with no restrictions had started to form. He stopped on nothing but a vague impulse and releasing the elastic band that restrained the poster it was allowed to unroll...

So on this spring morning in a parking area at Greycliffe the flamboyant movie poster heralding what was for generations an icon of modern cinema had slowly unfurled itself.

Who could not appreciate what it was set to advertise... 'The Wizard of Oz'.

Ian held the poster almost above his head and called aloud, 'There, Miss Cleary, as instructed by you and only you, this Ian Harbinger did follow my very own yellow brick road.' His outward response was leaving him dwelling on, what was my success? A question he knew was within, and really believed it will so remain.

Always without prior warning his mobile phone buzzed, alerting him that yet another incoming text message had arrived, it was becoming something of a habit!

Chapter 32

'The best laid plans of mice and men, that's what they say isn't it, Ian?' Fiona had made her point, even labouring on her involvement with the housing market on Friday, the day had been fraught with so much anxiety, but that was yesterday, and like all days it was finally concluded.

At last on the Saturday evening they were both together in the restaurant, not at the Globe & Rainbow which Ian continued to stay at but as she had indicated a few days earlier a newly refurbished establishment, that revelled apparently with both menus of Thai and Cantonese food.

With time for once on their hands they set to pass judgement on the meals about to arrive at their table. With so much to explain Ian had made a cautious decision to abridge certain events that had transpired since starting out in his quest of discovery. However at this moment it appeared an obvious fact that neither party could really contain their appetites as now hot baked rolls, a pre-curser to their meals were served.

Fiona had interrupted the conversation flow only a matter of three times, by what she was hearing the intrigue was bordering on the horrific, time and again it was leaving her replying, 'Why the constant pursuit made on you, Ian, by this ominous Karl Botha individual?'

'Don't really know, there's a link with my aunt years ago, he was incensed that wealth was for the taking in the remote Namibian desert, that was apparent when he followed us into those off the track regions, as likely as not the very birthplace of the Herero people.'

Ian was folding his napkin for no purpose other than making it into a neat square. He was still affected and shuddered at the thought of the ominous dry quicksand that had consumed Botha and his vehicle. If ever poetic justice was delivered then it was on cue for that sadistic fiend.

Fiona could clearly sense that he had drifted away from her. She rightly imagined it was concerning all of his incidents that had occurred in Namibia. With a degree tenderness she reached over and squeezed his hand. 'Ian, you're back and safe. Do consider what you have done for your aunt's memory. You know what I'm going to say, I mean it, how proud she would be of you her nephew.'

Before he could reflect and reply to her gratifying remark a fussy waiter arrived with their main course. 'That's it, Fiona, I'll close down for now and we can enjoy our meals, they do look rather good.'

Neither party was disappointed, they both commented that if these standards which such a diverse range of food could be continued to be implemented then the restaurant was on to an outright winner.

'Ian, I've had a crazy idea, it's about Homemead, you'll laugh I expect but hear me out.'

Ian smiled happy that Fiona could regain the ground with their conversation, he remained silent in anticipation for her to continue.

'When you called into the office, I cleverly used Homemead to throw off our beloved June Orpin from her busybody self, when you left I resumed the facade, shall we say borrowing the file from the boss's cabinet, listed properties are supposedly off limits, are you with me so far?' Her question was replied as a silent gesture by a wave of his wine glass.

'Anyway when I did get back again I had the time and privacy for a good look through, it doesn't make any sense, not from an estate agent's point of view, there's no real effort to sell the property. It's stood empty far too long, it's listed, lot of work needed, add all that up and you don't reach an answer, nothing you know stacks up.'

Fiona on completion of her rhetoric statements reached across serving herself the delicately and inspiringly cooked vegetables.

Ian wanted, as it would be perfect timing in lifting the clandestine activities of his secret visits made through the old pantry window at Homemead but decided to be prudent and still keep a silent tongue. It was not going to achieve much, and certainly would be unfair as Fiona was a member of the estate agent's staff.

'It doesn't end there, Ian, there's letters our Mr Jezzaid sent out to survey people months ago, of all things about hidden passages, priest holes and the like, all unnecessary to sell a property that's sticking, or put another way why did he need all of that?'

Ian quickly interjected. 'That's a waste of time and money, apart from an odd wall cavity there's no such things at Homemead as priest holes or whatever else. Because yours truly would have found them as a very inquisitive kid, remember all my summer holidays from boarding school were spent there.'

He knew he could play a further point based entirely on profit as Fiona had not offered a reply to his comments, so he resumed. 'Your Mr Jezzaid is aware of something, goodness knows what, possibly a future development, maybe even government aided and he's holding out for a healthy financial killing.'

Fiona waited patiently in readiness to play what she considered to be her trump card.

'There's more, Mr Harbinger, and I've an inclination it could even concern you, put it another way whilst you were tramping round Namibia, I was working on my ideas, like my father would say if a piece of grit gets inside an oyster's shell it will eventually transform it to become a pearl.'

Much as Ian was appreciating her profound interest in producing 'pearls of wisdom' concerning both Homemead and for that matter himself it was to a large extent getting maybe a little out of hand.

He had formed in his mind a reply, but suddenly without any previous idea a bizarre revelation shot across what was to be his potential response.

'Fiona your boss has he got a brother and is...'

Fiona almost thumped her wine glass down. 'Ian listen that's what I'm trying to get at... Yes he has an older brother and he lives or until his recent death out in your beloved Namibia, now you're allowed one guess to his name...'

Graham the chef was finding the heat from the kitchen was finally getting to him. He understandingly cursed the blatant fact that all the improvements were out in the restaurant. What about some consideration, like new ducting fans where the work's done? For all his cussing he knew only too well at the worst it was his employment, which was more secure these past few weeks. Trade had picked up remarkably no argument there, even a tenuous promise of a pay increase at the end of the month, coupled to this was his culinary skills that he had acquired as a chef working in the Far East.

The local radio station was blaring out an unlikely mixture of what they purported to refer as the 'cool spot', that really did rub 'salt' into his already sweat laden forehead. He was starting the last order, one of his sought after butterfly opened steaks adorned with Chinese style prawns, however the idiot of a customer had insisted it well done, in Graham's eyes that meant incinerated!

By now his assistant was starting to pack away, there was one object on Chef's mind that of a tall ice-cold glass of a certain lager, knowing only too well it would not end there as others would follow by way of complementary offers from those diners still at the restaurant's bar.

Then like all the other Saturday nights it would be a cautious crawl home on his scooter threading his way through the country roads. Perhaps one day he would relieve the bike of the L plates by finally motivating himself to pass his driving test?

But getting home was not what he desired, his family could not be classed as dysfunctional but they were in danger of heading in that permanent direction. Not the best of days, even his beloved football team had failed to get a result.

He removed from the grill his final cooking extravaganza suitably charred to what the customer had requested. The music had stopped; it was that time of night for the local radio to announce those life changing numbers, via the Saturday UK National Lottery.

Graham shouted at his assistant to do what was needed with preparing the serving plate, his concern was far more important, locating the pencil lodged behind his ear it was employed with a weekly task writing down the Saturday draw numbers.

An oil smudged corner on one of his completed order sheets allowed space for him to scribble down the digits. He pushed it aside adding even more cooking oil to the paper. Graham always varied his numbers week on week, so only when he wrote the current winning numbers would he be aware of his luck.

Through the kitchen's blue smoky atmosphere he completed his weekly task vaguely writing through yet another application of oil which caused the paper to slew almost in a full circle.

'Look at this, Rich, sodden lotto numbers, looks like I've written down birthdays... You know people's darn birthdays, don't bloody believe it.'

Graham the chef that had earlier provided two of his Saturday night diners with that of superb meals, allowing Ian to pass their compliments on to the chef and meant in all honesty. Strange the quirks of life, although he would never know that this very restaurant chef had stumbled on his part to resolve the conundrum of the current week's winning numbers, nothing more complicated than the dates of two people's birthdays that intrinsically merged as a line of numbers...

Ian had drifted from his surroundings, suffering from holding on to his usual visible charisma for life. Fiona could not fail to notice his change of temperament. 'What's wrong, Ian? You look like... you've seen a ghost.'

'Sorry... had an idea, I've maybe through your help solved I can only guess a family mystery.'

His annoying habit of forever rolling his table napkin was beginning to infuriate Fiona. 'Ian, stop that now, don't leave me hanging on the edge, what's this you've stumbled on?'

'Like a whole damn circus, Fiona, that's embroiled with Homemead. If I've got it right your Mr Jezzaid is the younger brother of the late Karl Botha, made worse as they were my aunt's two step-sons.'

She at that point raised the wine bottle intent to refill but her sole purpose was denied as it was empty. 'Yes I'm on to what you're saying, Ian, but names, their surnames they're not the same?'

Having made her statement she realised how futile the remark was. 'Yes of course, Marcus Jezzaid, how about if he had changed the family name when he first reached the UK?'

'Fiona maybe thanks to your, how shall we say, research is making the scenario fall into place... My aunt's second marriage by all accounts was nothing short of a screaming disaster. Leaving me thinking the ingredient was her new husband believing that his wife employed as she was surveying for mineral wealth in the remote deserts. So no prizes for the next bit, she would be aware what existed out in those regions. To put it basically, her husband was hell bent to get a piece of the action for himself.'

Reaching across he relieved Fiona of the empty wine bottle that she was insisting to hold. He mischievously wrapped his redundant napkin around the bottle's girth. The ever vigilant waiter anticipating a replacement arrived at their table with a new bottle. Ian knew his persuasive mood was invading.

'What do you think, Fiona? Is it making any sense with what you've seen on Homemead's file? This Marcus is trying to locate my aunt's maps, charts or the like, that as brothers they believe were hidden in the fabric of the building. That's what Botha was rambling on about to me as he was stuck on his disappearing truck, wanting me as a partner to what was out in the desert canyon, convinced I had all the knowledge and answers.' At this stage he purposefully stopped talking allowing Fiona some valuable space.

'It's getting maybe a bit deep, but it's feasible, one over here ever vigilant on the property and doesn't want it sold and the other out in Namibia ready for the action. My intuition, Ian, when you the 'nephew' which they must have being aware existed suddenly arrives on the scene, they're ready for you to open what they believe is a how shall I say, a can of worms.'

'Fiona you're my number one sleuth, it does make sense, when I appear out in Namibia, I now know why Botha found me in no time, he was behind the bogus switch with my desert guide, who by a quirk of fate went wrong, too greedy, that salt on those pack animals was worth a fortune… Whatever I think it's a mess, and lives being lost along the way…That's what I struggle to accept, I could have avoided the whole blessed issue.'

He was struggling not with his dramatic accounts of African deserts but rather the basic task of removing the already loosened bottle top, which eventually surrendered to his vague attempts with an end result of wine all over his fingers.

Fiona wanted at this stage literally to hit him, not because of his feeble efforts with the bottle but more profoundly, as by all his events he would be dead. It seemed crazy to her as if he was looked over by that of an 'angel', no it was not possible, but then try and prove me wrong. She wanted to forget all that, he was alive and that was all that mattered, more so as uppermost in her mind there was one singular reason, she loved him.

'Fiona this whole wretched saga started with me, yes me, watching a few chickens, months ago scurrying around like I knew as a kid with my aunt at Homemead…'

The remaining flame flickering from the expiring table candle created a virtual goodbye which exhibited a composure of light bathing her face. He could not fail to be visually moved by what he saw, perhaps for once all his estranged thoughts had left him?

Not ashamed to admit at least to himself that his sensual emotions for her were running at an all time high. In spite of his sensibility he was remaining remarkably composed, there was a dilemma escalating that allowed him one choice, that of his feelings of love he had for her.

But reality played its next move. From his jacket pocket containing his mobile phone there came its usual pulsing awareness of a new text, which could only be what he was expecting; a return contact from Canada in the guise of his loving daughter.

With wine spillage from the bottle as an irritating sticky mess on both hands, he had a genuine excuse in leaving the table. Cleverly he used this prime mover to his advantage as urgently he needed to discreetly know the content of Clare's reply.

Once inside the washroom there was good light, making it easier to read the phone's text, it was the reply he was hoping. For Dad nothing short of a Eureka moment, his daughter could get the time, only Clare could write such a descriptive reply on a 'drop everything' situation that Ian had presented to her less than 24 hours ago. Resulting in those rather magic words from both of them, Namibia here we come!

He smiled on how Clare had picked up his remark, 'get your sleeping bag', you will be using it under the stars. Next stop, in a sense will eventually find them both out in the deserts of Namibia.

Her description on how exactly she had managed to obtain last minute flight tickets to Jo-burg did not matter, they would meet up and an internal hop over to Windhoek would complete the deal, the rest he could organise through Mitch.

There was one singular question in her text that would undoubtedly hit the nerve, she had not unnaturally enquired how long they would be staying.

Ian was not acting on any preconceived impulse, he had to be open and truthful, he laboured to tap in a reply, it was short, but he knew if nothing else it would arouse an intake of breathe from his daughter. This was the vacation as Clare would realise he had always promised her. She would appreciate those desert skies awash with star constellations, that word she would use had to be 'awesome' he knew that, and he would lovingly accept it.

It was done, he wanted to quickly rejoin Fiona conscious she had been left rather long. His well ordered train of thoughts were invaded by a basic fact which was both patently clear and he was unable to ignore. Apart from their table two others still remained occupied, that was when he was forced to focus his attention on those particular tables. The couples having undoubtedly finished their meals were now in a process of what could be described as intimate small talk.

Ian's astute observation forced him into a situation in what he saw and that matter right on his chin of life. It was for him a realisation of age, it did not however stop there as it spilled over as a 'visual message' to himself and of course Fiona.

It did not take any working out those other occupants together with Fiona were of the same standing, but his more advanced age put him out on a limb. Perhaps deep inside this was a truth which had dawned on him more than once? He joined Fiona offering he thought an almost robotic form of apology for his time away.

His companion during the lull was updating her diary, on Ian's return knowing all of her previous mobile data was now non-existent, she requested his number. 'You've picked a good one there.'

Retaining any form of numbers was not his strong point, particularly as this was an entirely new 'special offer' mobile bought three days ago from a supermarket, and had an entirely new number.

In order to remember it was written in his pocket notebook. Retrieving it from his inside jacket pocket it was accompanied by a neatly folded sheet of paper.

Whatever it related was not uppermost on his mind, he had by this stage already hatched a devious and what he assumed was a necessary manoeuvre.

Removing a singular page he wrote the phone provider's code, but that's where the truth was to stop, the number which should relate to his phone was deliberately changed. Put simply he handed over to Fiona a faked made up number which on his part was a calculated gamble. A 'number' he could never be reached on!

He looked up and buried his guilt with a smile, in doing so he unfolded the sheet of paper fallen from the notebook exposing its mystery, none other than his infamous 'wish list'. That was not all, as within the cover of the same book was smaller slip of paper, more easily recognised as this night's lottery ticket. It slipped from his fingers elegantly gliding to his feet.

However the intervention of these events had not changed the direction by what he was prepared to think. Almost struggling behind the conversations and not to create an impasse between himself and Fiona.

He was in love, but what had to take place was for the well being of both parties. The responsibly was for him to reform on the grounds that it could not possibly last. Now, it was necessary to act before washed over by a tide of sadness, there had to be a break between Fiona and himself. It needed perceiving and he alone would have to do what was needed.

He did not pause again. Opening the folded paper revealing the precise detail of his 'wish list' the onerous amounts over the months had not changed. He was still acting on his astute impulse he picked up what was laid patiently at his feet. 'Here you are, Fiona, this is tonight's 'winning' lottery ticket.'

The thoughts of the 'Guardian' laying in the glutinous mud of the well become apparent, but to no avail as that belonged only to him and it was to remain buried for posterity.

'Fiona check it for me and out of the winnings settle up this list of my outstanding debts and the balance belongs in Scotland, family business, no arguments. I might, possibly be away for a few days, something has to be, you know settled?'

Every so often his proactive mind would attempt to slow down. What he had contrived was no way different than letting go or usurping the precious 'Guardian' crystal, except this for him was far more soul wrenching. Then let the heartaches stay with me, there had to be this break, was there any other way? As always for his predicaments there were never enough answers.

Fiona was bowled over with his play-acting, she had to admit it was somewhat puzzling having only asked him in the first place for a basic phone contact.

'But that's your ticket...' She was interrupted as he had lifted his empty glass offering her a toast.

'I picked loose change up in the street and bought the ticket with it. Fiona there's a saying, you'll win on borrowed money, trust me.'

She humoured him realising how late it had become. 'For you I'll check it in the morning, fingers crossed, like the sign.' Her captivating smile as always closed her promise for the future task.

He knew she had no idea of his devious move he could not let this relationship flourish much as he had wished, reiterating to his deep self what he understood. Perhaps returning to Namibia will eradicate the memories, but is that what I want to happen?

That thought livened his activity reminding him there was much to do, soon he would be boarding a flight making it possible, on meeting up with his daughter Clare to return to a part of the world that was offering an alternative direction in his life.

Would that ultimately become the solution and an answer to what he was seeking? Time and only time would expose a result.

Chapter 33

It was one of those mornings when the weather can really invigorate all those that venture outdoors. Warm sunshine against a backdrop of blue skies, maybe the pessimists would proclaim that it will not last; others would be more sceptical and call it a 'false' spring. Either way it was special and falling on a Sunday it was making Fiona McRae satisfied – it was an offering she really did need.

Having already decided on a Sunday morning drive, her justification was that life's too short. Briefly stopping to collect her Sunday newspaper she allowed the rest of the morning to belong to her, a much needed break. On an occasion like this she would be the first to admit that the Cambridgeshire countryside had an element of satisfaction, augmented by the influx of spring sunshine that only England is capable of replicating.

It was declared by her as a day of sheer escape from time stuck indoors at work, all those constant phone calls, appointments and whatever else. This chunk of peace and quiet, belongs only to me and definately no questions asked.

Fiona had more than once pondered on last evening in company with Ian, something deep down was not transparent and strangely unable to explain itself. During their meal he had certainly spent considerable time going over her own family's business involvement, which she appreciated.

But a paradox had all but existed, resembling a virtual cut off point at the latter part of the evening. When he had said goodbye on leaving the cab at his hotel, the situation had continued, surely there can be no doubt in his mind how I feel for him, nothing has changed. Now in the cold light of day she was still unable to think why all these events had occurred.

The only clue would have to be what he had undergone in Africa, relating for him as a life changing experience, and by his account you would not volunteer to face any of that. It's even affected myself indirectly, knowing the mystery younger brother to this Botha individual is right here in the guise of my own boss. Wow, what a thought to conjure, the stamp collecting Mr Marcus Jezzaid a 'villain' of the day. It's going to be interesting watching what could possibly unfold at Unwin & Hornby, patience as only time will tell.

She craved space and much needed private time, the letter accompanied with the set of ominous trading figures had arrived from the family business and was waiting her stringent scrutiny. It was early and the roads were empty; she was not going to argue with that, there was not a particular route in mind, but she was not prepared in finding herself gravitating towards Ian's beloved Homemead.

Knowing that the property was still as ever firmly on the market she pulled on to the driveway to be met by a reassuring noise from the gravel as the vehicle came to a halt. The result of which caused the bulky Sunday newspaper with its attendant magazine to flop down from the front seat into the passenger foot well.

Fiona reached for her coat which acting on caution she had thrown in the car, now she was prepared and definitely ready to face the day. As a member of the estate agents she had a right to negotiate even though it meant climbing the locked gate to access the sadly overgrown garden. The familiar derelict 'for sale' sign in the grass laid in an almost final resting place, but there was a difference, as this time she now knew the reason why.

It was causing her thoughts to return to Ian and that change of a character shift that she had witnessed from him last night in the restaurant. It was as if they were now both far more intrinsically linked, Ian with the deceased Karl Botha and as she was concerned with Marcus Jezzaid her own boss. I hold one piece of the mosaic, whilst Ian did once hold the other half, how strange the patterns of life can become.

It only seemed to her like yesterday that she was here showing the interested client Mr Harbinger round the house that meant so much to him. She sat on the edge of the well's wooden surround, there was a noticeable distraction, as the silence of this ambient spring morning was interrupted by a commanding and vibrant bird song.

Small wonder, as the ever present robin was proclaiming his aggressive dominance in jealously guarding his rightful territory. More so now as his mate was sitting tightly on her clutch of eggs, meaning as spring was arriving he would need to dominate his seasonal activities by collecting food for the ever hungry mouths.

She appreciated the intervention of the euphonic songster, not realising that the ivy covered wall behind where she sat was the location of the nest, and if she was not already occupying the well cover then it would be the garden's strongest character holding centre stage. But Fiona in the guise of a visitor was taking advantage of the directional sunshine allowing an intrusion of warmth, a precious and equally valued commodity at this fragile time of year.

Her eyes were closed listening to the array of sound on this special Sunday morning, that of the parochial robin, but even more, a faint but constant drone of bees which she assumed the newly found warmth had awoken from hibernation.

There was a sense of a closed cell about herself, an innocent victim captured in her own personal time capsule or so she liked to believe. Arguably her thoughts were replicating what she had known over those wild and inspiring parts of home in her beloved Scottish Highlands.

Although it was not directly her concern she could not fail to ponder as to whether the property of Homemead would ever sell? At this stage would the intrinsic connection that Marcus had with his late brother involved by that of a true hidden agenda with this piece of Cambridgeshire have a rightful closure?

One thing was for sure, its current state would not attract many buyers, give it a few more years at this rate of depreciation and it's into the derelict category. Suddenly a brain wave reached her. A report. What if I did a report for my boss, basic, not too much detail, what needs doing to sell Homemead? With summer on the horizon we can start by getting the grounds into shape. If I have to spend my working days as an estate agent, apart from suffering all the obvious jokes, might as well get something out of it. Anyway would be good to see his reaction.

On those pondering ideas she became aware of activity over the rough grass adjacent to the flint-embossed garden wall. A fluttering movement of yellow, it was tiny and had momentarily vanished from sight, but her patience was quickly rewarded as almost majestically there was its reappearance out into the sunshine. Now she could clearly discern what it was, that of a pristine butterfly.

Fiona had only a scant knowledge of what contributed to those butterflies that made up our indigenous species. However inspiration took over as this particular week's Sunday's supplement would give her the answer, as it was celebrating spring's arrival allowing the magazine to contain a leading article on none other than our own British butterflies.

By now her constant aerial companion was intently interested by fluttering over the battered downed well cover. She admired its colour bathed by the warm sunlight, excelling with lyre shaped wings of a soft sulphurous yellow hue, meaning one thing to her in particular, what a colour to dye up certain of her tweed wool. Fiona was intrigued as the singular butterfly was intent by continuing in remain close to the well. By now she was determined more than ever in establishing exactly what butterfly it would answer by name.

Fiona negotiated the property gate. She did not go unnoticed by as always the attention of the garden robin, but on this occasion the ensconced avian guardian had other priorities that would soon be hatching. But for now this intruder like all the others before was leaving his dominance.

The visitor to the garden paused removing the rust on her hands; a lasting residue from the corroding chain that held the gate. Her next concern was fumbling for the car keys in her coat pockets, wondering because of the short distance why she had locked the vehicle in the first place?

Searching her second pocket, the keys were located, they were lost in a sheet of folded paper. 'What's this?' Her puzzled concern was resolved by an easy answer, the blessed 'wish list' courtesy from Ian at the dining table, a glance left her mortified with its mind blowing content.

The sheer magnitude of Ian's personal debt illustrated on his 'need to pay wish list'. It was having such an impact on her, not even believing all those problems could be contained on one sheet of paper. It went one further in prompting Fiona to locate namely last night's lottery ticket and keeping her promise to check it for him.

It would have to wait for the moment as her interest was directed towards the newspaper's supplement determined in her search to identify that certain yellow butterfly. Her reward was made easy as the writer had gone to lengths in arranging a semblance of how the insects appear and for convenience in a chronological sequence.

This was easier still as the magazine's centre spread was totally self-explanatory whilst also dwelling on concerns with the current status of our British butterflies. There illustrated in the spring section was what she instantly recognised. That's it the brimstone. It further stated it is only the male of the species having the sulphur yellow colour. She was delighted, clever me… That's the very one.

The highlighted write up relating to the brimstone she momentarily ignored as her concentration was drawn in an intuitive direction to Ian's list. It had continued to literally take her breath away on realising the consequence of what was owed. It was all precisely itemised. That in itself was revealing, but dwelling on the bottom line figure, that was the sickening part. What that must be like, I'm so glad that's not me, Ian. Aware she had entered into a habit of talking to herself.

But she switched, inwardly laughing at herself and at the same time feeling instantly guilty. Fiona held up the singular lottery ticket. Men… With all that debt and he buys one, only one measly ticket. Does he believe in miracles?

The lottery ticket without so much as a thought was flicked on to the passenger seat. Her attention was drawn by female intuition in studying what was his comprehensive list of debts, able to trace the history with how his business fell victim to a massive embezzlement, instigated as she had been made aware by his two partners.

No one deserves that. How can he possibly work the scale of this debt off? What can I ever possibly say to him in a way of easing his predicament? It had started to occur to her remembering all of his attachment for Homemead as a youngster, yet this man wanted a viewing of the property, no way could he buy it, by what I see here he couldn't even afford the water well.

She adjusted the driver's seat giving her a view of those expansive and enigmatic skies, appearing as nothing short of unique. Then only a sadness of time was spoiling the scene, that of Homemead sprawled over by a forlorn state of emptiness, causing a melancholy appearance to descend over the house that it did not rightfully deserve.

The newspaper's bloated out sheets commanded her attention, the inside articles and features gained her grasp on events better than the depressing front pages. Soon she was actively engrossed with an article that appealed to her fashion sense. What the content was describing could be easily manipulated into her own tweed producing business.

Like most people that read Sunday papers sitting in parked cars they will eventually succumb to battling the folds of paper. On this morning Fiona was not excluded from that predicament. But even the TV pages and latest critic reviews of programmes were worthy of at least a glance. Only then did she notice the printed box representing the draws on last night's lottery results. With a smirk of laughter she reached over to pick up Ian's ticket and at long last finally checked it.

Not retentive with figures she had years back adopted a plan of caution, read and always re-read to confirm, even get someone else to check, but not an option on this particular morning. How many times she read the six numbers nobody would be aware. Also it would be difficult to understand if not impossible as why she jumped out of her car as if attacked by an 'alien creature'.

At first her voice, not that it was needed simply lost its power to respond. 'Numbers, they're the same, Ian. Your numbers all match. Heaven above you've won.' For her security for whatever reason made her scramble back inside the car and again to resume checking the ticket against the newspaper for the umpteenth time.

Her head was thumping, more so as she realised that inadvertently her mobile phone was left residing at home on the table of the kitchen diner, hell.

She desperately tried to remain calm and in control, easier said than done. Wait could there be errors? How many other winners? The paper had indicated this was a roll-over week. It's not real. No way can this be happening to me. Her pathetic solution was by pinching herself on the grounds, it has to be a dream.

It was her unreal state of isolation, having no phone that was making things worse. Ian needed contacting immediately, wondering if had kept a note of the numbers which she doubted. She vaguely remembered his remark, purchased from money he had picked up in the street? If all this is fact, then it would make a joke of his 'wish list'. Those debts would disappear in smoke, and more so what of his promise of capital for my family business?

What a morning, it's not right; no one gets this luck. She found herself for no reason taking the creases out of the precious lottery ticket and securing it in the glove compartment. More out of nerves she again tried folding or attempting with the ponderous layers of the paper. Given her current circumstances she gave up as a bad job. One thing she was able to achieve, to stare longingly towards the gate and onwards towards Homemead, as if help for her was laying in that direction.

Those harrowing depleted top windows had now caught the morning sunshine, through the glass panes there dwelt an indefinable sense of emptiness. Appearing as an arrangement of black ebony voids, that you would expect 'tears' to drain from.

Yet she momentarily noticed a shape that was not showing a few seconds ago, and the sunlight was in no way responsible. It wavered as a shimmering white tone like that of fabric. No it couldn't be, anyway it was gone.

Aware that it would need all her vigilant attention to actually drive, as at this stage she was seemingly overtaken in a true sense by the impact of the winning money. Now Fiona was praying that this was indeed fact and no mistakes had occurred? On starting the engine its noise in the quiet surrounds had a response of startling the splendid brimstone butterfly that newly out of hibernation was taking advantage by actively soaking in the sunshine radiated from the battens across the well.

It flew lazily fluttering over where it had spent the long months of sleep on the enclosed inner rim of the well in a void of darkness. The circle of the old grainy timber had a part where carved numbers remained, these enabled the creature to adhere and remain in a dormant phase through the tenuous cold of winter.

She was about to finally drive away, even in her elevated condition for some reason she looked at the magazine's open page, it pleased her that the identification was correct .

Almost to take her mind off her exasperating state she continued reading what related to this particular butterfly, further enhancing how they emerge from hibernation to greet the spring-like days. There was a reference that supported its old country name, on reading that she immediately fell victim to an almost unbelievable coincidence…

By now it was engaged in a crowning flight over the cover of the well, aspiring to hover savouring each moment as it passes embracing all that life has to offer. Stranger things on heaven and earth exist, maybe they are seldom discovered?

Numbers that were once carved on the well's internal wooden brace and now years later having come to light were replicated on to a modern perhaps rather insignificant ticket, for that of a certain lottery.

The wood carver who had inscribed those rudimentary figures years ago had since passed away, she rested in a far off country, a place that had lasting turmoil and changes during her life. For all those events it was her assignments with geological endeavours combined with personal altruism towards the people of the Herero that allowed this part of Africa to remain loyal in the heart of a lady named Anastasia.

When she had carved those numbers it was of a time when she, together with her second husband, had returned from South Africa for a holiday to be spent at Homemead. She was verging on desperation to leave a token at her old home that emanated from that of her deep emotion.

Her carving was all but hidden and discreet, consisting of the birthday dates of her first long gone husband and that of herself. Those actual numbers inextricably linked reflecting nothing more than a lasting sentiment to what they had meant to each other.

Moreover it was at that time when intimidation directed towards her from her recent husband had gained even greater heights. Realising her disastrous mistake together with the gravity of despair her latest marriage had created. There was no going back, all the weeping that left her in a lachrymose state would never alter anything that was discovered about her new husband and what were now her two step-sons...

Fiona looking from her car was drawn to stare at the singular exquisite sulphur colour of the brimstone, realising a word connection that she thought perhaps merits a paraphrase, 'sulphur and brimstone'. During all this extended time there was no concern for it wanting to leave its boundary of the well, as if a tangible purpose existed there.

The impact of the lottery win and how it had literally exploded into her special morning had understandably left her in a state of euphoria, further instrumental in what she believed she was now taking home. She laughed at her conjured thoughts, no need to be cynical when you can get comical.

As for the sheer humour bit for her, there is only one singular comment, it has to be, 'butterflies in my tummy'.

The car tyres as always crunched the gravel of the drive on leaving, for Fiona she was gratified with what she had only just read. The brimstone's other name, it was surreal, and so very apt, the male of the species that the country people for generations have because of its early arrival in the year known it to be called...

HARBINGER of SPRINGTIME

Chapter 34

Richard G was finally alone, throwing the file of papers on his desk in what could only be described as an act of disgust, in particular as they passed for top level 5 security. He muttered to himself rolling together words formulating into a caustic insult for those responsible. His remarks were polarised into a verbal statement only capable of falling on deaf ears. 'What a waste of my department's resources.' They should not be occupying priority on this desk, the direction we are all heading puts us in danger of being manipulated by a bunch of morons. That's to say nothing of what it's doing to my precarious blood pressure!

He had not only reached but considered as having passed his 'sell by date', resigned to accept that. Have a look at me though when I'm fishing and the mayfly are rising on my stretch of the River Test. It was true his retirement was not exactly imminent but akin to the proverbial 'carrot' dangling above his head it had now ceased to exist. To say he was mad would be a gross understatement, all year he had suffered this irksome state, knowing it was affecting his entire department.

There was a time when our country's national security was run by accountants, that was bad enough, now it had swung in the direction of morons struggling to be accepted as what they purported to be, that of politicians. Nothing more than ephemeral beings that would be better off kissing babies for their next electoral vote grabbing.

How many minutes he had stared at the covers of the bulging files he would have no idea. His only respite was the quality of the coffee which had just arrived. He found himself mesmerised by the huge wording the direct result of the rubber stamp, proclaiming over the grubby covers, 'Top Secret'.

He dwelt on his remit. I need you on this one, Richard, you have so much expertise with the Americans. He clearly remembered remonstrating cutting the conversation short, almost describing dealing with our American cousins as models of inert diplomacy. 'Inert' the operative word!

He jumped in, aggressively breaking the seal on the first file to reveal not so much its content but perhaps how quickly it could be resolved. Use video conferencing, no trips to the US. That would please him, it's true what my wife is saying, I'm getting too old for all this.

The coffee despite its heat retaining container had grown cold. He was drawn into a vortex which had rather seductively gained his interest not realising how close to home the investigation had transpired. Our own North Sea, right on our back yard. The US will love this one. Drilling rigs, Britain's self-sufficiency, happy days, he was starting to feel content to enter into a totally sarcastic frame of mind.

What happened to all our wealth? Aware of the transformation of his beloved countryside, his virtual hatred of contamination with the growth of wind farms.

The file's reference notes in the front portion gave him an immediate overview. He smiled, and that was a first for the day, something had raised its ugly head, up to now it had only consisted of a discovery years ago on the sea bed, certain artefacts that could offer no explanation? Now, guess what, guilty of musing inwardly to himself, they have all caught a 'bloody cold'. Didn't we learn anything from Roswell back in the '40s?

But this one's flying a British flag, not forgetting Viking longships, and lost relics that blatantly refuse to give up their ancient secrets, interesting. Now the Yanks have their bit of action to add, and by what they indicate their input is very recent…

Marjory knew if she was summoned to the fifth floor then it was important. Certainly more so than the emulsion paint in her recently decorated office that had failed to fully dry. She reluctantly tried the paint again, as the notice continued to indicate… 'Wet paint'.

'Richard.' Marjory was reluctant and certainly not wishing to be rude. 'We all thought you were retired?'

He looked up from the file, drawing at least a dose of stilted humour from their introduction. 'Hello, Marjory, yes… I'm a cardboard cut out, battery operated, talking, singing, what do you think?'

It was at best a viable icebreaker to start their discussion. She was used to him. 'Don't be such an arse, Richard. What's bugging you?'

'Maj, I need some delicate info without treading on our US colleagues' toes.'

She knew whatever the file he was fingering it would not be masquerading as some irritant. That's clearly why G had it assigned to him.

'You ask my department, Richard, name it and we can deliver, blood and guts if needed!' She never smiled. At least no one in her department had witnessed the event. At the moment she was craving for one of her dyspepsia tablets but they resided in her office cabinet. 'What's it about, Richard? Anything you can tell me?' But knowing only too well it was a pointless and equally futile question.

Marjory had taken one of the vacant chairs cluttering his office. Now she would bite her tongue and have no other course of action than await what was required, and that of her currently rather stretched department's staff.

She grew impatient, wanting this assignment. Her life revolved round her clandestine work, perhaps over shadowing the obsession with Persian cats. Right from her teens she knew that good looks had not been focused in her particular direction, but she had compensated by other means that bordered on the insidious. Now what Richard was about to offer her department would be nothing but sheer music in her ears!

'Maj, you want me to tell you? It's something big even out of this world, like Roswell and in the 21st century, you would be… off track.'

Now she had more than an inkling, cleverly supplied by G. She had accrued rather too many years in this profession. More than that she had the inborn skill of a woman's intuition. His covert answer was enough for her.

'Get your department on this like yesterday. Here's a list of people I need to, you know... interview.' His attention was divided by talking and at the same time scribbling names on his pristine notepad. 'Usual top level, I want them into Brecon HQ like their backsides never touch anything. Take care of all the details, Maj, I don't have to tell you.'

She was taken back, another big break for hers truly and for that matter her department. Hell why haven't I got those damn tablets when I need one.

'Work in alphabetical order, "SETI" over in America will be proud of us. They spend their time staring out into space, looking for extra terrestrials, guess you call them out of this world estate agents.' His insipid humour failed to find its mark, or she was far too intelligent to offer him any pleasure of false laughter.

'Let's see, this one was killed involved with oil exploration in the Gulf of Mexico, not long after the discovery, interesting, an accident they have recorded, I very much doubt that statement?'

Richard ran through all the catalogued details attempting to collate then in alphabetical order, although it was resembling more like a list of rather tired movie credits.

'Here's one, let's see, under H, an off shore oil rig engineer, that's an easy one, Maj... captive audience for you ...name ...Harbinger, Ian Harbinger...'

Fiona was suffering from lack of a decent night's sleep, a legacy since that certain morning now over a week ago at Homemead with the realisation of the lottery win. 'Crazy,' she thought. I could on Ian's behalf buy that property with one hand tied behind my back. But nothing was altering the state she was labour-

ing under, where is he? Indulging herself to proclaim aloud…
'You must be somewhere, Mr Ian Harbinger, the proverbial Harbinger of Springtime?'

It seemed to her that he had emigrated. No forwarding contacts left at 'The Globe and Rainbow'. She was continuing the search annoyed with him by his stupid and trivial mistake of not writing his phone number down correctly. It was absurd, the contacts from him since his return from Africa were either personal or by his mobile, but he had changed it, and now of course she had the incorrect number, which only added more frustration to the puzzle of his whereabouts.

However she had acted in a cautious if not shrewd manner when it became confirmed that his lottery ticket was a winner, also the only winner that night, it had hit big time, now his winning capital was secure. She acted as proxy on his list of debts as instructed, relishing how easy once you have the collateral to rule over any outstanding settlements. They were all waiting for final confirmation, but no matter, it was done.

She imagined his reaction once given the chance to explain what had transpired with the conclusions of his personal debt problems, namely fully solvent. Given the magnitude of what had been his debts a rather pointless remark, although for the present it humoured her.

Then that feeling of concern was invading her thoughts. What if anything had become of him? Surely not, his outward stamina, this veritable man of the world would defy that. She faced the fact in a prudent way, even if yet another 'worry bead' was hanging round her neck.

But there was one thing in particular she was radically sure about, that of making Ian Harbinger a business partner with her family. It might be one thing for him to become a volunteer, a benefactor donating his lottery winnings to her family's business. That was before he knew he had won, but it was worth more than that. She pinched herself in a sense of reality with the ominous duty to understand he does not even know yet, and as for all his debts, gone, wow, simply evaporated!

For Fiona it had become an involuntary time she had found herself transfixed. Strange one tiny piece of paper spaced out with numbers, a single lottery ticket had changed or would be altering lives. It was even more intriguing as it had been bought on borrowed or in this case 'found' coins, now does that make any sense?

She picked up the property viewing copies on her desk, noticing that Marcus had added to the pack of all things, Homemead? It was annotated with a firmly secured note, she read the comments in his inevitable neat hand writing. We were inviting a new approach to that of hopefully selling Homemead, she imagined that of lifting the property's image, interesting?

Looking through to his office Marcus was busy fussing over sale pamphlets, she could not fail to notice a change that had all but consumed him, his outward appearance, reinforced by a sense of growing confidence. This was a radical change, call it a metamorphism that had recently taken place. Then she knew the prime reason, his brother Karl was not just missing he was now finally confirmed as dead.

Purely by force of habit she assiduously checked for incoming phone calls, continuing to believe that he would be finally getting in touch...

Sadly nothing could be further from Ian's mind, much as he would have liked to hear from Fiona he was adamant, although devious in concept he needed to adhere to his plan. Their tentative relationship would never work out, his underlying reason why he had acted with his false trail of a wrong phone number, culminating he believed as disappearing without trace. For all that he knew only too well his regrets, but this course of action he personally over time would have to resolve...

For the approaching desert night they had gathered enough scrub wood for the fire. Ian knew it instilled a positive feeling of self-gratification by creating your campfire, the last two nights with this task he had found himself in a sense of friendly competition with his daughter. Noticeable to her father that she was enjoying the sheer impact of the deserts of Namibia, experiencing first-hand the rudiments that exist in remote regions of our world.

How the days had passed so quickly since they had met up at Johannesburg. Both parties had nothing but praise for flights and their connections, although on more serious reflection they agreed this would never in your wildest dreams become the norm.

On reaching Windhoek they made immediate contact with Mitch and his wife; the welcome they both received was nothing short of staggering. His Namibian associate was made aware of what he had in mind, this time Mitch had laid on transport with a definite upgrade, an almost new pickup truck. Otherwise all supplies for the proposed journey followed the same requirement as before. The master of logistics, Mitch, deserving his title as ever 'the organiser', who had one question and it was bottled up for his intrepid explorer. 'Take the lid off for me, Harbinger. What's all this fracking they've gone crazy on back home?'

That was an out of the blue remark from him, as Ian had really no interest on the latest in land based exploration with fossil involvement, but he owed his lifelong friend at least a cursory comment.

'Mitch I'm not dwelling on it, already it's reached government support, we saw it up on the North Sea, we've only one planet, but do we ever learn by what we do?'

Mitch knew instinctually he was not in a happy position to pursue his enquiry, as by this stage Ian was dangling a gift wrapped box in front of his face, that not even Clare was aware of its contents.

Ian had managed to find Mitch a perfect thank you gift for past times spent in his care. Consisting of a sought after piece of antique English silverware, his host was taken aback in surprise, commenting as reaching his veritable 'Achilles' heel' of expectation.

For all that Ian desperately wanted to start the journey. This time as they ventured out into the remote deserts, he had privileged knowledge to where at this time of year the Herero people would be located. Tomorrow they were all set to be off.

During their journey Clare noticed a subtle change gaining a hold over her father. By what she saw there was for her a growing concern. Not the sort to tread softly on such matters, a trait inherited from her mother, she decided with care and tact to challenge her father.

He listened intently, not failing to take his daughter's enquiring comments on board. Much to her relief he was content to explain his predicament. 'Clare, this is my nemesis. I'm going back to a people that, had I not gone out there in the first place, then their leader Jho-in would still be alive.'

She was taken aback by her father's soul wrenching and totally unexpected remark. Given the vehicle's cramped conditions she was cautious, needing no family disagreements or worse arguments, she thought carefully before attempting her reply.

'Wait to see what transpires in reality, it's that question, I suppose of destiny.' She paused, not her intention, however it allowed Ian to intervene.

'No, Clare it's not a cut and dried how can I say chapter of life. It happened, two men lost their lives by a course of action instigated by me, no arguments.'

She knew that to side step the subject would be futile, virtually on her part an act of verbal suicide.

'Dad, please listen up on this one. I work with a guy, a great news reporter. Some years back he missed boarding a plane vital for his news coverage, the plane crashed after take-off. You know what I have to say next, all killed, now that's fate, he wasn't meant to be on that flight, accept it, life's planned out.'

He listened, maybe his daughter's increasingly enhanced Canadian accent was hitting the right chord, at least it was acting in soothing his imminent dilemma.

Ian would never admit, his daughter's concerns were in effect allowing him to try and relax. 'You win, Clare, if I keep on guessing I'll never understand. It's all about those cameos of life we look back on.' He turned smiling to his daughter, it was now more than enough for her to realise things were going to be considerably easier, inwardly she felt a huge sigh of relief.

The Herero people knew of their impending arrival days before, sound from their vehicle was embodied to be carried over the desert winds. People living in one of the last wilderness on our sadly shrinking planet understood more than other civilisations could possibly comprehend.

Ian was now recognising the landscape which preceded to where the Herero settlement at this time of year would be located, he had acquired pensive feelings prior to their arrival, knowing these desert tribespeople do not send out invitations. Hopefully he was to be elated surmising the reception they would receive once the Herero laid eyes on his blonde daughter…

That was days ago, too much had been crammed in since then, his overactive offspring had seen to that, the limelight had not been focused on him. He had conversely decided with a discipline, that of taking for both of them any outside communication entirely out of the equation. Clare was taken by shock given the lifestyle of instant contact of Facebook she hung out on. Withdrawal symptoms for her were both tough and difficult. Ian in fairness to his daughter had to be in charge with any indifference she attempted to display.

Clare after her arrival rather eclipsed the centre stage of Herero settlement life, achieved by her skin colour. The Namibian women in particular could not argue with such a visual appearance. That was until the ritual the womenfolk bestowed on her, the red ochre, fine earthy colour powder inherent to certain parts of their country, an adornment in a form of paste that is smeared over the visible skin of their women. Clare was not allowed to escape such applications, but then her father knew she revelled in life traditions.

But her father had a definite agenda that was to be adhered to, come what may. There was one futuristic event that he was certainly keeping under wraps, when appropriate, nearer the departure time his daughter was in for one final surprise. It was a direct result of a constant process that he had laboured over for months, a life changing decision that the new Herero leader had welcomed from him. Now he was determined with his change of life direction…

With the onward journey they had now reached what Ian called the 'hidden valley'. What he was seeking, his return to the canyon of Taroo, the whole motivation of the journey, the embryonic place of the Herero, on this occasion shared in the company with his daughter. To reach the canyon obscured in the endless tracts of desert two young Herero guides had been assigned to them. Ian and Clare could not fail to see the feeling of pride these desert people exhibited towards the 'overseas excursionists'. It was impossible to note the feeling expressed by their guides, the language barrier was insurmountable, but all agreed that was not in any way a concern.

When they drove through the canyon entrance encircled by the treacherous dry quick sands Ian suffered rather badly knowing the ominous task of attempting that of facing his demons. After all those months he was hard pressed to believe what had transpired, almost within almost touching distance under the weight of tons of engulfing sand, the buried pickup truck and the entombed body of Karl Botha. But then Ian sensed the graphic events, remembering the horror associated with the leader of the Herero, shot to death in front of his own eyes by a bullet clearly intended for him.

As before they traversed the valley's floor finally making camp against the tall backdrop of the primeval outcrops. Ian had rather methodically explained who in the family was Aunt Anastasia. It was at first difficult for Clare to take things in given the complexity of families, and the Harbinger family was no exception.

She attempted to understand what it meant to her father, therefore the degree of empathy she wanted to express was not that of a chore, knowing how important for her to act in this direction. Maybe our modern world is becoming sadly lacking in a presence of human understanding, making her think, where had she heard that remark before?

Clare on first entering the caves to pay her respects to the burial places of the leaders of the Herero, became aware of the close propinquity to where Ian's aunt was entombed. She was not prepared for what came over her, that of unreal phobia, interpreting the whole experience as totally scary, not of this world, belonging to those unreal TV movies. She needed to redress these previous feelings which caused her to feel upset. Having openly explained to her father they both agreed and later she returned in a composed state of mind. Not just a case for doing it for her father, she alone in her own thoughts wanted to visit once more, this lady had after all belonged to her family…

Now the sun that had given them warmth was quickly setting. Clare continued to visualise the white silk scarf laid by the casket of their interned aunt. Clare had one highly motivated thought in her mind, she would not forget, when I get home I shall buy that same type to remember her, it will be worn in this lady's memory.

Tomorrow was to be the last day, they planned to break camp after dawn and make tracks back to the Herero settlement. What Clare was unaware was that from there it would be her, with their guides supposedly driving to return to Windhoek, where Mitch would collect her. Mitch as always would resolve any issues; he was privy to Ian's long standing agenda, already knowing that he was staying indefinitely with whom he privately referred to as his adopted people.

The Herero before had all but begged him to stay. He had become known to them as 'Life Giver of the Herero'. More so as the water he had brought forth had continued, a tribute to his endeavours. Their offer if that is how it should be described, by his decision would finalise into reality.

His daughter was more than content listening to whom she always considered as a man apart, that of her father, who now wanted nothing more than to hear her conversation. 'You know next year I've a chance to get up into the Rockies, with my uni lot want to do Kootenay Peaks, chance we can fly in, light aircraft stint, be awesome.'

Clare looked across the halo of firelight which performed shapes of flickering flames, mesmerised by its changing effects. It allowed teasing views of her contented father who had heard her word Rockies but no more, as now he was by the fires subtle heat overcome by the ingress of sleep.

His deep slumber allowed him a contentment of thoughts, although of no purpose other than glimpses of past memories, pursuing him into contortions that enabled him to slip into portals of time. Every so often there appeared through these apertures what he wanted to follow, but there were others that offered no more than isolated directions with no positive endings.

Eventually he explored one of the chosen portals which ending consisted of fields of hay, although much to his liking it caused him to become lost. It did not matter as now he sensed the sun-warmed grass around him; he lay hidden, the grass was swaying by zephyrs of a breeze. A schoolboy has all the time in the world, especially on summer holidays in those fields surrounding Homemead.

His aunt would never find him, he watched the skylarks' nest, it was hidden over by the quarry in cover of tall sedge grass, the bird was actively sitting on eggs. He wanted so much to have a peek, what colours would the eggs be? It was for Ian his perfect world, do I ever need to grow up?

The sound was faint but he knew his aunt was calling him. He imagined her standing by the kitchen door, in order to gain his attention she would walk out and bang loudly on the galvanised pail hanging on the water well, that chasm that disappeared into a dark void that any self-righteous school boy craved to explore. The noise that the pail proclaimed would always cause the starlings huddled on the storage sheds to fly away in an avian annoyance.

Ian in a state of sleep, enclosed within the comfort of his sleeping bag from a cold desert breeze originating from the very ancestral heart of Taroo. It grew with intensity almost apparitional, persevering on a journey, its sinuous form filtered into the entrance of the Herero burial caves. Empowered with an astral and upward momentum completing its direction by causing the silk scarf draping his aunt's burial place to create an ethereal shape of shimmering white silk. It was but a moment in time, a compelling and solemn task had been performed, then, as quickly the fabric resumed its original resting place.

The breeze was eventually sensed by Ian causing him to wake from that of his peaceful sleep. He looked above into the cold black void of the night sky, the desert vista acting out a drama of millions of piercing stars. Why so many? You could reach out and touch every single one. It was a spectacular and hallowed sight, what a privilege, but no answer would ever be forthcoming as why so many. That question in recent times had become a trademark for his own life; always too many questions and never enough answers.

He became transfixed with a futile practice of counting the contents of the heavens but he was losing the battle as a new approach of sleep was returning. He tried to resist this dilemma but could offer no contest to the arms of Morpheus that were gradually reclaiming him. His ingress of further dreams was waiting like that of loyal courtiers assigned to privileged royalty. He had no recourse other than to surrender…

That inherent unreal sensation was again sweeping through his body, this was the first time as the intensive perspiring took hold he could relate in an intuitive way to his unusual strength and additional power. It was within but not of a human form; an inheritance of the scorpion always accompanied with a sentiment of an arched and rampant tail that it was capable of displaying to his enemies.

He had survived the poison made from the creature's tail, but Sarnesa by her tribal potions and sedation combined by using her sexual power had struggled to save him from the brink of death. The price was that Ian had become invincible in his bouts of psyche as that of a 'scorpion', known only by the dutiful Herero saviour who by her sexual affinity had drawn away enough of the venom poised to kill her patient.

The human mind can retain endless images. As the survivor of the poisoning he was now experiencing during the times of his natural sleep that there was consistently surfacing the same face of a young Herero woman. Would he ever meet her in his world of reality…?

On this occasion he naturally had gravitated to the room at Homemead, his special bedroom, every school boy should be allowed that privilege.

Were the holidays of the long summer finally over, but why? They should never end. I don't need to return to boarding school, my Aunt Anastasia would like me to stay here. There are so many things I could do on the farm. I know she will be calling me soon, tea will be ready, it's my favourite, slices of scrumptious plum bread.

It was comfortable for him to focus on the bedroom's fireplace where above on the wall the framed embroidery resided. Now he wanted nothing more than to read the panel's compelling words. As always those of Edward Lear's enigmatic nursery rhyme. *The Owl and the Pussy Cat.*

Although drifting in his sleep from the present world consisting of the dark sky above the sands of the desert to the contrast of an encapsulated dream world of an enchanted childhood his eyes became trance like in his deep subconscious, his domain illuminated by the silver light of the ascending moon. Then at long last he remained contented to read the nursery rhyme, in particular those closing words that always belonged to his Aunt Anastasia.

…*Hand in hand on the edge of the sand they danced by the light of the moon*…

END

Rate this book on our website!

www.novum-publishing.co.uk

The author

In this, his debut full length novel, John Kelley draws on all his experience as an engineer working both in the UK and abroad. Born in the UK and already an established author of short stories and a renowned photographer, when he has time, Kelley also enjoys spending time driving rally cars in the UK. Passionate about writing and the planet, Kelley addresses many current global concerns in his novels which transcend any cultural differences.

novum 🔹 PUBLISHER FOR NEW AUTHORS

The publisher

> Whoever stops getting better, will in time stop being good.

This is the motto of novum publishing, and our focus is on finding new manuscripts, publishing them and offering long-term support to the authors.
Our publishing house was founded in 1997, and since then it has become THE expert for new authors and has won numerous awards.

Our editorial team will peruse each manuscript within a few weeks free of charge and without obligation.

You will find more information about
novum publishing and our books on the internet:

www.novum-publishing.co.uk